W9-BKE-199

DEBBIE MACOMBER

One of America's favorite storytellers!

Praise for Debbie and her previous novels:

"One of the few true originals in women's fiction."
—Anne Stuart

"Romance readers everywhere will cherish the books
of Debbie Macomber."
—Susan Elizabeth Phillips

This Matter of Marriage
is "so much fun it may keep you up till 2 a.m."
—*The Atlanta Journal*

"Popular romance writer Macomber has a gift
for evoking the emotions that are at the
heart of the genre's popularity."
—*Publishers Weekly*

"Debbie Macomber's name on a book is a guarantee of
delightful, warmhearted romance."
—Jayne Ann Krentz

"Well-developed emotions and appealing characters."
—*Publishers Weekly* on *Montana*

"Debbie Macomber is the queen of love and laughter."
—Elizabeth Lowell

Also available from MIRA Books and
DEBBIE MACOMBER

THIS MATTER OF MARRIAGE
MONTANA
MOON OVER WATER

HEART OF TEXAS SERIES

LONESOME COWBOY
TEXAS TWO-STEP
CAROLINE'S CHILD
DR. TEXAS
NELL'S COWBOY
LONE STAR BABY

Watch for the first book in
Debbie Macomber's Buffalo Valley trilogy

DAKOTA BORN

May 2000

DEBBIE MACOMBER

PROMISE
TEXAS

MIRA

If you purchased this book without a cover you should be aware that this book is stolen property. It was reported as "unsold and destroyed" to the publisher, and neither the author nor the publisher has received any payment for this "stripped book."

MIRA

ISBN 1-55166-502-6

PROMISE, TEXAS

Copyright © 1999 by Debbie Macomber.

All rights reserved. Except for use in any review, the reproduction or utilization of this work in whole or in part in any form by any electronic, mechanical or other means, now known or hereafter invented, including xerography, photocopying and recording, or in any information storage or retrieval system, is forbidden without the written permission of the publisher, MIRA Books, 225 Duncan Mill Road, Don Mills, Ontario, Canada M3B 3K9.

All characters in this book have no existence outside the imagination of the author and have no relation whatsoever to anyone bearing the same name or names. They are not even distantly inspired by any individual known or unknown to the author, and all incidents are pure invention.

MIRA and the Star Colophon are trademarks used under license and registered in Australia, New Zealand, Philippines, United States Patent and Trademark Office and in other countries.

Visit us at www.mirabooks.com

Printed in U.S.A.

To Irene Goodman
for one hell of an idea

Dear Reader,

I hadn't intended to write another book about Promise, Texas. When I finished the HEART OF TEXAS series, I was satisfied that I'd told the story of Promise, and solved the mystery around Bitter End. I was looking forward to new projects. New characters. Fresh plots and locations.

Then the letters started to arrive.

Such eloquent, beautiful letters. Letters that stirred my heart and made me feel both humble and privileged to be a writer. Letters that asked for more. My readers wanted more of Promise, more stories about these characters.

Thanks to my publisher MIRA (especially Paula and Dianne) for making this possible. I also want to thank Ann Cacciapaglia, friend, neighbor and vet-in-training. And thank you to my readers for validating my belief in the goodness of people everywhere and the pleasures of life in small-town America.

If this is your first trip to Promise, sit back and enjoy. If this is a return journey, be prepared to meet all your old friends and shake hands with a few new ones. This is the book you said you wanted! And my readers always seem to know my heart....

I eagerly look forward to hearing what my readers think about each book. You can write me at P.O. Box 1458, Port Orchard, WA 98366.

Debbie Macomber

HISTORY OF PROMISE, TEXAS

Promise is a fictional town located in the Texas hill country (the "heart of Texas"). It was founded more than 100 years ago, some distance from the site of the original community, which had been named Bitter End and now exists as a ghost town.

Bitter End had been established in the 1840s by a group of families who made the arduous trek from the eastern United States. It was a reasonably prosperous place until a few years after the Civil War, when a series of disasters befell the town. The residents were driven away and reestablished their town in 1881, calling it Promise.

For generations, very little was known about Bitter End. Descendants of the founding families knew only bits and pieces of the town's history and whispered that it had been "cursed" for some unknown reason. Most people didn't even know exactly where it stood, and not until the mid-1990s was the mystery of Bitter End solved.

The town of Promise (population about 1500) is in ranch country and is surrounded by a number of successful cattle ranches. Founding families like the Westons and the Pattersons still own the ranches their great-grandparents started. Other people, like Max Jordan and Ellie Frasier Patterson, continue to run businesses that have been in their families for many years. The strength of community and the feeling of "home"—this is why people stay in Promise, generation after generation.

And it's why people come here, too. Welcome to the pleasures of small-town life. Welcome to Promise, Texas!

THE PEOPLE OF PROMISE:
CAST OF CHARACTERS

Annie Applegate: Divorced bookseller and friend of Dr. Jane Patterson. Moves to Promise.

Nessa Boyd: Widowed sister-in-law of Dovie (Boyd) Hennessey.

Jeannie French: First-grade teacher. New to Promise.

Nell (Bishop) Grant: Ranch owner who runs a small dude ranch. Married to Travis Grant. Mother of Jeremy, Emma and toddler twins.

Travis Grant: Well-known writer who met Nell when he came to Promise for research several years ago.

Al Green: Sheriff's deputy.

Dovie (Boyd) Hennessey: Runs an antiques shop and is married to Frank Hennessey.

Frank Hennessey: Former sheriff of Promise.

Max Jordan: Owner of Western-wear shops.

Adam Jordan: Current sheriff of Promise. Was an Airborne Ranger for twelve years.

Val Langley: Ex-wife of Travis Grant. Lawyer who represented Richard Weston at his trial. From New York.

Wade McMillen and Amy (Thornton) McMillen: Promise Christian Church pastor and his wife.

Dr. Jane (Dickinson) Patterson: Doctor in Promise. Married to rancher Cal Patterson.

Cal Patterson: Partner in Lonesome Coyote Ranch with his brother, Glen.

Ellen (Frasier) Patterson: Owner of Frasier's Feed. Married to Glen Patterson.

Glen Patterson: Rancher. Brother of Cal.

Mary and Phil Patterson: Parents of Cal and Glen. Operate a local B&B.

Gordon Pawling: Retired judge from Toronto, Canada. Met Dovie Hennessey and the elder Pattersons on a cruise.

Lucas Porter: Widowed veterinarian. Recently moved to Promise, where his parents live.

Heather and Hollie Porter: Lucas's young daughters.

Louise Powell: Town gossip.

Savannah (Weston) Smith: Grady and Richard Weston's sister. Partner, with her husband, Laredo Smith, in the Yellow Rose Ranch.

Laredo Smith: Rancher and husband of Savannah.

Caroline (Daniels) Weston: Former postmistress in Promise. Married to rancher Grady Weston.

Grady Weston: Rancher, half owner of the Yellow Rose.

Richard Weston: Youngest of the Weston siblings. Currently in prison in New York City.

One

"Annie, I'm so sorry! I can't *tell* you how sorry I am."

Annie Applegate shifted the receiver to her other ear and blinked repeatedly. Jane Patterson's sympathetic voice had brought tears to her eyes.

"You should've let me know," Jane continued.

It'd taken Annie nearly twelve months to write her childhood friend about the disasters that had befallen her in the past two years. Jane had called the minute she'd read the letter; Annie was grateful for that, although even now, a friend's genuine sympathy threatened her shaky resolve in a way that indifference didn't.

"I...couldn't," she said. "Not right away."

Four years ago, Jane had left southern California—where Annie still lived—and moved to Promise, a town in the Texas hill country. She'd gone there to work in the local health clinic as partial payment for her medical-school loans. Her parents had been dismayed and delighted in equal parts when their only daughter married a local rancher and settled in the small community.

"What are you going to do?" Jane asked briskly.

She'd always had a practical, we-can-deal-with-this quality that Annie envied. "What are your plans?"

Annie wished she knew. The question was one she'd asked herself a thousand times since the car accident and everything that had followed.

"Do you think you'll stay in California?" Jane pressed when Annie didn't answer.

"I...I don't know. Probably not." Only she had nowhere to go, nowhere she needed to be, and no real family to speak of. Her friends here all seemed at a loss. They urged her to get on with her life; what they didn't understand was that she needed a completely different direction. A new sense of purpose. If she was going to pick up the shattered pieces that had once been her comfortable orderly existence and move forward, she had to make some real changes first.

"Come to Promise," Jane said, her voice unnaturally high with excitement.

"Texas?" Annie murmured. "You want me to go to *Texas?*"

"Oh, Annie, you'd love it! This town isn't like anyplace else in the world. The people are friendly and kind and there's a...a kind of caring here. Promise is small-town America at its best." Jane's enthusiasm was unmistakable—and contagious. "Small-town Texas at its best, too."

Annie smiled. "I'm sure a visit would do me a lot of good," she said, thinking aloud, deciding then and there to take Jane up on her offer.

"I'm not suggesting a visit," Jane said, interrupting Annie's musings. "I think you should move here. You need a change, a fresh start—you know you do."

She hesitated. "It might sound odd, but I have this feeling that Promise needs you, too."

Staring out the display window, Dovie Hennessey watched her husband hurrying along Promise's main street. He was headed toward her shop, and judging by the look on his face, he had something he couldn't wait to tell her.

"Dovie!" Frank barreled into the store a moment later, his eyes twinkling with amusement. At sixty-five, he remained muscular and fit, she noted with pride. Every time she saw him, he gave her heart a little thrill—even after three years of marriage. Their romance had begun more than a decade before they decided to "make it legal," as Frank put it. He'd initially been reluctant, since he'd never been married before and was afraid of losing what he'd thought of as his freedom. Dovie, who'd been widowed for years, had desperately wanted the comfort and respectability of marriage. In the end Wade McMillen, the local pastor, had suggested the perfect compromise: marriage with separate residences. It hadn't taken long, however, for Frank to move into Dovie's house full-time.

"My goodness, Frank, what's gotten into you?"

"Adam Jordan," Frank told her, shaking his head. "I swear I've never seen anything so funny in my life. Just wait'll you hear what that deputy did *this* time round."

"*Sheriff* Jordan," Dovie gently reminded him. Frank had retired five months earlier, and it had been an adjustment for both of them. After serving as the town's sheriff for almost fifteen years, he'd found it difficult to hand over the reins to someone else.

Especially when that someone had been such an unpromising specimen as a teenager. Adam Jordan had gotten into one scrape after another and had nearly worried his parents sick before he enlisted with Uncle Sam. Somehow the army had straightened him out. To everyone's amazement, Adam had thrived under the structure and discipline of military life. After basic training he'd applied and been accepted to Airborne Ranger School, and from there had gone on to serve a distinguished twelve years as a member of the elite outfit.

With the recent cutbacks in the military, Adam had returned to Promise. Much to the delight of his parents, who owned the local western-wear shop, he'd applied for a job with the sheriff's department. Frank immediately saw that he'd found his replacement. Al Green, who'd served as deputy for almost twenty years, had no desire to assume the responsibilities of the sheriff's position.

So Adam had arrived at precisely the right time. When Frank announced his retirement, the ex-Airborne Ranger had run for the office of sheriff and promptly been elected; that was almost six months ago now, in the November election. Frank continued to spend much of his time with Adam, helping, he claimed, with the transition. Dovie didn't know who required more assistance, Adam or Frank.

"Boy's made a fool of himself with that new teacher." Frank chuckled. "Again. Locked her keys inside her car trying to show her the importance of security."

Dovie groaned, embarrassed for Adam. Anyone could see he was infatuated with Jeannie French. Fresh out of college, the first-grade teacher had been hired the previous August, and Adam Jordan hadn't been the same since. He'd done everything he could think of to attract her attention, but according to rumor, he hadn't yet asked her out on a date. Some days, it was all Dovie could do to resist shaking some sense into the man.

"Naturally he had no way of knowing she always throws her car keys under the front seat," Frank explained.

"Why in heaven's name would she do something like that?" Dovie was exasperated with Jeannie, too. Surely the girl could figure out how Adam felt! She sighed; she could just imagine Adam's face when he realized what he'd done.

Frank shrugged. "Why do women do anything?" he asked philosophically. "She had her purse with her, as well as the keys for the school. Apparently she picked up the habit from her father. He's got a ranch a ways north of here. Not much concern about theft in a place like that. Or here, either."

So Adam was smitten and the new schoolteacher ignored him. The two of them had become a running joke around town. Jeannie was sweet enough, and a dedicated teacher, determined to make a difference in her students' lives. And Adam, for all his skills and talents, didn't know a damn thing about letting a woman know he was interested. Now, after a series of embarrassments, Jeannie refused to respond to Adam's overtures. Not that Dovie believed the girl should get involved in a relationship if she didn't

want to—but for heaven's sake, she could give Adam
a chance! The pair of them needed some guidance
and good advice, but Dovie didn't know who was
going to provide it. At one time that role would have
fallen to her, but these days, with her antique shop
doing so well, and Frank's retirement, she already had
more than she could handle. Then, there was the situation with her friend Mary Patterson, only she didn't
want to think about Mary just now.

"How'd Jeannie take it?" Dovie asked.

"Not too well. You'd think poor Adam had done
it on purpose."

"He was able to unlock the car, wasn't he?"

"Oh, eventually, but while he was fiddling with the
door, Jeannie was giving him a piece of her mind."

"Poor Adam," Dovie said.

"Poor Adam, nothing. That boy got exactly what
he deserved. He was showing off his authority, playing big man in town, and it backfired. Sure, his ego
got dented, but it was a lesson he won't soon forget."

"And you loved it."

Frank sobered. "I did," he admitted, "but not for
the reasons you think. That boy reminds me of myself
thirty-five years ago. Cocky as a rooster and high on
self-importance. He'll learn the same way I did—and
probably a whole lot faster."

Dovie wrapped her arms around her husband. He
was right—there *were* similarities between him and
Adam. She just hoped it didn't take Adam as long as
it had Frank to marry and settle down.

"By the way," he said, "I stopped at the travel
agency. Gayla had our tickets." Frank slid the airline
packet out of his hip pocket and set it on the counter.

This European vacation had been planned for months. It was going to be a combination of business and pleasure; Dovie and Frank would spend two weeks touring major cities on the continent, purchasing a few antiques, visiting a museum here and there. They considered the trip a honeymoon of sorts—although Frank was quick to insist that their entire marriage had been a honeymoon—plus a celebration of Frank's retirement.

"Hey," Frank said, tilting Dovie's head up so their eyes could meet. "You should be showing more excitement than this!"

"I *am* excited," she told him, and she was. They'd talked about this trip for years, dreamed about it, too. Dovie had assumed they'd take budget tours, but Frank had insisted they go first-class all the way. While he was willing to go to a couple of museums, shop for antiques and help her arrange shipping, he wanted to make sure they had ample opportunity to enjoy the sights. And each other.

"Dovie Hennessey, I know you too well to be fooled," Frank said, holding her gaze. "Something's troubling you."

It astonished her how well Frank did know her. She'd been married to Marvin Boyd for twenty-five years, and he'd always been oblivious to her moods. That certainly wasn't the case with Frank. There was an almost intuitive bond between them, one that marriage had honed and strengthened. She'd never expected to fall in love again, let alone experience a love like this. And the lovemaking, oh my, just thinking about the delights they'd found with each other...well, it made her heart beat triple time.

"It's Mary," Dovie said relunctantly.

"What's the problem with Mary?"

Dovie didn't know how to answer. Mary Patterson had been Dovie's best friend for most of her life. They'd graduated from high school together. She'd been Mary's maid of honor, and later Mary had returned the favor. Over the years Dovie had watched Mary and her husband, Phil, raise two fine sons.

It was Mary who had stood with her when Marvin was buried, Mary who'd helped her through the difficult months that followed. After Phil's heart problems were diagnosed, Dovie had encouraged the couple to hand over the management of their cattle ranch to their sons and move into town. Not ready to retire completely, they'd started a bed-and-breakfast—and no one was more surprised at its success than Mary and Phil themselves. For years she and Mary had spoken on the phone every day or so, saw each other often and shared all their joys and sorrows. Dovie felt the same way about Mary as she would've felt about a sister.

"You're not answering me," Frank said softly. His hands caressed her shoulders as he studied her.

"Because I don't know how."

"Start at the beginning."

If only it was that easy. "Something's...not right." There wasn't anything Dovie could put her finger on, nothing she could pinpoint other than a vague feeling. In fact, until this very moment, she hadn't intended to say a word, not even to Frank.

"How do you mean?"

"Not right" was nebulous, she realized, but it was the best she could do. "I don't know," Dovie had to admit again. "I just don't know. But it seems we're not as close as we used to be."

Frank took a few moments to consider this. "Do you think she might be a little jealous of our taking a trip to Europe?"

Dovie laughed outright at that, but then, Frank didn't know Mary the way she did. "Not in the least. Mary doesn't have a jealous bone in her body."

"So, what do you mean you're not as close as you used to be? Seems to me you two are constantly chatting on the phone."

"Yes, but..." What her husband said was true enough, yet lately their almost daily talks had felt strained. Even *strained* was too harsh a word—this change had begun months ago, very slowly, only Dovie wasn't sure how she knew that. The difference was subtle, but somehow Mary seemed less attentive, less interested in their conversations.

That very morning was a perfect example. One thing Mary and Dovie enjoyed was sharing recipes and ideas about food and decorating. Both of them took an unabashed delight in everything domestic— the Martha Stewarts of Texas, Frank called them. Mary had been instrumental in convincing Dovie to open the small tearoom inside the antique store and had encouraged her to serve some of her special recipes. Because of Mary, Dovie's chocolate-dipped peanut-butter cookies and the buttermilk crust for her apple pie were two of the town's favorites. Yet this morning, when Dovie had mentioned a new coffeecake recipe she planned to try, Mary had sounded...indifferent.

"But what?" Frank asked when she didn't continue.

"I just don't know," Dovie said, starting to feel a bit desperate. "Something's wrong. I feel it in my bones."

"Come to Promise," Annie Applegate repeated Jane's invitation aloud as she drove down the narrow Texas highway toward her new life. Her friends thought she was crazy to pack up everything she owned and move to Texas, to a town she'd never even seen. Perhaps they were right, but it felt good to be taking some positive action.

When they were teenagers, Jane Dickinson had been one of her best friends. Correction, Dr. Jane Patterson. It was hard to remember that Jane wasn't simply Jane any longer, but a fully certified physician. Not only that, Jane was married—and Annie wasn't. Oh, she *had* been, but a serious car accident had left her with a permanent limp and a husband who found himself incapable of loving a woman whose once-perfect body was now marred by ugly, red scars.

No, Annie told herself, she was not going to dwell on Billy, although that had become nearly impossible since she'd learned his new wife was pregnant. What hurt most was that Billy knew how much she'd longed for a child. Before the wedding, they'd frequently discussed the family they'd have—at least three kids, close together. As an engineer, Billy earned enough to support a wife and children; he'd claimed he was willing to forgo extra cars and trips and other luxuries. Annie had thought of little else but quitting her job at the library and becoming a full-time wife and mother.

During the five years of their marriage, Billy had put her off with a detailed list of reasons they should wait before starting a family. In retrospect, it was a blessing children hadn't been involved in the divorce.

Annie had wanted to put all the pain and betrayal of the marriage behind her; she'd done that symbolically by reverting to her maiden name.

The car accident had cost her six months of employment, three operations, physical therapy and almost constant pain. But those were minor inconveniences compared to the death of her marriage.

"Make a new life for yourself in Promise," Jane had suggested. "Our library has a limited budget and is only open part-time. This town needs a good bookstore."

In the weeks since, they'd exchanged countless letters and talked endlessly, running up huge long-distance bills. Annie had learned about cowboys, cattle and ranchers. She'd learned that Texas cuisine included barbecue, chili without beans and lots of hot peppers. At least, she was already familiar with Mexican food—which she loved; according to Jane, there was a good *and* authentic Mexican restaurant in Promise. Jane had told her to listen to some country-and-western music, especially Willie Nelson. Her friend had described the people of Promise, the community itself, and her own role as physician in the town's only clinic. Hearing Jane's enthusiasm for Promise, Texas, Annie understood her decision not to return to California.

In some ways, Annie already felt part of the community. She knew the town and its history; she knew something about every family in the area. And thanks to Jane she could almost talk like a Texan. Their lengthy phone sessions were usually punctuated with high-spirited giggles that were reminiscent of their high-school days.

And now she was ready.

She'd sold or given away what she couldn't carry, and the U-Haul trailer was packed to the brim. When she finally reached the town limits, the church steeple was the first thing to catch her eye. The bowling alley was next, then the city park, followed by the post office.

Annie pulled into the bowling-alley parking lot and cut the engine. It was exactly as Jane had described, complete with a Greyhound Bus sign and a neon light advertising the café and a $1.99 breakfast special.

Jordan's Town and Country Western Wear sat on the corner across the street—and there it was, the empty space next door. She'd put down money to lease, with an option to buy. The place had originally been a real-estate office, but some time ago the company had moved to larger quarters. Jane had assured Annie that this would be the perfect spot for a bookstore; Annie had contacted the rental agent and they'd quickly reached an agreement. A bookstore was just what the town needed, it seemed, and Annie could think of no better way to invest her insurance settlement.

Best of all, there was a small apartment above the store. It had a large picture window that looked out over Main Street and the city park. Jane had arranged to have the place painted for her, and they'd decided on sage-green walls. This was to be Annie's home.

Jane had asked Annie to stop by the clinic the moment she arrived. The two of them had planned every aspect of this move, and Jane wanted to be the first to welcome her.

Annie climbed out of the car and methodically eased the ache from her arms and legs; the hours of driving meant stiff cramped muscles and pain deep in her bones. She glanced around, absorbing the feel of the town. She studied Main Street with its row of old-fashioned streetlights, decorated with baskets of May flowers. Vehicles, most of them battered pickup trucks, angled in from the street and filled the parking spaces. People strolled leisurely about, stopping to chat with each other from time to time.

The sun shone brightly for early May. Annie could hear birdsong everywhere. She noticed a bed of roses, already in bloom, around the base of a statue that stood in the center of the park. Jane had told her that her friend Savannah Smith had planted those roses.

It was a nice town, Annie decided. Everything she'd anticipated and more.

"Howdy, ma'am," a man said, touching the rim of his cowboy hat as he walked past. "Can I help you find something?"

"No, I'm fine, thanks." The town was friendly, too, but then, Jane had prepared her for that. She'd just sampled what Jane had written about so often—something she called "real Texas hospitality."

Yes, Jane was right; Promise would indeed make her a good home. With that in mind, Annie headed toward the clinic. Her pace was slow; although her limp often wasn't noticed—unless she was tired or had been on her feet for hours—the long drive had had its effect. The intermittent pain and the scars were as much a part of her now as her features or her personality.

As luck would have it, Jane was talking to her receptionist when Annie stepped inside the clinic.

"Annie!" Jane hurried toward her, smiling hugely and engulfing her in an enthusiastic hug. "You look wonderful!"

"So do you," Annie returned in all honesty. Jane was six and a half months pregnant although she barely looked it, especially wearing the loose white jacket. Annie knew how excited Jane was about this baby. Because of her contract to work at the clinic, she and her husband, Cal, had delayed starting their family. The town had recently hired another doctor, and Jane planned to work part-time after the birth.

"Jenny," Jane said as she turned toward the receptionist, "this is Annie Applegate, one of my best friends. We grew up together."

"I'm so pleased you're here," Jenny said, her smile encouraging. "Dr. Jane's been talking about it for weeks."

"I've got fifteen minutes or so between appointments," Jane said, tugging at Annie's hand. "Come and meet Dovie, and if there's time I'll take you over to meet Ellie and—"

"Already?" Annie protested, but not too strenuously. She'd been hearing about the women of Promise for months…no, years. She couldn't wait to meet them—even if she didn't know how she'd keep them all straight.

"Dovie baked scones this morning, and I promised Ellie I'd give her a call the minute you got here. Savannah's dying to meet you, too. She's the one who grows roses."

Annie nodded. She remembered who Savannah was. Dovie, an older woman, owned an antique shop, and Ellie, she recalled, was married to Cal Patterson's brother, Glen. Moments earlier, Annie had been exhausted, but five minutes with Jane and she was raring to go. "I want to see my store as soon as I can. The apartment, too, of course."

"Max Jordan has the key for you—that's his western-wear store. By the way, his son was recently elected sheriff." She paused as though she'd just thought of something. "He's single, if you're interested."

"I'm not," Annie assured her, but had to laugh. It was almost as if they were back in high school. Jane, with her boundless energy for life, was always trying to organize everyone else.

"Oh, Annie, you're gonna love it here!"

Annie was counting on that.

"And I'm going to love having you here."

"Another Californian," Annie teased, although she was well aware that Jane considered herself a Texan now.

"Cal says I might not have been born in Texas, but I got here as soon as I could. He'll be saying the same thing about you before long."

Arm in arm, they crossed the street to Dovie's shop. "Dovie," Jane called as she opened the door. "Annie's here!"

A lovely white-haired woman stood in a corner of

the store, working on a display. She stopped instantly and made her way across the room, her eyes brimming with warmth. "Annie, I've been looking forward to meeting you. In fact, Jane's told me so much about you, I feel as if we're already friends." She smiled. "This town certainly needs a bookstore...and now you're here to start one. That's terrific."

"I'm excited about it," Annie admitted, letting her gaze wander about the room. She'd never seen antiques displayed in such an artistic and creative way. Accessories and smaller items had been arranged on and around the furniture. Fringed silk scarves and long jet necklaces spilled out of open drawers. There didn't seem to be anything Dovie didn't sell, from exquisite stationery and reproductions of classic jewelry to dining-room sets and gorgeous mismatched pieces of china.

"Come sit for a spell and have a cup of tea," Dovie invited. "The scones are still warm. I want you to taste my homemade strawberry jam."

No sooner had Annie sat down at a table in the small tearoom than Dovie delivered a plate with scones, plus a small pot of butter and another of jam.

"It looks like you intend to fatten me up," Annie said with a laugh.

"You could use a few pounds," Jane whispered. "I'd love to give you some of mine."

"Nonsense," Annie whispered back.

Dovie poured tea all around. "Now, Annie, tell me about yourself. There may be details Jane left out."

Annie laughed again. "Well, as you probably already know, Jane and I are the same age."

"In the prime of our youth," Jane inserted, putting an extra spoonful of jam on the warm scone.

"I'm...divorced." Annie faltered over the word. Even after a year the reality of her dead marriage produced a sense of failure and pain. When she'd spoken her vows, she'd meant every one of them. It seemed that Billy, however, hadn't. The "for worse" and "in sickness" parts hadn't meant much to him. Annie had done everything possible to save her marriage, but as determined as she was, Billy was more so. He wanted out. In the end, she'd had no choice but to give in. That he'd remarried within a month following their divorce had come as a bitter blow and the ultimate humiliation. It'd been obvious that he'd already been involved with someone else well before their split, maybe even before her accident.

"I'm so sorry about your divorce. I know you also suffered the loss of your mother at an early age," Dovie murmured.

Annie nodded. "My mother died when I was seven," she said. "My dad and his wife are in San Diego, but I don't see them much." Annie had often wondered how different her life might have been had her mother lived. People cared about her—aunts, uncles, grandparents—but they had their own lives and had lacked the time or patience to deal with a confused little girl who didn't understand why her mother was gone. Even her own father had deserted her, burying his grief in his job. He hadn't remarried until Annie was in her final year of high school. She'd been raised by a succession of housekeepers who'd moved in and out of her life; it was difficult to remember all their names.

"How sad," Dovie said with genuine sympathy. "About your mother...and your father."

"It made me strong," Annie returned, "and independent." That was one of the reasons Billy had divorced her, Annie believed. Perhaps if she'd needed him more, had been weak and clingy, he would have stayed. No, it wouldn't have mattered. Billy would have left her, anyway.

"But you're here now," Jane said, "ready to start a new life."

"That's true," Annie agreed. She reached for a scone, scooping on a thick layer of jam. "In fact, I'm *more* than ready."

Two

Both her children were down for their afternoon naps, and that meant Savannah Smith had an hour to herself. She poured a cup of tea and reached for the mail, which one of the hands had delivered before lunch. Early afternoon was her favorite part of the day. With two children constantly underfoot, it seemed the house was rarely quiet—not that Savannah had cause for complaint. She adored her children and loved her husband deeply. There'd been a time when she'd despaired of ever being a wife and mother, and then one day when she least expected it, she'd met Laredo. From the moment she'd picked up the handsome hitchhiker along a deserted stretch of road, her life had changed.

Her life had become what she'd always wanted it to be.

She sifted through the envelopes, automatically setting aside the bills and tossing the advertisements in the trash.

Then she saw it, her address scrawled in a familiar hand—and froze.

The letter was from Richard, her brother. The name of the correctional institution was stamped on the back of the envelope, along with a warning that the letter had not been inspected.

Savannah needed several minutes to calm her pounding heart before she found the courage to tear open the envelope. Even then, she couldn't bring herself to unfold the one thin sheet of paper. In the three years since Richard had been incarcerated, this was the first letter she'd received from him. Typically, he blamed Savannah and her brother, Grady, for his troubles. He wouldn't have written if he didn't want something. She knew that without a shred of doubt.

Richard, the youngest of the Westons, was a constant source of pain to the family. After his last visit to Promise, during which he'd wrought havoc and brought disgrace into their lives, Savannah had searched carefully for an explanation, some event in their childhood that had shaped Richard into the man he was now. The thief, the scoundrel, the felon, preying on the weak and helpless. The man who gave no thought to the well-being or rights of others. In the end, she'd discovered nothing that could explain it. He'd been born into the same family, attended the same schools, lived in the same community. Richard, Savannah and Grady had all been equally nurtured and loved by their parents. Granted, her mom and dad had spoiled Richard a little, making fewer demands of their charming younger son than they did of their older children. But what youngest child wasn't just a bit indulged?

Savannah had come to accept that there wasn't any single thing that could account for the way Richard was. He'd made a series of small selfish decisions through the years; each one, she suspected, had led to the next. Each irresponsible act made the next one possible. And over time, those selfish actions had grown bigger and bigger. But for years, Savannah— if not Grady—had excused or overlooked his behavior.

The first major and truly unforgivable demonstration of Richard's character had occurred shortly after their parents' deaths in a flash flood. The day of the funeral, Richard absconded with the cash their father had left his heirs to cover the hefty inheritance taxes on the ranch. Richard had taken the money and simply disappeared. As a result, Grady and Savannah spent years scrimping and sacrificing to hold on to the land that had been in their family for more than 130 years. Savannah never learned what had happened to the forty thousand dollars, but guessed that Richard had squandered it, as he had his life.

Then one day, six years after he'd disappeared, Richard had mysteriously returned, full of regret—or so he claimed—for the pain he'd caused them. At first he seemed to be his old self again—fun-loving, charming, sociable. Before long, the ranch house was full of music and laughter, the way it had been when their parents were alive. Within a few months, though, Richard had revealed what he really was. Savannah had learned the ugly truth—her brother hadn't changed at all. He disappeared again, owing thousands of dollars to local businesses. This time he holed up in Bitter End, a ghost town buried deep in the hill country, miles outside of Promise. Not until later did they learn that Richard was on the run from the law.

He'd hidden out in Bitter End for weeks. Savannah

was convinced he would have stayed there indefinitely if not for the accident. A stairway had collapsed in one of the old buildings, trapping him. He could have died, *would* have, if he hadn't been discovered by Dr. Jane and Cal Patterson. Nearly dead, Richard had been airlifted to a San Antonio hospital, and once he'd recovered, he was returned to New York to stand trial. His crimes had included defrauding and forcibly confining illegal immigrants; he was sentenced to twenty-five years in a New York state prison. Until today, Savannah had heard nothing from him.

Now this.

She braced herself emotionally and unfolded the letter.

Dear Savannah,

I imagine you're surprised to hear from me after all this time. It's taken me this long to come to grips with everything and realize how wrong I was. I never was a quick study, was I?

Prison life is worse than you probably think. Much worse. But it's what I deserve. I can almost hear Grady agreeing with me and I don't blame him. I know I've been here for three years and I apologize for not writing sooner, but I didn't have the courage to ask you to forgive me. I'll understand if you decide not to answer this, but I hope you will. Could you find it in your heart to bury the past and start again?

One thing I've learned in this hellhole is the importance of family. I don't know what I'd do without my memories of you and without the money you sent for Christmas and my birthday.

Thank you. Now that I'm stripped of everything else, I've discovered how much you and Grady mean to me. You're all I have. I'm sure Grady won't forgive me—but will you? I'm paying for my crimes, and will continue to pay for the next twenty-two years. I can't undo the pain I caused you or repay the money I stole, but I can tell you how truly sorry I am.

Write me, Savannah, please. Tell me about the Yellow Rose—how's life on the old ranch? What's happened to Bitter End? I worry about some of those old buildings and fear another one might collapse. That place is dangerous and should be shut down. I certainly hope you haven't been back there on one of your "rose-rustling" expeditions!

You and Laredo are parents now. That's wonderful. A girl and a boy. I'd love to see photos. I imagine Laredo is a proud father, and I already know what a good mother you must be.

Don't let me down, Savannah. Please answer. I wouldn't ask if it wasn't necessary. You're all I have.

Love,
Richard

Savannah read the letter a second time and was so caught up in what her brother had written that she didn't hear the back door open.

"Savannah, can you..." Her husband's words died when he saw her with the letter, tears streaming down her cheeks. "What's wrong?" he asked urgently, kneeling down in front of her.

She lowered her head. "It's a letter from Richard." Her voice was shaky despite her efforts to control it, and she felt more than heard Laredo's sigh.

"What does he want?"

Rather than explain, she handed him the letter. Savannah watched her husband's expression as he read it, knowing he trusted Richard even less than she did.

"How come he knows about Laura and Matt?"

She looked up. "I've mailed him a Christmas card every year." Savannah knew she shouldn't have, and while Laredo wouldn't have forbidden it, he obviously didn't approve, either. But if Grady had learned what she'd done...well, he would've hit the roof. Her older brother tended to be volatile when it came to Richard, and he'd said over and over that he wanted no further contact. Nothing.

Richard's action had hurt Savannah, but it was Grady who'd mortgaged their cattle ranch, the Yellow Rose, to pay the inheritance tax, and then slaved for six years to become debt-free. It was Grady who'd personally paid back every penny Richard had charged in town, rather than tarnish the good name of Weston. Grady who'd been robbed of the best years of his youth, paying for the sins of his brother while Richard squandered their inheritance—and then returned for more.

Laredo set the letter aside. "What are you going to do?"

"I...don't know." And she didn't. Richard hadn't asked for anything other than her forgiveness and the promise that she'd write with news of home.

How could she refuse? And yet how could she

open that door and give her wayward brother another opportunity to abuse her family?

"Are you going to tell Grady?"

"I don't know," she said again. She wasn't sure of anything at the moment. She could only imagine what Grady would say if she told him she'd been in touch with Richard. On the other hand, she didn't feel she should keep it from him. After all, she and Laredo were Grady's partners in the Yellow Rose; Laredo and Grady were not only breeding quarter horses together, they were good friends. And despite Richard's faults, which were many, he *was* their brother.

"Grady has a right to know," her husband reminded her gently.

"A right to know what?" Grady asked as he stepped into the kitchen.

Veterinarian Lucas Porter leaned against the porch railing and drank deeply from a glass of iced tea. Ranchers Cal and Glen Patterson stood next to him, enjoying the peacefulness of the moment. The day had been exhausting, and Lucas was tired to the bone. Tired but also exhilarated, following the complicated birth of a foal. The mare was a favorite of Cal's and he'd been worried. Lucas was glad Cal had enough common sense to call him when he did. Another hour and it would've been out of his hands.

"She's a real beauty," Cal boasted.

"She's something, all right," Lucas couldn't help agreeing. Over the years, he'd assisted in bringing a number of foals into the world. His sense of wonder never seemed to dim. He could be reeling from lack of sleep, but it never failed. Any birth immediately gave him a renewed sense of joy in life.

"Aren't you going to call Jane and tell her?" Glen asked his brother. "Annie'll want to know, too."

Annie. Annie Applegate. This wasn't the first time Lucas had heard the woman's name. Apparently she was a lifelong friend of Jane's who'd recently moved to Promise.

"Annie—she's new in town, right?" Lucas asked, entering the conversation. "The one who's opening the bookstore?"

"Yeah," Glen said. "Friend of Jane's. Cal likes her. So do I," he added, meeting his brother's eyes.

Cal nodded. The more taciturn of the two, he didn't seem to mind Glen's answering for him.

Lucas envied Cal and Glen their close relationship. They ranched together, and between them ran one of the most prosperous herds in the county. They'd begun experimenting with crossbreeding cattle, together with their neighbor Grady Weston, and had achieved some real success. Lucas was impressed with their research, which had been written up in agricultural journals as far away as Scotland and Australia. The Patterson brothers and Grady Weston were fast making a name for themselves.

"What's Jane doing?" Glen asked. "I thought this was her day off."

"It is. She's with Annie. Since Jane talked Annie into moving here, she feels personally responsible for the bookstore's success. I made her promise not to lift anything and she said she wouldn't, but I know my wife. She's working as hard as half a dozen men about now."

Lucas gathered that the women in Promise were thrilled with the idea of a bookstore. Just that morning, he'd gone into the café at the bowling alley for coffee, only to find a sign-up sheet for reader groups by the cashier. Annie already had three or four such groups forming, and the bookstore hadn't even opened yet.

Lucas didn't understand the point of reading groups. He didn't want anyone telling him what he should or shouldn't think about a book. He was quite capable of forming his own opinions, thank you kindly. Women, though, seemed to look at it differently. There was a group to talk about the classics and one for romance novels; there was even a group to discuss "simplicity" books. *Simplicity?* If women found it so all-fired necessary to simplify their lives, they might start by cutting out all these unnecessary groups and weekly meetings. But then, no one had asked for *his* thoughts on the matter.

"Have you met Annie yet?" Glen asked, glancing casually toward Lucas.

"Not formally," Lucas said before taking another long swallow of iced tea. He'd seen her around town a few times. She was tall and fragile-looking. From what Cal had told him, she'd been involved in a car accident a while back, followed by a bad divorce. Apparently it was the need for a new beginning that had brought her to Promise.

New beginnings were something Lucas understood. Three years ago, after his wife's death, he'd returned to Promise, seeking a fresh start for himself and his children. He'd spent the first ten years of his life in Promise; then the family had moved to Oklahoma

City. His parents had retired in Promise soon after he graduated as a veterinarian. When his wife died, his mother had urged him to make the move back, promising to help him care for his two young daughters. And she had. He couldn't have made it this far without his parents' help. If only Julia...

Pain tightened his chest at the thought of his wife. Julia had been dead for almost four years, but the ache inside him never seemed to diminish. True, the sharpness of his loss had dulled with time, but not the empty feeling deep inside him. At night especially, the loneliness was more than he could bear.

Losing their mother had been terribly hard on Heather and Hollie, who continued to weep for Julia. Not as frequently now as in the beginning, but often enough to remind him that neither girl had forgotten her mother or ceased to miss her. Lucas pushed away the memories and tried to resume an interest in the conversation.

"Personally, I don't know what it is with women and their books," Glen was saying. "Ellie's downright excited about this new bookstore." He shook his head. "I can see what's going to happen already. Tumbleweed Books is gonna be just like Dovie's place. I'm gonna feel like a bull in a china shop the minute I step inside. You know what else I figure? She'll start selling other stuff besides books. There'll be trinkets and smelly women things, and coffee with stuff in it. Like *vanilla*." He shuddered. "I say it's time a *man* opened a shop in Promise."

"Men don't buy that many books."

Lucas raised his eyebrows. "Maybe you don't, Cal, but I happen to read quite a bit."

"I didn't say men didn't *read*," Cal objected. "I said they don't buy books. Did you realize that seventy percent of all books are bought by women?"

"When did you become such an expert on book sales?" his brother asked sarcastically.

"Since I've been talking to Annie. She knows about books—used to work in a library. And she knows about business. She did her research before deciding to open her bookstore."

"Good for her," Glen said. "But what about a store for us men? Where a guy can smoke a good cigar and buy new boots at the same time."

That sounded like a great idea to Lucas, but from personal experience he knew that what Cal had said was true. Only it wasn't limited to books. Women took real pleasure in shopping. And pride—it apparently required great skill to scout for bargains. Hell, whenever *he* had to buy jeans, he wasn't willing to check out prices in three or four stores first just to save a few pennies. His time was too valuable to waste on bragging rights for a pair of denims. In his dad's words, "Women shop. Men buy." That always made Julia laugh—no, he wasn't going to think about Julia now.

"It isn't only the women Annie's catering to, you know," Cal continued. "Besides her reader groups, she's hoping to start a creative-writing group and Saturday-afternoon storytelling for kids. You might be interested in that for your girls. She's already got Travis Grant lined up."

This was one of the longest speeches Lucas had ever heard from Cal, and he appreciated the information.

Travis Grant was a local writer with a wide national audience for both his children's books and adult adventure series. Lucas had been looking for ways to encourage Heather to read, and this sounded perfect. He hadn't managed to convince her that reading was fun, not a chore. However, getting Heather to read was the least of his worries at the moment.

At Cal's mention of the girls, Glen turned his attention to Lucas. "How's it going with your new housekeeper?"

Lucas shrugged. He paid top dollar for Mrs. Delaney and found the woman to be adequate, but little else. She watched the girls before and after school, cooked their dinner and did light housekeeping. Although Mrs. Delaney was kind enough to his children, she didn't offer them any real comfort. And she wasn't enthusiastic about much of anything. She didn't read to the kids or play with them.... He shrugged again.

"That says it all," Cal muttered.

Lucas nodded in agreement. "Sometimes I think it'd be easier to find myself a wife."

"Then why don't you?" Glen asked. "There's got to be someone within a hundred-mile radius who'd be willing to have you."

Lucas slapped his hat against his friend's side, and Glen laughed. Despite his own grin, Lucas saw no humor in his dilemma. His parents, Carl and Elizabeth Porter, had been looking after the girls, but caring for two youngsters had taken a toll on his mother and she needed a break.

His mother felt she was letting him down, but Lucas was the one who insisted his parents travel for a while and enjoy their retirement. They'd done far too little vacationing since he'd moved to Promise with his girls. It was time.

"Things are bound to get better," Lucas said. He sounded more certain than he felt.

"Yeah," Glen concurred, and Cal nodded.

For the sake of his sanity, Lucas hoped his friends were right.

Three

Grady Weston had been in a bitch of a mood all afternoon, and he knew why. It was because of Richard and that damn letter. Just when Grady was beginning to feel his life was finally free of his brother, Richard turned up again. Like a bad penny. Interesting how many relevant clichés there were, he thought grimly. A rotten apple. A bad seed. A thorn in his side.

Richard's most recent effort to weasel his way back into the family's favor infuriated him. Grady knew he needed to talk to Savannah and soon, otherwise Caroline was going to start asking questions. He'd never been good at hiding his concerns from his wife. He hadn't mentioned the letter, which meant she'd probably hear about it from Savannah. He wanted to avoid that. Even now, after three years of marriage, he couldn't shake a niggling fear that was tied to Caroline's past connection with his brother.

At the end of the day, Grady didn't head back to the house as was his normal routine. Instead, he turned off the main road toward Laredo and Savannah's place.

Grady parked the pickup, then walked to the rose garden, where he knew he'd find Savannah. While she prepared the earth for new plantings, three-year-old Laura was busy filling a yellow plastic bucket in the sandbox and nine-month-old Matthew was contentedly chewing on a toy in his playpen.

His sister stopped her work, leaning on the hoe when she saw him approach, almost as if she'd been expecting him. A large straw hat shaded her face, preventing him from reading her eyes. One thing he'd say about Savannah: she certainly had a way with roses. A profusion of color marked the rows—deep reds, pale pinks, whites and yellows. Even from a distance, he caught their scent. Savannah's roses had an unforgettable fragrance.

She had a thriving mail-order business that specialized in antique roses. She was what some people called a "rose rustler"—or "rose rescuer," as she preferred to describe it. She visited abandoned farmhouses, old churches and even cemeteries to find long-forgotten roses, many of them a century old. She scoured ditches and detoured onto rambling dirt roads. It wasn't unheard of for Savannah to drive two hundred miles to track down old roses. More than once, she'd stood up to demolition crews and halted highway construction work. She'd do whatever it took to find and rescue surviving rosebushes. She'd bring them home and restore them to full health and beauty, then propagate them for sale to other rose lovers— whose numbers continually astonished Grady.

"Hi, Grady," Savannah finally said. She slowly put aside her hoe before walking out of the garden, stopping to scoop Matthew out of his playpen first.

The child offered Grady a toothy grin, showing off four front teeth. In all his years, Grady didn't think he'd ever seen a youngster who resembled his father as much as young Matthew did, in personality as well as appearance. Even at nine months, Matthew displayed a stubborn strong-willed nature. Although, come to think of it, Caroline said much the same thing about *their* son, three-year-old Roy. Except Caroline attributed those traits to Grady, often saying Roy was "just like his dad."

"Everything all right?" Savannah asked. She sat down at the wrought-iron table outside her garden and motioned him to join her. There was a tray holding a pitcher of iced tea, along with two empty glasses—and again Grady had the feeling she'd been expecting him. She poured tea into both glasses, sliding the second one in his direction.

Grady declined with a shake of his head and remained standing. "I'm here about Richard's letter," he said abruptly. He didn't want to be distracted by social niceties before he'd explained the reason for his visit.

"Yes," she said with a soft sigh. "It's been on my mind, too."

At those words, Grady pulled out the empty chair and sat. "Have you answered him?"

"Not yet."

"Are you going to?" This was the more important question.

Savannah hesitated. "I...haven't decided."

"Don't," Grady advised, apparently louder than he'd intended, because Laura looked up from her construction project in the sandbox to stare at him.

"He didn't ask for anything," Savannah said.

She'd offered to let Grady read the letter, but he'd

refused. He wanted nothing to do with Richard. As far as he was concerned, his brother was dead. If Savannah chose to have contact with him, contrary to his advice, that was her choice, but he felt obliged to give her fair warning.

"You know he's just trying to use you," Grady muttered. He was well aware of Richard's game. His brother intended to slither back into their lives a bit at a time. All he had to do was find an opening—and Savannah, with her soft heart, would most likely provide it. Then, once again, Richard would get what he wanted. And he *did* want something; Grady would stake his life on it. Richard *always* wanted something.

"He asked us to forgive him," Savannah said. "I do wish you'd read the letter, Grady."

"I don't need to."

Savannah sipped her tea, but in a way that told him she was concentrating on something else. To his surprise, he noticed a smile edging up the corners of her mouth. "I'd forgotten how hardheaded you can be."

That reputation annoyed him, especially since he didn't feel he deserved it. True, he held some firm opinions and stuck to his convictions...but he was willing to listen to argument. He considered himself a fair man. And smart about Richard, if nothing else. He'd been burned one too many times by his worthless brother.

"Take my advice, little sister," Grady said curtly, wanting to make himself clear. "Don't answer that letter."

"Oh, Grady, do you honestly believe Richard is incapable of regret?"

"Yeah, I do." In fact, he didn't have a single doubt. His brother was a user and an abuser.

"You don't think three years in prison has taught him anything?"

"Oh, I'm sure it has," Grady conceded with more than a hint of sarcasm. "I can only imagine everything he's learned."

Savannah's shoulders rose and fell as she sighed again. "He didn't say, but I had the feeling Richard's found God."

Grady snorted, unable to hide his disgust. "They all do."

A pained look came over her. "Oh, Grady," she whispered, her eyes full of disappointment. "When did you become this cynical?"

The question didn't require a response. "Don't let him use you, Savannah."

"He's our brother," she protested.

"And he's done nothing but abuse our family and ruin our name. Not once, but twice. Don't let it happen a third time." Grady figured he'd said his piece, let her know his thoughts; what he couldn't do was insist she ignore Richard's letter. That decision belonged to Savannah alone. With a brief salute and a smile for the children, Grady headed toward his truck.

"Grady!" Savannah called after him.

He turned back and met her gaze.

"How can I not forgive him? That's all he wants. He's lonely and he's asking for news of our family. That's reasonable, isn't it?"

This pulled Grady up short. "*What* did you say?" He returned to the table in just a few strides.

Savannah blinked, apparently surprised at his reaction. "Richard asked me to write him and tell him about the family."

"The hell you will!" That did it, as far as Grady was concerned. He slapped the table hard enough to send pain shooting up his forearm.

Savannah jerked and Matt let out a startled cry. Savannah comforted him and sent Grady an accusing glare. Grady regretted frightening the baby, but he didn't regret saying what he had.

"Under no circumstances are you to tell Richard anything having to do with Caroline, Maggie, Roy or me. Not one damn word. Is that understood?" Anger churned in his gut.

"But—"

"I mean it, Savannah. Write him if you must. You can bare your soul to him, if you're foolish enough to think he's changed. But I forbid you to write so much as one word about me or my family."

"Grady, I'd never—"

Frightened by the loudness of his voice, Laura climbed out of the sandbox and raced toward her mother.

Savannah drew her daughter close. "If I do write him, I won't mention a word about you, Caroline or the kids."

He waited for his pulse to return to normal, then nodded. "Thank you." Sorry he'd frightened his niece and nephew, Grady crouched down at Laura's level. The little girl tentatively met his eyes.

"You still my favorite girl after Maggie?" he asked, his voice coaxing.

Laura grinned.

"Good. Now give me five." He held out his palm,

which she slapped with her own hand. Standing, Grady kissed the top of Matthew's head. "I'll talk to you later."

"All right," Savannah answered.

It came to him then, what he needed to say. What he should've said earlier. "If Richard's so keen on seeking our forgiveness, why didn't he write me, too?"

His sister couldn't answer that.

Adam Jordan waited a couple of days before apologizing to Jeannie French; he wanted to give her a chance to cool down before he humiliated himself further. He flushed with embarrassment every time he thought about locking her keys inside her car. It'd been an accident—but he'd acted like an idiot. And if that wasn't bad enough, he'd done it in front of Frank Hennessey. He was tempted to hand in his badge. Not that there was any chance Frank would let him.

Parked in his patrol car outside Promise Elementary, Adam waited until the school buses rolled out of the parking lot. A few of the town kids lingered in the playground, swinging on the monkey bars, the same ones he'd swung on as a child. The children stopped when they saw him step out of his car.

One little girl waved, and he waved back. Soon the kids were back to playing their games.

Walking through a side entrance, Adam made his way to the first-grade classroom, heavy shoes pounding against the floor. When he got to the room, he glanced inside. Jeannie was busy rinsing paintbrushes at the small sink in a corner of the classroom.

Every time he saw her he found it hard to swallow or even breathe. His heart seemed to speed up, as though adrenaline was surging through his body. He supposed it was; after all, that fight-or-flight response was a familiar one to him, given his military background. For twelve years, as part of a close-knit army unit, he'd been capable of making life-and-death decisions. His training had taught him to trust his instincts and to react quickly. Yet whenever he was in the vicinity of Jeannie French, those same instincts clamored that she was the woman he'd been waiting for. A woman to share his life.

His mother had been after him to settle down, not because she feared he couldn't fend for himself, but because she was blatantly in pursuit of more grandchildren. Adam's older sister had stopped at one child ten years ago, so the responsibility had fallen upon Adam's shoulders. Thus far, he'd been a disappointment to Margaret Jordan.

Now that he was back in Promise, his mother's hints had grown less than subtle. Years ago Adam had come up with a defense, telling Margaret he'd know the woman when he saw her. He wasn't sure that was true, but it seemed to satisfy his mother, however temporarily.

Then it actually happened. He met Jeannie French, and it felt like a bullet between the eyes. Adam had never experienced anything close to this kind of feeling. His stomach started acting up, he couldn't sleep, and every ounce of finesse he'd ever possessed deserted him. Here he was, a man who could leap out of a plane, rope a calf, and curse in five languages. But when it came to asking Jeannie out on a date, he reverted to the insecure teenage boy of twelve years ago.

What puzzled Adam was the realization that, objectively speaking, Jeannie couldn't even be described as beautiful. Attractive, perhaps pretty, but she certainly didn't have a face or figure that would stop traffic. She was average in height and weight. About five-five, maybe five-six with shoes. Mid-length brown hair, brown eyes. Round face with a small mole just above her lip on the left side. Kind of cute, he'd say. And sweet-natured. A perfect teacher for first-grade students. He'd dated women far more beautiful, far more sophisticated, but not one of them stood out in his mind the way Jeannie did.

She must have felt his scrutiny because she turned around and met his look, mild surprise showing in her eyes.

"Hello, again," Adam said.

"Sheriff Jordan." Glancing away, she straightened, then set the clean paintbrushes aside, as if she wasn't completely comfortable around him.

After everything that had happened, Adam didn't blame her. He stepped into the room, prepared to begin his apology. "I thought I'd come by and make sure you didn't have any problems with..." His voice faded when he realized he made no sense. She'd been driving back and forth to school in the same car all week, so clearly there'd been no trouble because of his stupid trick.

"Everything's fine," Jeannie told him. She pulled a paper towel from the dispenser and wiped the brushes dry before storing them upright in a glass jar.

"I, uh, wanted to let you know how sorry I was

for causing you any inconvenience.'' Adam could feel
the heat gathering around his ears.

''You couldn't possibly have known I'd tossed the
car keys under the driver's seat,'' she was quick to
assure him, which gave Adam hope. ''It's a dumb
habit, I know.''

''We don't have much crime to speak of here in
Promise, but it's a good idea not to tempt fate. You
wouldn't want to make it easy for someone to steal
your vehicle.'' Adam relaxed, grateful that her an-
noyance had faded since he'd last seen her.

''You're right, of course,'' she said politely. ''I'll
be more cautious in the future.''

She seemed to be waiting for him to leave, even
wanting him to go. Instead, Adam walked between a
row of impossibly small desks. ''Mrs. Schneider was
my first-grade teacher,'' he announced, and instantly
wanted to kick himself. He must have sounded like
an idiot. He'd been looking for a way to make conversation, to gradually introduce the question he
wanted to ask. He should have known better. Small
talk wasn't his forte.

Jeannie folded her arms and nodded.

''Since you're new, I, uh, wasn't sure anyone told
you the sheriff's office generally meets with the elementary students every year. Either Deputy Green or
I'll be making an appearance within the next month
or so.''

''Oh. Well. That's a very good idea.''

''We want the students to know the sheriff is their
friend.'' He yearned to tell her he wanted to be *her*
friend, too, but couldn't figure out how to do that
without sounding like he was making a pass. Which

basically he was, only he'd rather not be so obvious about it.

"I'm sure the children will enjoy your visit very much." She remained standing with her arms folded. She continued to look as if she was waiting for him to leave, but he ignored her signals. This was the longest conversation they'd had without a major embarrassment on his part, and he wanted to take advantage of it.

"I...hate to be rude," she said after a moment, "but I have a dentist appointment at four this afternoon." She glanced at the clock.

Adam's spirits sank. *Ask her,* his mind shouted. A movie on Friday night, perhaps dinner afterward. Just how difficult could it be to get the words out?

"Before you go," he said quickly, then remembered *he* was the one expected to leave. "Actually, I'll be going, not you.... I was thinking—no, I mean hoping, that you'd let me make it up to you."

She frowned. "I'm sorry, I don't understand."

"Locking your car keys inside your car."

"Sheriff, really, it isn't necessary." She refused to meet his eyes, which flustered him even more.

"How about dinner on Friday night?"

"Sheriff..."

"If not dinner, maybe you'd be interested in seeing a movie. I hope you like butter on your popcorn."

"I love buttered popcorn." Her eyes softened with a smile, and Adam saw for the first time how truly beautiful her big brown eyes were. Jeannie French wasn't the least bit ordinary; she was beautiful, stunningly so. Funny he hadn't recognized that earlier.

"Great." He felt like leaping up and slamming his

hand against the door frame, the way he'd done in sixth grade. "How about dinner *and* a movie? I'll pick you up around five on Friday and we'll catch the early show at the theater and then go out—oh, maybe to the Chili Pepper. What do you think?" He wanted to groan at the thought of all these wasted months. They should've been dating since at least January. The only reason they weren't was that he'd been a fool—and a repeat offender, at that.

"Oh, Adam—"

It was the first time she'd used his given name, and she made it sound like the most incredible name a man could have.

"—I don't think that's a good idea," she continued awkwardly.

"No?" Surely there was some mistake. He waited for her to explain.

"There're some people who just don't...gel together," she blurted. "Certain people who aren't meant to be more than friends. I'm honored that you asked me out, but I just can't see the two of us...dating." She paused and glanced guiltily in his direction, as if to determine the amount of damage her words had inflicted. "Don't misunderstand me— I like you."

"Obviously not enough."

"I'm sorry...."

"Listen, Jeannie, if you don't want to go out with me, all you have to do is say so." Which she had. Adam set his hat back on his head and hurried for the door, eager to escape.

"I'm sorry," she said again.

In an effort to save face, Adam shrugged as though it was of little consequence. "No harm in asking."

"None," she agreed earnestly. "It was very nice of you to be so understanding."

Adam didn't think that remark deserved a response and made a quick getaway.

Driving through town, he stopped at his father's western-wear shop. He should have known, Adam decided. Women like Jeannie French didn't date guys like him. Hey, maybe she had a boyfriend in Brewster. Some cowboy or other. She hadn't said so, but it was certainly possible. And just his luck.

"How's life treating you?" Max Jordan asked when Adam walked in.

"Fair," Adam muttered, suddenly wondering why he'd bothered with this impromptu visit.

Max Jordan leaned both elbows on the counter and studied him.

"What?" Adam demanded sharply.

Max sighed heavily. "She turned you down, didn't she?"

"Who?"

"That new teacher you've had your eye on for the last six months. You finally worked up your courage to ask her out, and then she turned you down."

"You know how I feel about Jeannie?"

"Are you kidding? Half the town knows."

Great, just great. No wonder Jeannie had been rushing him out the door. She knew how he felt—just like everyone else in town, apparently—and had been trying to spare him further embarrassment.

"She doesn't want anything to do with me," Adam

told his father, disgusted with himself for not having figured it out sooner. It'd taken thirty years to find the right woman, only to learn she wasn't interested in him.

vold his father disguised with himself for not having

figured it out sooner. He'd make one?s peace to end

the right moment, only to learn she wasn't interested

in him.

Four

"**Y**ou want me to meet you at the café at noon?"
Jane Patterson asked her husband, although the question was more of a reminder for Cal.

It was Saturday, a beautiful May morning, and he'd
parked the pickup on Main Street. Jane had the dis-
tinct feeling Cal hadn't heard her, and it wasn't the
first time this had happened lately. "Is something
bothering you?"

Cal's gaze drifted to her rounded abdomen and he
grinned. "Not a thing," he said, and briefly kissed
her cheek. "We'll meet at noon."

"Right."

They simultaneously opened the truck doors and
climbed out, then headed in opposite directions, Cal
to visit his parents at the local bed-and-breakfast and
Jane toward Tumbleweed Books to see Annie.

The moment Annie Applegate had opened her
doors for business, she'd been swamped with eager
customers. Jane was delighted to see Annie's venture
already a success—and delighted to have her company again.

Jane chatted with friends and neighbors as she
strolled down the sidewalk. It seemed every rancher
in the area made a trip into town on Saturday morn-

ing. Once she was inside Tumbleweed Books, Gina Greenville, the high-school girl Annie had hired part-time, rang up the book Jane had ordered—the latest blockbuster by their local writer, Travis Grant. Travis was very much part of the Promise community and something of a hero. It'd been Travis and his wife, Nell, who'd solved the mystery at Bitter End, the original settlement that had been abandoned in the 1880s and reestablished as the town of Promise.

Annie sat in the back of the shop, surrounded by a circle of children for Story Time. Among the ten or eleven gathered there, Jane saw Heather and Hollie Porter; they were huddled together, close to the front, their father, Lucas, leaning against the back wall.

A chapter from Beverly Cleary's book, *Ramona the Pest,* had the children's rapt attention. Hardly a sound could be heard above Annie's voice. Jane hadn't seen her friend look happier or more at peace with herself since their high-school days. Annie held the book up so the children could see one of the drawings, and caught Jane's eye as she did. Annie smiled as if to thank her.

The bookstore was Jane's first stop, and she hadn't intended to stay more than a few minutes, but she couldn't make herself leave. On Saturdays she crammed in as many errands as she could, and this morning's schedule was heavier than usual. The baby was due in about two and a half months, but she was only now buying clothes and equipment for the nursery. She'd be able to take time off both before and after the birth; besides the physician Promise had under contract, there was a midwife who'd been hired because of the town's recent population explosion.

The children gathered around Annie were testament to that.

Three-year-old Joey McMillen crouched next to Roy Weston, Grady and Caroline's boy. The two were the very best of friends. Johnny Patterson, Ellie and Glen's son, was only a few months younger. Jane saw all three mothers—Amy, Caroline and Ellie—chatting animatedly at the other side of the store, near the children's book section. From what she'd heard, watching those three boys was like looking back thirty years and seeing Cal and Glen Patterson with Grady Weston. The three ranchers had been close friends their entire lives.

Jane knew she needed to leave, but was mesmerized by the story and by the simple joy of seeing her friend this happy.

"How's it going, Dr. Jane?" Lucas Porter asked quietly.

"Great," she whispered back. "How about you, Dr. Luke?"

"Fair to middlin'," he said, keeping his gaze trained on his daughters.

"Your girls certainly seem to enjoy Story Time."

"That's not the half of it," Lucas muttered. "Annie is all they talk about these days. It's Annie this and Annie that. They'd come to the bookstore every day if they could."

It did Jane's heart good to see those motherless children bond with Annie. Of all the women in town, Lucas's children had found the one who could really understand them, the one with whom they shared a common experience. It seemed as though the two little girls intuitively knew that Annie had also lost her mother when she was young.

All at once Jane saw the romantic possibilities between Annie and Lucas. It made sense; they were perfect for each other. Cal would probably be furious with her if she told him what she was thinking—but what he didn't know wouldn't hurt him. She'd invite them both for dinner, she decided, and nudge them in the right direction—just as Dovie and Ellie had once steered her toward Cal.

"Annie's really terrific with kids, isn't she?" Dovie commented, coming up behind her. "I knew we needed a bookstore, but I had no idea it was going to be this popular."

Jane nodded happily. It looked as if the bookstore was about to become the new gathering place in town. Maybe Annie should buy an espresso machine and sell cappuccino and *latte*. It was time Promise caught up with the rest of the country in that regard, although she couldn't imagine Cal or any of the other ranchers sipping a tall, skinny, double-sweet *latte* with a dash of Madagascar cinnamon.

Jane's eyes connected with Dovie's and held. She pointedly slid her gaze toward Lucas, then Annie. She couldn't believe she was the only one to notice the romance potential between the widower and her friend. Odd that it'd taken her this long to see it.

Dovie frowned.

Jane's eyes widened as she repeated her maneuver, glancing from Lucas to Annie. She gave Dovie a moment to catch her meaning, then raised her eyebrows in mute comment.

Jane knew the instant Dovie understood. The older

woman's mouth formed a small O. Then she winked, letting Jane know she was in full agreement.

"You're right, the girls seem to like Annie," Jane mentioned casually as she sidled closer to Lucas.

Oblivious to what Dovie and Jane were plotting, he nodded.

"You're sure everything's okay?" Jane asked.

"At home," Dovie added.

A frown clouded his face. "I guess so."

"The new housekeeper's working out?" Jane asked next.

Lucas lifted one shoulder in a shrug.

"I imagine you could use a break now and then," she continued.

"Get out, spend a few hours with another adult," Dovie elaborated.

"Yes, I suppose, but—"

"Have you ever thought of asking Annie out?" Jane asked point-blank. She was already behind schedule with this matchmaking and didn't have time to be subtle. Besides she'd been married long enough to realize men were dense creatures—often loving and wonderful but sometimes dull-witted, especially where romance was concerned. She knew Cal appreciated it when she came promptly to the point; subtlety was usually wasted on him. After conversations with her friends, Jane had concluded that her husband wasn't unique.

"Out? Like on...a date?"

"Why *not* date Annie?" Jane said quickly.

Lucas sent her a stricken look.

"Come on, Lucas," Dovie cajoled, "it would do

you both good. Annie hasn't taken a break since she arrived last month.''

"The girls…''

"Frank and I would love having them for the evening," Dovie volunteered.

"Cal and I would, too," Jane said, although she probably should have checked with Cal *before* offering.

"You would?" Lucas resembled a man who'd been thrown a lifeline, but didn't know what to do with it.

"Ask her," Jane urged.

The story ended, and the children started milling about the store in search of their parents.

"You think I should?" Lucas said in a hesitant voice.

"Yes," Jane replied, perhaps a bit too emphatically.

"I'm sure Annie would enjoy your company." Dovie spoke lightly, as though this was merely a suggestion on their part.

A minute later Lucas's daughters had found their father and begun chattering excitedly about the story.

"Daddy, Daddy…''

Jane noticed that Lucas's assessing gaze followed Annie as she moved here and there, answering questions, helping customers. "Maybe I *should* ask her out," he murmured before turning his attention back to his children.

Jane reached for Dovie's hand and squeezed it hard.

Not long afterward, Jane left the bookstore grinning widely. Oh, yes, Lucas and Annie were *perfectly* suited. She felt pleased with herself as she hurried on to her next destination.

Shortly after noon, when Jane walked into the café at the bowling alley, she immediately saw Cal sitting in a booth toward the back of the room. She made her way toward him and unloaded her packages before sliding into the opposite seat.

"I had the most fabulous idea." She hadn't planned to tell him, but she couldn't resist. "Annie and Lucas."

Her husband looked at her blankly.

"Lucas was at the bookstore with his girls this morning and I suddenly realized..." Her voice faltered as she noticed his frown. "Well, I suggested Lucas ask her out and I think he's going to do it."

"Jane, for the love of heaven—"

"I know—I shouldn't interfere. Just this one time, though." She paused. "Don't be angry with me, but I volunteered us to watch Heather and Hollie when they go out."

He shrugged and muttered something she didn't catch, then reached for the menu tucked behind the napkin dispenser.

"What's wrong?"

"Nothing." He studied the menu like a legal document, even though he was as familiar with it as he was with the current price of beef.

"I stopped off at the JCPenney catalog store and looked at some stuff for the nursery. We need to get that order in soon."

He nodded.

Jane chatted for a few more minutes about Dovie and Annie's story hour and various people she'd seen, then stopped abruptly. She'd become aware that Cal wasn't upset with her over this matchmaking issue; in fact, he was barely listening. Something else was on his mind.

"All right," she said sternly, "what is it?"

He stared at her a moment, apparently uncertain about whether or not to speak. "It's Mom and Dad," he finally said. He sighed, but seemed relieved to talk about it. "I found out they aren't accepting guests at their bed-and-breakfast anymore. Glen was as shocked to learn about it as I was."

"But why aren't they taking guests?" Jane asked. She adored her in-laws, and Mary and Phil were terrific grandparents to Johnny, Ellie and Glen's son. They were thrilled that Cal and Jane were expecting.

"I haven't got a clue." Cal looked away. "I wondered what was happening. The last couple of times I've stopped by, there weren't any guests, but I didn't think much of it. Then this morning when I was there, the phone rang and Dad answered and said they weren't accepting reservations. When I asked him about it, he didn't really answer. Said he and Mom had decided to take a few months off."

"Maybe they need the break," Jane suggested, not understanding her husband's concern. "They might have a trip planned."

"No," Cal shook his head. "If they were going to leave town, they'd at least mention it to Glen and me. Something's going on, something they don't want to talk about."

Jane wondered if he was overreacting, but that wasn't like Cal. If he suspected something was amiss, then he was probably right. "Do you know what it might be?"

Cal took her hand. "I'm afraid that after nearly forty years, my parents' marriage is in trouble."

Savannah hadn't heard a word of Pastor Wade McMillen's sermon on Sunday morning. When the singing started, signaling the end of the worship service, she hardly knew where the time had gone. She'd been confused and distracted since receiving Richard's letter, which she hadn't answered yet. He wanted her forgiveness, and she could see no way to refuse him that, although she knew both Grady and Laredo would prefer she not respond.

"If you don't mind, I'd like to talk to Wade," Savannah whispered to her husband. The church started to empty.

"I'll collect the kids," Laredo said as they slipped out of the pew.

"I won't be long."

Almost everyone had left by the time Savannah reached Wade and his wife, Amy, who stood in the foyer and spoke to as many of their flock as possible. Wade's eyes met hers, and Savannah felt as if he'd read her heart.

"Do you have a moment?" she asked, her hand still in Wade's.

"Of course."

Amy made an excuse and was about to leave them to talk in private when Savannah stopped her. "No, please, I'd like you to stay."

Both the pastor and his wife gave her their full attention.

"It's about Richard," she began.

Wade sighed and shook his head. "Something told me this had to do with your brother."

"He wrote for the first time. He said these three years behind bars have given him a perspective on the wrong he committed. He's asking for my forgiveness."

"And Grady's?"

Savannah shook her head. "He wrote only to me."

"I see."

"Grady doesn't want me to answer him. He's afraid it'll open the door to…something else, and he doesn't want Richard back in our lives. I don't blame him. I love both my brothers, but Richard's brought us nothing but pain and embarrassment. He's hurt our family and our community. I'm ashamed that people know the things he's done."

"But you feel you can't ignore his plea?" Amy asked.

"God's word is full of forgiveness." Savannah couldn't stand inside a church and say otherwise. That was what made this situation so difficult. Truly forgiving Richard meant forgetting everything he'd done. She wasn't sure that was possible.

"It's in forgiving others," Wade said quietly, "that we learn to forgive ourselves."

"Sometimes it isn't as simple as it sounds," Amy said. "Shortly after Joey was born, I heard from my mother. She told me she wanted to mend fences."

Savannah knew how deeply Amy had been hurt by her mother, who'd abandoned her when she was pregnant, leaving her to face the world alone.

"As soon as she learned I'd married Wade and that

he'd adopted Joey, she wanted back in my life. It took me a long time to be able to forgive her for deserting me when I needed her most.'' Wade placed his arm protectively around his wife's shoulders. "But I *have* forgiven her. I can look back now and not feel that pain anymore. Yes, I know the type of person my mother is. But while I love her and have forgiven her, I avoid contact with her. I have to be realistic about it. She's a selfish, self-destructive person, addicted to drugs and alcohol. I love her, I pray for her, but I've chosen not to make her a part of my life.''

Savannah let the words settle in her mind. The way Amy felt about her mother was the way she herself felt about Richard. She wanted a better life for him, but not at the risk of her own or her family's. "Thank you,'' she said, and hugged Amy.

Wade hugged her next. "Your heart will tell you what to do,'' he assured her.

The minute she'd finished with the noon meal and tucked Laura and Matthew in their beds, Savannah sat down in front of the computer and typed a letter.

Dear Richard,

After three years without a word from you, I'll admit your letter did take me by surprise. I'm glad to hear you regret the crimes you've committed and the pain you've caused Grady and me—and those poor helpless immigrants in New York City. My prayer is that this realization is a new beginning for you.

You asked about home, and I'm pleased to be able to tell you that the Yellow Rose is thriving. The partnership between Grady and Laredo has been a good one.

As for Laredo and me, our marriage is very happy. Laura and Matthew keep me busy, and my rose gardens take up the rest of my time. I've raised several prizewinners in the past few years. My catalog business continues to blossom (pun intended). Laredo splits his time between ranch work and raising quarter horses. He has a gentleness about him that children and horses instinctively respond to. I married a good man.

I want you to know that I do forgive you, Richard. You're my brother and I could do no less—but forgiveness is all I have to offer you.

You rejected your home, your family, your heritage, and that can't be undone with a mere apology. The trust that used to exist between us has been destroyed. Not once but twice, and that isn't easily repaired. I can forgive you, Richard, but I can't trust you.

Savannah

When she'd finished, Savannah read the letter through, then saved it. She glanced up as she heard the sound of footsteps.

Laredo had moved into the room and now stood behind her. He placed his hands on her shoulders. "You answered him?"

"Yes," she said tentatively, knowing he might disapprove.

"Tell me what you think," she said, and scrolled the letter back onto the monitor for him to read.

"Well?" she asked a few minutes later, wanting his opinion.

He kissed her cheek. "I knew you'd answer. You're much too kindhearted to ignore Richard's plea for forgiveness."

"But I can't allow him back in my life," she said, and experienced an almost overwhelming sense of sadness. The brother she loved was someone she no longer knew. In the years since their parents' deaths, he'd become a stranger.

"Are you going to let Grady read your letter?" Laredo asked.

"Yes," she said, "if he wants to. He has a right to know what I told our brother." It wouldn't be easy for Grady to accept her decision. He had his own demons to confront when it came to Richard.

It took Lucas almost a week to find the nerve to approach Annie Applegate about dinner. Friday morning, he sat on the edge of his bed, rubbed his face with both hands and heaved a deep sigh, promising himself he wouldn't put it off any longer. He just had to make sure he explained himself clearly.

Since the day Jane and Dovie had suggested he take Annie out, he'd made a dozen excuses to visit Tumbleweed Books.

He'd bought two more stories by Beverly Cleary for the girls, an atlas and a biography of Abraham Lincoln. But he still hadn't spoken to Annie.

At one time he'd had it all, and then his wife had died from cancer. For two years he'd railed against the unfairness of life; now he merely felt empty. He hated to disappoint Jane and Dovie, those two great romantics, but he wasn't interested—not in a romantic relationship, at any rate. He intended to be honest with Annie about that. Despite what he'd said to the Pattersons a few weeks ago, he wasn't planning to remarry.

The truth of the matter was that he was lonely, and he thought maybe, just maybe, Annie was lonely, too. Two lonely people who might share an evening out sometimes. Two people who could each benefit from someone to help break the monotony of everyday life. Someone to laugh with. A friend. He didn't quite know why he hesitated about approaching Annie. After all, they had several things in common. They were both newcomers to the community, although he'd lived in Promise as a child and returned there a few years ago. More important, Annie Applegate was alone, the same way he was, and she might be open to a just-friends arrangement.

Both his daughters now loved books. Heather, who'd recently been a reluctant reader, spent her entire allowance on books every week. Hollie, who was only learning to read, followed Annie around the shop like a shadow. Lucas marveled at Annie's patience with his daughters. He appreciated it, too.

Today was the day, Lucas promised himself. Jane had reminded him twice about her offer to watch his girls, and so had Dovie. A single father didn't get baby-sitting offers all that often; he'd be a fool to turn this one down.

Dr. Jane had made no attempt to be subtle about setting him up with her bookseller friend, and that worried him. But as long as he and Annie understood each other, it could work. The problem was, how exactly did a man convey that to a woman without disappointing or insulting her? Still, he had to try.

With a sense of resolve, Lucas readied himself for his day, paying extra attention to his appearance. When he'd finished, he studied his reflection for several minutes, scrutinizing himself with a fresh eye.

He concluded that at thirty-five he hadn't lost his looks. True, he was a little rough around the edges, but after everything that had happened in the past four years, plus his responsibilities at home and work, that was to be expected.

He possessed a full head of dark hair, with a few gray strands. But not many; he deserved more. The shadows beneath his eyes revealed too many sleepless nights and a grief that would haunt him to the grave.

All morning as he went about his duties, Lucas searched his soul...and thought about Annie.

He also thought about his wife.

It seemed an eternity ago that he'd dated Julia. They'd been college classmates and had married before he entered veterinary school. She'd worked to support them while he completed his training. Once he'd graduated and joined a practice, they'd started their family. Everything had been so well planned, so carefully worked out. Then Julia had become ill and was soon diagnosed with cancer. Within six months she was dead—and so were all his dreams.

Driving into town, he parked his pickup, then quick-marched down the street toward the bookstore. He burst inside, determined to be done with this once and for all.

"Annie." He hadn't intended to sound quite so demanding—or so loud.

Belatedly, and thankfully, he realized she was alone.

Startled, she looked up from the cash register. "Lucas?"

"No," he said. "I mean yes, it's me. Obviously." He groaned inwardly. "I...I was wondering..." He stopped, not knowing how to proceed. This was even worse than he'd envisioned.

"You were wondering..." Annie prompted.

Before he could say another word, the bell above the door jangled and Louise Powell walked in. Oh, wonderful—the town gossip. One thing about Louise, her timing was impeccable. He could only imagine what she was thinking. Here he was, hat in hand, stuttering with awkwardness. Louise paused when she saw him, and that sly knowing look came over her features.

"Hello, Louise," Annie said cheerfully. Too cheerfully, Lucas thought.

He didn't have a thing to feel guilty about, but he might as well have been a cat standing in a froth of feathers. Lucas cursed silently at the interruption.

Louise stared at the two of them, as though waiting for them to continue their conversation. "*Hello,* Lucas."

"Louise..." His gruff response did little to disguise his displeasure. Damn woman was about to ruin everything.

Louise glanced from one to the other. "Did I interrupt something?"

Annie shook her head. "Not at all. How can I help you?"

"As a matter of fact, you did interrupt something," Lucas muttered. Taking the woman by the elbow, he escorted her to the door. "I'm sure you won't mind coming back at a more convenient time."

Based on his experience, it wouldn't matter *what* he said or did from this point forward; Louise's version of what had happened would be all over town within minutes, anyway. That was the last thing he wanted, but he wasn't about to let this old biddy stop him now.

"Well, really..." Louise clucked as he escorted her out the door and then locked it after her. To be on the safe side, he reached inside the window and flipped the Open sign to Closed.

"Lucas?" Annie stared at him as if he'd taken leave of his senses. "What's going on?"

The problem was, he didn't know. He drew in a deep breath, switched his hat from his left hand to his right and then rammed his fingers through his hair.

"What's going on?" she demanded.

"Do you like to eat?" he blurted out, immediately cursing himself for asking such an inane question.

"Eat... Of course. Doesn't everyone?"

"The Mexican Lindo—or what about the Chili Pepper? And there's always the café at the bowling alley."

Her eyes narrowed. "Are you asking me to lunch? Is that what this is all about?"

"No, not lunch," he snapped before he could stop himself. God help him, he was making a mess of this.

"Oh?" Her confusion apparently matched his own.

"Dinner," he said, and fearing what he might say next, clamped his mouth closed.

Some of the bewilderment left her eyes. "If I understand you correctly, you're not asking me to lunch but to dinner, right?''

By this time, Lucas was afraid to say another word. Nodding seemed the best form of communication.

''Any day in particular?''

All of a sudden Lucas felt the need to sit down. He sank into one of the overstuffed chairs she'd placed throughout the store. Hoping to make a fresh start, he ran his hands through his hair, disarranging it further, and inhaled deeply. ''Annie, I apologize.''

A hurt look flickered over her face. ''For asking me to dinner?''

''No, for making a fool of myself. It's been a long time—years. Jane and Dovie suggested that I—'' He stopped. One thing he didn't need to tell her was that the entire idea had come from someone else. ''I wouldn't blame you if you decided you never wanted to lay eyes on me again. But in case you do, how about dinner?''

Her smile was warm and forgiving. ''I think that would be wonderful.''

''You do? You'll go?'' He bounded to his feet. ''Great—that's really great.'' Feeling jubilant, he headed toward the glass door, pausing only long enough to change the sign to Open.

''Lucas.''

He turned back, but not before he caught a glimpse of Louise Powell peering in through the display window, her hands cupped in front of her face.

''Is there any particular night you'd like to go?'' Annie asked.

''How about...'' He paused, afraid to suggest an evening without first clearing the date with Jane and

Cal. "Is it all right if I get back to you? There's... some other stuff I'd like to talk to you about, as well." In light of how poorly this had gone, it seemed best to wait before he introduced the "just friends" idea.

"Sure."

"You won't change your mind?" he asked.

"Not unless you do."

Lucas rolled his eyes. "Trust me, after all this, it ain't likely."

Annie smiled, and for the first time since entering the bookstore, Lucas felt like grinning himself.

Louise Powell was still standing on the sidewalk outside Tumbleweed Books. He stopped, debating whether to say anything, then decided against it and hurried toward his truck.

Five

Dovie couldn't believe everything that needed to be done before she and Frank left for Europe. Vanessa Boyd—always called Nessa—her sister-in-law from her first marriage, had agreed to fill in for Dovie at the shop. Amy McMillen, the pastor's wife, had volunteered to collect the mail and newspapers and keep an eye on the house. Appointments, errands, deadlines crowded on top of one another until the thought of leaving for two weeks overwhelmed her.

Frank was no help. He took all her crises in stride and insisted everything would take care of itself. His problem, in her opinion, was that he'd married too late in life to learn the importance of worry. She'd told Mary Patterson that, anticipating a big laugh, and hadn't gotten one. Her strained friendship with Mary continued to bother her. Another item to add to her growing list of concerns.

"You look exhausted, and you haven't even packed yet," Nessa commented when she entered the shop that morning. She was spending a couple of weeks working at the store to get a feel for the job before replacing Dovie.

"I *am* exhausted," Dovie confessed. She poured them each a cup of tea and placed her feet on the chair across from her. The ovens had been on since four o'clock that morning. No one seemed to appreciate how much effort went into preparing for a vacation, least of all Frank.

"Oh, Dovie, you're going to have the time of your life! Think about it—Paris, London, Amsterdam..."

Dovie knew Nessa was right. She should be excited. Happy. But she wasn't; she was tired.

Nessa had been a godsend. The previous fall, her sister-in-law had returned to Promise after a long absence. For nearly thirty years she'd followed her oil-executive husband, Marvin's brother, around the world. In their twenties, Nessa and Dovie had been as close as sisters, but then Leon had started work for one of the big oil conglomerates, and the couple had traveled frequently. Their three children, now grown, had settled in different parts of the country. And then, shortly before he was due to retire, Leon suffered a heart attack and died.

Nessa hadn't known what to do with herself afterward. Her children each had their own opinions about what was best for their mother. Judging by the phone calls Dovie had received from Nessa's oldest daughter, Sylvia, they obviously thought Nessa was incapable of making rational decisions. But she wasn't. After a few months, much to Sylvia's distress, Nessa decided to leave New Orleans and move back to Promise, and Dovie was delighted she had.

Despite her daughter's displeasure, Nessa packed up sixty-three years of life, which included a trunk full of mementoes from the family's travels. She bought the house that had once belonged to Ellie Patterson and moved in. All without the aid of her children, who continued to bicker among themselves. Dovie found it wryly amusing.

"You're going to love London," Nessa promised, stirring her tea.

"And Paris."

"Ah, Paris," Nessa said dreamily. "The City of Light. There's nothing like it, Dovie. Nothing."

Dovie knew she'd enjoy Europe once she got there, although at the moment her feet hurt and her head was full of all the tasks she had yet to complete. "It's just that I've got so much to do."

"I'll help. Why do you think I'm here?" Nessa stood, prepared to carry her half-empty teacup to the kitchen. "Now, where would you like me to start?"

Dovie motioned her back to her chair. "You might be ready to get up, but I'm not through sitting yet." Especially after an entire morning spent baking ten dozen scones to freeze so Nessa could serve them while Dovie was in Europe.

Without complaint, Nessa sat down again. "At least let me dip the peanut-butter cookies for you."

"All right," Dovie agreed. A few years earlier, she'd taken her peanut-butter cookies and half dipped them in a pot of melted chocolate. The result had made her cookies the most popular in town. She'd spent the day before baking a triple batch, hoping Nessa would have enough to last for the two weeks she'd be away.

"You haven't got a thing to worry about," Nessa assured her. "I promise I'll watch over the store as if it were my own."

"I know." Dovie was grateful, too. Nessa's return to Promise had been perfectly timed. Normally she

would've asked Mary Patterson to step in for her. Not
now. If Mary had wanted to help, she would have
volunteered. And...she hadn't.

"I'm afraid that when we're on our trip, I'll be so
tired all I'll want to do is sleep." Especially if this
week was anything to go by.

"You're going to be much too excited to sleep,"
Nessa said. "Traveling's a wonderful adventure, and
the memories will last you a lifetime."

"I'm sure I'll feel better once we've actually left.
All the work leading up to this vacation is what's
driving me nuts. Frank and I—" She stopped
abruptly, realizing how thoughtless she must sound.
Nessa had been a widow for only a year. "Nessa, I'm
sorry."

"Sorry?" Nessa repeated. "For what?"

"You traveled all over the world with Leon, and
here I am dragging up those memories."

Nessa dismissed that idea with an absent wave of
her hand. "Don't be silly. The memories I have are
happy ones. I loved my husband and never regretted
a day of our lives together. But I've adjusted to life
without Leon. It took me six months to regain my
balance and decide where home would be. I don't
know why Sylvia thinks she needs to watch over me
twenty-four hours a day. I'm not a child."

"What's Sylvia up to now?"

"Nothing new. She seems to think I'm the type of
woman who needs a man in her life."

Dovie had rarely met a woman as capable as her
sister-in-law.

"Lately she's been suggesting I remarry. She said
she wouldn't worry about me so much if I wasn't

living alone. Have you ever heard anything more ridiculous in your life?''

"She's joking, right?"

"I wish. She's already lining up men for me to meet when I visit this summer. I told her I wasn't interested, but that's never stopped Sylvia before and I don't expect it will now."

"Are you going to put up with it?"

Nessa laughed. "No, but I'll have to go through the motions. She's got her brothers involved in the great manhunt now."

"Oh, dear."

"Don't worry, Dovie, I know how to handle my daughter."

"Perhaps I should talk to her," Dovie suggested.

"I don't think so, seeing that you're to blame."

"Me?" Dovie gave a small shriek. "*Me?* What did I do?"

"Nothing much but find happiness after losing your husband. Sylvia says you're a perfect example of a woman who's gotten on with her life."

"I was a widow for eleven years before I married Frank," Dovie protested.

"I know." Nessa fell silent for a moment. "Actually, I have only myself to blame for this. After Leon died, I was a mess. His death came as such a shock. He kissed me goodbye that morning, and by noon he was dead. Like I said, for six months I wasn't myself—I hardly slept or ate or anything else. Then one day I woke up and realized Leon was dead, but I had the rest of my life to live. After all the moves and adjustments we'd made over the years, I figured

I could do it one more time. Do I miss Leon? Damn straight I do. But he's gone and I'm alive.''

"Oh, Nessa, you're so wise."

"Not really." She laughed and shook her head. "Now, what is it you need me to do this morning?"

"Were you serious about dipping the cookies?" It would be a great help, and one less headache for Dovie. They froze so nicely, too.

"Of course I was serious."

"Oh, good."

The door opened and Frank walked in, looking as if he hadn't a care in the world. "How are my two favorite women this fine morning?" he asked, strolling leisurely across the room. He wrapped his arms around Dovie's waist and nuzzled her neck.

"Frank," Dovie chastised him, embarrassed at the open display of affection. In the years since their marriage, he'd become more demonstrative.

He chuckled and gave her a small squeeze before he released her. Dovie cast an apologetic glance at Nessa, but their eyes didn't meet. Before Nessa could hide her response, Dovie viewed the pain on her sister-in-law's face as clearly as if it'd been written in ink.

Annie was surprised by how much she was looking forward to her luncheon date with Lucas Porter. Because of their busy schedules, it seemed impossible to find an evening they were both available. Between the children's needs, including parent-teacher interviews, and extended office hours at the animal clinic, Lucas had no evenings free. And Annie still spent every night checking inventory, studying publishers' catalogs, reading *Publishers Weekly*. Her free time co-incided with his only once—on Wednesday afternoon of the following week. So they agreed to meet for lunch.

By one o'clock, when she joined him at the Chili Pepper, she was nervous and uneasy. She could see that he was, too. After they'd been seated and ordered their lunch, the conversation came in fits and starts.

"I don't know what it's been like for you since your divorce," Lucas said, shifting his silverware from one side of his plate to the other. "But since Julia died, I've sometimes felt starved for lack of adult conversation. At least, conversation that isn't strictly work-related."

"It does get lonely," Annie admitted.

"For me, too," he muttered. "That's why..." He hesitated and glanced in her direction, as if to gauge how much to say. "It'd be good to have a *friend*," he said in a rush. "Someone who understands how damned lonely it can get. I'm not looking for anything more."

She nodded, unsure of what else to do. He didn't need to paint her a picture. He wanted a friend. Okay, fine. An occasional lunch date. No problem. Someone to talk to, another adult who understood. She wanted that too, so she really had no reason to feel disappointed.

"I'm not interested in remarrying any time soon, if that's what concerns you," she told him.

"You're not? Great." His relief was evident.

"Friends," she said, and held out her hand for him to shake.

"Friends," he said, reaching across the table.

Until today's lunch, Annie hadn't quite known what to make of Lucas Porter. She had the impression that he was a good father; his daughters clearly adored him. And the way he'd botched asking her out had actually been quite endearing.

Once Louise Powell had spread her news at a frenzied pace, half the people in town seemed intent on telling Annie what they knew about the widowed veterinarian and how much he'd loved his wife. Each recounted tales of what he'd been like three years earlier when he arrived in Promise, grief-stricken and depressed.

Until now, Annie had been convinced this lunch was a mistake. She'd predicted to herself that they'd spend the entire time talking about his dead wife, her illness, her sterling character. And if not her, the conversation was sure to center on his two daughters.

But Annie was wrong. After they agreed that being friends would be the extent of their relationship, they talked about books. Both were voracious readers and had read many of the same titles. After the initial awkwardness, their discussion during lunch was lively and animated, with a friendly argument or two. For instance, he thought a particular much-hyped new author was intellectually pretentious; she disagreed. Over coffee, the conversation flowed naturally to other subjects. They discussed similar experiences they'd had and exchanged observations. They talked about how moving to Promise had changed them. Normally shy, Annie was amazed at how much they had in common and how comfortable she felt with him.

Eventually, they talked about the ghost town some

miles outside Promise. Jane had written long letters telling Annie about Bitter End and the story behind it, so Annie knew the town had been the first settlement in the area. She remembered that shortly after the Civil War, disaster had befallen Bitter End and driven all the inhabitants away. They'd established a new settlement, which they'd named Promise, and the town had flourished from then on.

Their lunch hour flew and almost before she was aware of it, they discovered it was time to leave.

They continued to talk as he escorted her back to Tumbleweed Books. Reluctant to part, they found their steps slowing as they reached the store.

"I had a great time," Annie told him at the entrance. "I only hope we lived up to the rumors Louise Powell's been spreading about us."

Lucas grinned. "I don't know if that's possible."

Annie smiled, too. Poor Louise was destined to be disappointed.

"I'm kind of surprised myself," Lucas admitted, looking mildly guilty. "I had a good time, too...."

"Ah, so the truth is out. Enjoying yourself came as a shock, did it?"

They stood smiling at each other until Annie finally broke eye contact. "Thanks again, Lucas."

"Thank *you*," he said. Then, as though it was an afterthought, he leaned forward and, in full view of anyone who might be watching, kissed her cheek.

A kiss on the cheek. Fair enough, since they'd decided they were friends and nothing more. "Bye," she told him quickly, starting inside.

"Annie." Lucas stopped her, his voice urgent. "Would you...are you willing to do this again?"

She nodded without hesitation.

"When?"

She gave a little shrug. "What works for you?"

"How about now?" he asked. "I'm working to-morrow evening, so I can take the afternoon off. Just let me call my assistant first." He paused. "You said you'd never been to Bitter End. Would you like to go?"

"I'd love to! Give me ten minutes to change clothes and talk to Gina." Because she was a high-school senior, Gina's class schedule allowed her to work at the bookstore two afternoons a week. The teenager was perfectly capable of tending the store for the rest of the afternoon. Besides, Annie was intensely curious about Bitter End.

She still remembered reading Jane's long account of her own initial visit to Bitter End, and the eerie feeling she'd experienced when she first stepped onto the main street. As Annie recalled, Jane and Cal had had quite an adventure, complete with dramatic rescue. It was Jane who'd discovered a badly injured Richard Weston hiding out there.

"I'm assuming Jane told you about her experience in Bitter End?" Lucas asked as they headed out of town in his truck.

"She wrote about finding Richard Weston there, nearly dead after the staircase in the old hotel collapsed on him." That particular letter had been riveting. If Jane and Cal hadn't arrived when they did, Richard would surely have died. "You've been there?"

"A couple of times," Lucas told her. "Wade

McMillen's held church services out there the last Sunday in August for the past two years. Speaking of Wade, did you know Joey McMillen was born in Bitter End?''

''Really? A preacher's son... Didn't a preacher's son die there, a hundred-plus years ago? Wasn't that the story?''

Lucas told her what he knew of how a preacher's son had been hanged by a group of drunken men. When the preacher discovered what had happened, he'd placed a curse on the town. In time, everyone who'd settled in Bitter End was driven away by plagues and disasters, and Bitter End had been virtually forgotten.

Lucas parked the pickup, then led Annie through a field of bluebonnets toward a worn pathway. Holding her hand, he guided her down an embankment. Because of her injuries from the car accident, Annie proceeded cautiously, watching her step. When she looked up again, she went abruptly still at the sight of Bitter End nestled below. Two rows of buildings, mostly stone and some of wood, cut a swath through the heart of the town. A church and cemetery stood at one end, a large corral at the other, with hitching posts and water troughs. For its age, the church, which was the most prominent building in town, seemed to be in good condition. The hotel, with its second-floor balcony, appeared in the worst shape, leaning precariously as if ready to topple at any moment.

Annie stared at the colorful array of rosebushes in bloom. She took in the other plants, some in window boxes and others in flower beds that bordered the buildings and splashed bright colors against their drab exteriors.

"I remember Jane told me about this—but I still can't believe it," she said, astonished at the vivid flowers everywhere she looked.

"Frank mentioned once that the town used to be completely dead," Lucas said as he slowly navigated their way down the embankment. "A genuine ghost town. He said it was really something, what happened after Joey McMillen's birth. Some folks think that having a preacher's son born in the town is what broke the curse. Others—of a less romantic bent— talk about an underground spring breaking free." He shrugged. "For whatever reason, everything started to grow again."

"What an incredible story," Annie said, awed. "Did anyone think of restoring the old place and making a tourist attraction out of it?"

"Apparently there was quite a debate about doing that," Lucas told her, "but the council voted it down. On the other hand, no one wanted to let the place deteriorate, either. The history of Promise is rooted in Bitter End."

"So what happened?" She gestured around her.

"Frank told me that slowly, one by one, families started visiting the old town. Soon they were making improvements. The steeple on the old church got re-built. That's where Pastor McMillen holds the annual service. The church has been cleaned out and the pews straightened. A couple of the buildings, like the hotel, are boarded up because they're unsafe, but the old stone structures are still solid."

"Everyone's done a wonderful job."

He nodded. "The last time I was here, I noticed that a number of families have put furniture in the buildings—stuff that was handed down to them from their grandparents and great-grandparents."

"I imagine Savannah planted all these roses," Annie said.

"She was the one who started it all, you know. It was her search for old roses that brought her to Bitter End. Soon after, others came, and later when word got out about Richard hiding here, people got really curious. Bitter End was what originally brought Travis Grant to Promise."

Annie proudly featured his books at her store, and he'd already come to speak once. Travis wrote best-selling children's books as T. R. Grant and had written two blockbuster adult novels as Travis Grant. It'd been a thrill to meet him, along with his wife, Nell, and their children, including a pair of adorable two-year-old twins.

"Nell and Travis were the ones who solved the mystery," Lucas went on to explain.

Annie had known that, but she hadn't heard details.

As he led her into the buildings he knew were safe, Lucas described the search Travis and Nell had undertaken, which involved interviewing descendants of Bitter End's residents, going into newspaper archives on the Internet and piecing together an antique story quilt.

When Lucas and Annie finished exploring, they sat in two rocking chairs placed on the boardwalk outside the mercantile. The scene was a pleasing one. Annie could imagine what it must have been like 130 years ago, and her thoughts slid pleasantly back in time.

They sat in companionable silence for a while, the subject of Bitter End apparently exhausted. Lucas glanced at her and said, "I hope my girls haven't made pests of themselves. They'd be at the bookstore every day if I let them."

"Pests? Heather and Hollie? Never!"

"They like you."

"Well, I like them. I hope you'll let them come as often as they want." She wanted to add that he was welcome too, but didn't.

Lucas chuckled. "I don't think I could keep them away."

Annie recognized the girls' need to be noticed and nurtured and loved. As a motherless child, that was what she'd sought herself. Whatever she could do to comfort them, to assuage their sense of loss, she would.

Lucas looked at his watch. "We should probably think about heading back."

Annie knew he was right, but she hated to leave the tranquillity of Bitter End. Nor was she ready to give up this time with Lucas.

By tacit agreement, they returned to the truck. Lucas walked ahead of her, assisting her as she made her way carefully up the embankment. When the terrain became steep, he reached for her hand. She smiled her appreciation and was rewarded with a lazy grin, which unaccountably sent her pulse skittering. Friends, he'd said, and she'd agreed—yet it seemed somehow that they'd already gone beyond friendship.

She was well aware that Lucas was a handsome man, especially when he smiled. But it wasn't his good looks that impressed her. Billy, her ex-husband, had been known as a heartthrob in their college days. But unlike Billy, Lucas Porter was a man of character, a man of inner strength. When his wife became ill, he hadn't turned his back; instead, he'd remained steadfastly at her side. When she'd died, he hadn't handed his children over for others to raise, but had uprooted himself and moved to Promise to be closer to his parents. This was the kind of man who would accept her scars. A man who wouldn't turn tail and run at the first sign of trouble. Friends, she reminded herself. That was all they'd be and that was fine by her. Wasn't it?

As they traveled back to town, they talked about the old families—the Westons and Pattersons and Frasiers—who'd left Bitter End and come to Promise. Truly a place for new beginnings, they decided. Lucas parked behind Tumbleweed Books and walked her up the stairway that led to her small apartment above the store.

She unlocked the door and was about to invite him in when he said, "Thanks, Annie, for a very enjoyable afternoon."

"Thank you." She held her breath, hoping he'd ask her out a second time right then and there.

He didn't. Instead, he tucked his hands into his pants pockets, nodded and walked away.

Apparently the interest she felt wasn't mutual.

Six

Glen Patterson knew his brother well enough to recognize when there was something on his mind. And this past week, Cal hadn't been himself.

For several years following the breakup of his engagement to Jennifer Healy, who'd walked out on him less than forty-eight hours before the wedding, Cal had been withdrawn, uncommunicative. Then Jane Dickinson came to Promise, and his brother's personality was gradually transformed. That was four years ago. After meeting Jane, Cal had become more optimistic and relaxed about life. It was increasingly obvious to Glen—if not to Cal—that his brother had fallen in love. Glen was, to say the least, relieved. In his view, marriage to Jane was the best thing that could have happened to Cal. Jane had restored the person he used to be, before Jennifer. But Glen sensed that something was wrong now, and he prayed it wasn't with his brother's marriage.

They were in the process of branding cattle and had finished for the day. They climbed into the pickup, then headed toward the barn in silence. Glen made a few brief attempts at conversation, but Cal's lack of responsiveness unnerved him. No teasing, no laughing, no jokes. Every once in a while, he studied Cal surreptitiously, unsure what to say.

"Everything all right with Jane and the baby?" he asked as casually as he could, when Cal parked the pickup behind the barn.

"Fine," Cal snapped.

"Don't bite my head off," Glen snapped back. "If you wanna be mad, then be mad, but I'd like to know what you're mad about. I'm funny that way."

That comment elicited a weak grin. Then, for no reason Glen could discern, Cal turned abruptly and walked into the barn.

"You been to see Mom and Dad lately?" Cal asked when Glen followed him. He sat down on a bale of hay, removed his hat and leaned forward, resting both arms on his knees.

"Of course I have." He was the brother who lived in town, after all. Glen saw their parents every week, sometimes two or three times. He and Ellie bowled in a couples' league on Thursday nights and his parents baby-sat Johnny. He often stopped by for a quick visit. And they saw each other at church on Sundays. Come to think of it, though, his parents' attendance had slipped in the past few months.

"Notice anything different?" Cal asked next.

Glen considered their last few visits and shook his head. "Not really."

Cal gritted his teeth. "Is the entire world blind?" he muttered. "Am I the only who can see there's something going on?"

"What's wrong with Mom and Dad?" This was beginning to irritate Glen.

"I told you they aren't accepting reservations, didn't I?"

"Yeah. But that's their decision, don't you think?"

Cal ignored his question and asked another. "How long has it been since they had guests?"

"They want a break," Glen said with a shrug. "Frankly, it's none of our business *what* they do."

Cal was silent a moment. Then he asked, "When was the last time you sat down and actually talked to them?"

"I do every week." But did he? Glen paused to give the matter more thought and realized that when he and Ellie dropped Johnny off on Thursday nights, they rarely spent more than a few minutes chatting with his parents. After bowling, it was too late for anything other than a quick exchange.

"I can't remember the last time Mom had us over for Sunday dinner. Can you?"

Now that he thought of it, Ellie had said something along those lines earlier this week. He hadn't really responded. He figured he saw his parents often enough without their inviting him over for dinner. It wasn't a big deal. Was it?

"Then you really haven't noticed..." Cal sounded less sure of himself now.

"Noticed what?"

Cal didn't answer immediately. "I'm not sure I want to say."

"If you're so all-fired worried, then why don't you ask Mom and Dad yourself?" Glen suggested.

Again Cal hesitated.

"Obviously something's really bothering you here—even if I can't figure out what. You need to talk to them. Hell, I'll go with you, if for no other reason than to get this burr out from under your saddle.''

"Fine." Cal nodded. "Come on," he said as he walked briskly toward the barn door.

Glen stared at his brother in disbelief.

"There's no time like the present," Cal went on. "I'll tell Jane where I'm going and meet you at Mom and Dad's.''

"All right," Glen sighed. "If that's the only way to clear this up." Privately, though, he saw it as wasted effort.

By the time Glen arrived in Promise, he'd convinced himself his brother was imagining things. Their parents had never been better. Five years ago their father's heart condition had given them all a scare. But Phil wasn't even out of the hospital before his ever-resourceful wife had taken matters under control.

Rather than sit in his truck, waiting for Cal to arrive, Glen knocked on the back door and let himself in. Whistling, he moved into the kitchen—then suddenly stopped. His father was standing at the stove, an apron tied around his waist. Glen couldn't prevent his mouth from dropping open in shock. Never in his entire life had he seen his father cooking.

"Glen!" His father was definitely surprised to see him.

"Where's Mom?" Glen asked.

"Upstairs," Phil answered, as if that explained everything.

"You're...cooking." So much for stating the obvious.

"Nothing wrong with that," his father returned, sounding defensive.

The back door opened and Cal walked in. His reaction to seeing his father in an apron was the same as Glen's. "Where's Mom?"

"Upstairs," Glen and his father answered.

"What are you boys doing here?" Phil slid the pork chops onto a cookie sheet and placed them in the oven. With one quick motion, he jerked the apron free of his waist.

"Cal has something to ask you," Glen said, glancing at his older brother. He crossed his arms and leaned against the kitchen counter. Cal was the one with the questions; let him do the talking.

Cal opened the cupboard door and reached inside for a coffee mug. With his back to his father, he asked, "So, how are you and Mom getting along these days?"

"What kind of damn fool question is that?" Phil exploded. "Your mother and I've been married nearly forty years. If we were going to have problems, they would've shown up before this, don't you think?" The sharpness of his words conveyed distress as much as anger. "What's with you two, anyway? I don't go asking you questions about your relationships with your wives. Don't pry into my private affairs and I won't pry into yours."

His loud rebuke had taken Glen aback. Cal seemed equally shocked. Before either could respond, their mother came into the room.

"Phil?" she said with a puzzled look. "Why are you yelling?"

"No reason." Phil shrugged apologetically.

"Can you help me?" she asked next, ignoring both Cal and Glen.

"The boys are here, sweetheart." He gestured toward them.

She smiled in their direction. "We don't see you nearly as much as we'd like," she told them. She frowned. "Do we, dear? Now, Phil, have you seen my needlepoint? For the life of me, I can't find where I put it." She sounded distracted, Glen noticed. That was unlike her.

"In a minute, Mary," Phil replied. His father's voice changed, becoming patient and gentle. Quite a contrast to the tone he'd used with them, Glen thought.

His mother started to leave the room, but then turned back and said, "Come again, boys, you understand?" With a little wave, she wandered off, toward the stairs.

As soon as she'd left, Cal looked directly at his father. "What's wrong with Mom?"

Glen had felt it, too. There *was* something wrong. His father's attitude, his mother's odd vagueness—they added up to something. But what?

"First it's our marriage, now it's your mother?" Phil said in a cold restrained voice.

"Dad—"

"Perhaps it'd be best if we continued our discussion another time," he said, and all but ushered them out the back door. Glen couldn't help noticing the weariness in his father's eyes.

Cal and Glen stood staring at each other as the door closed.

"Well?" Cal asked. "Am I right? Is something wrong with Mom and Dad?"

Glen shook his head. "Yeah, you're right, but I have no idea what's going on."

"I think we should find out, don't you?"

Glen didn't know how to answer. He didn't want to pry into his parents' lives, but at the same time, he'd begun to worry about them.

In fact, he was just as worried as Cal.

Sheriff Adam Jordan hadn't been in the best mood since that last visit with Jeannie French. He was still trying to figure out why she didn't want to see him. Either she was interested in someone else or she was already involved—maybe, as he was beginning to suspect, with some guy from Brewster. She didn't wear a ring, though. And as far as he knew, she wasn't seeing anyone from around here. But a woman this special, this attractive, didn't go unnoticed. Not in Promise, Texas. Not *anywhere* in Texas.

Adam sat at his desk attempting to do his paperwork, but in reality he was mulling over his options, which appeared to be damned few. Jeannie was off-limits; she'd said as much herself. He had to respect her wishes. He might not like it, but there wasn't anything he could do about it. He'd just about decided to accept his fate when Frank Hennessey walked into the office.

"You look sadder'n a dead mule," Frank said. Without waiting for an invitation, he grabbed a chair and dragged it beside Adam's desk, which had been Frank's not so long ago. "Don't tell me that pretty little teacher's still got you down."

Adam couldn't see any reason to pretend. Frank had a way about him that made it impossible to hold things back. It was one reason he'd been the best damn lawman Adam had ever known. Frank had the ability to look a man in the eye and without a word make it perfectly clear that he would settle for nothing but the truth. Even the most accomplished liars—like Richard Weston—quailed under Sheriff Frank Hennessey's basilisk gaze.

"I think there's someone else," Adam said. It was easier to accept than the excuse she'd given him.

Frank shook his head. "Who? I don't remember hearing that she's hooked up with anyone."

That was the problem; Adam didn't, either. "There has to be some other guy. Why else would she tell me she wasn't interested?" Adam refused to believe her rejection had been personal. On the other hand, if she *was* seeing someone, wouldn't it be simpler to say so? Hmm. Maybe she had to keep the relationship a secret because—

"You know what I'd do if I were you?" Frank asked. He leaned back in the chair and folded his hands behind his head.

"What?" Not that Adam really wanted to know.

"I'd ask her a second time. School's gonna be out soon. So you better get movin'."

Adam dismissed that concern. "I heard she's staying in town for the summer. But what if I ask her out again and she refuses?" Adam had already thought about trying again, but there was such a thing as pride. Without much effort, Jeannie had managed to stomp all over his, and he wasn't sure he was up to more of the same. "She's already kicked me in the teeth once."

"Well, so what if she turns you down? It won't kill you." Frank gave a short bark of a laugh. "Show her you've got a little gumption. After all, you haven't exactly put your best foot forward with that girl."

"What do you mean?"

"You locked her keys in the car!"

"That was an accident," Adam protested.

"You looked like a numbskull."

Adam flushed. Frank was right, and locking her keys in the car wasn't the worst of it, either. The first time they'd met, he'd been following her down a flight of stairs and inadvertently stepped on the hem of her dress. If not for his quick reflexes, she would have fallen. Her skirt had ripped, too. Frank didn't know about *that* one. And not so long ago, he'd walked up behind her at the post office. He hadn't meant to frighten her, but when she turned around and found him there, she gave a small yelp and her mail went flying in every direction. He hadn't known what to say, so he'd helped her gather her mail, then stood back helplessly and watched her race out of the building as if she couldn't get away fast enough. So asking her to dinner again didn't seem like a very good idea.

Adam scowled, preferring to change the subject. He didn't want to think about Jeannie French, yet she was constantly on his mind.

"Aren't you and Dovie leaving for Europe soon?" he asked pointedly.

"Yup. We'll be out of your hair soon enough,"

Frank said agreeably. He grinned, and Adam wondered if Frank was deriving some kind of twisted pleasure from making him uncomfortable.

"Did you stop by for an actual reason?" he asked with exaggerated politeness.

Frank narrowed his eyes and shook his head as if to say it was a sad day in Promise when the community elected Adam Jordan to the office of sheriff. "She's been in town what—about ten months now, right?"

"Right," Adam concurred with a sigh. "About that." Obviously Frank wasn't going to let the matter drop.

"The Cattlemen's Dance is coming up in June," Frank said, examining his fingernails. "Seems to me a new schoolteacher's kind of obliged to make an appearance at one of the town's biggest social events of the year. Don't you think?"

Adam's spirits lifted and he straightened. One thing was certain; if he didn't ask her to the Cattlemen's Dance, someone else would. If she was going to reject him, well, so be it. But he wanted to be first in line in case she had a change of heart.

Adam sprang from his chair and scooped his hat from the peg on the door.

"Where you goin'?" Frank called after him.

Frank should be able to figure it out, but Adam told him, anyway. "To ask Jeannie French to the Cattlemen's Dance. Where else?"

Frank nodded approvingly. "Don't take no for an answer, either, you hear?"

"That's up to Jeannie," Adam said. He passed Al Green heading into the station and laughed out loud when he heard Frank ask the deputy if there were any crises that needed handling.

Adam was driving toward Promise Elementary when he saw a deep-blue Toyota that looked just like Jeannie's turn into the Winn-Dixie parking lot. He made a left hand turn himself, hoping fate was with him for once.

It was. He waited as Jeannie got out of her car and entered the store, all the while rehearsing what he'd say.

True, the grocery store didn't allow him any privacy, but he wanted this invitation to seem spur-of-the-moment. As though he'd run into her by chance. As though asking her to the dance had occurred to him the very second he spoke to her.

Feeling better than he had in days, Adam loped into the store and collected a cart. The office was about out of coffee; he might as well add a package of filters, too. Never mind that the department had about ten thousand of them stacked in the kitchen.

It took him fifteen minutes to locate Jeannie French. By then, he'd added cookies, coffee cream, paper towels and a number of other things to the cart. He'd be lucky to escape for under fifty bucks. The woman was already costing him money—and she hadn't even agreed to go out with him yet!

"Ms. French," he said as he pulled his grocery cart alongside hers. He noticed she'd chosen the same brand of pecan cookies he had. He saw this as a positive sign.

"Good afternoon, Sheriff." Her greeting was cordial, if a little reserved.

To Adam, she seemed prettier every time he saw

her. Today she wore a white silky blouse with frothy strips of lace bordering the row of buttons on either side. She'd paired it with a slim black skirt that reached midcalf. She looked elegant, sophisticated, classy. Adam approved.

"I, uh, was wondering if you had a few minutes," he said, when he realized he was staring.

"Ms. French! Ms. French!" Emma Bishop, Travis Grant's stepdaughter, raced up just then, a look of panic in her eyes. "I can't *believe* I found you. Do you know where the spare key to the card catalog is? I volunteered to work in the school library this afternoon and I can't remember where I put it."

"Emma, of course. The spare key's in my purse. Oh, dear, I do hope you haven't lost the other one."

The two carried on an animated conversation over the missing key while Adam was left to twiddle his thumbs.

"Excuse me." A grandmotherly woman approached him. "Can I tempt you into sampling our new barbecue sauce?" She led him to a card table draped in a red-checkered tablecloth and holding several trays of small white cups. These were filled with nibbles of chicken speared on tooth picks and liberally doused with Texas Fred's Sizzlin' Barbecue Sauce.

It'd been several hours since lunch and Adam didn't object to trying a piece of chicken. He helped himself to a cup and had to admit it was some of the best barbecue sauce he'd ever tasted.

"Take one for your lady friend," the woman suggested.

Adam hesitated, then thought it couldn't hurt his

cause. It was never a bad idea to come bearing gifts, even small ones. He could see that the conversation between Jeannie and Emma was almost finished. Jeannie had handed the girl a key, and Emma was nodding solemnly.

Adam started toward Jeannie at the same time as the girl turned down the aisle, moving rapidly in his direction. Seconds later she slammed into him. The force of the jolt knocked him back a couple of steps, but he maintained his balance. However, the accident was not without consequences. The small white cup filled with chicken and barbecue sauce flew out of his hand. Adam watched in horror as it soared between him and Jeannie and landed squarely in the middle of her chest. In the middle of her lacy white blouse.

She screamed and leaped back as the bright red sauce spattered her and the paper cup fell to the ground.

"Oh, Ms. French!" Emma cried in fright, covering her mouth. "I'm so sorry! I shouldn't have been running."

Jeannie's shocked disbelieving gaze was riveted on her blouse.

Adam pulled his handkerchief from his hip pocket. "Here," he said.

Jeannie bit her lower lip. "This is the first time I've worn it."

"Oh," Adam murmured, holding the cloth in one hand and his heart in the other. Every time he was anywhere near this woman something awful happened. Something for which he was responsible.

Jeannie accepted the handkerchief. She seemed

about to cry. She did her best to dab off the worst of the mess, but that only made the stain worse.

"It's my fault," Emma wailed, sounding close to tears herself.

"No one's to blame here," Jeannie said, but she refused to look at Adam. "I think it might be best if I just went home."

"I'll drive you," he offered, figuring that was the least he could do.

"Thank you, but no." Her voice shook slightly.

"Is there *anything* I can do to help?" He was willing to offer her his life savings, his badge, his—

"No," she said miserably. "You've already done quite enough."

Days like this it was pure pleasure to be a writer. The words flowed effortlessly onto the computer screen as Travis Grant worked on the latest in his T. R. Grant series, called *Billy the Kid and Jessie the Teen.* His publisher was sure to change the title, but it was fine for now. He always needed a working title, no matter how clumsy.

Nell's writing desk was placed against his; that meant they faced each other when they worked on their respective books. After winning first prize in the local chili contest a few years ago and selling the use of her recipe to a restaurant in town, Nell had gathered together her family's favorite recipes. Sometime within the next year, her first Texas cookbook would be published. Travis was very proud of her.

Nell had run an emergency errand in town after Emma had phoned about some disaster concerning a key for the library. She hadn't returned yet.

Leaning back in his chair, Travis threaded his fingers behind his head and read the computer screen, convinced he was a genius. Either that or a fake. No one should get paid the amount of money he did and enjoy his work so much.

The phone on his desk pealed, disturbing his moment of self-appreciation. He grabbed it rather than risk waking the twins from their nap. Dianna and Devon had recently turned two.

"Hello," he said absently.

"Travis, is that really you? My goodness, you sound as if you're in the next room, instead of the wilds of Texas."

He looked up from the computer at the sound of his ex-wife's voice. It'd been months—no longer, perhaps a year—since they'd talked. While the divorce had been friendly, or as friendly as any divorce was likely to be, he didn't have any reason to keep in touch with Val. He would always be grateful to his ex, though. Indirectly, she was the person responsible for his meeting Nell. Val would never have guessed that when she persuaded him to go to Texas to check out Richard Weston's story about a ghost town.

"What can I do for you, Val?" he asked a little warily.

"Aren't you going to ask how I am?" she responded sweetly.

"No." No use pretending, Travis thought.

"Well, then I'll ask you. How are you? How's the family?"

She wanted something. Travis recognized the slightly pleading sound in her voice. They had been married for eight years, after all.

"You and Nell had twins, right? Boys? Girls? One of each? I can't remember now, but it was a real surprise, wasn't it?"

"One of each," Travis supplied. "Dianna and Devon."

"How cute. Planning any more additions to the family?" she asked, ignoring the lack of welcome in his voice.

Travis didn't think that was any concern of hers. "What makes you ask?"

"I don't know. Just curious, I guess."

He decided to change the subject. "How's New York?"

"You'd know if you visited more often."

After he'd married Nell, Travis had decided to keep his Manhattan condo, but his visits had become few and far between. Once last year and twice the year before. He didn't like being separated from Nell and the children. As it was, promotion tours kept him away more than he liked. In fact, he was seriously considering putting the condo on the market. Perhaps that was the reason for Val's unexpected call, something to do with the apartment.

"Did you hear Charlie and I divorced last year?" she asked.

So Val was already through marriage number two. "No. I'm sorry."

"I'm not. I never should have left you."

Travis didn't believe her, not for a minute. He'd been a struggling young writer when they first met, while she'd recently passed the bar. They'd fallen into bed and then into marriage, far too soon to know their own minds. It had been a stupid mistake on his part, one he'd paid for dearly in the years that followed. Val had scorned his writing and his chances of success, and soon left him for one of the senior partners in her law firm, Charles Langley. A year or so after she'd remarried, Travis's children's-book series had begun to succeed—beyond his expectations, and certainly beyond hers.

"Did you phone to cry on my shoulder?" he asked, remembering the many arguments in which she'd urged him to "get a real job."

"Of course," she joked, and laughed lightly. "Actually, I do have another reason."

"I thought you would."

"Do you and Nell still have that dude ranch?"

Now, what reason could she possibly have for needing to know that? The dude ranch was in operation, but only on a limited basis, and only in late summer. Mostly it catered to senior citizens. Since Nell no longer needed the income, several retired ranchers had more or less taken over the operation. They delighted in leading groups of greenhorns around the countryside. Travis got a kick out of watching these men and women in their sixties and seventies get on a horse for the first time in their lives. Granted, the horses Nell gave them were generally ready for retirement themselves, but the "senior dudes" enjoyed the sense of adventure, the camaraderie and the outdoor experience. His mother-in-law, Ruth Bishop, managed all the paperwork, plus tagged along as cook.

"Why?" he asked bluntly. He hated to sound suspicious, but he simply didn't trust Val.

"I was thinking of taking a small vacation and visiting your area."

"*You're* coming to Texas?" He didn't try to hide his surprise. Val was as urban as they came. "Whatever for?"

"I need some time away and you seem very impressed with the great state of Texas. I figured I'd have a look for myself."

Travis counted to ten to keep from saying something he might later regret.

"I was hoping you'd be willing to rent me a room," she went on.

"There's a wonderful bed-and-breakfast in town," he suggested.

"I tried booking a room there, but apparently the Pattersons aren't taking guests these days."

Travis hadn't heard that, but Val must've called them; otherwise she wouldn't have known their name. "I don't think it's a good idea for you to come to Promise," he finally said.

"Why not?" Val challenged.

"If you're so interested in Texas, try San Antonio," Travis murmured. "Or Dallas. Or Houston— plenty to entertain you there." No way in hell did he want Val anywhere near Nell and his family. The two women had never met and that was the way Travis preferred to keep it.

"But I want to see the hill country," Val purred, just like she always did when she was intent on getting her own way. It astonished Travis that he could ever have thought himself in love with this woman.

"Goodbye, Val," he said firmly.

"I'll phone back in a couple of days." He heard her words as he replaced the receiver.

"That was Val?"

Travis glanced up to find Nell framed in the doorway. She was a large woman, tall and big-boned, but graceful. From the beginning, he'd seen real beauty in her strong features and honest expression. It seemed a miracle that they'd found each other. He'd been soured on love and marriage; Nell was a widow who'd still grieved the only man she'd ever loved. Nell and her family had welcomed him into their home on a stormy night, his first night in Texas. That storm was the beginning of his new life....

"She wants to visit Texas." Travis answered his wife's question before she could ask.

"Dallas? San Antonio?"

"No, Promise." Travis had trouble believing it himself. "Furthermore, she wants to rent a room from us. Apparently Phil and Mary aren't accepting reservations."

"I see," Nell said.

Travis stood and walked across the room and drew Nell into his embrace.

"What did you tell her?" she asked, wrapping her arms around his neck.

"I wanted to suggest she take a flying leap and—"

"Travis..."

He sighed deeply. "I urged her to play tourist somewhere other than Promise." Then he kissed his wife, his lips lingering on hers.

Nell's eyes were closed. "I think we should."

"So do I." He nibbled her ear.

"Travis! Not that. I think we should let her stay here."

"You're joking, right?"

"I've never met Val."

"I'd rather keep it that way."

"We owe her. If she hadn't represented Richard Weston, you'd never have come to Texas."

Val had been the attorney assigned by the court to defend Richard, who had told her an incredible story about a ghost town called Bitter End. Val had passed it along to him—one of the few favors she'd ever done him.

It happened that Travis had been plotting a book around a ghost town at the time, so he'd gone to interview Richard. Weston had fed him a convoluted story about the town and some buried treasure. Travis had listened skeptically, but in the end, he had indeed discovered treasure. He'd met Nell and fallen in love.

"I don't mind, Travis," Nell assured him.

"You actually *want* to meet her?"

Nell smiled and nodded. "You love me, don't you?"

"You know how much."

"Then there's nothing to be afraid of. We have the space here, and as far as I'm concerned, she's welcome to rent it the same as anyone else."

Travis held his wife close. He wasn't convinced that allowing Val into their lives was a smart thing to do, but he'd never been able to refuse Nell anything. If she wanted to meet his ex-wife, then so be it.

Seven

Dovie and Frank hadn't been gone two days, and already Nessa felt right at home running Dovie's antique store. There'd been a couple of messages for Dovie on the store's answering machine; the man's name wasn't familiar. But other than that, she'd handled the customers and their requests very nicely, if she did say so herself.

Nessa had always felt close to Dovie but had never been fond of Leon's older brother, Marvin, Dovie's first husband. She'd found him selfish and self-absorbed. Over the years she'd seen the longing in Dovie for a child, but Marvin hadn't been willing to even consider it. Nessa knew her own children had helped ease that ache in Dovie's heart. She'd been a wonderful aunt and was certainly a favorite of Sylvia's. In the past year aunt and niece had clashed over Sylvia's attempts to control Nessa's life, but they continued to maintain a healthy respect for each other.

In fact, as Nessa had told Dovie, it was because of her marriage to Frank that Sylvia had decided her mother should remarry. She cringed every time she thought about it.

Good grief, Dovie and Frank had been together for

at least ten years before they got married. But Sylvia just ignored that little reality.

Nessa wasn't in any hurry to venture into a second marriage—if ever. She'd loved Leon too much for that. They'd traveled all over the world together and experienced such incredible adventures. Nessa had memories she wouldn't trade for anything. Hiking in the Alps with her family. Riding elephants in India, dogsleds in Alaska. She'd swum among stingrays in the Caribbean and climbed Mayan ruins in Mexico. For part of that time their children had been with them, attending local schools in London, Argentina, Labrador, the Middle East. As much as possible, Leon had kept his family at his side. He'd been a wonderful father, a devoted husband. No, Nessa wasn't likely to find another man like Leon. And frankly, she wasn't looking.

The bell above the door sounded, and a distinguished older man entered the shop.

"Good afternoon," Nessa greeted him. She didn't recognize him, but then she hadn't lived in Promise for many years.

"Good afternoon," he returned. He glanced about the shop with interest and obvious approval.

"Can I help you find something?" Nessa asked, walking toward him.

"I'm looking for Dovie." He continued his perusal, his gaze wandering from one display to another. "Dovie Boyd."

"I'm sorry, but Dovie's traveling in Europe."

"Oh." She could tell he was disappointed. "I did try to phone, but when I couldn't reach her, I thought maybe the shop hadn't opened yet and..." He let the rest fade.

"Is there anything I can do for you?"

He nodded toward the tearoom. "A cup of something hot would be wonderful."

She gestured to the small group of tables. "I was about to sit down myself. In fact, the water's just boiling for tea. Won't you join me? I'm Nessa Boyd, by the way."

"Dovie's sister?"

"Dovie and I are—were sisters-in-law. Our husbands were brothers."

"Ah, that explains it."

Nessa poured the steaming water into an antique Spode pot and carried it to the table with a plate of Dovie's special peanut-butter cookies.

"I'm Gordon Pawling," he said. "Dovie and I met a few years back. On a cruise."

"Oh, *you're* the man who left those messages." She glanced at him speculatively as she poured tea into bone-china cups. She liked the way Dovie used mismatched bits and pieces of old tea sets.

Gordon stirred sugar into his tea. "Tell me, did Dovie marry her sheriff friend?"

"Yes. More than three years ago."

Gordon seemed taken aback. "Good grief, it has been that long, hasn't it?"

"Frank and Dovie are vacationing in Europe and I'm watching the shop." Nessa slid the plate of cookies in his direction and was gratified to see him take one.

"I'm in San Antonio for a few days for a conference—international law—and I remembered Dovie. I had the day free, and when I wasn't able to reach her by phone yesterday or this morning, I decided to take a chance and come anyway,'' Gordon said. "I met the Pattersons on that cruise, too, but they also seem to be out for the afternoon.''

"I know Dovie will be pleased that you visited,'' Nessa assured him. "I do hope you'll take the time to see Promise. It really is a lovely town.''

"I will,'' he said, and met her look. "So, you're new here yourself?''

"Not exactly new.'' Nessa went on to explain that she'd recently returned after many years away. When she mentioned being a widow, he made a point of telling her he was a widower. In the course of their conversation, Nessa learned that Gordon was a retired judge from Toronto, Canada; he'd been invited to the legal conference to participate on a panel. He had one son who was the same age as Sylvia.

"This store is just the way I pictured it,'' Gordon told her over a second cup of tea.

"It's very like Dovie,'' Nessa agreed.

"I'm glad she's happy.''

They chatted for what seemed to be only moments, but when Nessa checked the time, she was stunned to realize it was half an hour past closing. She finished telling him about Frank and described their small wedding. "Now my children seem to think I should follow Dovie's example and remarry,'' she added wryly.

Gordon carefully returned his cup to the saucer. "What is it with children these days? My own son has been harping on that very subject. He was the one who insisted I take the cruise.''

"My daughter, Sylvia, already has a whole lineup of men she wants me to meet. I don't understand it. You can't imagine what I went through to convince my own children that I'm perfectly capable of making my own decisions."

"Your Sylvia has an evil twin in my son."

Nessa laughed.

"It's taken me a while to understand why it's so important to him that I get married again."

"Tell me, please," Nessa begged. "Perhaps it'll help me understand my own children."

"Miles and his mother were very close," Gordon said, his look thoughtful. "He misses her a great deal."

"My children miss their father, too," Nessa murmured.

"What it all comes down to is that Miles wants a mother. He might be thirty-five, but he still needs his mother. Since Evelyn's gone, I suspect he's convinced himself that any woman I choose to be my wife would fit the bill."

It was a theory worth considering, but Nessa wasn't sure it applied to her situation. "I don't know if that's the case with my children," she told him. "I'm afraid I raised chauvinists. My children seem to feel I need someone to take care of me. I thought the three of them would have a conniption when I told them I'd bought a house in Promise."

Gordon chuckled. "I've been a disappointment to Miles, as well."

They laughed and chatted some more, then Gordon glanced at his watch. "My goodness!" he said, in a shocked voice. "Look at the time."

Nessa didn't want him to leave and was about to suggest he have dinner with her. Afterward she could give him a quick tour of the town.

"I should've left two hours ago," Gordon muttered, swallowing the last of his tea. "There's a banquet I'm supposed to attend. I'm going to be late."

It was ridiculous to feel disappointed, but Nessa did. They'd spent nearly three hours talking nonstop, and it felt like three minutes. She didn't think she'd ever grown this close to anyone this quickly. She could almost persuade herself that *she* was the one who'd met Gordon Pawling three years ago on a Caribbean cruise. That *she* was the one he'd driven all this way to visit.

"I don't know where the afternoon went," Nessa said, making small talk as she carried their cups to the sink.

"Me, neither."

She didn't tell him the shop normally closed an hour earlier.

"I hate to rush out, but..."

"Go—don't worry."

She understood his need to leave, but it didn't diminish her feelings of regret. She walked him to the door and then outside, where he'd parked his rental car, a large luxury model.

He hesitated before climbing inside. "I haven't enjoyed an afternoon this much in years."

She crossed her arms. "Same goes for me."

"It was a pleasure to meet you, Nessa Boyd."

"You, too, Gordon Pawling."

He got into the car and started the engine. He waved as he headed down Main toward the highway;

Nessa waved back. She should have returned to the shop then—there were all kinds of things she had to do before closing. Instead, she stood on the sidewalk and watched Gordon's vehicle disappear.

With an unaccountable sense of loss, she walked back into the shop and flipped over the sign to read Closed.

As luck would have it, Adam Jordan's visit to the first-grade class at Promise Elementary was scheduled for the last week of school in late May. Adam hadn't seen Jeannie French since the barbecue-sauce episode. He'd avoided her, but probably not nearly as avidly as she'd avoided him.

Every time he remembered the look of horror on Jeannie's face, he felt sick at heart. He'd called himself every name in the book and vowed that from then on he'd stay out of her life. The fates had made it clear: they weren't to be together. Not ever. He was to look elsewhere. Forget her. Maybe he wasn't meant to be married at all, which was fine by him. The one and only time he'd been really attracted to a woman, he'd done nothing but make an idiot of himself. Oh, yes, he intended to stay well away from Jeannie French. For the sake of his sanity and her wardrobe.

Then he saw that he was scheduled to talk to the kids at Promise Elementary.

"You feel like visiting the school this afternoon?" he casually asked Al Green.

The deputy glanced up from his desk with a look of surprise. "I thought you enjoyed talking to schoolkids."

"I've got a lot to do today." He didn't, but it was

the best excuse he could come up with on short notice.

Al hesitated. ''I don't get along with kids all that well.''

''You have five of 'em,'' Adam reminded him.

''I like my own—it's everyone else's who get on my nerves.''

Adam grumbled under his breath. He could order Al over to the school, but a lot of good that would do. Al would resent it, which could jeopardize their working relationship. And all because Adam was embarrassed to see Jeannie French. Of course, he *could* contact the school and ask for a delay, but that didn't seem fair. Not when the other teachers had planned their days around his visit.

''All right,'' Adam said in a resigned voice. ''I'll do it.''

Al nodded. ''Seeing as you're the one who volunteered for it, that only seems right.''

Leave it to Al to remind him of that. Well, he'd be in and out of that first-grade class so fast, Adam promised himself, that Jeannie would barely notice him.

When Jeannie French saw the afternoon schedule and noticed that Sheriff Adam Jordan would be speaking to her class, her first instinct was to take a day's sick leave. *Not again.* He'd already ripped one skirt and ruined the most beautiful blouse she'd ever owned. Jeannie wasn't normally rude, but she'd never met anyone who had this kind of effect on her. Every time he even came close, something happened. Something ridiculous and embarrassing. She supposed she couldn't blame *everything* on him, but still... Some people just didn't mix, and that appeared to be the case with her and Adam Jordan.

Until recently, it seemed that everywhere she went, the sheriff was sure to follow...just like Mary's lamb in the nursery rhyme. She'd been flattered; he was certainly good-looking and actually seemed quite nice. But then he'd ripped her skirt, frightened her out of her wits, locked her keys in the car and destroyed a beautiful new blouse.

Oh, yes, it was best to acknowledge that any relationship with Sheriff Jordan was doomed before it started. There was another reason she was less than interested in Adam—Will Osborne, a local ranch hand who was handsomer than any man had a right to be. Now if *he'd* asked her out, there'd be no question about how she'd respond. Will was charming, a little risky and a lot sexy. They'd had a couple of conversations, but nothing had evolved beyond that. Jeannie hoped to see him again soon.

The morning passed quickly. Jeannie was crazy about her students and they returned her affection in full measure. The minute her first-graders were back from lunch, she found herself watching the clock, knowing the sheriff was due at any time.

As it turned out, he left her classroom for last. When he entered the room, the children stared up at him, at his uniform, his weapon, his hat, and their eyes filled with awe.

"Boys and girls," Jeannie said, standing at the front of the class. "We're fortunate to have Sheriff Jordan visit us this afternoon. He has some important information for us, so let's give him our full attention.'' She stepped aside and Adam stood before the children.

Jeannie walked to the back while he reviewed basic safety information. Barely a murmur could be heard. She realized that Adam had become every boy's hero and every little girl's knight in shining armor. She looked at him critically. Yes, as she'd noticed before, he was attractive enough. Very fit. About six feet tall. A kind face. She squinted and looked at him a second time, almost hoping she'd feel something. Anything.

She didn't.

When he'd finished, he asked for questions, and the children's hands shot up. The question-and-answer session continued until the bell rang, signaling the end of the school day. A minute later the classroom emptied as the children raced toward the waiting buses.

So Jeannie found herself alone with Sheriff Jordan yet again.

''Thank you,'' she said, knowing she sounded stiff. ''The children enjoyed your talk.''

He nodded. ''I wanted to apologize about the blouse,'' he said hoarsely.

''Don't worry about it.''

''I'd like to pay the cleaning bill, if you'll let me.''

''That isn't necessary.'' She'd already taken it to the cleaners and they'd promised to do the best they could, but they could offer no guarantees. The blouse had cost her nearly seventy bucks—a real extravagance for her—and now there was every likelihood it was ruined.

Silence again. It seemed so loud she wanted to shout that he should either say something or leave.

''I'd hoped to ask you...a question at the Winn-

Dixie. I realize you—'' He stopped and his shoulders moved in a deep sigh. ''What I'd...'' He started over. ''The community has a big dance every June sponsored by the Cattlemen's Association,'' he finally got out.

Jeannie had heard about it from the other teachers. It was said to be quite the affair. Nearly everyone in Promise made an effort to attend.

''I know you said you didn't think the two of us gelled—was that the word? I'm not exactly sure what you mean, and...I figure you should go out with me once before you can be sure of that.''

This was quite a speech for the sheriff. She could well imagine what the evening would be like— strained, awkward and potentially painful. He'd probably step all over her feet if she danced with him. Not only that, she'd have to bring an extra set of clothes.

''I will be going to the dance. Janice Reynolds mentioned it last week.''

The sheriff's eyes brightened with enthusiasm. ''Everyone in the community goes. It's the biggest event of the year.''

''That's what Janice said, but—''

''Then you'll go with me?'' he asked, not giving her a chance to finish.

Jeannie felt a surge of anger. He made this so damn difficult. ''Please don't make me say it again, Sheriff.''

He stared at her blankly.

''Please don't make me tell you I'm not interested in dating you,'' she said as kindly as she could. Why was the man so dense? Didn't he know she'd wanted to avoid exactly this?

His expression tightened. "I see. I'll make sure there's no repeat of this. Goodbye, Ms. French."

"Goodbye, Sheriff Jordan."

With his head high and his back straight, he walked out of her room. Jeannie should have been glad. He'd promised he wouldn't approach her again, which was the result she'd wanted to achieve. She'd taken the honest but painful path, not letting him trap her into attending the dance with him. She expected to feel a sense of relief. But she didn't. Instead, she felt as if she was the cruelest, most wretched woman on the face of the earth.

Eight

Lucas held the San Antonio paper in his hands, but he wasn't reading. The dinner dishes were done, and Heather and Hollie were in their bedroom playing. He cherished the silence, knowing it wouldn't last, and returned his attention to the front page.

His thoughts soon wandered from the headlines to his afternoon with Annie Applegate the previous week. He hadn't expected to enjoy it as much as he had. Their lunch, followed by the visit to Bitter End, had stayed in his mind ever since. Annie had a gentleness about her, and a sincerity. It was easy to see why his girls were so drawn to her.

He wanted to see her again, yet resisted asking. He wasn't sure why, but it seemed important that he put some distance between them.

With that in mind, he'd made an excuse not to take his children to the bookstore on Saturday morning. They could still go, but not with him. He didn't want to appear too interested, too eager. So he'd arranged for the girls to go with Caroline Weston and her daughter, Maggie. When Heather and Hollie returned shortly after noon, they'd been full of chatter. He longed to ask if Annie had mentioned him, but didn't.

The big Cattlemen's Dance was fast approaching

and he knew he was expected to attend. He'd had a miserable time last year. He'd felt so alone, watching his friends hold their wives on the dance floor. Watching the comfortable intimacy between them. He'd been so painfully aware of his loss that night. He'd never stopped missing Julia, and lately he seemed to miss her more than ever.

Lucas didn't want to think about the dance, didn't want to remember how badly his children needed their mother, how desperately he needed his wife. He felt those needs, those fears, every night, lying alone in the dark. He didn't want to remember them now.

Annie. It was better to think about Annie. She reminded him of Julia in some ways—her ease with people, especially children, her wholehearted commitment to the projects she undertook. In other ways, she was very different. Lucas realized he'd grown up with Julia. He'd been nineteen when they met and twenty-three when they got married. There'd never been anyone else from the moment they first kissed.

"Daddy! Daddy!" Hollie called out to him from the other room. "Heather took my Barbie."

"Heather, give Hollie her doll back," he said automatically.

"It's *my* doll."

"It's *mine*."

The argument was escalating fast. Setting aside his newspaper, Lucas hurried to the bedroom. "All right," he said, standing in the doorway, "what's the problem?"

"Heather took my Barbie," Hollie said again.

The girls must have had ten Barbie dolls each. "Can't you play with another one?"

"No!" Hollie wailed. "This one's got the party dress. My other Barbies can't go to the Cattlemen's Dance without a party dress."

It seemed to Lucas that Heather owned a Barbie in a party dress, too.

"Hollie's Barbie is in the bathtub," Heather reminded him. "Hollie took off the dress and now she wants mine. Tell her she can't have it, Daddy. Tell her." She stared up at him with pleading brown eyes.

"Hollie?"

The five-year-old's lower lip quivered as she returned the Barbie in the fancy dress to her older sister.

"Thank you," Lucas said, praising her sense of fairness. He held out his arms and, sobbing, she raced toward him. He held her until the storm of tears had passed. With some effort and the three of them searching, they eventually located the other party dress, buried at the bottom of the toy chest. Hollie's Barbie was rescued from the tub and made resplendent once again. Peace was restored. After their baths, Lucas read to his girls, listened to their prayers, then tucked them in for the night.

Usually he turned on the television once they were asleep, and that was his plan. To his surprise, he found himself reaching for the telephone, instead. After connecting with Directory Assistance, he dialed Annie's home number.

"Hello?"

For the life of him Lucas couldn't think of a single reason for calling. And now that she was on the other end of the line, he panicked, not knowing what to say.

"Hello," she repeated.

"It's Lucas."

That announcement shut her up. Well, great. They could stay on the phone for hours, neither of them saying a word. That was one way to spend an evening.

"How are you?" he asked. So much for witty repartee.

"Fine. And you?"

"Oh, just fine."

"I missed seeing you this morning."

She had? Suddenly that seemed encouraging, although he'd rather not think about why. "Has anyone mentioned the Cattlemen's Dance?" Until the words were out of his mouth, Lucas didn't realize he intended to invite Annie. But it made perfect sense. They understood each other. They'd each experienced a devastating loss. They had a lot in common. They were friends. Who better to invite to the biggest community event of the year?

"Jane said something about the dance," Annie told him.

"Would you like to go?"

"I was thinking about it."

"With me," he added.

Her hesitation threw him. "That is...I mean, if you'd rather not, I understand. It'd only be as friends. It's just that..." First he couldn't manage to get a word out, and all at once they were spilling out so fast they didn't make sense.

"I think that's a lovely idea, Lucas. I'd hate going by myself."

Thank God. Being friends with a woman was difficult enough without having to deal with rejection, too.

"Only..."

His spirits took an immediate dive. "What?" He wanted her to say it—tell him what he'd done wrong.

"Lucas, I don't dance very well."

That was it? She was concerned about her ability to dance? His relief was so great he nearly laughed out loud. "Actually, I'm not all that light on my feet, either," he said to reassure her.

"It's because of the car accident."

"Don't worry about it, Annie. In fact, we don't even have to dance."

Annie's laugh was almost musical. "Darn, and I was hoping we could whirl around the floor, barefoot and wild."

The image of the pair of them shoeless in the middle of the dance floor made him smile.

"I'll get the tickets and call you back about the time," he said, grateful the ordeal of asking her was over.

"Great. Thank you, Lucas."

Lucas was still smiling when he hung up the phone. He returned to his favorite chair and picked up the television's remote control. He watched a nature program, and then the news.

Once he was in bed, he read for a while, but found his thoughts drifting to Annie. He turned off the light. Even after all this time of sleeping alone, he continued to stay on his side of the bed out of habit. An oddly consoling habit, one that was hard to give up— although there was no reason he couldn't sleep in the middle, claim the entire bed if he wanted.

The darkness and silence settled in around him. He waited, as he did every night, for the loneliness to come crashing down on him.

Tonight it didn't.

Richard's second letter in three years was a shock to Grady Weston. Because it was addressed to him, not Savannah. He didn't think his brother had the guts to write him. Not after what he'd done. The only feeling Grady had left in his heart for Richard was pity. His brother was in prison, and that was exactly where he belonged. Exactly where he would remain.

Caroline was aware that a letter from Richard had arrived that day, marked as it was with the prison stamp, warning the recipient that this was uncensored mail from a penal institution. She'd seen it, but hadn't questioned him about it. Still, she knew he was disturbed by the letter—the way she always knew when something troubled him.

Grady was tired; his day had started at three in the calving barn. It hadn't helped that Richard's letter was waiting for him when he came in from a long day spent moving the herd to its summer pasture. Now, after dinner, he'd holed himself up in his office to read it. No need to ruin his meal.

The letter said precisely what Grady had expected Richard would say. That he was sorry. Terribly, terribly sorry—Grady had heard all that before. Then Richard went on for a couple of paragraphs about how much he needed his family. Same song, second verse. Grady trusted his brother about as much as he did a rattlesnake. Sad though it was to admit, Richard had destroyed every ounce of trust Grady had invested in him—trust that couldn't be restored. In fact, he'd spent his entire adult life destroying his family's faith in him.

There was a light knock at his office door and Caroline stuck her head inside.

"Come on in," he told her. He'd known she'd come to him eventually wanting to talk about the letter.

She entered and closed the door. "Maggie and Roy are asleep," she said.

Grady glanced at the clock, surprised it was that late. Generally they tucked in the kids together and listened to their prayers. "You should have called me."

"Not tonight, Grady."

He nodded, grateful as always for her wisdom and sensitivity.

Caroline didn't take the chair across from him as she usually did. Instead, she crawled into his lap and wrapped her arms around his neck. It felt good to have her this close.

"Are you going to tell me about it?" she asked, her head on his shoulder.

Grady hesitated, then shrugged. "The usual—Richard being his persuasive self," he told her. "So very sorry for all the pain he's caused everyone, et cetera."

"He might be sincere this time."

"Fine, he can be sincere from prison. If Savannah wants anything to do with him, that's her decision. I don't."

Caroline's fingers were in his hair. "Do you hate him so much?"

Grady gritted his teeth. "Yes... Hell, I don't know.

All my illusions about Richard were destroyed the day I buried my parents.'' He shook his head. ''He says he's sorry, but he's said it before. All he talked about in that letter was himself. *His* circumstances, *his* feelings, *his* mistakes. Richard's entire world revolves around Richard. I wasn't fooled when he came back to Promise four years ago, and I'm not fooled now. Richard will always be Richard.''

Caroline held his face between her hands. ''You have nothing to worry about, Grady. Maggie is your daughter in every way that matters, and I'm your wife.''

Grady knew what she said was true. Nevertheless, one small hidden part of him battled back the dread and the fear that somehow, his brother would slip back into their lives and claim his daughter. Would entice Caroline away from him. His doubts weren't based in reality. Not once since they'd married had Caroline given him cause to doubt her love. Not once.

''I'm just afraid he's going to waltz into this house and steal you and Maggie away,'' he admitted reluctantly.

Caroline gave a short harsh laugh. ''It'll never happen. Never,'' she emphasized. ''He doesn't even know Maggie is his child.''

Grady wanted to believe it, but he couldn't be entirely sure. Not after Richard had inadvertently stolen the child and kept her overnight in Bitter End. He *must* have guessed. Must have suspected.

Richard had seduced Caroline one night, soon after their parents had died. Seduced her and left her. It sounded melodramatic, Grady knew, but it was the simple truth. Yeah, that was Richard for you. His persuasive, seductive brother. His irresponsible, selfish bastard of a brother.

All his life, until now, Richard had managed to get whatever he wanted—which almost always belonged to Grady. He couldn't lose Caroline and Maggie. Richard wasn't coming back here ever; that was all there was to it. That was the only way he'd never be a threat.

"Are you going to answer the letter?" Caroline asked.

He laughed as if she'd made a joke. "No way."

She nodded.

"My instincts are screaming he's not to be trusted—the same as they did the last time."

He half expected Caroline to argue with him and was grateful when she didn't. He groaned. Damn, it felt good to hold her in his arms. It seemed a shame to waste these precious moments. He twisted his head until his lips met hers. Her mouth parted in welcome and the kiss deepened.

His fingers fumbled with her shirt buttons, then groped to find the clasp of her bra.

"Grady," she mumbled, dragging her lips from his. "There's another reason I needed to talk to you tonight."

"Tell me later." He knew she'd been looking for a way to reassure him of her love, and he'd come up with the perfect solution.

"I...thought...you'd...want...to...know...now." She got the words out between kisses.

"Why?" If he delayed her long enough, it wouldn't matter. His quest was complete when he managed to free her magnificent breasts.

"Grady," she moaned. "I'n. 'ate."

"No, you aren't, sweetheart, your timing is perfect." He sought her nipple—and then her meaning hit him. His head snapped up. "Late?"

She smiled dreamily and nodded.

"How late?" he asked. "When?"

"Last month sometime."

"But…" His heart was thumping with excitement. They'd talked about another baby, and both had decided they wanted to add to their family. But he'd expected it to happen long before this. Roy was already three and Caroline had gotten pregnant practically on their wedding night.

"Don't tell me you're surprised." Happiness radiated from her.

"No." He couldn't very well be, seeing that they were a healthy married couple and deeply in love. "Just happy."

"Oh, Grady, me, too. I can barely contain myself."

"But isn't it too soon to know for sure? What about one of those kits you can buy or, better yet, making an appointment at the clinic?"

"I'm sure," she insisted. "I *know* I'm pregnant. I can feel it." She grinned. "Besides, I did buy one of those kits and all it did was tell me what I already knew."

Shifting the weight of her in his arms, Grady stood and carried her out of the office.

"Where are we going?"

"We have some celebrating to do," he said, walking into the main part of the house and past the dining room.

His wife smiled knowingly when he rounded the

corner and headed down the long hallway that led to their bedroom. He loved this woman and would spend the rest of his life proving it.

It didn't take Savannah long to get wind of the letter Richard had mailed Grady. Somehow, he wasn't surprised. She came by the house later the following day to drop off a loaf of freshly baked bread and a bouquet of long-stemmed red roses. Savannah and Caroline had been friends for years, but it soon became apparent that Savannah wasn't there just to visit with Caroline. She wanted to see Grady, too. He was in the calving barn, bottle-feeding a newborn calf whose mother was too weak to nurse.

"He wrote?" she asked, leaning against the enclosure.

"If you're asking about Richard, yes, I heard from him."

"He told you how sorry he is?" she asked, watching him.

"Oh, he said he was sorry, all right."

Savannah didn't say anything for a while. Neither did Grady. She reached over to stroke the calf. His sister had always had a special love for babies, human and animal. Their vulnerability brought out not only her gentleness but her strength.

"You won't be answering him," she eventually said.

"No." Grady didn't need to think twice before responding. He glanced up, expecting her to chastise him or insist it was his duty. When she didn't, he wasn't sure why.

"Caroline's fairly bursting with your news."

"Yeah." Grady's chest swelled with pride. "Looks like she's pregnant."

"That's so wonderful."

"I wish Mom and Dad were here to know their grandchildren." They'd died together in a flash flood a decade earlier, but not a day passed that Grady didn't remember his parents in one way or another.

"They *are* here," Savannah whispered. "I believe that with all my heart."

Grady sighed. "I know you think I should write Richard—"

"No," Savannah said quickly, cutting him off. "I don't think that."

"You don't?"

"He's up to something. I don't know what, but he needs us for some reason."

Grady suspected as much himself and was amazed that his tenderhearted sister shared his opinion.

"Whatever it is, I don't want any part of it," Grady said without emotion.

"I don't, either," Savannah said.

Nine

Nessa's day had been full. She'd waited until business slowed midafternoon, then called the Pattersons to learn what she could about Gordon Pawling. Phil remembered him well.

"Of course I know who Gordon Pawling is," Phil said. "We've been exchanging Christmas cards for three years."

"But he didn't know Dovie and Frank were married."

"He didn't ask and I didn't say anything," Phil continued. "It wasn't my place to let him know. Why are you asking?"

"He stopped in last week."

"Gordon Pawling was in Promise? Why didn't he phone?"

"He did, but apparently you were out that day."

"Oh, too bad. He's a hell of a nice guy."

Nessa thought so, too. "He was disappointed Dovie was away."

"Why didn't he let us know he was going to be in the vicinity?"

"I can't say for sure," Nessa said, nodding at Ellie Patterson when she walked into the store. "I think it was a last-minute decision."

"Still, I wish I'd known."

Selfish though it sounded, Nessa was grateful to have had those special hours with Gordon, grateful he hadn't needed to rush away to meet with others. Whenever she thought about their afternoon together, a feeling of warmth came over her. It had been like a reprieve, a time out of time. She'd felt, briefly, as if the problems facing her had melted away and she was young again. But she wasn't a schoolgirl; she was a mature woman, a widow with a complicated life and manipulative children.

"I have to go," Nessa said. "I've got a customer— your daughter-in-law, Ellie."

"Give her a hug for me," Phil told her.

Ellie had come for scones to take home for Glen and was soon gone, and Nessa was once again alone with her thoughts. She was glad she'd talked to Phil about Gordon, although some of her questions about the man remained unanswered. One thing Nessa did know—her afternoon with Gordon had been wonderful. However, she hadn't heard from him since and suspected she wouldn't. If only he hadn't left in such a hurry. If only they'd been able to exchange addresses. If only...

The following morning, when Nessa was counting out cash for the register, the phone rang. Absently she reached for it while sliding the twenties into their slot.

"Dovie's Antiques," she said, tucking the receiver between her shoulder and her ear as she continued the task.

"Is this Nessa?"

Nessa's hands went slack. "Gordon?" The pounding of her heart was so fierce she hardly knew how she managed to stay upright.

"Then you do remember me?"

As if she was likely to forget him! "Of course. You're Dovie's friend," she said, more to remind herself than him.

"I'd like to believe I'm your friend, too." He sounded a bit sheepish, as though her comment had caught him off guard.

"You are," she said, her voice strained and unfamiliar even to her own ears.

"I had the most enjoyable afternoon in Promise, thanks to you."

"I wish you'd been able to see the town."

"I do, too. In the past week I've wanted to kick myself for rushing off the way I did, but I had no idea how swiftly the time had gone."

"Did you make it to your banquet?"

"Unfortunately, I was an hour and a half late and ended up eating in my room."

"Oh, dear," Nessa said. "That afternoon just flew by, didn't it?"

"I wanted to thank you for making me feel so welcome."

She pressed the receiver hard against her ear, as if to get closer to him. "It was my pleasure."

"I would've phoned sooner, but I had to make an unexpected trip to Vancouver. My brother-in-law died suddenly."

"Oh, Gordon—I'm so sorry." She felt a pang of regret, remembering how quickly her husband's life had been snatched away.

"Yes, it was quite traumatic, and a reminder of

how precious life is. We shouldn't waste time, not knowing how much or how little we have.''

Nessa heard the pain in his voice.

"Actually, losing Paul was what prompted me to call," he said. "I'm not usually as comfortable with anyone as I was with you. The truth is, I tend to be somewhat reserved.''

He paused and Nessa smiled, almost enjoying his discomfort. "Uh-huh,'' was all she said.

"I met Dovie three years ago. It was the last night of the cruise, and I kept wishing we'd found each other sooner. Before she decided to marry her sheriff. I refuse to do that again, waste time that way. So I have to ask—did you enjoy our afternoon as much as I did?''

"That afternoon was one of the best I've spent in years,'' Nessa replied honestly.

He chuckled warmly. "I haven't stopped thinking about it since.''

"Me, neither.''

"For most of my working life I sat in judgment of others,'' he went on. "That was my job, but it gives a man a false sense of thinking he knows what's right. I worked too hard, spent too many hours away from home. I realize now that my son suffered, and I'm sorry to say my wife did, as well. Now I see Miles making exactly the same mistakes. Even so, he claims to know what I need and isn't afraid of telling me.''

"My children are the same. Are you saying I was the one who taught them this? What a horrifying thought.''

They both laughed and it felt amazingly good.

"I want to call you again, Nessa. That is, if you don't mind."

"I'd like it very much." She gave him her home phone number and wrote down his.

They chatted a bit more and then Gordon confessed, "I couldn't sleep last night, thinking about talking to you again, wondering what you'd say and hoping you wanted to get to know me better, too."

"Oh, I do!" She paused. "I spent the evening reading the book you recommended. The novel by Kaye Gibbons."

They talked for almost thirty minutes before a customer entered the store and Nessa had to go.

"Can I phone you at home this evening?" Gordon asked.

"Please. I'll look forward to hearing from you."

And that was how it started. From then on, they talked every night, precisely at seven. Nessa felt like a kid again. There didn't seem to be anything they couldn't talk about. Even though they'd met only once...

Two weeks after his visit, a few days after they'd begun talking every night, Nessa heard from Dovie.

"Nessa," Dovie complained, "there must be something wrong with your phone line. I tried for over an hour and all I could get was a busy signal."

Had she really spent an entire hour talking to Gordon? Oh, my, she hated to think what his phone bill would be.

"Dovie, it's so good to hear from you," Nessa said, rather than explain there was nothing wrong with the phone system. "Where are you?"

"New York. Frank and I landed earlier this afternoon. We're staying here for the night and then flying into San Antonio first thing in the morning. We'll be back in Promise by nightfall. How is everything?''

"Wonderful."

"You sound good."

"Actually, business has been excellent," Nessa said, steering the conversation away from anything personal. "Slow but steady. I sold the two trunks from Hong Kong and the marble table."

"That's great, because we're going to need all the room we can get. Just wait'll you see all the incredible antiques Frank and I found in France and England." Her excitement spilled over as she recounted the items she'd purchased and shipped home. "And Paris—oh, Nessa, you were right. It has to be one of the most beautiful cities in the world."

"Yes. Romantic, isn't it?"

"Did anything happen while I was away?" Dovie asked next.

Nessa hesitated. Dovie deserved to know that Gordon had stopped by the store to see her. In three years he hadn't forgotten her. Three years! The first question he'd asked Nessa had been about Dovie and Frank Hennessey.

"Nothing out of the ordinary," Nessa said, berating herself already for her lie of omission.

Not until the line had been disconnected did she admit to being jealous. Her feelings were silly and irrational. Dovie was far more than her relative. She was her friend. Her closest friend. She had every right to know that Gordon Pawling had come to Promise. But Nessa hadn't told her....

But she would, Nessa promised herself. The next time she saw Dovie, she'd tell her everything.

Dianna and Devon sat on the kitchen floor banging pots and pans while Nell put the finishing touches on a triple-layer chocolate rum cake. Travis's favorite. The racket was almost deafening, but it was the sweetest of music to Nell's ears. The twins' happy chatter reinforced her sense of her husband's love and commitment to her. Since Val Langley's phone call, Nell needed that reminder.

She wanted to kick herself now. Oh, sure, she'd said, tell Val we'll rent her a room. How stupid can you get? While it was true the two women hadn't actually met, Nell had seen plenty of pictures.

Travis's first wife was beautiful. If Val hadn't chosen a career in law, she could have been a model. Nell felt like a linebacker compared to the dainty Val. Where this woman had curves, Nell had muscles. Where Val had bouncy carefree curls, Nell had thick straight braids. The sophisticated New Yorker would take one look at her and think Travis had married some hayseed.

Nell could think of no possible reason Val might have for visiting Promise other than to lure Travis back. She'd made a mistake in divorcing him for another man, and now she was divorced again. In the years since she'd left Travis, his career as a novelist had skyrocketed—no doubt making him seem even more desirable.

Clearly Val had seen the error of her ways and was determined to win him back. And Nell, gullible naive soul that she was, hadn't guessed the other woman's intentions until it was too late. She knew full well that she'd probably be involved in a battle for her husband, yet here she was in the kitchen, doing boring unsophisticated countrified things. She might soon be fighting to save her marriage—and her ammunition of choice was chocolate cake.

Boy, did she have problems! She'd better get some counseling.

Generally she wasn't emotional, but the more she thought about what she'd done, the more she worried. The last three and half years had been a gift she'd never even hoped to receive. When Jake died, Nell hadn't believed she'd be able to love again. Or that another man would love *her*. Then Travis had come to Promise in search of a story. They'd met and fallen in love. She remembered what her life had been like after he'd returned to New York that first time. It would have been better, she'd decided then, if he'd never come to Texas. The emptiness inside her had seemed greater than ever before. She couldn't go through that again. She couldn't lose Travis, she just couldn't.

"What smells so good?" Travis asked, walking into the kitchen. "Is it what I think it is?"

Nell hadn't expected him back this soon. Sniffling, she grabbed a paper towel to wipe her nose, praying he didn't notice the tears glistening in her eyes.

Travis reached down and lifted first Dianna and then Devon for a quick hug before he made his way toward her. He kissed the back of her neck and slid his arms around her waist, hugging her against him. "Don't tell me that's your chocolate rum cake?"

"Yup." She swallowed past the lump in her throat.

"It isn't my birthday, is it?"

"Nope."

"Christmas? Our anniversary? Did I miss something I shouldn't have?"

"Of course not." She forced a laugh.

"Then what did I do to be worthy of this monumental effort?"

"It's a declaration of war," she admitted.

"War? What do you mean? War against whom? What's wrong?"

Nell continued frosting the cake, although her hand trembled. "My mother told me long ago that it may be old-fashioned, but it's true—the most direct route to a man's heart is through his stomach."

"A truth if I ever heard it," he agreed, then went quiet. "You have my heart, Nell."

"Do I?"

"Honey, how can you even think otherwise?"

"Val wants you back and like an idiot I practically invited her into our home! How could I have been so stupid. How could you have let me *be* so stupid?"

Travis turned her around so that he could see her face. Nell met his gaze, but tears blurred her vision.

"Nell. My sweet, beautiful Nell."

"I'm not beautiful!" she cried. "That's the whole point."

"Don't ever say that," Travis said in a rare display of anger.

"Not compared to Val."

"Val?" He spit out the name as if it left a bitter taste in his mouth. "She's vain, selfish, manipulative and conceited."

"But she wants you back!"

"Nell, I have three things to say." Travis laughed. "First, I love *you*. Second, why would I want a woman like Val even if I wasn't remarried? And third, I don't believe she wants me back at all. She wants something, all right, but it's not me."

"Then why is she coming here?" Nell blew her nose. "What *does* she want?"

"I can't be sure. With Valerie, who knows?" Travis frowned. "She claims she's curious about life in Texas. Says she needs to get away for a while."

"I'd think Val's the type who'd be more at home in London or Los Angeles."

Travis agreed with a quick nod. "It does make me wonder."

"So we come full circle. She wants *you*."

He laughed outright at that. "Well, she can't have me."

"Not without one hell of a fight."

That seemed to amuse him. "Maybe I should take her out to Bitter End and let her find her own way back."

He'd never do that, Nell knew, but it did ease her mind to know her husband wasn't any more anxious to see his ex-wife than she was.

Still holding her, Travis nuzzled her neck. Nell felt a tug and glanced down. Dianna and Devon were staring up at their parents. Devon had his arms wrapped around his father's legs and Dianna's plump fingers clutched Nell's apron.

Travis reached for Devon and Nell reached for Dianna. "Leave you and my babies?" He shook his head vehemently. "That's the biggest joke of the year. No way, Nell. Not in this lifetime."

* * *

The conversation with Nell remained in Travis's mind long afterward. He'd tried to talk his stubborn wife into letting him call Val and tell her to find other accommodations, but difficult as it was to understand, Nell refused.

It wasn't in her to turn tail and run, which was a quality he deeply admired in his wife. She faced every challenge head-on, every problem without backing down. She was resourceful, and she never gave up. If it hadn't been for Nell, he would never have uncovered the mystery behind Bitter End or understood what had driven hardened pioneers from their homes more than a hundred years earlier.

From the first she'd been quick to credit him. The limelight always made Nell uncomfortable. Even the year she'd won the chili cook-off...

His thoughts returned to his ex-wife. He couldn't imagine why she'd be interested in Texas. Thinking about Val, Travis recalled his meeting with Richard Weston. At first it was hard to believe anyone this likable, this clever, would end up behind bars facing a twenty-five-year sentence. They'd met through Val, who'd been his court-appointed attorney. Generally she hated these cases and gave them the least amount of effort. She must have ticked her second husband off royally for him to hand her this case. As a senior partner in the law firm, Charles would have been the one to make the decision. Travis had merely been relieved that Val was some other man's headache, but now Charles Langley had apparently seen the light himself.

Still, none of this explained Val's curiosity about Texas. He'd asked her about it, and she'd made up some silly excuse about wanting to see the state ever since she'd read one of his books. *Yeah, right,* he'd almost snorted. The only book of his *she'd* have any interest in reading was his bankbook.

He'd rather she wasn't coming, wished he'd been able to convince Nell to deny her room and board. But Nell wouldn't hear of it. Not his Nell.

Jeannie French knew that discouraging Sheriff Jordan's romantic interest in her had been the right thing to do, although it hadn't been easy. Nevertheless, the look on his face when she'd turned down his invitation to the Cattlemen's Dance still haunted her.

In the days that followed she found herself thinking about him more and more, and wondered if there'd been a gentler way of refusing him.

On the last day of school, Bernie Benton, the fifth-grade teacher, came into her classroom after school.

"Hey, how's it going?" he asked casually, hands stuck inside his pants pockets.

Jeannie knew Bernie had been born and raised in Promise and had taught at the school for the past five years. She'd heard someone say he'd graduated in the same high-school class as Adam Jordan, although she wondered if that was wrong. Bernie appeared to be a few years older, but maybe that was because of his receding hairline.

"Hello, Bernie."

"I was wondering if anyone's told you about the Cattlemen's Dance next week."

This dance, Jeannie thought, was all anyone mentioned these days. The last dance she remembered hearing so much about had been her high-school prom.

"Are you going?" Jeannie asked.

"Of course. What about you?"

She had the impression she was expected to go, even though no one had come right out and said as much. "I thought I'd drop by." She hadn't run into Will Osborne and suspected she wouldn't. Even if she did, Jeannie could think of no way of letting him know she'd welcome an invitation from him. Often she wished she were more sophisticated, more worldly. Then she wouldn't worry so much about hurting someone's feelings or give a second thought to rejecting a man like Sheriff Jordan.

"Do you have a date yet?"

Bernie was married, with three young children, yet it almost seemed as if *he* was inviting her. "I didn't know I had to have a date."

"You don't," Bernie was quick to explain. "It's no big deal if you go alone."

"I'm glad to hear it." Seeing that there was every likelihood she'd end up doing just that.

"I was thinking maybe you'd like to ride along with me," Bernie suggested lightly.

"You and your wife?"

Bernie looked uncomfortable. "Actually, Cheryl and I've recently separated."

"Oh...I'm so sorry."

"Yeah, well, it's just one of those things."

"Still, it must be very difficult for everyone." Especially his children. Jeannie didn't know why some people thought children under a certain age wouldn't be affected by divorce. Her limited time teaching had shown her that all children, regardless of age, were subject to the tensions created by family problems.

Bernie shrugged. "So what do you say? Want to ride along with me or not? I mean, I'm going and you're going. There isn't any reason to take two separate cars."

Now it was Jeannie's turn to be evasive. She'd rejected one man and wasn't about to enter a dead-end relationship with another, a fellow teacher at that. "I don't think it's a good idea."

"Why not?" Bernie seemed surprised, as if she, of all people, would appreciate the logic of his argument.

Was this guy as dense as Adam—or was it just the men in Promise? "Well," she began, "you might be separated, but you're still married. You have a wife and three beautiful children who need their father."

"Yes, but...Cheryl doesn't understand..."

"Bernie, listen, I don't think it'd be fair for me to hear the particulars of your marital problems. I hope, and I'm sure you do, that the two of you can work things out and in that case, going to the dance with me won't help the situation. Also—" she took a deep breath "—I don't mean to be unkind, but you and I work in the same school. It seems to me that someone who didn't know the two of us might believe I was somehow involved in the breakup of your marriage."

"That's ridiculous!"

"People might not think so if I turn up with you at the biggest dance of the year. How is anyone to know I'm not your date?"

"Oh." He buried his hands deeper in his pockets. "Cheryl's going."

"With a date?" If so, that would explain everything.

He hesitated. "I don't know."

That was it, Jeannie thought. If his wife did attend the dance with another man, he wanted to prove that he was capable of finding himself a partner, too.

"Bernie, listen," Jeannie said as gently as she could. "I'm sorry about you and Cheryl, really sorry, but I don't think showing up with me at the dance would be very smart. You have children. Don't throw away your marriage by doing something that stupid."

"Who are you—Dr. Laura?" Although the question was sarcastic, his look was sheepish.

"No, just someone who cares about families."

Bernie lowered his eyes. "You're right."

"Ms. French?" Emma Bishop poked her head into the classroom. "Oh, hi, Mr. Benton," she said. "There's a message for you in the office, Ms. French," she announced. "Mrs. Caldwell asked me to let you know."

"Thanks, Emma."

"I'll talk to you later," Bernie said, and left her classroom, his expression so woebegone it was painful to see.

On her way out of the school, she stopped at the office.

"The message was from Mr. Jordan," Martie Caldwell, the secretary, told her.

Oh, no. What now? "Sheriff Jordan called for me here at the school?"

"No, it was Max Jordan, from the western-wear shop next to Tumbleweed Books. He told me to tell you your order's in."

"But I didn't order anything."

Martie shrugged. "You'll have to ask him about that. All I did was take the call."

Jeannie felt a headache coming on. Her temples throbbed, and she was in no mood to deal with what was sure to be a waste of time. Whatever had been ordered had nothing to do with her, but it meant a trip to the store to sort out the misunderstanding. A trip she wasn't pleased to make.

First Bernie, now this.

She was lucky enough to find a parking space in front of Jordan's Town and Country Western Wear. She'd met Max Jordan briefly at a church dinner in August, shortly after she moved to Promise. She remembered him as a pleasant kindly man.

"Hello, Mr. Jordan," she said calmly, careful not to let her irritation show.

"You got my message, then?"

"Yes, but I'm afraid I didn't order anything."

Max reached behind the counter and produced a box. "It arrived this afternoon."

"But I didn't place the order."

"I know. Adam did. Funny thing is, I couldn't get my son to deliver this." He shook his head. "Came in here one day a couple weeks back, real upset with himself. I tried to get him to talk about it and he damn near bit my head off."

"What's in the box?" Jeannie asked when Adam's father paused long enough to take a breath.

"A blouse."

"Blouse?"

"That's right, a fancy silk one. Real pretty, I might add. Adam described it for me and asked me to find

a blouse exactly like it." He gestured toward the box.
"He knows I don't carry women's wear other than
the western variety, but he insisted I try. It took me
some time, but I did manage to locate one that resembled the picture Adam drew." He opened the box and
lifted out a blouse exactly like the one that had been
ruined by the barbecue sauce.

"That's it!" Jeannie cried.

"Adam seemed to think so."

"But he didn't need to do that."

Max frowned. "I don't know what's going on between you two, but I've never seen my son this
twisted up over a woman."

"*Nothing's* going on," Jeannie said firmly.

"So Adam claims." Max shook his head again. He
returned the blouse to its box, tucking it inside the
protective tissue covering.

"Thank Adam for me," she told him when he
handed her the package.

"You can't tell him yourself?" he asked. "Do I
look like Western Union to you two? Adam asks me
to tell you this, and you ask me to tell him that. Seems
a bit ridiculous."

Jeannie had to smile. "You're right, Mr. Jordan.
I'll let Adam know at the first opportunity."

Max's face broke into a wide grin and he nodded
approvingly. "You know, you two would make a fine
couple if you gave each other a chance."

Ten

"The castles in the Loire Valley," Dovie said, closing her eyes as if she were visiting them all over again. "Nessa, I swear I've never seen anything more spectacular in my life."

Nessa agreed. She'd felt the same way on her first trip to France. The summer homes of royalty...well, they were like something out of a fairy tale.

Dovie hadn't stopped talking about the trip all morning. "We're going back," she insisted. "Soon. Next year."

"Once just isn't enough, is it?" Nessa asked, wishing she and Leon could have had the opportunity to visit France again before his death.

"I don't know why Frank and I waited as long as we did, and the antiques...oh, Nessa, it was like walking through the doors of paradise." She closed her eyes again and smiled ruefully. "I'm making a nuisance of myself, aren't I?"

"Nonsense." Nessa enjoyed Dovie's bubbling enthusiasm and if she wasn't responding as excitedly as her sister-in-law thought she should...well, there was a good reason. While Dovie was talking, Nessa was trying to find a way to tell her about Gordon's visit.

"I know how it is when people return from vacation," Dovie said as she flitted from one end of the store to the other, unable to stay still. "They expect everyone else to feel the same as they did."

"But I do," Nessa assured her, and it was true. "I loved going to France. I loved visiting Provence, I loved sitting in a café in Marseilles—they say if you're there long enough, you'll see the whole world go by. Most of all, Dovie, I loved walking in Paris."

Dovie nodded. "Walking along the Seine at dusk, with Frank's arm around me, hearing music in the background..." Dovie sighed, then shook her head. "Time to get back to the real world. I can't thank you enough for taking such good care of the shop while I was away."

"It was my pleasure, Dovie. I mean that."

"I wish you'd let me pay you."

Nessa wouldn't hear of it. She inhaled deeply, her hands tense at her sides. It was now or never. "Actually, while you were away, I met a friend of yours— well, more of a former friend, someone you might even have forgotten—"

The phone rang just then, and Dovie whirled around to reach for it.

Nessa didn't know who was on the other end, but Dovie spoke excitedly for several minutes. Then she was silent, murmuring occasionally, as the other person spoke. "That was Savannah," she said, hanging up the phone. Her look was pensive, sober.

"Is something wrong?"

Dovie walked into the kitchen and poured herself a cup of tea. "Want some?" she offered, but Nessa shook her head. Dovie added sugar to her cup, stirring slowly. "I haven't heard from Mary, not once. I phoned and left a message, but she didn't return my call, and now Savannah tells me she hasn't talked to Mary in weeks.''

"Did Mary know when you and Frank were due back?" Nessa asked.

"She knew," Dovie murmured, clearly hurt that her friend hadn't called.

"Call her again," Nessa suggested. It seemed the obvious solution.

"I know I should, but I'm the one who's always phoning. I've asked Mary a hundred times what's wrong and she insists nothing is. Even Phil seems defensive when I talk to him. Ellie tells me that Cal and Glen have noticed things aren't right with their parents, too. Frank and I are just baffled. Cal thinks his parents might be getting a divorce, but I doubt that."

"Still, something isn't right." Nessa felt Dovie's concerns were legitimate.

"Did she drop in while I was away?" Dovie asked next, still stirring her tea, although the sugar had long since dissolved.

"No, come to think of it, she didn't." When Nessa had first moved to Promise, Mary had helped find her house, which hadn't been listed. The couple who'd purchased Ellie's family home had recently been transferred and were looking for a quick easy sale. Nessa would never have heard about it if not for Mary. They'd known each other casually for a number of years, and Nessa had been delighted to resume their acquaintance. However, in the past few months, the relationship had fallen off. Mary just never seemed to call anyone these days or go anywhere by herself, or even with Phil.

"I'm beginning to think it might be a medical problem," Dovie said, staring sightlessly into the distance.

"Could be," Nessa concurred. "Why don't you ask Phil?"

"I couldn't do that! If Mary or Phil wants to tell me, well, that's one thing. But since they prefer to pretend nothing's wrong, what can I do?"

"I don't know how to advise you." Nessa told her sister-in-law. "I just don't know."

Nessa left the shop midmorning and spent the rest of the day berating herself for being a sneak. She wished desperately that she'd mentioned Gordon's visit when Dovie had phoned from New York. Because she hadn't, the entire episode had taken on gigantic proportions in her mind. Before Savannah's call, she'd mentioned meeting Gordon and managed to get out everything but his name—the most important part. And after the call, they'd been caught up in the situation with Mary and there really hadn't been the opportunity to talk about anything else.

By the afternoon, Nessa had reasoned it out and was content once again. Dovie was happily married; she wouldn't care if Nessa and Gordon were friends. And since it made no difference one way or the other, Nessa saw no urgent reason to tell Dovie immediately. Or so she convinced herself.

That evening, when Gordon's call came precisely at seven, Nessa settled in her favorite chair. They talked for a few minutes the way they always did at the beginning of a conversation. Gordon would tell her a little something about his day, then ask about hers.

"Dovie's back." She mentioned this in an offhand tone, awaiting his response. Even after talking to him every night, getting to know him, sharing her life and thoughts with him in lengthy conversations, Nessa wondered what he'd say, how he'd react.

"I suspected as much when you said you wouldn't be working at the store any longer."

"She had a wonderful time."

"I imagine so. My first trip to Europe was special, too." He went on to tell her about the months he'd spent in Germany and Italy, and soon the conversation flowed as it always did with them. Soon they were laughing, sharing impressions, exchanging experiences.

"I didn't tell Dovie about you." Her admission came reluctantly. Nessa felt she should tell Gordon what she'd done—or rather, what she *hadn't* done. "I know it's silly, and I can't even explain why I didn't."

Gordon went silent and Nessa's heart raced fearfully for a moment. Then he laughed. Amusement was the last response she'd anticipated.

"You find this funny?"

"No, not funny. It's just that you and I are more alike than I realized. I didn't mention meeting you to Miles, either. The fact is, he knows nothing about my visit to Promise."

"Oh, and I didn't say a word to Sylvia, either." Nessa laughed, too. "What's wrong with us?" she asked, feeling considerably better in light of Gordon's confession.

"Nothing's wrong with us," he replied. "We have a right to our privacy."

Nessa wasn't entirely sure she agreed. Certainly Sylvia wouldn't. And Dovie?

"Once when I was a kid I found a beautiful rock," Gordon said slowly. "At least I thought it was beautiful. It glittered blue and green and gold. I put my rock in a cigar box my grandfather had given me and I didn't tell anyone about it. I knew everyone would ooh and aah when they saw this treasure, and I'd be the envy of all my friends, but still I didn't tell."

Nessa closed her eyes and listened, feeling like a child who'd happened on a treasure herself.

"Even now, I can't explain why I didn't brag about that rock to my friends. If I had to make a guess, I'd say that in my five-year-old mind, I'd decided I wanted to keep something so wonderful to myself."

"You were afraid that anyone else who saw it might try to diminish its beauty," Nessa said quietly.

"Yes, that too," Gordon concurred.

"I think that's why I couldn't bring myself to tell Dovie." It made perfect sense now. It was the same reason she hadn't told Sylvia or her sons that she'd met someone. She didn't want to hear their comments or speculation, didn't want to answer their questions. She didn't want them to make this *ordinary*.

"By nature I'm not an impulsive man. I don't know what came over me the day I reached Dovie's answering machine and drove to Promise, anyway. But whatever it was, I'm grateful."

"I am, too," Nessa murmured. She hesitated. "Are we being a pair of old fools, Gordon?"

"Perhaps, but if the way I feel about you is considered foolish, then fine—I'll be foolish. I haven't felt this alive in years.''

''Me, neither.''

''You mentioned that big dance next week.''

''Yes.'' She'd told him a great deal about the community and the people of Promise.

''I never was much of a dancer. Oh, I can manage my way across a dance floor, but I'm no Fred Astaire. And yet…''

''Yes?''

''Last night as I drifted off to sleep, all I could think about was dancing with you. Holding you in my arms.''

''Oh, Gordon.''

''Maybe I should come back to Promise.''

''For the dance?'' Nessa's heart surged with excitement. ''Could you? Would you?''

''When exactly is it?''

She told him and heard his sigh of regret.

''I'd be there if I could,'' he told her. ''Unfortunately we'll have to do it another time.''

Jane Patterson sat in her rocking chair counting stitches on her knitting needle when Cal walked into the room. Her ankles had swollen with the pregnancy and she'd propped them up on the ottoman.

Cal waited patiently until she'd finished. ''That was Glen on the phone. He and Ellie are coming over.''

''Tonight?'' It was unusual for Cal's brother to make a social visit, especially on a midweek evening, since he was at the ranch every day. Because Ellie owned the local feed store, they lived in town and Glen commuted to the ranch, which was the arrangement that made the most sense for them. The two couples saw each other fairly often, but for the most part, Jane and Cal drove into town, instead of the other way around.

"Is everything all right?" she asked. Cal had been restless and short-tempered for weeks now, worrying about his parents. She understood his concern, yet wasn't sure how she could help. She'd been giving it some thought, though. Maybe she could get in touch with a geriatric specialist she knew in California....

"Glen and I've been talking," Cal said.

"You talk every day."

"About Mom and Dad, I mean."

Jane set her knitting aside. Savannah had recently taught her to knit, and she'd finished her first project a week earlier—a lovely yellow baby blanket. Now she was moving on to booties and a sweater.

"Did you notice anything different about Mom last Sunday?" Cal asked. It was a question he asked with increasing frequency. "You're a doctor, you should be able to tell when someone's ill."

Jane had noticed a number of things about her mother-in-law and she had her suspicions. But she couldn't give a medical diagnosis unless Mary took the proper tests. Nor did she feel comfortable sharing her suspicions.

"Your mom *looked* healthy," she said, hoping that would reassure him.

"But not happy," Cal added, frowning.

"She did make an effort," Jane reminded him.

"My dad made an effort, too, and everyone could see it was an effort."

"Cal," she said, trying to calm him, "let's not

jump to conclusions here. We need more evidence before we—''

''These are my *parents*, Jane, and I'll tell you right now, I don't appreciate your attitude.''

''My attitude? What—''

''You think I'm overreacting.''

His accusation stung. ''Have I said that?''

''No, but I can tell what you're thinking.''

Jane got awkwardly to her feet. ''I don't know when you became a mind reader. You must've missed your calling in life, Cal Patterson. It just so happens I'm worried about your parents, too!''

''You certainly have an odd way of showing it.''

Jane pinched her lips, refusing to continue the argument. ''This isn't helpful, Cal.'' She walked out of the room.

''Where are you going?'' he demanded.

''To make coffee.''

''These are my parents, Jane,'' he said again, following her into the kitchen. ''How would you feel if this was happening to your mom and dad?''

''*What's* happening?'' she cried. No one had had any real proof of anything. Cal and Glen had been talking, working themselves into a frenzy of worry, making illogical assumptions. They'd dragged Dovie into it, too. For the past week her husband had talked more with his mother's friend than he had with her, his own wife.

''You know something's wrong.'' He paused and stared at her. ''You know something and you're not telling me.''

''Cal, I know nothing.'' Not for certain, and she

wasn't about to heap additional worry on his already burdened shoulders.

"You're a doctor," he said again.

"That doesn't make me a magician."

Her husband dragged out a kitchen chair and sat down at the table. Taking several deep breaths, Cal closed his eyes. "It seems as if I'm the one looking after my parents now." He shook his head. "Or trying to."

"Your mom and dad are getting older. This is what sometimes happens—a kind of role reversal."

"Mom's depressed."

Jane walked over and placed her hand on Cal's shoulder. "I think you're right. Your father seems depressed, too. But it's not an uncommon side effect of aging."

"It's more complicated than the two of them not getting along."

"I suspect so."

A vehicle could be heard pulling into the yard. "I don't know what to do to help them," Cal whispered. "That's what's so frustrating."

"I know."

Soon Ellie and Glen joined them in the kitchen. Johnny was home with a sitter, which told Jane the conversation was a serious one.

Once Jane had poured coffee and passed around a plate of Dovie's cookies, they all sat at the kitchen table.

"Dad told me today that he and Mom won't be attending the Cattlemen's Dance this year," Glen said.

Cal nodded. "I don't know why that surprises you.

Mom and Dad have avoided all social functions for at least six months. Can anyone remember the last time they went out with their friends?''

"Dovie says Mom barely talks to her anymore," Ellie supplied.

"Tell them what happened earlier this morning," Glen urged his wife.

Ellie stared down at her coffee. "Mom and Dad came into the feed store to pick up some fertilizer for the garden, and Dad was chatting with Lloyd Bonney about something or other. While Phil was busy, I was talking to Mom about Glen's birthday, which is next week."

"She didn't remember the date," Glen cut in. "She actually had no clue what time of year I was born."

"Mom hasn't been herself in months," Cal said. "She's depressed, forgetful, sometimes disoriented. This is more than the normal aging process, isn't it?"

All three looked at Jane. "I couldn't possibly answer that without giving her a full medical exam and arranging for some tests." She couldn't say the dreaded word—Alzheimer's. Not yet.

"Even if you did know, you wouldn't say," Cal muttered accusingly.

Jane disregarded the pain she felt at his anger and refused to answer such a loaded question. There was nothing she could do unless Mary submitted voluntarily to those tests.

The following afternoon Jane left the clinic and made an unexpected visit to her in-laws. Phil answered the door, but didn't show any pleasure at seeing her. He stood in the doorway, blocking her entry into the house.

"Do you have a few minutes?" she asked, surprised when he didn't step aside or invite her in.

"Actually, I was just leaving."

"I'd love to visit with Mary," Jane said.

"She's coming with me."

Jane hesitated, then walked over and sat down in one of the big wicker chairs positioned on the veranda. She gazed out at the town park for a moment, with its stately oaks and lush green foliage.

"Is she that bad?" Jane asked softly.

Phil tensed, then walked over to the porch railing, his back toward her.

"Don't insult my intelligence by telling me I'm imagining things," she said. She'd suspected for several months that Mary's problems were related to the onset of Alzheimer's disease.

Phil was quiet so long she wasn't sure he was going to speak. "How did you know?" he finally asked.

"I've wondered for a while. Wasn't it a year ago that Mary hurried out of church, positive she'd left the freezer door open?"

"About then."

"And it wasn't open, was it? I remember everyone laughed about it."

Phil nodded miserably.

"The last time I saw her by myself, she couldn't recall the phone number to the ranch."

"We had that phone number for nearly thirty-five years." The sadness in his voice was enough to break Jane's heart.

"There've been changes in her personality," Jane

said. "Small ones at first." Mary had always possessed a sharp wit, one Jane had admired. These days, Mary was vague and she often wore a confused look. A number of times Jane had been certain that it took her mother-in-law a moment to place her, to remember that she was Cal's wife.

"So you've noticed the difference in her personality, too?"

"I'm afraid so, Phil."

"If you have, then so have others," he mumbled. "You can't protect her forever."

"I know." He turned around and sat in the wicker chair next to Jane, then buried his face in his hands. "The other day she got dressed and forgot to put on her brassiere. When I told her, she got so embarrassed and upset, I didn't know what to do."

"You're doing the housework and cooking?"

He nodded. "At first she couldn't remember the recipes she's made for years. She'd leave out an ingredient or two, and we'd laugh it off. Then she damn near burned the house down, leaving a pot on a burner."

"There are medications that can help."

"I know all that. I'm looking into it, doing everything I can."

Jane didn't want Phil to think she was being critical. "Is she under a doctor's care?"

"Dr. John Curtis in San Antonio. We made our first visit two months ago."

Jane had heard the name and knew he was a respected physician who specialized in geriatric care, especially with Alzheimer's patients. "How long do you intend to keep this from Cal and Glen?" she asked, wanting him to realize what the situation—and his secrecy—was doing to his family. His sons had a right to know, and it wasn't her place to tell them.

"I'll talk to them soon."

Jane patted his hand gently. The stress had taken its toll on Phil—that much was obvious. He'd lost weight and the shadows beneath his eyes were testament to his ordeal. "Please, Phil. They deserve the truth about their mother," she urged. "And once they know, they can help her—and you."

"I know I should have told them before."

Jane agreed with a nod, but didn't judge him. It was his love for Mary that had made Phil hide her illness.

"Promise me you'll let me be the one to tell Cal and Glen, in my own time and my own way."

Jane hesitated.

"Promise me," he pressed. "Mary is the mother of my sons. I should be the one to tell them."

"I agree with you, and I promise," Jane said. She just hoped he'd talk to them within the next few days. She would keep Phil's secret, and pray that Cal never learned how much she knew.

Eleven

The hall at First Christian Church was crowded with women, their chatter echoing inside the cavernous room where many social functions were held.

The annual June quilting bee was one of Savannah's favorites. The finished quilts were auctioned later in the year and the money given to local charities. Laredo, Savannah's husband, joked that quilting bees were just the women's excuse to visit, and to some extent, Savannah thought he was right. These days, she rarely had this much undivided time to spend with her friends.

Amy McMillen, Nell Grant, Jane Patterson and Savannah worked together at one table, cutting pieces for a quilt top, while Caroline, Ellie and other women sewed them together. The sound of their machines hummed pleasantly in the room.

Savannah looked up from her task to note that her group seemed rather solemn compared to the other tables. "Hey, guys," she said cheerfully, "we should be having fun."

"I'm having a great time," Nell insisted with a dour look.

"Me, too," Amy echoed forlornly. "A really great time."

"So am I," Jane added, sounding equally miserable.

Savannah put her scissors down and folded her arms. "All right, what's wrong?"

"Nothing," Jane answered. "Not a single solitary thing."

The truth was, Savannah's spirits were low, too. Thoughts of Richard weighed her down, despite her best efforts to forget him. Perhaps if she stopped dwelling on her own troubles...

"Amy, you look kind of discouraged. Do you want to talk about it?"

The pastor's wife met Savannah's gaze haltingly, but it wasn't long before she glanced away.

"A burden shared is a burden lightened," Nell said.

"Exactly," Jane agreed, then seemed to realize what she'd said and quickly closed her mouth.

"Okay." Amy finally said. "It's my mother again. She phoned just so she could tell me that I'm doing a terrible job being a mother to Joey and Sarah."

Outraged cries echoed around the table, and Amy's spirits appeared to lift. "I *know* I'm a good mom and I love my children, but this kind of conversation is typical of my mother. I know I shouldn't let her get me down—but I can't help it. She's always attacking me, making me feel bad about myself. It's one of the reasons I only invite her to my home once or twice a year. She's so negative and she can't let a single conversation pass without making a derogatory comment about me or my family." She sighed. "I don't tell Wade all this because he'd just refuse to let my mother visit at all. And tempting as that is, I do feel sorry for her, and I feel…some obligation, I guess.''

Everyone offered words of encouragement to the pastor's wife, who was much loved by everyone in Promise. Savannah could well imagine what Wade would say if he knew what kinds of things his mother-in-law said about his wife. The thought of his reaction was enough to bring a smile to her face.

''Okay, Nell,'' Savannah said, ''what about you?''

''Me?'' Nell protested. ''Oh, all right.'' She stiffened her spine and Savannah noticed the way her fingers tightened around the scissors. ''Travis's ex-wife is coming to visit.''

''Here in Promise?''

Her announcement was followed by a chorus of groans.

''That's not the half of it,'' Nell muttered, cutting a piece of yellow floral fabric with determination and speed. ''The worst part is *I* was the one who invited her to stay with us.''

''Why's she coming?'' Amy asked.

Nell shrugged. ''I don't really know—but I think she's decided she wants Travis back.''

Savannah scoffed at the idea. She'd seen for herself the love in Travis's eyes every time he looked at Nell. He was crazy about his wife and family and wasn't afraid to show it.

''You haven't got a thing to worry about,'' she said.

''I know that in my heart, and then I remember the picture I once saw of Val and…well, she's beautiful.''

"Don't discount yourself," Savannah advised her friend. "And remember *you're* the one Travis loves."

Nell smiled, and she did seem a little relieved.

"What about you, Savannah?" Jane asked. "You haven't been yourself all morning."

"I haven't?" she said, although she knew Jane was right.

"Yeah, you," Amy confirmed. "You're not going to escape this."

Savannah hesitated, wondering how much to say. "Grady and I recently heard from Richard."

That captured her friends' attention.

Jane was incredulous. "After all this time?"

Savannah nodded. "Let me tell you, his letter was something of a shock."

"What did he have to say for himself?" Amy wanted to know, then added, "That is, if you don't mind talking about it."

"No, I don't. Richard said what he always says. He made a lot of sincere-sounding apologies and promises."

"So what does he want this time?" The skeptical question came from Nell who, unlike most people in town, had never been fooled by Richard.

"Nothing, or so he claims. Just that he's sorry and he's changed his ways."

"Don't you believe it," Nell insisted.

"Grady and I don't."

"So he's seen the error of his ways, has he?" Jane was no less skeptical.

"Well, it's what he *says*," But Savannah had believed Richard before and paid dearly for her faith in him.

"It must be hard, when you so badly want to believe him," Amy said. "I've been thinking a lot about your brother since you mentioned him and that letter. Both Wade and I've been praying about the situation."

"Thank you," Savannah said. Forgiving Richard was one thing, but making her family, her friends and herself vulnerable to him was another entirely. Had there been any evidence, something that proved the truth of his claims—like an effort to reach the very people he'd hurt most—she might be inclined to trust him, at least a little. But she knew that wasn't the case.

"Jane?" Nell looked at her, and to everyone's surprise Jane's eyes welled with tears.

"Jane," Savannah said, taking her hand. "What is it?"

She shook her head, clearly embarrassed by the emotional display. "Cal and I had an argument before I left the house. It was nothing and I'm sure everything will have worked itself out by the time I get home. It's just that…with the pregnancy and all…"

"You're more emotional than usual," Nell said.

Jane nodded and dabbed her eyes with a tissue.

Savannah wasn't nearly so sure. Usually by the sixth month, a woman's hormones were more balanced.

"The big dance is next Saturday night," Amy said. "I say we shake off our worries and kick up our heels."

"Forget all our troubles," Nell added.

"Hear, hear," Jane said between sniffles.

Savannah laughed. "You're right. We're going to have the time of our lives."

"What's the matter, Daddy?" Heather asked Lucas as he placed the dinner plates in the dishwasher.

Hollie handed him her silverware and gazed up at him. "Are you sad, Daddy?"

Lucas wasn't aware his worries were this noticeable to his children. "Mrs. Delaney is moving to Kansas to live with her son," he told his daughters. The housekeeper had given her notice that night when he got home.

"Yeah, we know," Heather said. "Mrs. Delaney is going to live with Larry and his wife. She's real excited about it, too."

Apparently his children knew more of the details than he did himself. But apparently they hadn't yet made the connection—if the housekeeper left Promise, she wouldn't be there to look after them.

"She's got three grandchildren in Kansas." Hollie relayed additional facts with all the finesse of a television reporter. "She misses them, too."

"I know she does." But not nearly as much as Lucas was going to miss Mrs. Delaney. What on earth would he do now? Especially with school out for the summer.

"We know who we want to be our new housekeeper," Heather said as she carried her empty milk glass from the table.

This was encouraging news. Perhaps the girls knew about someone he didn't, a school friend's mother or older sister. "Who?"

"Annie!" Heather shouted gleefully.

"Annie!" Hollie chorused.

Lucas groaned. This entire situation was impossible. Mrs. Delaney had promised to stay on until he found a replacement, which was a relief, but at the same time he didn't want to keep the older woman away from her grandchildren. He intended to place an ad in the local paper and start the interviewing process, but he hated the thought of turning his daughters' care over to strangers.

"We like Annie more than anyone around here," Hollie said, "and she reads real good. If she was the housekeeper, she could read us a story everyday. Not like Mrs. Delaney."

Lucas was trying to find a way to explain to his daughters why Annie couldn't be their housekeeper. "Well, Annie has a job, you know, a job that's very important to her. She runs the bookstore and that means she has to work every day."

Heather regarded him thoughtfully. "Could Annie be our new mother, then?" she asked.

Hollie's eyes instantly lit up. "Could she, Daddy, could she?"

"Ah..." Lucas didn't think he'd ever been so taken aback by any of his daughters' ideas. "I don't think so."

"Why not?" they asked in unison.

"Well, because—"

"We like her better than any lady in the whole world, not including Mommy and Grandma Porter," Heather said.

"Yes, but—"

"Will you think about it?" Heather asked, pleading with him.

"That won't do any good."

"Please, Daddy, oh, please," Hollie begged, folding her hands prayerfully and looking up at him with an intensity that almost broke his heart.

"Don't say no," Heather added, "not until you think about it."

"This isn't like getting a toy from the toy store," he said, wondering why he bothered trying to explain. "Annie has other plans for her life."

"But we want her," Hollie said in that matter-of-fact way of hers.

"*Promise* you'll think about it, Daddy," Heather said again. "Please?"

He'd think about it, all right. For two seconds.

It was the day of the Cattlemen's Dance, a day that dragged by slowly. Annie hadn't seen or talked to Lucas since he'd called to invite her. Sometimes she wondered if she'd imagined the entire conversation. But he'd left a message on her answering machine, saying that he'd pick her up at six. He'd sounded... curt. Businesslike.

However, there were plenty of signs that she was on his mind, as he was on hers. Heather and Hollie showed up faithfully each Saturday morning for Story Time, but without Lucas. Caroline Weston always brought them with Maggie.

Both girls were full of excited chatter about their father. The previous Saturday Hollie had whispered to Annie that Lucas had talked about her. The five-year-old hadn't said anything else, leaving Annie to wonder what Lucas could possibly have said.

The most telling sign, though, she'd learned in a conversation with Jane earlier in the week.

"Lucas was asking about you," Jane had mentioned in an offhand way.

"About me?" She shouldn't be this glad.

"Actually, he asked Cal."

"What did he want to know?" It did seem to Annie that if he had any questions, he should come to her.

"Cal didn't exactly remember. That's men for you. It was something about your plans, I think. Or your past."

Annie wasn't sure if she should be insulted or excited. "He already knows about the car accident and the divorce. What more is there to say about me?"

Until she came here, her entire world seemed to revolve around the events of the past two years, as if there'd never been anything else in her life. That was one of the reasons she'd moved to Promise—to escape the glances, the unspoken questions, the pity friends leveled at her.

She'd come to Promise to make a fresh start, to escape the past. A past that grew more and more distant as she grew more and more involved in this new life. She hadn't given Lucas much detail about the accident or the divorce. The woman who'd been in a car crash, whose husband had left her—she didn't want Lucas or anyone else to define her by those things.

"You like him, don't you?"

The directness of Jane's question had caught her off guard. Annie nodded. She did like Lucas, more than she cared to admit. He wanted them to be simply friends, and that was fine with Annie. Since the divorce she'd dated a few times, but she hadn't been ready for a new relationship. Moving to Promise had sped up the healing process considerably; still, a full-fledged romantic relationship was intimidating. No, she figured being friends was all she could handle for now.

"He's a good man," Jane had told her, then gently squeezed Annie's hand. "He'd never do the things Billy did."

Intuitively Annie recognized that.

They talked a little longer, and Annie noticed that her friend didn't seem as energetic as usual, but when she pressed, Jane made excuses and left shortly afterward.

By six o'clock the night of the dance, Annie was eager to see Lucas again.

He rang her bell and smiled when she opened the door. She liked the look in his eyes when he saw her. Her dress was new and expensive, and the way his eyes widened with appreciation made it worth every budget-crushing penny.

"Would you mind very much if we talked first—before heading over to the dance?" He seemed nervous, almost ill at ease.

"Of course I don't mind. Come on in." She held the door for him, and wondered if tonight would end in disaster. Perhaps she'd put too much stock in Lucas's invitation. "Would you like a cup of coffee?" she asked. "Or a glass of wine?"

He shook his head as he walked into her tidy living area, then restlessly paced the room.

"Please—sit down," she said, motioning toward the furniture.

"Sit down? Sure." He chose the chair by the end table, where she kept a stack of reading material.

Annie took the sofa, sitting on the edge of the cushion, her hands clenched together. "What's wrong?" It seemed to her *something* must be.

"Nothing." His reassuring smile was all too brief.

Annie waited, puzzled by his mood.

"I have…a question to ask you," he said at last.

"All right."

He stood, walked around the room again, then sat back down. "You know, I'm really grateful you're being this patient with me."

"Is your question that difficult?"

He snorted a laugh. "As a matter of fact, it is."

"Ask away. I promise not to bite your head off."

His face relaxed in a smile. "That's good because… You might not think that once I…" He hesitated, shook his head. "I wasn't going to do this. It would've been much better to wait until after the dance, but I realized as I was walking up the stairs that I couldn't. The whole night would be miserable if I didn't get this off my chest right away."

"It's all right, Lucas, really."

He nodded and seemed to gather his nerve. "I thought maybe you and I—" He stopped cold, a look of horror on his face.

"Thought what?"

"I've advertised for a housekeeper."

"You want me to give up the bookstore and become your housekeeper?"

"No," he protested. "I can hire someone to clean my house, but I can't hire anyone to love my children. Not the way you seem to. And they love you. I've never seen anything like it. From the moment you moved to town, Heather and Hollie knew.''

''Knew what?'' But she thought she'd already figured out the answer. His daughters had recognized that she, too, had been motherless. She understood the empty feeling that invaded a lonely child's heart.

''Knew they wanted you for their stepmother,'' Lucas answered.

Annie's head snapped up. She was wrong. ''They want me for their *stepmother?*''

''I can only imagine what you must be thinking and, frankly, I don't blame you. I told you I didn't want anything more than friendship, and I don't... well, I do, but...'' He abandoned that line of thought. ''We barely know each other. It's too soon. I still love Julia and you've just come out of a disappointing marriage. People will think we're both nuts.'' He closed his eyes and shook his head, as if he could hardly believe what he was saying.

Annie felt numb. This had to be a joke. ''Are you asking me to marry you, Lucas?''

He glanced away. ''Pretty pathetic proposal, isn't it?''

Annie wasn't going to lie to him. ''Yes.'' But then, she'd already had romance—all the romance she could handle in this lifetime.

''I apologize, Annie. I don't have any excuse for approaching you like this.''

Annie stood. ''Do you still want to go to the dance?''

He looked up at her and nodded. Slowly Lucas came to his feet. Annie reached for her purse and together they headed for the door. He didn't speak again until they'd made their way down the stairs at the back of the building and outside, to where he'd parked his truck.

"Naturally it'd be a marriage of convenience," he said, resuming the conversation.

"Your convenience, you mean." She wasn't being rude, only truthful.

He opened the passenger door and paused. "You're right. But, Annie, I'd do whatever was necessary to make this marriage worthwhile for you, too. My children need a mother and I need…a friend. Someone to come home to in the evenings, someone to talk to at the end of the day. I'm well aware that I have no right to ask you something like this. But we could make it work, I know we could."

"You mean that? You'd do what you could to make this marriage worthwhile for me?" Annie asked.

"Anything." His gaze was intense. "*Is* there something I can do for you, Annie?"

She accepted his hand and climbed into the truck cab. "As a matter of fact, there is."

He held her look, waiting, wondering.

"I want a baby, Lucas. If you agree to give me a baby, then I'll marry you."

Twelve

Jeannie French heard the music drifting through the open doors long before she entered the Grange Hall, where the Cattlemen's Association held their dance every year. The cars parked along both sides of the road must have stretched half a mile in each direction.

Bernie Benton's suggestion that they bring only one vehicle made sense; she could see that now. But she'd come alone, having received two invitations and declined both.

She liked both men, but Bernie was married and Adam, well, she was afraid she might have been unfair to him. But who could blame her? Every time he got near her something unpredictable happened. Usually something embarrassing.

As she approached the hall, Jeannie noted a number of people, mostly men, milling around outside. Some were smoking, some had brought out their drinks. All of them seemed to be watching her. That made Jeannie a little uncomfortable. *Gee, I hope they approve of my outfit,* she thought with sarcastic humor, and that made her feel better.

After much deliberation Jeannie had chosen the silk blouse Adam had so thoughtfully replaced. She wore it with a long black skirt and matching vest with small silver buttons. This was about as fancy as she got. She'd paid special attention to her hair and makeup and knew she looked good, although she wasn't really sure who she was trying to impress. Not these guys, anyway. As for Will Osborne, she hadn't seen him in weeks.

The hall itself was crowded, but many of the townspeople were either on the dance floor or standing around the edges. Long rows of chairs were set against the walls, and Jeannie saw that some of the town's older folk had gathered there. Tables were scattered about the room, but each one seemed filled to capacity.

"Jeannie, over here." Bernie Benton raised his arm.

She could pretend she hadn't heard him, but decided against it. With so many people pressing in around her, having somewhere to go gave her a feeling of security and of belonging. She'd seen other teachers and their husbands at his table.

"Hello, everyone," she said when she got within hearing distance. Her friends and fellow teachers good-naturedly shifted their chairs to make room for her at the table.

"Do you want to dance?" Bernie asked, tucking his hand under her elbow.

"No, thanks. I just got here." She had to lean toward him to be heard above the music.

Bernie nodded, but she saw the disappointment in his eyes.

"Don't let him pressure you into dancing," Martie, the school secretary, whispered on her other side. "He's feeling upset just now. See the woman in the long pink dress? That's Cheryl. Apparently she came with someone else.''

"Oh."

"It's not your problem."

Jeannie nodded, but as she watched Cheryl Benton dance, she caught sight of another familiar figure. Adam Jordan. He was dancing with someone she didn't recognize and seemed quite agile on his feet. The woman with him appeared to be captivated by whatever he was saying.

She'd promised Max Jordan she'd personally thank Adam for replacing her ruined blouse, but the opportunity hadn't yet presented itself. She'd do it tonight. It should be easier now that he'd apparently found someone else.

"Who's that with—"

Before she could complete the sentence, Martie answered. "Cheryl's with Lyle Whitehead," she murmured with a frown. "I don't know what she sees in him. Lyle's bad news." At Jeannie's puzzled look she added, "He's a known troublemaker."

"I meant who's dancing with Sheriff Jordan."

"Oh, sorry." Martie half stood and glanced to her right, then her left before sitting down again. "The sheriff's with Dovie Hennessey. I thought you knew Dovie."

Jeannie did. Obviously he'd changed partners.

Bernie had disappeared, and she was pleasantly surprised when someone else asked her to dance. But the music was so loud that other than getting the man's name, Billy Joe Durkin, Jeannie couldn't talk to him. When the song ended, they applauded politely.

"Thank you, Billy Joe."

"No, ma'am, I'm the one who should be thanking you." He tipped his hat and escorted her to the table.

"Billy Joe's something of a lady's man," Martie told her when she sat back down. "He considers it his duty to make sure that every woman here gets the opportunity to dance with him."

"What about Will Osborne?" she asked. "Is he here tonight?"

"You didn't hear?" Martie seemed delighted to pass on some gossip. "He married a waitress from Austin a couple of weeks ago."

"Oh." Jeannie felt foolish for having asked. It wasn't that she was so keen on Will. They'd talked a couple of times, that was all. The only man in Promise who'd shown the least bit of interest in her was Adam Jordan.

Jeannie was about to comment when a ruckus broke out not far from their table. She turned around to see Bernie Benton nose to nose with Lyle Whitehead. Bernie's face was red with anger.

"Let's settle this outside," Lyle shouted.

"Fine with me," Bernie shouted back.

"But not with me," Adam Jordan said, stepping forcefully between the two men. "The problem is, no one bothered to ask me, and I strongly object. In fact, I've made it my mission to be sure everyone gets along and has a good time this evening. Are we all clear on this, gentlemen, or do we need to discuss it further at my office?"

"Whitehead made a move on my wife," Bernie protested, hands clenched at his sides.

"She asked for it," Whitehead snarled. "It isn't

my fault she married a wimp who doesn't know what a real woman wants.''

"Oh, no," Martie said from behind Jeannie.

"Let me at him," Bernie cried, and would have gone at the other man with his fists if not for the sheriff.

With one quick graceful movement, Adam stopped the teacher's forward progress. At that very second Lyle pulled out a knife.

Jeannie sucked in her breath, along with everyone else, and strangled a cry as Lyle swung the blade at Adam. She jerked her head away, unable to watch. The crowd roared with disapproval and someone shouted a warning. It wasn't necessary. Whatever Adam did, he had Lyle flat on the floor almost immediately. Half a minute later, the knife was out of his grasp and he'd been handcuffed.

Deputy Al Green made his way through the crowd and dragged Lyle to his feet before escorting him outside to a chorus of hisses and catcalls.

"Lyle's going to end up in jail this time," Martie muttered as the music started again. "It's where he belongs."

Jeannie didn't know or care about Lyle; she couldn't take her eyes off Adam. *This* was Adam Jordan? The same man who couldn't utter a complete sentence in her company? The man who'd ripped her skirt, frightened her out of ten years of her life, locked her keys in the car and spattered her with barbecue sauce? Tonight she'd certainly seen a different side of him.

For the rest of the evening Jeannie watched him. Not once did he look in her direction. Not once did he give any indication he even knew she was there. He seemed to dance with every woman present, but not with her.

When a ladies' choice was announced, Jeannie shocked herself by boldly crossing the room to Adam's side. "Sheriff?"

He looked at her as if he didn't know who she was.

"Would you like to dance?" she asked, trying not to sound as nervous as she felt.

Wordlessly he led her onto the dance floor. His hold was loose and he gazed somewhere over her shoulder.

"I wanted to thank you," she told him.

"For what? Not asking you to dance all evening?"

"No," she said, mortified he'd think such a thing. "For replacing my blouse. You didn't need to do that."

He snickered as if he didn't believe her. "Well, I was the one who ruined it."

"That was an accident," she said. "At any rate, what you did was very thoughtful, and I want you to know I appreciate it."

He didn't speak during the rest of their dance. Jeannie wished he'd relax, but he held himself stiffly away from her. When the music ended, she wanted Adam to ask her to dance the next round with him; instead, he politely brought her back to the table with Martie and her friends.

"Thank you," she said, hoping her disappointment didn't show. She couldn't very well blame him after the number of times she'd rejected him.

"My pleasure." He touched the rim of his hat and began to move away.

"Adam," she called out impulsively. But when he turned back, she couldn't think of anything to say.

His smile unnerved her. "Don't worry, Jeannie, you've done your duty." Having said that, he turned and walked away.

Cal knew he was being an ass, but he couldn't seem to stop himself. He'd been worried sick about his parents and had taken his impatience and frustration out on Jane. He'd tried to apologize, tried to tell her he didn't mean the things he'd said, but every time he opened his mouth he only made matters worse.

When he grumbled about the dance, she'd offered to let him off the hook. Her offer was sincere, although he knew she'd been looking forward to this evening for weeks. He was tempted to take her up on it, but he figured he owed her. As it was, they arrived late; it was nearly nine-thirty when they left the house.

They barely said a word all the way to the Grange Hall. "Are you sure you're up to this?" Cal asked as he drove around searching for a parking spot.

"I'm sure."

It wasn't like Jane to be this quiet. Sure, he'd been a jerk lately, but he loved her and she knew it, at least he prayed she did. "Honey," he said miserably, filled with regret, "I'm sorry."

"For what?"

Damned if he knew. "Whatever I've done to upset you."

"You haven't upset me."

"You're absolving me from all wrongdoing, then?"

She gave him a quick smile. "I wouldn't go as far as that."

He laughed and squeezed her hand, and she smiled again, but he could tell her joy was fleeting. He was the cause, and the knowledge weighed down his heart.

Unexpectedly he found a parking space relatively close to the hall. A long walk wouldn't have bothered him, but he didn't want Jane to have to go far. She rarely complained about being uncomfortable with the pregnancy, but he knew these past few months had drained her physically and emotionally. He was sure his moods hadn't been any help, either.

He was excited about having a baby, but it all seemed unreal to him. He recognized that soon he'd be a father and he was determined to be a good one; he just wasn't sure when fatherhood started. Jane was already a mother. Her body proved as much. But he didn't feel any different now than he had when she'd told him she was pregnant. His elation had lasted a long time, but at the moment, all that was required of him seemed to be this infernal waiting. He wasn't very good at it.

The hall was crowded, the way it always was for the annual dance. Cal slid his arm protectively around his wife as they walked in.

"Glen and Ellie are over there." Jane pointed.

His brother was standing and waving his arms above his head to attract their attention. Glen had secured a table; Grady and Caroline Weston and Nell and Travis Grant sat with him.

"You're late," his brother said as he neared the

table. Glen slapped him on the back. "Mighty fine duds you're wearing."

"Should be, seeing that I borrowed 'em from you."

The music was loud, too loud for extended conversation. Glen left to get them each a drink—a cranberry juice for Jane, a Lone Star beer for Cal.

Cal pulled out Jane's chair and draped her shawl over the back. "Look," she said close to his ear once they were both seated, "Annie's dancing with Lucas."

Cal glanced toward the dance floor. Sure enough, there they were. He studied them for a minute, wondering if he was witnessing the start of a romance. Jane certainly seemed to think so. Cal wasn't sure. Lucas had asked him some questions about Annie early on and a couple more that week. So the vet asked a few questions. Big deal. Didn't prove a thing. Jane, however, saw this as a clear indication that something might happen soon.

"Annie's with Lucas?" Ellie asked, raising her voice to be heard.

"Jane's already got them engaged," Cal informed his sister-in-law.

"I do not," Jane protested. "It's too early to tell."

Cal rolled his eyes, thinking he was being clever, but he caught the look on Jane's face and saw that he'd hurt her. Again. Another on his growing list of sins.

The band began a ten-minute break then. "I'm going over to talk to Dovie and Frank," she told him, and excused herself to the others.

"I'll go with you," Ellie said, slipping past Glen and Cal.

The women left the table and Glen moved into the chair Jane had vacated. "What's going on with you and Jane?" his brother demanded.

"What do you mean?" Cal asked irritably. Even if he'd been sure of what it was, he wasn't going to discuss it with his brother.

"She isn't herself."

That, Cal already knew.

"Neither are you," Glen added.

"Me?" This surprised Cal; then again, it didn't. The problem with his parents had been consuming him for weeks. At first everyone had discounted his concerns. More recently he'd felt vindicated, but being right in this instance brought damn little satisfaction.

"How's Jane feeling?" Glen asked next.

"She says she's fine."

"Ellie was really moody when she was pregnant with John."

"Jane isn't the moody type," Cal snapped.

"No, but you are!"

Cal refused to dignify that with a response.

"You missed seeing Lyle Whitehead make a fool of himself," Glen told him, changing the subject. "Adam put him in his place quick enough."

"What happened?"

Glen described the incident, and as his brother spoke, Cal surveyed the room, seeking out Jane. This was supposed to be a night of celebration, a night to enjoy, and here he was talking to his brother, while his wife stood on the other side of the room with Dovie. It wasn't right.

"Hey—where are you going?" Glen muttered when Cal got to his feet.

"To ask my wife to dance."

"You're *volunteering* to dance?" Glen made it sound as if the band should do a drum roll before he walked onto the floor. Under normal circumstances Cal wouldn't volunteer, not when he possessed two left feet, but he needed to have Jane all to himself for a little while.

Jane looked up with surprise when her husband approached. "How you doing, Dovie?" His mother's friend was a favorite of his. He exchanged handshakes with Frank. "Hear you two had a great time in Europe."

"It was wonderful," Dovie said rapturously.

"Sit down," Frank urged.

"Actually, I came to steal my wife away. I thought we'd dance."

Jane cast him the same shocked look he'd gotten from his brother. He smiled and held out his hand.

"You *want* to dance?" she asked as Cal led her toward the floor.

"Anything wrong with that?"

"Not wrong, just unusual."

He couldn't argue. His timing was perfect, he noted with some relief; the first number was a slow one. All he had to do was put his arms around Jane, shuffle his feet back and forth, and that passed for dancing. Good enough for him.

Jane walked into his arms, and it felt so damn good he nearly groaned aloud. He hadn't held her like this in weeks. What was happening to them? Whatever it was had to stop. He needed his wife and loved her beyond measure.

Breathing in the scent of her hair, he closed his eyes and gently swayed with the music.

"I love you," Cal whispered.

She nodded, tightened her arms around his neck and buried her face in his shoulder.

It took him longer than it should have to realize she was crying. "Jane, love…what is it?"

She shook her head silently.

"You're crying because I love you?"

She nodded.

That was when it happened, when he felt the solid unmistakable kick against his ribs. His child had belted him. "Did you feel that?" he asked excitedly. He remembered Wade telling him how the same thing had happened when Amy was pregnant with Joey— at this same dance, too—but Cal hadn't understood the significance. He did now.

Jane gave an amused shrug. "Yes. He likes music, I guess."

"She," he corrected. From the first Jane had been convinced the baby was a boy. He'd never understood why; the ultrasound hadn't indicated one way or the other. "It has to be a girl. If it was a boy, he wouldn't be this happy about being on a dance floor."

Jane laughed sweetly, softly and his heart felt so full he thought it might burst wide open.

Flattening his hand against her stomach, he nearly laughed out loud when the baby kicked, harder this time. That incredible surge of emotion, of love, happened all over again.

"That answers my question," he whispered.

"What question?" She leaned her head back far enough to give him a quizzical look.

"When a man starts to feel like a father. I did just now—that's my child punching at me."

"Our son," Jane said with a happy smile.

"Daughter," he murmured, and seeing the love in his wife's eyes, he knew what he had to do next.

Jane frowned when he stopped dancing and took her by the hand. "Where are we going?" she asked as he tugged at her arm.

"Outside."

"Why?"

"Because I need to kiss you so much right now, it's either embarrass us both or get off the dance floor."

"Cal," she protested weakly as they wove their way through the crowd, "we're married!"

"So? Is that a problem? Does that mean I can only kiss you at home?"

Her eagerness as she followed him out the side door told him she needed this as much as he did. They needed each other and always would. They were a team, a couple, a family. Lovers and friends, confidants and companions. And now, parents.

As soon as they were out of sight of everyone else, Cal drew her into his arms. She opened her mouth to him in a kiss that started gentle, but quickly became intense. Jane tasted like heaven, sweet and passionate, her arms wrapped tightly around his neck.

Cal didn't know how long they kissed before he was aware that they weren't alone. He dragged his mouth from hers and stared into the shadows, where he saw another couple. It took him an instant to identify them—Bernie and Cheryl Benton. The last he'd heard, they'd separated. Now, apparently, they'd worked out their differences. He fully intended to resolve any differences in his own marriage—without the help of a knife-pulling idiot like Lyle Whitehead.

Whatever was wrong, he intended to fix it or die trying.

Thirteen

Sunday morning after the dance, Annie Applegate lay in bed and thought about what she'd done. She'd agreed to marry a man who didn't love her. She expected, in the clear light of day, to feel some regrets; to her astonishment, she didn't. She'd accepted the proposal of a man who was looking for a companion, and a mother for his children. It had seemed a straightforward arrangement—until *she'd* complicated it. By asking him to get her pregnant. He'd said nothing about sharing a bed; she'd in effect made it a condition of the marriage. More than anything, she wanted a baby. And Lucas had agreed to be the father.

Annie hadn't told anyone, not even Jane. Last night, Lucas hadn't mentioned the wedding again until the end of the evening, and then he suggested they seek out Wade McMillen. They'd managed to corner the pastor by himself, and if he was surprised by their news, he didn't let it show. The short conversation ended with Wade making an appointment with them for Monday afternoon.

Annie supposed that some ministers might refuse to marry them. Their marriage agreement was unusual, but she sensed Wade understood that they were two lonely hurting people, seeking to find solace in each other. They weren't in love, but they respected and cared for each other, and both wanted the best for Lucas's children. Besides, Annie had married for love the first time, and the feeling hadn't lasted.

Midafternoon on Sunday, Annie phoned her father.

"Sweetheart, it's good to hear from you," Brandon Applegate said. He rarely called her. Annie never doubted his love, but often wished he were a different kind of person. A different kind of father. They'd never been close and she didn't know how to bridge the emotional distance between them.

"I thought I should tell you I'm getting married," she said.

Her news was greeted with a brief silence. Then a somewhat startled "Married? To whom?"

"His name is Dr. Lucas Porter. He's a veterinarian. A widower with two daughters."

"You knew him before you moved to Texas?" her father asked, as if that would explain her sudden desire to leave California.

"No, I met him shortly after I arrived."

"But it's only been a couple of months." He sounded appalled.

"I know."

Brandon's sigh was deep enough to be audible. "I hope you know what you're doing."

"I do," Annie assured him. "I'm not sure when the wedding will be, but I'll let you know as soon as I can."

"This is a busy time of year for me," her father said. It was his way of telling her he wouldn't be attending the ceremony. He probably figured he'd done his duty the first time round, and one wedding was his limit, Annie thought with some amusement. Eventually he'd send Annie and Lucas his congratulations, together with a generous check, confident he'd fulfilled his role as her father.

Monday afternoon Lucas showed up at the bookstore a full hour before their scheduled appointment with Reverend Wade McMillen. He walked in and studied her for a moment, as if he half expected her to tell him she'd changed her mind.

"Hello," she said. Countless questions had occurred to her since Saturday night, and all she could think to say was, "You're early."

"I know. I just wanted to make sure you're still willing to go through with this."

"I'm willing. Are you?"

He nodded firmly. "I'm not sure it was a good idea to say anything this soon, but I told the girls."

Her one hesitation had been Heather and Hollie. How would they *really* feel? Would they resent her, think she was trying to replace their mother?

"They're thrilled," Lucas told her. "I am, too. I'm grateful, Annie. Incredibly grateful."

"Me, too." She smiled. "I phoned my father."

Lucas tensed, as though he anticipated an argument. "He was opposed to the idea, wasn't he?"

"No. All he wanted was my assurance that I know what I'm doing."

Lucas glanced away. "Do you, Annie? *Do* you really know what you're letting yourself in for?"

Lucas didn't understand. His proposal offered her an opportunity she'd stopped hoping for. He was going to marry her, complete with her flaws and her scars, both physical and emotional. He'd be giving her a family, two lovely little girls who needed her, and a baby of her own. It was enough. More than enough.

"I talked to my parents, too," he confessed.

"What did they think?" Annie remembered they had a travel trailer and were parked somewhere in the Florida Keys, spending a lot of time deep-sea fishing. She'd met them shortly after she arrived in Promise, but only in passing.

"My mom was a bit concerned that it's too soon."

"By anyone else's standards, it *is* too soon."

"I told her I hadn't called to ask her permission. Both Mom and Dad like you, and that helps. Dad seemed to think we'd be able to make a good marriage. I agree with him."

"And your mother?"

"She advised us both to think this through very carefully."

"I already have," Annie said.

He grinned, satisfied. "I have, too."

They discussed a few details while they waited for Gina Greenville to arrive. Once she got to the bookstore, Annie and Lucas left for their meeting with Wade.

Annie noticed the curious stares as they walked the short distance from the store to the church rectory. She felt self-conscious, as if everyone in Promise had already guessed they were getting married.

"Hello, Lucas. Annie," Louise Powell trilled when they passed her on the sidewalk.

"Hi, Louise," Annie said. Lucas merely nodded.

"Great weather we're having, isn't it?"

"Yeah, great," Lucas echoed without enthusiasm.

"Where are you off to?" Her eyes flashed with undisguised curiosity.

Annie looked at Lucas, wondering how he'd respond.

"To see Wade McMillen about a wedding."

"Yours?" She offered the suggestion with a laugh, turning it into a joke.

"As a matter of fact, yes," Lucas supplied, and his hand squeezed Annie's.

"I knew it. I knew it all along," Louise chanted gleefully. "The minute I saw you together, I could smell romance in the air. I went home and told my husband it wouldn't surprise me if you two got married by the end of the year. When's the date?"

"Soon," Lucas told her shortly.

In truth, Annie would have preferred they not tell anyone until they'd spoken to Wade. Other than her father, she hadn't told a single person, not even Jane. Well, if nothing else, the fact that Lucas had shared the news with the town busybody meant he was serious about this wedding. She guessed that if Wade refused to perform the ceremony, they could find someone who would.

"Word'll be all over town by the time we finish talking to Wade," Lucas said as they climbed the stairs to the church rectory. "You don't mind, do you?"

"No," Annie said. And on second thought, why should she? They'd made their decision; they both wanted this marriage.

Martha Kerns, Wade's secretary, seated them in the pastor's office and explained that Wade would be with them in a couple of minutes. Then she quietly left the room and closed the door.

"Have you given any thought to when you'd like the wedding?" Lucas asked.

"No." She glanced at him. "Have you?"

Lucas shrugged. "Is two weeks enough time for you?"

They'd already agreed it would be a small private wedding. "All right with me, if it is with you."

He grinned. "That's long enough for me. Mom and Dad asked to be included, and that'll give them the time they need to drive back from Florida."

"I'd like Jane to be my maid of honor."

"I was thinking of asking Cal to stand up for me."

"Heather and Hollie will be there, won't they?" Annie asked, wanting to make the girls feel part of things.

"I'd like them to be," he told her, "if you're okay with it."

Annie nodded.

Their eyes met and they smiled slowly. Lucas reached for her hand, raising her fingers to his lips. "You won't be sorry, Annie," he promised. "I'll do everything in my power to be a good husband to you."

Annie believed him.

The door opened then and a breathless Wade McMillen rushed in. "Sorry, I'm late," he apologized as he pulled out the chair at his desk. "Now, what's all this about a wedding?"

"Mother, are you seeing someone?" Sylvia had arrived unannounced at lunchtime—highly unusual for the middle of the week.

Nessa had been expecting her daughter's question. "Seeing someone, dear?" she repeated, keeping her voice low as she pierced a piece of lettuce with her fork. Sylvia had driven from her home in New Orleans for a "quick visit." Nessa didn't know what she'd said during their last phone call to raise her daughter's suspicions, but whatever it was had Sylvia packed and on the road within twenty-four hours.

"Mother, please, either you've met someone or you haven't."

Her daughter was far too direct, Nessa mused. "What makes you ask?" Sylvia was a dear girl, but she did tend to be dictatorial.

"Well, for one thing, your phone's busy for at least an hour every evening. For another, you've been acting strange all weekend."

"Is the latter an observation or a criticism?" Nessa asked, rather enjoying this exchange. Unnerving her daughter wasn't an everyday occurrence. After weeks of listening to Sylvia campaign for the idea of remarriage, Nessa had come to a rather startling conclusion. Her daughter *did* want her to see men, but only men she'd selected herself.

"Just answer the question, Mother."

"Have I met someone?"

"Yes, Mother." Sylvia's sarcastic tone reminded Nessa of some rather difficult years when all three of her children had been teenagers at the same time. Back then, Sylvia had developed an obnoxiously superior attitude. By the time she was twenty, she'd gotten over that—well, mostly.

"Sylvia, sweetheart, I've met any number of people since moving back to Promise."

"A man, Mother, I mean a man."

"Several." Nessa dug into her salad with gusto. It was either that or laugh out loud.

"Is there any *particular* man you've met? One you're—" Sylvia's mouth twisted as she said the word "—*attracted* to?"

Gordon. Oh, my, yes. Their telephone conversations continued on a nightly basis, sometimes lasting as long as two hours. If it wasn't happening to her, Nessa wouldn't have believed any couple could have this much to say on such brief acquaintance. They talked about their lives, their children, their marriages. There didn't seem to be anything they *couldn't* talk about. Nessa lived for his calls; her entire day was focused on hearing his voice. She felt young again, young and vibrant. In love.

The thought brought her up short. My goodness, it was true. She'd fallen in love with Gordon.

"Mother," Sylvia insisted, louder this time. "My goodness, what's come over you?"

"Nothing, dear," Nessa said, although she was flustered. Her face felt warm and her hands cold. Her appetite unexpectedly deserted her. Carrying her plate, she got up from the table and walked into the kitchen.

Sylvia finally stopped the incessant questioning.

"I was thinking of doing a little shopping this afternoon," she said.

"That's nice, dear." Nessa claimed her favorite chair and reached for her knitting. "Be sure to go see your aunt Dovie."

"I will." Sylvia's expression was grave, and before long she left the house.

As soon as she did, Nessa sighed in relief. My goodness, Sylvia was a troublesome child.

Dovie was humming to herself as she lifted the pie plate with one hand and ran a knife around the edge, cutting off any crust draped over the sides. Apple-and-date pie made with her buttermilk crust was one of Frank's favorites, and she was planning to surprise him. Her husband was playing cribbage down at the seniors' center and she didn't expect him back for a couple of hours. Plenty of time to make that pie.

As a new retiree, Frank had claimed no one would find him at the seniors' center, but he'd quickly enough had a change of heart. Now he routinely dropped in there once or twice a week. Recently he'd told her he'd volunteered to give a safety workshop geared toward senior citizens.

This was exactly what Dovie had hoped would happen. Frank had floundered a bit when he'd first retired and spent far too much time at the sheriff's office. Dovie was grateful for Adam Jordan's patience. Every day Frank had returned from his talks with Adam to tell her about all the mistakes the young sheriff had made and how he would've handled things differently.

But after a few months, Dovie had begun to notice a gradual change in Frank. He hadn't participated in Lyle Whitehead's arrest. Frank had been confident that Sheriff Jordan and Deputy Green could adequately handle the situation, and they'd proved him right. She felt Frank had truly retired now. The official date had been early January, but his retirement hadn't really taken effect until the night of the Cattlemen's Dance.

The doorbell chimed and Dovie set aside the pie to answer it. "Sylvia!" She let out a cry of delight, and the two hugged for a long moment. Never having had children herself, Dovie cherished Nessa's oldest daughter. She disagreed with the way Sylvia treated Nessa these days, but that was between mother and daughter, not aunt and niece.

"How are you, Aunt Dovie?" Sylvia asked as she followed her back into the kitchen.

"Never better." Dovie slid the pie inside the preheated oven and put on water for tea. "Your mother said you were here for a visit."

"I'm heading home tomorrow morning."

"I'm so glad you took the time to come by. I don't see you often enough." Dovie brought down her favorite teapot from the pine hutch and two matching cups and saucers. "How are you and Steve and the kids?"

"Great," her niece responded without elaborating.

As soon as the tea was ready, Dovie added a plate of her peanut-butter cookies and carried the tray into the formal living room.

"Aunt Dovie, have you noticed anything strange about my mother lately?"

Dovie had to stop and think. She was prepared to defend Nessa had Sylvia said her mother seemed anxious or depressed. But strange? "What do you mean by strange?"

Sylvia took her time answering. "She's...happy."

Dovie paused in the task of pouring tea. "Being

happy shouldn't be considered strange. Nor is it a matter for concern.''

"Have you looked at her lately? Really looked?'' Sylvia demanded.

Everything was a crisis with this child. Dovie had always thought she was destined for the stage, since Sylvia made a drama of the most mundane incident, the most trivial problem.

"Mother's always wearing a silly grin. That's not like her.''

Dovie carefully put the teapot back on the tray. "Now that you mention it, Nessa does seem… brighter, more energetic.''

Sylvia nodded.

"It involves a man,'' she said. "I just know it.''

Dovie merely raised her eyebrows.

"Has she mentioned anyone?'' Sylvia pressed.

Dovie thought about the past few times she'd seen Nessa. "No, I can't say she has.''

"That's what I figured,'' Sylvia muttered darkly. "You haven't seen her date anyone, have you? Or heard any rumors?''

Once again, Dovie was left to do a mental review of when and where she'd seen her sister-in-law, and with whom. Nessa had been out with various friends, including her, and she'd attended several community events—although not the dance, now that Dovie thought of it. But to the best of Dovie's knowledge, she hadn't been seen in the company of any man. "I don't know if your mother's dating or not,'' Dovie confessed. "I don't *think* she is, but…''

Sylvia looked as if she was in pain. "You're sure of that?''

"My dear child, I don't actually keep tabs on Nessa."

"But she talks to you more than anyone."

"True…"

Sylvia reached absently for a second cookie. The girl had been watching her weight for as long as Dovie could remember. It was almost unheard of for her to eat two cookies at one time.

"What exactly are you upset about?" Dovie asked.

"Aunt Dovie, don't you know what this means?" Her hand returned to the plate for an unprecedented third cookie. Crumbs attached themselves to the corners of her lips.

"I'm afraid I don't." While she was deeply fond of Sylvia, she felt the girl was definitely overreacting. Fine, so Nessa was happier and livelier than she'd been in a while. There was a simple reason for that. She'd adjusted. It'd taken her some time to find her footing after Leon died, but now that she had, Nessa was ready to get on with her life.

Dovie recalled that first bleak year after her own husband's death and how desperately she'd searched for something to give her life purpose. That was when she'd opened the antique store.

"Don't you see?" Sylvia cried. "My mother's seeing a man."

"But, Sylvia, I thought that was what you wanted."

Her niece ignored the comment. "She didn't attend the dance, did she?"

"No," Dovie said.

"Doesn't *that* tell you something?"

"Tell me what?" Dovie hated to appear obtuse, but she didn't know what Sylvia was talking about.

"My mother," Sylvia whispered, closing her eyes, "is having an affair."

"Don't be ridiculous, child," Dovie chastised immediately. She was sure Nessa was doing no such thing.

"Mark my words, Aunt Dovie," Sylvia said. "She's seeing someone she doesn't want us to know about. He must be married. What other reason could she have for not telling us?"

Fourteen

Sheriff Adam Jordan's days off usually fell in the middle of the week. He'd developed a habit of checking the movie schedules every Wednesday. If something new was playing that he particularly wanted to see, he often went to the early-evening show.

He wasn't as interested in this week's movie, a comedy starring Jim Carrey, as he was in a couple of hours' distraction. He was still thinking about the previous Saturday and how shocked he'd been when Jeannie French invited him to dance. Okay, she'd had a reason. She'd wanted to thank him for replacing the blouse, but she needn't have asked him to dance to do that.

Adam wasn't all that fond of dancing, but he made a point of partnering as many women as he could for a spin around the floor. It was either that or spend the entire evening ogling Jeannie. He'd never seen her look more beautiful. Apparently it was his lot in life to get stuck on a woman who wanted nothing to do with him.

He'd seen her dance once with Billy Joe Durkin and nearly suffered a heart attack. Billy Joe was a ladies' man, and if ever a woman was capable of capturing a cowboy's attention, it was Jeannie. She'd danced with a few other men, too, and it was damned difficult to stand back and watch. Since that night all he'd done was think of Jeannie. He needed a distraction, so an afternoon at the movies suited him just fine.

Ticket in hand, Adam purchased a bag of buttered popcorn and a tall drink, then headed into the air-conditioned theater. The nice thing about catching the first show of the night was how empty the theater was. Many times there was only a handful of people.

Carrying his snacks, Adam discovered the theater completely unoccupied. A few more patrons would arrive in short order, they always did, but by then he'd have his choice of seats. That was the good news. The bad news was he'd prefer to share a movie with someone. But most of his friends didn't have the same days off. And if they went to a weekday showing, it was usually the later one, well after dinner.

Adam had settled in his seat when the doors opened and a second person entered. A woman, he noted absently, taking a sip of his drink. Not until she walked past him did Adam recognize Jeannie.

"Jeannie," he said aloud, then wished he hadn't. So much for playing it cool. So much for acting nonchalant. Blurting out her name in a surge of sheer joy wasn't going to impress a woman who'd made her views on dating him extremely clear. Painfully clear.

"Hello, Adam," she said, looking equally delighted to see him. That was a switch.

Rather than say anything else that would embarrass them both, he stuffed a handful of popcorn in his mouth, then wiped his greasy palm down his thigh. When no one immediately joined her, he glanced over his shoulder, finding it difficult to believe she was alone.

She hesitated, then sat two rows ahead. With the entire theater empty, she'd chosen to sit almost directly in front of him. Was this a signal? Was this her way of letting him know she regretted her previous attitude? Adam wasn't going to risk asking.

"Want a Milk Dud?" she twisted around to ask.

His mouth was full of popcorn, so he shook his head.

"I was hoping you'd save me from eating them all myself. I can do without the extra fat."

If she was hinting that he should tell her she had a perfect body, he wouldn't comply, although heaven knew it was the truth. Everything about her was perfect. Time and again he'd tried not to think of her; until last Saturday, he'd almost succeeded. Then she'd asked him to dance, and the feel of her still lingered in his arms.

Offering him a piece of candy could be an overture. A friendly gesture. But he knew himself well enough to recognize that he wouldn't be satisfied with a casual friendship. He wanted more. A whole lot more.

"Actually, I much prefer the popcorn," Jeannie was saying. "But Milk Duds are the lesser of two evils."

"Buttered popcorn?"

"Buttered," she agreed.

Adam wasn't sure what possessed him. He knew he'd kick himself later, but he stood up, carrying the bucket of popcorn and the drink, and moved to her row.

Jeannie smiled as he took a seat three away from her. "I've come to rescue you," he said.

"Rescue me?"

"From eating the Milk Duds. If you're going to consume unwanted calories, make it something you'll truly enjoy."

She seemed about to argue, then suddenly said, "You're right."

Grinning, he tilted the popcorn in her direction.

Jeannie helped herself to a handful, then savored each kernel. "This stuff is going to clog my arteries, add fat to my hips and get stuck between my teeth."

"You can always refuse," he reminded her.

Her hand stilled above the bucket. "I'll do without lunch tomorrow and promise to floss after the movie."

Adam chuckled.

"Here," she said, handing him the Milk Duds.

"What's this for?"

"My gift to you," she said, her eyes twinkling.

The theater darkened then, and the previews began. A few more people entered and chose seats far from where they sat. Adam wasn't sure who moved first, but by the time the movie started, he and Jeannie had each shifted one seat over and sat side by side.

The comedy was undeniably silly, and Adam howled with laughter. Jeannie did, too. The popcorn slowly disappeared and not long after, "The End" flashed across the screen. Then the lights came on, and they glanced at each other self-consciously.

But neither Adam nor Jeannie made any attempt to get up.

"That was great," Adam said, and he wasn't referring just to the movie. This was what he'd envisioned a date with Jeannie would be like. Laughing together, enjoying each other's company. It had happened by accident. However, he wasn't sure what to suggest next. If anything.

"I haven't laughed this hard in months," she said.

He thought of asking her to dinner, but dismissed the idea immediately. No need to set himself up for more rejection. If Jeannie suggested something, though, that would be an entirely different matter.

She didn't.

Adam finally stood. "Good seeing you again," he said casually.

"You, too." Jeannie got to her feet, as well, but neither made a move toward the aisle.

"I'd better be going now," he muttered.

"Yeah, me too."

Adam forced himself to turn and start out of the theater, determined not to look back.

"Adam?"

He whirled around at the sound of her voice, cursing himself for appearing so eager.

"I thought you handled the situation with Lyle Whitehead beautifully...at the dance."

"Thanks." He lingered, wanting to say something and not knowing what. If only he'd had more experience, more finesse. "Did you, uh, enjoy the dance?" A question seemed the best way to continue the conversation.

"It was great." Jeannie joined him in the aisle and they walked out of the theater together. "I learned more about the people of Promise in those few hours than the entire time I've lived here."

"How's that?"

Her smile was slow and it charmed him completely. "I saw my colleagues and my students' parents outside the classroom—that was a real eye-opener."

Adam chuckled.

"Now I know why certain children behave the way they do."

They walked into the warmth of the late-June evening. Once again Adam toyed with the idea of inviting Jeannie for dinner. Once again he decided against it.

"Well, nice seeing you," he said—for what? the third time?—and was about to turn away.

"You, too...Adam," she said, slightly breathless. "I..." She paused and offered him a shaky smile. "Listen, you and I started off on the wrong foot, it seems."

He waited.

"I was thinking maybe...you know, we could be friends."

He thought about it for a moment. She'd opened the door, but not damn near far enough. Friends. She wanted to be friends. "No thanks, Jeannie."

"No?" She looked stunned. "But I...I hoped..."

He'd also hoped, and it'd been a disaster. "You see, I want the popcorn, too. I'm afraid I'm not interested in the Milk Duds." Adam could tell from her frown that she didn't understand.

"I hate it when people talk in riddles," she said. "I can't figure them out."

"You will," he told her. Then he turned and strolled away.

* * *

Gordon Pawling was as giddy as a schoolboy. It'd been fifteen years since his wife's death and he'd never expected to fall in love a second time, certainly not this late in life. He felt so young, so happy now. Since meeting Nessa, he felt full of purpose; he had a reason to get out of bed in the morning. His interest in the world around him grew. He found himself looking up old friends he hadn't talked to in months, playing chess again. His passion for golf returned.

His son had been after him to get back into law. Since his retirement, Gordon had acted as a legal adviser, reviewing cases and offering opinions and recommendations, but he'd let that slip away. Let most things slip away.

Before he met Nessa, he'd simply been waiting to die. Not in a morbid sense, but as the natural end of human existence. He'd lived a productive life, had a fulfilling career, married, fathered a son, served his community and retired. He'd completed his purpose. Death was the next logical step. He didn't fear it, didn't dread it.

But thanks to Nessa, Gordon had discovered a new enthusiasm for life. He greeted each day with anticipation. Their telephone conversations had become his secret addiction. He'd never been much of a talker, especially over the phone, but all that had changed. The phone was his only contact with Nessa, and it had become essential to spend part of every day with her.

"Dad." Miles walked into the den, surprising him. "I thought you must be home, but you didn't answer the door."

"I didn't hear it." Caught up in his plans and reveries as he was, the sound of the doorbell must have escaped him. A visit from Miles was rare indeed. "Sit down. What can I get you to drink?"

His son sank into the matching chair on the opposite side of the fireplace. "I thought you must've been reading and dozed off."

Gordon didn't confirm or deny his son's comment. It would be a bit embarrassing to admit he'd been deep in thought—about a woman.

"What are you drinking?" Miles asked.

Gordon had forgotten about the glass on the end table at his side. "Wine. It's a merlot."

"I'll have some of that."

Gordon stood and headed for the dining room, checking the time as he went. Nessa would be expecting his call in a few minutes. He got another goblet from the buffet and poured his son a glass, then hurried into the kitchen to use the phone there.

Nessa answered on the first ring.

"Miles is here," he explained. "I'll call you back as soon as he leaves."

"Oh, do," Nessa said, sounding stressed. "Please. No matter what time it is."

"Is everything all right?"

"Yes," she said, then added shakily. "I don't know…Sylvia's gone, but Gordon, I feel like such an old fool."

"If you're a fool, then so am I. I'll phone as soon as I can. Goodbye for now, my darling." It was the first time he'd said the endearment aloud, although that was certainly the way he thought of her.

He returned to his son a moment later and was

surprised to find Miles standing at his desk. Miles glanced up with a mildly guilty expression and stepped forward to accept the goblet.

"Something on your mind?" Gordon asked as they both sat.

"Work. Kids," Miles said, resting his head against the cushion and closing his eyes. "There just don't seem to be enough hours in the day. I need a vacation."

"Take one," Gordon advised. "It'll do you good. Karen, too."

"I was thinking the same thing."

Gordon was proud of his son, who had a number of fine traits and qualities. Most of those had come from his mother, in Gordon's opinion, but his keen legal mind and good business sense he'd inherited from his father, if Gordon did say so himself.

"You enjoyed the cruise you took a few years back, didn't you?" Miles asked.

"Very much." But not for the reasons his son assumed. Gordon had agreed to the cruise under protest. The idea had been Miles and Karen's, and the tickets were given to him as a gift. They were making an effort, he'd realized, to lift his sagging spirits. So he'd gone. He'd found the experience moderately enjoyable, but the best part of the cruise had taken place the last evening, when he'd gotten to know Dovie. They'd stayed up nearly the entire night talking. She was in love with her sheriff friend and took pains not to mislead him, for which Gordon was grateful. That night had been a valuable lesson for him; spending time with Dovie had proved he could still feel attracted to a woman. Could still enjoy music and moonlight and a bit of flirtation.

It seemed ironic—and somehow right—that he'd met Nessa through Dovie.

"Karen's been looking at brochures."

"Take a cruise," Gordon said. "Perhaps as an anniversary gift. I could—"

"Dad, no. Thank you, but no."

Miles had a stubborn streak. "All right, if you insist, but I'd be more than happy to pay for it."

"Didn't you meet someone special while you were in the Caribbean?" Miles continued, not looking at him.

"Special?"

"A woman," his son elaborated.

"Dovie Boyd," Gordon said.

"From somewhere in Texas, right?"

"Promise, Texas," Gordon replied. "Why?"

"You really liked her, didn't you?"

"As a matter of fact, I did," he answered, wondering at this line of questioning.

"Whatever happened with you and Dovie?" Miles persisted.

Gordon sighed and sipped his wine. "She married the local sheriff soon after she returned from the cruise."

"She's married." Miles straightened, and the sly smile he wore vanished. "Married!"

"It happens every day, son. People in love get married."

"I see." Miles muttered, and sadly shook his head.

"I probably didn't mention it, but that's because I only found out myself."

"I see," Miles muttered again. "You were recently in Texas, weren't you?"

"Last month for that international law conference," Gordon confirmed. He was about to explain that he'd rented a car and driven to Promise. But before he could, Miles's cell phone rang.

"Miles Pawling," he said, flipping open the compact telephone with the dexterity of a frequent user.

Gordon could tell from his end of the conversation that the caller was his daughter-in-law, and that something had gone awry.

"I have to go," Miles said, snapping the phone closed and slipping it into his pocket. "Chrissie's sick and Karen needs me to stop at the drugstore on my way home."

Gordon walked him to the door. "Take my advice, son, and book the cruise."

Miles stared at him as if he hadn't heard a word Gordon said. As if he didn't recognize his own father.

"Is everything all right, Miles?"

His son rubbed his face. "Oh, yeah," he replied with a tinge of sarcasm, "everything's just fine."

Shrugging, Gordon closed the door and returned to the den. He knew Nessa was waiting, so he sat down at his desk, reached for the phone and punched out her number. Shifting papers, he saw the phone bill and groaned. Even with a special long-distance service, these daily calls were expensive.

"Hello," Nessa answered, sounding more cheerful.

"It's Gordon."

"Did you mean what you said earlier," she asked without preamble, her voice soft. "Am I your darling?"

"If you want to be. Do you?"

"Yes." She didn't hesitate. "Oh, yes."

Relaxed now, Gordon leaned back in the chair and set the phone bill aside. These moments with Nessa were worth every penny. "Tell me about your daughter's visit," he said—and suddenly remembered Miles standing at this very desk. Was it possible his son had seen the telephone bill with page after page of long-distance calls to Promise?

Fifteen

The engagement of Annie Applegate and Lucas Porter didn't come as any surprise to the community of Promise, thanks to Louise Powell, who took delight in being the one to spread the word. If anything, people seemed genuinely pleased.

In the last week of June, Annie did more business at the bookstore than at any time since she'd opened. Almost everyone in town dropped by to offer congratulations and best wishes. Talk of their engagement was all over town. People assumed it was a love match, and the jokes about the brevity of their courtship flew fast and furious.

Both Annie and Lucas took the teasing in stride. She didn't let it bother her and knew Lucas didn't, either. Other than Wade, no one needed to know the details of their agreement. Annie didn't tell anyone, not even Jane.

The two weeks between the Cattlemen's Dance and the wedding passed in a blur. Annie sewed identical dresses for Heather and Hollie, went shopping in Austin with Dovie and Jane for her own wedding dress and spent the rest of the time packing up her tiny apartment to move in with Lucas and the girls.

Mrs. Delaney left for Kansas with a clear conscience. Heather and Hollie spent almost every day with Annie. She loved these girls and they in turn loved her.

On the day of the wedding, Savannah brought a lovely wedding bouquet filled with delicate white rosebuds to Annie at the church. She hugged her close. "I hope you'll be happy," she whispered.

"I intend to."

While the ceremony was small and private, the reception would be in the church hall later the same day. Annie was astonished and pleased at how many people had asked to be invited. Dovie had baked the wedding cake, and the women's church group provided the decorations.

"Are you ready?" Jane asked Annie when she arrived at the church with Cal.

Annie inhaled deeply. "I think so." She wore an antique-white suit that fitted her perfectly. Dovie had been the one to find it. This wasn't the type of outfit Annie would normally have chosen, but she'd tried it on at Dovie's insistence. The minute she saw her reflection, Annie knew. It felt as if the suit had been especially designed for her and this day.

"You're beautiful," Jane said softly, her voice full of emotion. "I wish your dad had come."

"It isn't necessary." Annie understood and accepted her father's detachment.

Lucas and the girls, along with his parents, arrived next. As soon as Heather and Hollie saw Annie, they raced to her side, their new patent-leather shoes tapping in the vestibule.

"Oh Annie, you look so pretty!" Heather cried.

"So do you," Annie said, and bent down to hand

each girl a small bouquet of pink roses. They were serving as her bridesmaids and looked angelic in their pink floral dresses with wide satin sashes.

"Does everyone know where to stand?" Wade asked, signaling that it was time to start the ceremony. Annie had decided not to walk down the aisle; with such an informal wedding, it seemed unnecessary. Grandiose.

The small group gathered at the front of the church. Annie hadn't paid much attention to Lucas until then. He wore a dark suit and looked wonderfully handsome, if a little nervous.

She could hardly take it in—a few minutes from now, she'd be this man's wife and stepmother to his daughters. At some time in the future, she'd bear his child. From this day forward, Lucas and the girls would be part of Annie's life.

Perhaps she should have been more nervous, more uncertain, but she wasn't. She stood confidently beside Lucas, waiting for her future to begin.

Wade McMillen opened his Bible, and with a warm engaging smile, looked first to Annie, then to Lucas.

After a few introductory words Wade said, "Lucas, if you'll repeat after me. I, Lucas James Porter, solemnly promise to love, honor and cherish Ann Marie Applegate in sickness and in health..."

Lucas shifted his weight from one foot to the other, then held up his hand. "Could you stop?" he murmured.

Annie's gaze flew to the man she'd agreed to marry, her heartbeat echoing in her ears. From the way he avoided looking at her, Annie knew.

Lucas had changed his mind.

"Son?" Carl Porter, Lucas's father, sent Annie a quick nervous glance. "Is something wrong?"

"I don't know." Lucas sounded ambivalent. Unsure.

"You don't want to go through with the wedding, Lucas?" Wade asked gently, without censure.

He didn't answer. "Would it be all right if I spoke to Annie privately for a moment?"

"Of course," Wade told him.

Annie saw Jane and Cal exchange looks as she accepted Lucas's hand and walked with him, her heart in her throat, all the way to the back of the church. Not knowing what to expect, Annie waited for him to explain.

"I can't do it, Annie."

Of all the things she could have thought just then, what came into her mind was the fact that her dress had cost nearly three hundred dollars. She was worried, too, about moving all those boxes back into the tiny apartment above the bookstore. Crazy concerns. Mundane meaningless problems.

"Are you saying you want to call off the wedding?" she asked, doing her best to remain calm.

"No," he said, his expression utterly miserable. "I want us to do this—more than anything—but I can't vow to love you. I can't stand in this church and, before God, promise you something that isn't possible."

Annie's knees were about to collapse, and she lowered herself onto the closest pew. Her hands gripped the bridal bouquet with a ferocity that numbed her fingers.

"I have little enough to offer you as it is," Lucas

said in a low hoarse voice. "The benefits of our union seem to be almost completely one-sided. I refuse to mislead you. I'll never love you—not the way you deserve, Annie. I buried my heart with my wife."

"I see," she whispered.

Wade joined them. "Is there a problem I can help with?"

"It's the vows," Annie explained, when Lucas wasn't immediately forthcoming. "We aren't in love."

"Ah, I see," Wade murmured. "Would you be more comfortable if I omitted the word 'love'?"

"Can you do that?" Lucas seemed at a loss. "I'll cherish Annie and honor her as my wife. I'm willing to commit my life, my resources and my future to her. Is that enough?"

Wade looked to Annie for the answer.

"It's enough," she told him.

Lucas relaxed visibly. "Thank you."

Wade patted Lucas on the back. "Shall we continue, then?"

"Please," Annie said. She stood and placed her hand in Lucas's. She'd had all the words about love before, and they'd been hollow. To anyone else it might seem she was being cheated, but Annie felt no such loss. She was prepared to pledge her life to an honest man who refused to mislead her in any way. He would honor and cherish her, and that was more than any other man had given her.

Jane studied Annie as if she wanted to pull her aside for a second consultation. Annie tried to reassure her with a smile. "It's fine," she whispered.

"You're sure?"

Annie nodded.

The ceremony proceeded without further pause and was immediately followed by the reception. Many of the people there Annie barely knew. The support from the community she'd lived in for such a short time was a blessing she hadn't expected. For three wonderful hours, there was laughter, music and good food. Wade and Cal offered toasts to the newlyweds. Carl Porter spoke to Annie in such a welcoming way she was moved to tears. And then it was time to leave. Amy and Jane accompanied Annie when she went to change out of her wedding dress.

"There's something very special about Promise," Amy McMillen said when Annie mentioned her surprise at the number of people. "I arrived in Promise only a few years ago myself," she continued. "At the time, I felt as though I didn't have a friend in the world. But somehow…it was as though the entire town wrapped its arms around me. It felt almost as if everyone had been…waiting for my arrival."

"Wade certainly was," Jane teased, joining them.

Amy grew still. "I thank God for my husband. I love him more every day."

"I thank God for mine, too," Jane said, and rested her hands on her very round stomach.

"I'm grateful for Lucas," Annie admitted, and the three women hugged each other.

"Darn it, you're going to make me get all weepy," Amy mumbled. "I know you'll be happy with Lucas, Annie. You're both such special people."

Come to Promise, Jane had written all those months ago. *It won't be long before it'll be like home.*

Two months after her arrival, and Annie felt she

was part of a real family for the first time since her mother's death.

Jeannie French had hoped Sheriff Jordan would show up at the reception for Annie and Lucas Porter. But she hadn't realized how many people would be there. Everyone she knew in Promise had crowded into the church hall to wish the newlyweds happiness. Jeannie didn't know either Annie or Lucas well, but she admired Lucas's reputation and was fond of his daughters. Heather would be going into the third grade, and Hollie would begin first grade. Annie Applegate seemed both pleasant and sincere; her bookstore was a boon to the community and a place Jeannie visited often. Annie had helped her find several hard-to-locate books on the history of the Texas hill country. History, particularly state history, was a passion of Jeannie's.

Jeannie was in the mood for romance, in the mood for real-life love and happy endings. She also recognized that she'd completely misjudged Adam for months because of some trivial incidents and minor accidents. Now she'd ruined any chance with him. What she needed was a way to let Adam know she was interested. That she'd revised her opinion. If he *did* attend the reception, she might have an opportunity to hint at her feelings. So far, he was nowhere in sight.

The church hall was beautifully decorated, with flowers everywhere. A table, set off to one side, was stacked high with exquisitely wrapped gifts, and the wedding cake was lovely. Not until Gina Greenville served her a piece did she realize this wasn't a traditional white cake, but cheesecake with a basket-weave frosting made of sweetened cream cheese.

Jeannie had just taken her first bite when she finally saw Adam. He was standing on the opposite side of the room, wearing his uniform; he'd apparently stopped by either on his way to or from work. She wondered why she hadn't noticed earlier how attractive he was. He looked great—masculine and authoritative—and it wasn't just the uniform.

Her mouth closed around the plastic fork, and she simply stared. He must have felt her gaze because he glanced up and their eyes connected. Jeannie swallowed the bite of cake, which slid down her throat like a solid piece of cheese. Her heart pounding, she attempted a friendly smile.

In the two weeks since they'd met at the movie, she'd thought almost constantly of Adam. She'd hoped to hear from him and was disappointed she hadn't.

She'd attempted to be kind in her earlier rejections, but knew she'd hurt his pride. Her one fear now was that Adam wouldn't be inclined to accept her apology.

She made an effort to look casual as she worked her way across the room. "Been to any good movies lately?" she asked him a few minutes later.

"None to speak of."

Before she could continue the conversation, he moved off, joining a cluster of men that included Cal Patterson and his brother, Glen. Jeannie tried to ignore her disappointment. She chatted with Martie, the school secretary, all the while searching for Adam, hoping she wasn't being too obvious. She couldn't believe he'd leave so soon.

"Are you eating Milk Duds or popcorn these days?"

Jeannie whirled around to find the sheriff standing behind her. "Popcorn."

He smiled in approval. "Plain or buttered?"

As she'd told him earlier, she'd never been good at word games. But she waded in, anyway. "Buttered," she told him. "The real thing, too."

"Same for me," he murmured.

Jeannie suspected more was being discussed here than snack-food preferences—which was fine with her.

"Well, I see you two are finally talking to each other."

Jeannie hadn't noticed Max Jordan until he spoke. Both of Adam's parents joined them, looking pleased with themselves, as if they were solely responsible for this moment of potential romance. Margaret smiled benevolently at Jeannie, hand tucked inside her husband's elbow.

"Glad to see it," Max said. "Always thought it was a damn shame that my son—"

"Dad," Adam warned in a low growl.

"Go on," Jeannie urged Max, wanting to hear what he had to say.

Max glanced between her and his son. "On second thought, I think Adam would prefer to do his own talking."

"Thank you, Dad," Adam said stiffly.

The four of them stood there for a few minutes and made small talk about the weather, the loveliness of the bride, and the annual fourth of July Willie Nelson festival, which would be held once again without Willie's presence. A few years earlier, the star had unexpectedly shown up at the annual rodeo and chili cook-off and people still talked about it. As soon as Max finished a story about Cal Patterson and an ornery rodeo bull, Margaret looked at her son. "Well, are you going to ask her?"

"Ask her what?"

"To dinner," his mother said patiently.

"Personally, I think you ought to take Jeannie out to see Bitter End," his father suggested. "Have you visited the old town yet?" he asked her.

"As a matter of fact, I haven't—" she smiled at Adam "—and I'd very much like to."

"Adam can arrange that, can't you, son?" Max said.

"Perhaps," Adam agreed. "Now, if you'll excuse me..."

For the second time that night, Jeannie's spirits fell with Adam's departure. Everything had seemed to come together nicely once his parents joined the conversation, but then Adam had walked away again. Jeannie felt deflated. She'd never been any good at this romance thing. Finding the right man seemed easy enough in love stories. Usually the heroine recognized him in the first few chapters—but not Jeannie. She flailed around, ignored a good man and then insulted him, and now she didn't know how to set things straight.

Lucas and Annie were getting ready to leave for their honeymoon when Jeannie saw Adam step out of the hall. She gauged her time carefully and followed him into the parking lot.

"Sheriff Jordan," she called out as he neared his patrol car.

He turned at the sound of her voice.

Fortunately no one else was there. "Do you have a minute?"

"I..." He glanced at his watch, but she didn't give him the opportunity to respond.

"Good. First, I want to say I'm sorry. Earlier, you said you were interested in dating me and I told you I didn't think that was a good idea. I'm afraid I might have spoken...hastily." She couldn't get much more direct than that. It was up to him now.

He seemed to consider her words, then he nodded, turned and walked away. Again. Well, that answered that.

By the time Jeannie got home, she felt even worse. It was for times like this that chocolate was created, as every woman knew. Not wanting to leave the house on a chocolate run, she scrounged around the kitchen. The best she could come up with was a half-full sack of stale chocolate chips. She tasted one, then threw them out.

Okay, no chocolate. Desperate to find comfort, she ran bathwater and emptied an entire bottle of a perfumed bath concoction under the faucet. Bubbles exploded and grew to a frothy towering mass.

Jeannie didn't care. She waited until the bubbles died down a little, then stripped off her clothes and sank into the hot water, sighing deeply.

Eyes closed, she soaked for probably an hour, replenishing the hot water from time to time. She soaked until her skin was wrinkled and prunelike. And then she had to stand under the shower to rinse off the soapy residue of the bubble bath.

With her head wrapped in a towel and her terry-cloth robe securely cinched around her waist, she wandered barefoot into the living room and turned on the television. Lucas and Annie were about to embark on their honeymoon, and the best *she* could do was reruns of "Law & Order."

The show had just started when the doorbell chimed. Peering through the peephole, she saw Adam Jordan standing there. Under any other circumstances she would have hurled open the door and greeted him enthusiastically. But not when she looked like this!

That was her problem, Jeannie decided. Her timing was all wrong. He was interested and she wasn't. Now she was interested and he wasn't. Hell, she didn't care *what* she looked like, she wanted to know why he was at her front door.

Doing her best to pretend her appearance was perfectly normal, she opened the door. "Hello, Sheriff," she said as nonchalantly as she could.

He squinted at her, but didn't speak.

"Yes?" she urged.

"Do you still want to go to Bitter End?"

She brightened. "Yes."

"Is tomorrow all right?"

She nodded. "That would be perfect. Two o'clock?"

"Two o'clock." He stepped away from her porch.

It was all Jeannie could do not to toss off her towel and dance a jig.

Sixteen

Any attempt at a honeymoon had seemed farcical to Lucas, but his mother, a hopeless romantic, had insisted the newlyweds at least take the weekend to themselves; the girls would stay with his parents. Lucas talked it over with Annie, and they'd decided to spend the weekend in San Antonio. Annie had never seen the Alamo or the famous River Walk, with its shops and restaurants. Their choice thrilled his mother, who thought San Antonio was the most romantic city in Texas.

It was dark by the time they checked into their downtown hotel. He'd reserved a room with two queen-size beds; although he'd agreed to father a child with Annie, he assumed she wouldn't be ready for intimacy this soon. Not when he'd stopped their wedding to tell her he'd never be able to love her. It astonished—and humbled—him that she'd been willing to proceed with the ceremony.

"Would you like to take a walk?" he asked. It was far too early to turn in for the night. He recognized his suggestion for what it was—a delaying tactic. He didn't know if she intended to sleep in the same bed with him, and hadn't yet worked up the courage to ask her. Although he suspected the answer would be no.

"A walk sounds perfect," Annie said, reaching for her purse.

Out on the paved walkway, they held hands and strolled leisurely past the nightclubs, hotels and restaurants. The full moon lit the darker areas and Tejano music—the music of south Texas—created a lively festive atmosphere. Flat-bottomed tour boats cruised lazily up and down the old canal.

Lucas hoped that while they walked he could apologize for stopping the wedding; he just wasn't sure how to explain what had happened. Annie might prefer he say nothing, considering how much the episode must have embarrassed her.

But Lucas felt he had to speak. "I'm sorry about…earlier—at the wedding," he said after they'd walked for ten minutes or so.

"It was the right thing for you to do."

That was all she said. He waited for her to continue, but she didn't. He wanted to say that he needed her, cared for her, but couldn't make vows that would be impossible to honor. Apparently she didn't want to hear it. He sighed, not realizing until that moment how nervous he'd been about her reaction. She *seemed* to accept what he'd done. But how did she really feel?

They walked in companionable silence for another thirty minutes, then turned and headed back in the direction of the hotel. The uncomfortable issue regarding their sleeping arrangements hadn't been settled. It was a difficult subject to broach. However, the sooner he understood what was expected of him, the better.

"The room has two beds," he said, hoping he sounded casual.

"I noticed."

"Do you…are you planning to sleep alone? Would you prefer we not share a bed yet? I realize eventually we'll be involved, uh, physically, but…" It occurred to him then that she might assume he intended to make love to her that very night. "Not that I was expecting we'd…I'm not planning on anything…happening—"

"Lucas—"

"Not unless you wanted to, of course," he rushed to add. He wished they'd decided all this before the wedding.

"How about if we start by sleeping in the same bed?" she suggested.

That was fine with Lucas. Other than Julia, he hadn't had much experience with women. He'd much rather move slowly. He yearned to do the right thing by her and, as he'd already discovered, that wasn't always easy.

By the time they neared the hotel, Lucas felt as though a huge weight had been lifted from him. He'd let her know he felt badly about putting her in a difficult position during the wedding, and they'd arrived at a decision about their sleeping arrangements. Not a bad beginning, he felt. At least they were able to communicate.

He noticed, however, that Annie's steps slowed the closer they got to the hotel, until eventually she came to a stop.

"Lucas, there's something I need to tell you before we go back to the room."

"Okay." He could see that whatever it was concerned her deeply. Annie held herself stiffly and her hands were clenched.

"You already know I was in a car accident."

"Yes." But he wasn't about to ask questions. Any details would have to be freely offered by Annie herself. She hadn't pried into his marriage to Julia, and he wasn't going to investigate her past, either.

"I..." She hesitated, pulling her hand free of his and wrapping her arms around her waist. "Before we go to bed, you should know that I—" She turned away from him.

"Annie?" He wanted to hold her, comfort her, reassure her, but wasn't sure he had that right. And he wasn't sure she *wanted* his comfort. Or his touch.

She turned back to face him, her shoulders squared, her face blank, revealing no emotion. "The accident left scars, Lucas. Ugly scars. A lot of them. They won't fade and they won't go away."

So that was it. He reached for her hand and kissed her fingertips. "I have scars, too, Annie, just as many, just as ugly, only you can't see mine."

She blinked, and he smiled and slid his arm around her waist, drawing her near. "It's those scars that brought you into my life," he reminded her.

He'd made a wise choice in marrying Annie Applegate. A very wise choice, indeed. His children—and his friends—had recognized the possibilities long before he saw them himself, but Lucas had certainly come to appreciate the idea.

An hour later, after a quick shower, Lucas pulled

back the sheets and climbed into bed. The lamp on the nightstand beside him was on, and while Annie had a bath, he flipped through a glossy restaurant-and-shopping guide he'd found in the room.

Slowly the bathroom door opened, and Annie walked out in a white floor-length Victorian-style gown that was as beautiful as it was simple.

Lucas felt his heart slam against his chest. Apparently he was more ready for the physical side of their marriage than he'd realized. He hated to stare but couldn't take his eyes off her.

"Do you normally sleep on the left side of the bed?" she asked.

Somehow, he managed to break the trance. "If you want, I can switch." His voice sounded higher than normal.

"No, this is fine." She busied herself folding back the sheets.

"Shall I turn off the light?" he asked once she'd slipped into bed. She lay rigidly on her back with her arms outside the covers.

"If you'd like."

Lucas reached for the switch and the room went dark.

"How long do you think we're going to continue being this polite with each other?" Annie asked, a smile in her voice.

"I don't know. I guess we should enjoy it while we can."

The silence stretched between them. This was their honeymoon; it didn't seem right just to say good-night, roll over and go to sleep, but he didn't know what Annie expected of him. He wished again that he could hold her, tell her how grateful he was that she'd married him.

He hesitated, not wanting her to misread his suggestion. Finally he said, "Annie?"

"Yes?"

"Would it be all right if I moved closer to you?"

Lucas heard the almost imperceptible sigh of relief. "I wish you would. I had no idea a queen-size bed had this much room in it."

Annie rolled onto her side, facing him, and he shifted toward her. She was warm and soft and smelled faintly of jasmine.

"That's much better," Annie said, placing her hand in his, lacing their fingers together.

It was a vast improvement as far as Lucas was concerned, too. He closed his eyes and as he drifted off to sleep, it occurred to him that this had been his wedding day and he hadn't kissed his bride even once.

Adam didn't think he'd ever been as upset with his parents as he was at the wedding reception. Their attempt to arrange a date between him and Jeannie had been the worst kind of embarrassment. He'd been forced to leave rather than say something he'd regret later. To his amazement, Jeannie had followed him into the parking lot.

She wanted to apologize, she said, wanted to get to know him. Fine, only he wasn't so sure he wanted to date her anymore. At least that was what he'd tried to tell himself. It'd taken him a good two hours to admit that he was being an idiot. This was exactly what he'd been praying for since last August. This was the woman he'd idolized from afar and humiliated himself over. Now Jeannie had practically come right out and told him she was interested. And he wasn't? *That* was a joke if he'd ever heard one.

Sunday afternoon he picked her up at her small rental house a few minutes before two. She answered his knock immediately, dressed in jeans that hugged her slender hips and a loose T-shirt.

"I'm ready," she said, grabbing her shoulder bag.

"Me, too." But his throat was dry and his heart alternately beat fast, then slowed.

"I'm so glad I'm finally getting to see Bitter End," she told him as they headed toward his truck. "The crazy thing is, I must've lived here three months before I even heard of it. I've read extensively about the hill country but didn't know about the town until one of the children happened to mention it."

Adam opened the truck door for her and helped her inside before hurrying around to the driver's side. "I lived here my entire life and didn't hear more than vague rumors about it until I came home, after I was discharged from the army," he said as he started the engine.

"How could you not?" She seemed stunned by his revelation. "The older kids talk about it all the time."

"It's only been the last few years that anyone knew much about the ghost town," Adam explained. They made their way out of Promise and down the long stretch of county highway.

"I've been wanting someone to go out there with me, but didn't know who to ask," Jeannie said.

Adam was infinitely pleased that he was the one who'd be taking her, although he wasn't sure how effective a tour guide he'd be. The ghost town wasn't a place that especially thrilled him. He'd been to Bitter End any number of times since his return, heard the story behind the curse, as well as local speculation that the birth of Wade and Amy's son had broken it. In his view, that was probably one myth replacing another, a new story replacing an old one. He had no problem with that—he loved a good story as much as anyone—but he did think the town was dangerous. It wasn't restored the way some ghost towns were in Arizona and Nevada. Those places had been commercialized and set up for the tourist trade. Not Bitter End. The old town was made up of stone buildings and wooden ones. Some of them were in deplorable condition. A few of the wooden structures seemed ready to collapse, and while the others were in somewhat better shape, they had their problems.

He also wondered if Jeannie would be disappointed when she saw the old town, and said as much.

Jeannie insisted that Bitter End couldn't possibly disappoint her. "My minor was in history," she explained. "I tried to research Bitter End when I learned about it. Naturally, reading Travis's new book helped."

Adam had read the book, too. Travis had written a suspense novel for adults, a story completely unlike any in his popular children's series. The best-seller had featured an abandoned town similar to Bitter End. It had become an insider joke around Promise. Everyone knew he'd written about their local ghost town but maintained the secret, as he did, in an effort to keep Bitter End from being commercialized.

"Did you learn anything new?" Adam asked. "In your own research, I mean."

"Probably nothing that Travis and Nell don't already know. What I found was mostly on the Internet and in a couple of fairly obscure books Annie managed to get for me."

"My ancestors weren't among the very first homesteaders," Adam told her, "but they came to Bitter End soon after it was established. They settled there and then moved on to Promise. My father's taken quite an interest in the old mercantile, and he's brought a number of artifacts to put on the shelves. Last year the junior-high kids toured Bitter End as part of their history class. My dad and some of the other merchants in town dressed in historical costume. Apparently it was a big hit with the kids."

"What a great idea." Jeannie's eyes lit up with interest, and it was all he could do to keep his truck on the road.

Adam gripped the wheel more tightly to steady himself. After all these months of wanting Jeannie and being rejected, this time together didn't seem real. He could think of only one thing: how much he wanted to kiss her.

When he reached the turnoff onto the dirt path that led to Bitter End, out of sight of the highway, Adam brought the truck to a stop.

"We're here?" Jeannie sat up straighter and glanced about.

"No, not even close. It's a couple of miles yet."

"Then why'd we stop?"

Adam clenched the steering wheel. "Go ahead and be mad...."

"Why would I be mad?"

"Because of what I'm about to do."

Jeannie laughed softly as if she thought this was all a joke.

Without saying anything else, Adam simply pulled her into his arms. She caught her breath as her eyes met his and she understood what he wanted. Had she protested, Adam would've turned away, but her wishes seemed to be completely in accord with his.

He bent forward, bringing his lips to hers. The kiss was slow and deep, and Adam felt it all the way to the soles of his feet.

Jeannie wrapped her arms around his neck and leaned into him. As her breasts nudged his chest, an urgency filled him, and he pressed his mouth more hungrily to hers, concentrating on the taste and feel of her.

At last they broke apart, and Adam dragged a deep breath into his oxygen-starved lungs. "Wow."

"That was my line," Jeannie whispered. Her eyes were still closed.

Adam's hands trembled as he reached for the ignition key. Jeannie was probably waiting for him to say something. Well, if he could've explained what had prompted this sudden need, he would have. As it was, he just kept his mouth shut.

Jeannie hung on to the door handle as Adam sped toward the ghost town. The truck bounced over the uneven road, jolting them this way and that, but he didn't slow the pace.

When he arrived at the place where they'd park and continue on foot, Adam noticed another vehicle.

"Someone else is here," Jeannie said, sounding

breathless. This was the first either had spoken since the kiss.

"That's Travis Grant's truck."

Adam turned off the engine and hurried around the cab to help Jeannie out. His eyes met hers, and when she rested her hands on his shoulders, she smiled. "Do you want me to apologize for kissing you?" he asked, needing to know.

"If you do, I'll be furious."

Adam relaxed. "It would've been a bold-faced lie."

Her smile created dimples on either side of her mouth. "I'm glad to hear that."

It demanded every bit of restraint he possessed not to kiss her again right then and there. Instead, he took her arm to lead her along the rocky path to the limestone outcropping from which they could see the town.

"Oh, my," she whispered.

He moved closer to her and was gratified when she took his hand and entwined her fingers with his.

"It's just the way I imagined it would be," she whispered, gazing at the view for a few moments before clambering eagerly down the steep trail.

Adam saw that Nell was with Travis; she waved when she noticed them.

"Howdy," Travis called from the church's graveyard. Nell and Travis walked out of the cemetery to meet them in the dusty main street.

"Adam was kind enough to offer me a tour of Bitter End," Jeannie said. "I've never been."

"We're here on another research mission," Nell

told them, "although we aren't really sure what we're looking for."

"This place feels so—" Jeannie seemed to be having trouble finding the word she wanted "—historic." She shrugged. "Well, you know what I mean."

Actually, Adam was grateful to run into Nell and Travis, who knew much more about Bitter End's history than he did. "I don't think I'll be able to answer all of Jeannie's questions."

"Give Jeannie the grand tour," Nell suggested, "and when you're finished, come and join Travis and me over by those benches. I brought along a thermos of coffee. If you don't mind sharing a mug you're welcome to have some. We can sit down and chat then."

"Thank you. We'd love to," Jeannie said excitedly, answering for both of them.

As they wandered down the street, Adam did the best he could, telling Jeannie all the facts and stories he remembered. Businesses lined each side of the main street, but the most prominent building in town was the church. The old wooden hotel had been boarded up with a large sign warning against exploration. As Adam expected, Jeannie had question after question, many of which he couldn't answer.

"This place is thrilling," Jeannie announced when they rejoined Travis and Nell. "I feel privileged to be here."

"Jeannie's an amateur historian," Adam told the other couple. He and Jeannie sat on the second bench outside the mercantile.

Jeannie dismissed his claim with a wave of her hand. "I took as many history courses as I could, and

I've always been fascinated with the Old West. It's one of the reasons I enjoyed reading Travis's book so much.''

"Why don't you start by telling us how you two solved the mystery of Bitter End?" Adam said.

Nell poured tall mugs of coffee, and since she'd only packed two, shared hers with Travis, while Adam and Jeannie shared the other one.

"You already know that Bitter End was settled after the Civil War, right? The pioneers decided to build the town here after a long and difficult journey."

"Tradition says that's how the town got its name," Nell inserted.

"For a time the community prospered," Travis said.

A glance down the main street was proof enough of that.

"But everything took a turn for the worse when a preacher's son was hanged by a band of drunken men because he tried to protect a saloon girl from their attack. His father came looking for him some time later, and when he learned what had happened, he cursed the town. No one took him seriously until a series of disasters led the community to believe they were doomed."

"From what we've learned since, the people left in a panic," Nell added. "They must have. We found tin cans still on the shelves, clothes, all kinds of things. Once the decision had been made, they just abandoned the town."

Jeannie appeared fascinated by the tale. "That's an incredible story." She took a deep breath. "Actually, I read something recently that might interest you," she told the small group, "if you're not already familiar with it. Have you ever heard of One-Eyed Jack?"

They all shook their heads.

"I came across him in an out-of-print book Annie recently found for me. It was privately published in the early 1920s, and there were only about a thousand copies. I don't even want to *tell* you what I paid for it." She gave a mock shudder. "Anyway, it seems that this Jack Benson was a Confederate soldier who lost an eye at Gettysburg. Apparently that was how he got his oh-so-clever nickname. According to the story, he turned to crime after the war and started running with a gang of misfits and undesirables, spreading havoc across Texas. It was said he'd kill a man for the pleasure of watching him die."

Adam grinned, enjoying Jeannie's storytelling ability.

"He and his band roamed the territory," she continued, "terrifying the residents. It's believed he was killed in a shoot-out with Texas Rangers after robbing a Union paymaster."

"So many young men turned to a life of crime after that war," Nell said sadly.

"I read a rather nice story having to do with the Civil War myself," Travis said. "In fact, it was a diary published in the 1890s. This diary had been written by a woman named Carrie Erath, who was employed as a seamstress for the Union army. Day after day she sewed those blue uniforms. She must've had a creative imagination, because she couldn't help wondering about the men who'd be wearing her uniforms and what would happen to them once they were in battle.'' He paused. ''Apparently she took to writing short letters of encouragement and stuffing them in the pockets. Later she received a letter from a young soldier in response to one of her notes. After the war they met and were married.''

''That's really sweet,'' Nell said with a sigh.

''True,'' said Travis. ''If I was writing historical romances, I might find a way to use it.''

''Whatever happened to Carrie Erath and her soldier husband?'' Jeannie asked.

''That's the sad part. Her husband was stationed out West and brought her and the children with him, and then he was killed in an Indian raid.''

''Oh, no...''

''You're researching a book?'' Adam reminded Travis of his earlier question.

''Well, not exactly,'' he answered. He and Nell glanced at each other as if gauging how much to say. ''Actually, we're more curious than anything else. Someone we know has shown some—shall we say, unusual—interest in Bitter End and we're trying to figure out why.''

''Another history buff?'' Jeannie asked.

''No.'' Travis appeared certain of that.

After a few minutes' silence, Jeannie said, ''There's another story I read recently about a woman known as Betty Bountiful.''

''The dance-hall girl?'' Travis asked. ''Yeah, I've heard of her.'' He chuckled. ''Betty's exotic fan dance brought them in droves.''

''She was talented in other areas, as well,'' Jeannie teased, and they all laughed.

Once again, Adam was impressed with Jeannie's

knowledge of the Old West. She and Travis exchanged another half-dozen stories until Nell looked at her watch. "It's nearly six!" she said, obviously shocked at the time. Adam was, too; the entire afternoon had disappeared.

Jeannie talked nonstop on the ride back into town. Her enthusiasm for Bitter End was contagious, and Adam soon found himself agreeing to escort her back. But then, he would've been willing to visit the garbage dump if she'd wanted to go there.

"Adam, I had the most wonderful day. Thank you so much for bringing me," she said as he opened the truck door for her.

"It was my pleasure." He meant that.

"And, Adam…" She paused and looked away.

"Yes?"

"If you wanted to kiss me again, I…wouldn't object."

That sounded fine to Adam, who needed no further encouragement.

Mary Patterson sat in her rocker, staring at the television, surprised to see that the screen had gone blank. Where was Phil? Oh, yes, she remembered now. He had to go out on an errand—somewhere—but he'd promised he'd be back soon.

What about her grandson? Johnny had been with her, too, hadn't he? Glen's two-year-old son was the joy of her life, even though he could be a handful.

"Johnny," she called, looking around. Glen and Ellie left him with her and Phil every week when they went bowling. Mary lived for Thursday nights—or was it Friday? Not that it mattered. What fun they had, she and Johnny. He loved the silly games they played and the songs they sang. Sometimes he remembered the words better than she did, and that made him feel smart.

So where could he be? Confused and suddenly concerned, she walked from room to room, calling his name, her voice growing more urgent.

He was gone. Her grandson was gone. A sick feeling attacked the pit of her stomach. He'd been with her only a few minutes ago. Johnny needed constant supervision, and here she'd forgotten all about him. The last thing she remembered was Phil kissing her on the cheek, telling her he was running to the store. She was to keep an eye on their grandson.

"Johnny," Mary cried, more loudly this time. Gripping the banister, she carefully made her way up the stairs and was winded by the time she reached the top step. She hardly ever climbed these old stairs anymore; it was just too hard on her knees.

"Johnny, don't scare Grandma like this," she pleaded. "Come out, come out." Her heart felt as if it might explode. "Please, please," she begged. Phil would be angry with her. He'd gotten angry with her recently because she'd forgotten something. She couldn't recall what it was now, only that Phil had been upset.

"Johnny...oh, Johnny..." She couldn't find her grandson anywhere. They'd all be angry with her. She loved Johnny so much, and if anything happened to him, it'd be her fault. Her fault. Everything seemed to be her fault lately.

Johnny would have answered by now if he could. If he was in the house. If he was all right. Mary knew something must have happened and she'd be blamed. Sobs welled up. Deep sobs, too deep to hold inside.

She had to hide, had to find someplace no one could find her because if they did, they'd never forgive her. Never.

Cal had one eye on the weekend newspaper and the other on his wife. The baby was supposed to arrive eight days from now, although Jane had told him only about ten percent of babies were born on their due dates. Which meant it could be even later. Cal shook his head. He'd never seen a woman look as pregnant as Jane. She'd insisted they attend the annual Willie Nelson picnic on the fourth of July— which they had. No Willie, but they'd had a great time nonetheless. She just refused to slow down, despite the advanced state of her pregnancy. With the days getting longer and warmer, he'd watched her struggle to find a comfortable position in which to sleep. Rolling over in the middle of the night seemed to require a massive effort.

The phone rang, and with a sigh he got up to answer it.

It was his father, and his voice was shaking with panic. "Cal, I can't find your mother."

"What do you mean you can't find her?"

"She's gone, I'm telling you."

"Gone?"

"I can't find her. I was out working in the garage and I came inside to check on her. She's nowhere to be found! I've searched this house high and low. No one saw her leave. Dear sweet heaven, where could she be now?'' His voice cracked with strain and worry.

''I'll be right there.'' Cal replaced the receiver and discovered Jane was staring at him.

''What's happened?'' she asked urgently.

''Mom's disappeared. I don't know what the hell's going on here, but I've never heard my father sound so scared.''

Cal was already halfway to the door when Jane announced that she planned to come along. He didn't have time to argue with her. It was probably just as well; this late in the pregnancy, he didn't feel good about leaving her alone.

''Are you going to tell me what's going on?'' he demanded once they reached the highway. He made an effort to keep his voice calm. He wasn't angry with Jane or even his father. He just wished to hell someone would have the decency to tell him what was wrong with his mother.

''Your father promised me he would.''

''It's Alzheimer's, isn't it?'' He had to ask, although he'd begun to realize it must be.

Jane nodded.

''How long have you known?''

She hesitated. ''I've suspected it for a few months now, but I didn't dare say anything without the tests. Not long ago your father confirmed my suspicions, but he begged me to let him be the one to tell you and Glen.''

Cal took her hand, knowing how difficult this must have been for her.

''Please don't be angry with me,'' she said softly.

"I'm not. Dad was only trying to protect Mom. I'd do the same."

"He's doing the best he can," Jane said, "but I think it's gotten much worse lately."

"Poor Dad."

Glen and Ellie were already at their parents' home by the time Cal and Jane arrived. Cal found his father sitting at the kitchen table, his face in his hands.

"I've been through every room in the house," Glen told him. Cal noticed how pale his brother was and guesed that Phil had told him the truth about their mother's condition.

"Then I suggest we call Sheriff Jordan," Cal said.

"No," Phil cried, his face pale and drawn. "I don't want anyone else to know."

"Glen!" Ellie shouted from the top of the stairs. "I found her!"

Cal, Glen and their father rushed up the stairs to find Ellie standing with her arm around Mary's waist. Cal saw how lost and confused his mother looked. Seeing her like this nearly tore his heart out.

"Where was she?" Phil demanded.

"Crouched inside the closet."

Phil stared at her. "You were in the closet?"

"Are…are you mad at me?" his mother whispered, her eyes red and swollen with tears.

"Why would I be mad?"

"I lost…Cal. I can't find him anywhere."

"Mom, I'm right here."

His mother frowned. "No…it was someone else I lost. Someone I love." She started to weep again, huge sobs that racked her whole body. His father moved protectively to her side and with both arms around her, helped her down the stairs.

The small group followed and watched as Phil placed her in the rocking chair, then sagged onto the sofa, looking worn and broken.

"I can't do it anymore," he whispered. "I just can't do it alone anymore."

Seventeen

Miles had phoned the previous evening and invited Gordon for lunch, which was a pleasant surprise. The reservation was for noon at Scaramouche, a restaurant they'd always enjoyed. By the time Gordon arrived, his son was already seated. He looked up from the menu when Gordon joined him.

"This is very nice," Gordon said. Then he frowned. Something was obviously bothering Miles. During their last conversation his son had seemed overworked and suffering from stress; he'd asked about the cruise, then left as soon as Karen phoned. Gordon couldn't help wondering if there was a problem with his son's marriage.

"How's Karen?" Gordon asked, attempting a less-than-subtle approach.

Miles glanced up from the menu. "Good."

"The kids?"

"Fine."

The waiter approached and they both ordered the baked salmon with pecan crust and a glass each of a Niagara chardonnay.

"Actually I asked you to lunch this afternoon to talk about *you*," Miles said, pausing when the waiter returned with the wine. "I never thought I'd be having this kind of conversation with my own father, but apparently it's necessary."

Gordon squared his shoulders, gazing at Miles over the rim of his glass. "Is something wrong?"

"You tell me."

"What in heaven's name leads you to assume I have a problem?" He was feeling better about life than he had in years.

Miles took a moment to smooth his linen napkin across his lap. "Then let me be frank," his son said. "Are you involved with a woman?"

How Miles knew about Nessa, Gordon could only guess. "As a matter of fact, I am." He fully intended to tell Miles about Nessa, and would have the night he'd stopped by the house if his son hadn't left so suddenly.

"That woman in Texas?" His mouth was pinched and his tone disapproving.

Gordon tensed, disliking his son's tone. He didn't understand how Miles could object to Nessa, since he'd never even met her. "She has a name, son."

"I already know her name."

"You do?"

"I know more than you think I do, Father," Miles continued stiffly. "I happened to see the telephone bill on your desk the other night. You two seem to have quite a thing going."

Gordon wasn't accustomed to being chastised by his son, and he didn't appreciate Miles's attitude.

"Are you planning an affair with a married woman?"

Gordon had never heard anything more outrageous in his life. "Have you gone mad?"

"What else am I to believe?"

Gordon nearly laughed out loud when he realized the misunderstanding. "You think I'm involved with Dovie Hennessey, don't you? It might interest you to know it isn't Dovie I've been phoning every night. My lady friend's name is Nessa Boyd, and she's Dovie's sister-in-law."

Miles frowned at Gordon as if he didn't believe him. "Why didn't you mention her before now?"

"Nessa and I decided not to say anything," Gordon explained, "not at first, anyway. It's a bit embarrassing to feel this strongly about someone you've spent such a short time with, and...well, Dovie doesn't know." Gordon paused when it became apparent Miles wasn't willing to accept his explanations. "I thought you *wanted* me to see women," Gordon said. "Wasn't that the point of sending me on a cruise?"

"Yes, but I'd prefer it if you'd chosen a widow."

"Nessa is a widow."

"So you say, but ask yourself this, Dad. What kind of woman asks you not to mention you're having a relationship? There's got to be a reason. She doesn't want her sister-in-law to know you're—"

"Talking. That's all we've done," Gordon said. Miles's assumptions were beginning to anger him.

"Have you had her checked out?" Miles asked.

"I'm not buying a used car!" Gordon's anger turned to fury.

"In this day and age—" Miles started, but Gordon cut him off.

"That might be how you handle your personal affairs, but I refuse to act in such an underhanded way.''

''Don't be stupid, Dad. She has to know you're a wealthy man.''

''She knows nothing of the sort.''

A muscle twitched in Miles's jaw. ''You're going to do it, aren't you?''

Gordon glared at his son. ''Do *what?*''

''Marry her. Promise me you won't do anything that stupid without talking to me first.''

Their meals arrived, but unfortunately Gordon's appetite was gone. He placed his napkin on the table and sat back in his chair.

''Now what?'' Miles said, then noticed the discarded napkin. He motioned at Gordon with his fork. ''For heaven's sake, eat your lunch.''

''It's been a long time since anyone's treated me like an ill-behaved child, and I refuse to put up with it now. You're not my mother and you're certainly not my guardian.''

''No, I'm your son, and I'm doing everything I can to stop you from making an ass of yourself.''

''Then I suggest you worry more about being one yourself.'' Before their argument could escalate further, Gordon stood and walked out of the restaurant.

This was the day Nessa had dreaded for weeks. She'd put off telling Dovie about Gordon much longer than she should have. Really, it was ridiculous to have worried about it at all. She waited until Saturday afternoon, when she knew Dovie would be home by herself.

Ever since Dovie and Frank had returned from their

European vacation, Nessa had avoided her sister-in-law. That on its own was silly. How much easier everything would have been if she'd told Dovie the first time they'd talked. Now she had only herself to blame for these feelings of guilt.

Nessa had purposely timed her visit so Frank would be away from the house. He'd gotten more and more involved with organizing activities at the seniors' center and spent much of his free time with his friends.

Dovie answered the doorbell almost instantly. "Nessa, come on in! I've hardly seen you in weeks." She held the screen door open wide, then led her into the kitchen. "Would you like coffee or tea?"

"Do you have anything stronger?"

"Iced tea?"

Nessa laughed. "I was thinking more along the lines of a rum and Coke." Under normal circumstances she wasn't much of a drinker, but she needed it just then to bolster her courage.

Dovie hesitated. "Any reason you're looking to sample the hard stuff in the middle of the afternoon?"

"As a matter of fact, there is. Oh, Dovie, I should have done this long ago."

Her sister-in-law dragged the step stool to the refrigerator, climbed up and reached into the cupboard above, bringing down an unopened bottle of rum. It was the dark variety; Nessa suspected Dovie had purchased it on the cruise when she'd met Gordon. That was three years ago. Obviously hard liquor didn't see much use in this household.

Dovie poured a liberal dose of the rum into two glasses, then opened a bottle of cola and added that.

"Okay," she said, holding one glass and handing the other to Nessa. "I'm ready. Tell me."

The words tumbled out of Nessa's mouth. "I'm in love with Gordon Pawling."

"Who?" Dovie asked with a frown.

"Gordon Pawling. You met him on the cruise ship a few years back. He stopped here to see you while you and Frank were in Europe and well...Gordon and I've been talking by phone ever since."

"I see." Dovie sat down on the stool and gave her an odd look.

Oh, my, this was worse than Nessa had feared. "I didn't mean to fall in love with him," she blurted. "It just happened. And I do love him, Dovie, really and truly."

"Gordon Pawling," Dovie repeated as if she had trouble taking it in.

"He's asked me to meet him in Kansas City next week."

"Why Kansas City?" Dovie asked. She still hadn't tasted her drink, but Nessa had downed nearly half of hers.

"It's neutral ground for us both. He's away from his home and family and friends, and I'm away from mine. We need to see each other again—to test how we really feel."

"You love him?"

Nessa nodded. "If he asked me to marry him, and Dovie, I pray that he does, I'll leap at the offer."

"Good for you." Dovie hugged her.

"You don't mind?"

"Good grief, why should I? I'd forgotten Gordon's

name, but I do remember him. He's a real sweetheart.''

"I think so, too," Nessa whispered. "But when you first realized who I meant, you got the oddest expression on your face."

Dovie blushed. "I'm afraid I was beginning to believe Sylvia."

"Sylvia?" Nessa couldn't imagine what her daughter had said to Dovie.

"She thinks you're having an affair and frankly, I was beginning to have my suspicions, too."

Nessa smiled. "Well, now you know. But we've only met once—the day he came to the shop—and then it was just three or four hours. That's why we're meeting in Kansas City. We need to know if we'll feel the same way when we see each other again."

"All I want is for you to be happy," Dovie told her.

Nessa hugged her sister-in-law. Happiness was what she wanted, too, but it seemed to be getting more and more complicated.

The last communication from Val Langley had come at the beginning of July. It was a perfumed note informing Travis of her arrival date—today. Nell had been scrubbing and cleaning the house all week. No easy task with a pair of two-year-olds underfoot, plus fourteen-year-old Jeremy and twelve-year-old Emma. While she might not be able to compete with Val in looks and sophistication, Nell was an excellent housekeeper. If ever there was a time she wanted her home-making skills to shine, it was now.

Homemade bread and cinnamon rolls lined the

kitchen countertop. A load of cotton-blend sheets hung from the clothesline. The windows sparkled, the floors shone and a bouquet of fresh flowers decorated the kitchen table.

"I wish you'd relax," Travis muttered as he came into the kitchen. He'd spent his morning writing, with frequent stops to refill his coffee mug. "You don't need to do anything to impress Val."

"I'm not doing this for Val," she protested.

Travis eyed her quizzically, as though he doubted the truth of that.

"I'm doing this for me," Nell said. "Val's going to arrive looking like she walked off the pages of *Vogue,* and I'm going to look—and feel—like a country bumpkin."

"I'll have you know I'm madly in love with the woman you're calling a bumpkin."

"Good, and don't you forget it."

The front doorbell chimed, and Nell felt panic rise up in her. They weren't expecting any dude-ranch visitors at the moment, and all their friends and neighbors knew to come to the back door. It had to be Travis's ex-wife.

"Would you stop?" Travis groaned. "Val has nothing on you."

He said it with such vehemence, she was inclined to believe that *he* believed it, anyway. The twins started to fuss, and grabbing her youngest daughter and son, Nell held their hands, pulling them with her as she followed Travis to the door.

As she suspected, the visitor was Valerie Langley. The woman was everything Nell had feared: petite, slender and sophisticated. Picture-perfect in what was obviously a designer suit, which probably cost more than Nell's entire clothing budget for the century. This woman was every wife's basic nightmare.

"Travis!" Val cried, and threw her arms around his neck. You'd think she'd waited years for precisely this moment, Nell thought sardonically. "How good it is to see you again."

She noticed that Travis extracted himself from the hug with a haste that bordered on rudeness.

Val smiled warmly at Nell and the children. "This must be Nell and those precious twins."

"Hello," Nell said, struggling to hold on to Dianna who wanted only to escape. Devon stared solemnly at the other woman, as if she were an angel who'd graced the earth with her presence.

"Would you like something cool to drink?" Nell asked once she'd collected her wits.

"That would be delightful. You wouldn't *believe* how long it took me to get the rental car and find my way here. You guys don't exactly live close to anything civilized, do you?" She laughed lightly. "You'll see to my bags, won't you, Travis?" she said, trailing Nell into the kitchen.

"Something wrong with your arms?" Travis asked as he went to the kitchen, too.

"Travis," Nell murmured, secretly glad but preferring that her husband display at least minimal politeness.

"Fine. I'll take your things to the bunkhouse," he told his ex-wife.

"Bunkhouse?" Val repeated, as if the notion came as a shock. "But I thought this was a dude ranch."

"It is," Travis assured her. "All guests sleep in

the bunkhouse, unless they're driving the herd, in which case they're required to sleep under the stars.''

Val pinched her lips together. ''I'm sure the bunkhouse will be just fine.''

How she really felt about accepting accommodation in the bunkhouse they'd probably never know, Nell mused, smiling to herself.

''I'm sure it will,'' Travis told her, his voice cool. ''The price includes two meals a day.''

''I'm grateful you were willing to put me up,'' Val assured them both. ''You'd think a town this size would have a few more options than a bed-and-breakfast and a dude ranch out in the boonies.''

''That's what makes it a dude ranch,'' Travis said, not bothering to hide his sarcasm.

''I'll get you some iced tea,'' Nell told the other woman, and headed for the refrigerator.

''My,'' Val said, glancing about, ''you're certainly the...domesticated type.''

''Well, I do bake all our own bread,'' Nell said. What had made her feel proud only a short while ago left her feeling gauche and old-fashioned now.

''How...quaint.''

''Some women are willing to invest that kind of time and love in their families,'' Travis said.

''Ouch.'' Val spoke out of the side of her mouth. ''I think that little barb was intended for me.''

Nell grinned, pouring Val a glass of tea. She had every intention of clearing the air before Jeremy and Emma returned from an outing with their grandmother. She didn't want her two oldest children exposed to the hostile undercurrents that were bound to continue if Travis and Val went on exchanging insults. "I'm hoping we can be friends, Val."

"That would be nice," Val agreed, but she sounded as though she considered it highly unlikely.

"I'll show you to the bunkhouse," Travis said. "It has a communal bath and a two-seater outhouse."

"Travis," Nell protested, then turned to Val and added, "We don't have any other guests currently, so you won't be sharing the showers. There's no need to use the outhouse, either. You can use the bathroom here."

Val looked vastly relieved as she drank her tea. Putting down her glass, she announced, "I believe I'll go freshen up. What time would you like me for dinner?"

"We eat a whole lot earlier than eight," Travis informed her.

"Six, if that's convenient," Nell said, glowering at her husband.

"I'll be here with bells on," Val promised.

"We don't dress for dinner," Travis said. He reached for a bread stick, and munched on it loudly. "I suggest you leave the bells in your suitcase."

Nell waited until Valerie and Travis had left the house before quickly making the twins' lunch. After that, she sat in the rocking chair with them for a few minutes before putting them to bed for their naps. Travis returned just as she finished rocking them to sleep. He carried Dianna and she took Devon. They placed the sleeping children in their beds and quietly tiptoed out of the room.

"Travis, what's gotten into you?" Nell asked. "You were so rude to her."

"I didn't like her attitude toward you."

"I appreciate your concern, but I can take care of myself." Her protective feeling toward Travis's first wife came as a surprise. She hadn't expected to like Valerie, but she sensed a vulnerability beneath the polished exterior. "Don't be so hard on her."

Travis sighed. "I guess she's not so bad."

"You know, I think she has a strong need to impress others, which usually stems from insecurity."

Travis nodded. "Seeing her now makes me wonder how I could ever have loved her. I find it hard to believe we were once married."

At the moment Nell was wondering what her husband had ever seen in *her,* compared to the beautiful Valerie.

"She asked if you and I would set aside some time this evening to chat with her," Travis said.

"About what?" Nell couldn't help being curious.

"I'm not really sure. She asked about Grady and Savannah. I can't imagine why she'd come all this way to meet them. Surely it couldn't have anything to do with Richard, not this long after the trial."

"I thought she wanted to know about Bitter End."

"She did, but now I wonder if that was only an excuse to come to Promise. She hasn't mentioned it yet."

Nell shrugged. "Then why do you think she's here?"

"Well, she's after something," Travis murmured thoughtfully. "And it sure as hell isn't me. I know her better than that," he said in response to Nell's anguished look.

"If she's interested in anything about me, it's the

success I've had," he told his wife. "The money I've made. Not me."

"Good thing, because she'd have one hell of a fight on her hands."

Travis's laughter filled the kitchen, and he wrapped his arms around Nell's waist and kissed her in a way that made her grateful she was a married woman. She felt the kiss go through her like warm honey.

"Travis," she whispered, her eyes closed, "what was that for?"

"I love you, Nell, and I want to be very sure you know it."

"I do." She supposed her feelings were the same as any second wife's would be after meeting wife number one. Perhaps a bit more complicated, seeing that Val was light-years ahead of her in the beauty department. It helped that Travis cherished her enough to want to reassure her.

"I don't know why Val's here," Travis whispered, holding Nell close. "I just don't know."

Annie and Lucas had been married for two weeks. They remained polite, almost comically so, especially in the bedroom. Every night he held her close, and every night she grew more accustomed to sleeping in his arms. He kissed her when he left for work in the morning and again before they went to sleep at night. Light kisses, more a quick touch of their lips than a real display of affection.

Annie was happy with this state of affairs. It was early yet, she reasoned, and they had a lot to learn about each other.

The girls accepted her without qualms and were

excited to have a new mother. Annie lavished them with love and attention, and they thrived right along with Annie, who felt a new confidence, a new serenity—the result, she knew, of being needed and loved.

What with settling in, Annie had little time to spend with Jane, whose baby was due any day. Jane's parents had decided to come after the birth, so Annie had volunteered to help the midwife when her friend went into labor. Lucas had promised to tag along in case Cal needed someone there for him.

The call came early Monday morning soon after Annie had opened the bookstore. "It's time," Cal said calmly.

"I'm on my way." Annie told him, and immediately phoned Lucas. Her second call was to her in-laws to ask if they could watch the girls.

When he pulled up in front of the bookstore, Lucas seemed a lot more excited than Cal had sounded on the phone.

"How's Cal doing?" he asked with a wide grin as she slipped into the seat next to him.

"Fine," she said, and shook her head. How typical of a man to inquire about the father, instead of the mother!

The drive from town to the Patterson ranch took forty minutes—and that was with Lucas risking a speeding ticket. Cal threw open the door to the back porch the minute they arrived.

"Smile, Cal," Annie told him after giving him an affectionate hug. "A beautiful baby is about to be born."

"It's going to be a difficult birth," Cal muttered, pale with concern. "I'm sure of it. And Jane refuses to go to the hospital in Brewster. The woman is too damn stubborn for her own good.''

''You don't know what it's going to be like,'' Annie said, wanting to reassure him. ''Relax, will you?''

''But we *do* know,'' Grady Weston countered. He and Caroline, along with Glen and Ellie Patterson, had both come to lend their support. ''The baby's going to take after Cal, and everyone knows what a big head Cal has.''

Glen hooted with laughter.

''But Jane's overdue,'' Cal said in serious tones. ''The baby's going to be big. Huge. Has anyone noticed her belly recently? She should be in the hospital.''

Annie had heard all this before. How could anyone say a baby was overdue? It seemed to her that Jane's son or daughter would arrive at exactly the right time, despite what others predicted.

''Who's with Jane?'' Annie asked. She assumed Cal would want to be with his wife.

''Leah Collins, the midwife,'' Cal told her, then added sheepishly, ''Jane kicked me out. She said if all I was going to do was argue with her, she wanted me out of the room.''

''Go to Jane,'' Lucas told Annie. ''As soon as Cal's willing to admit his wife knows more about birthing babies than he does, I'll send him in.''

Annie was halfway to the bedroom when she stopped. ''Did anyone think to call Jane's parents?'' The Dickinsons would be anxious to hear the news. Jane was, after all, their only daughter.

''Yes, I'd better let them know,'' Cal said, and

headed for the phone. He cast Annie a look of gratitude.

Despite Cal's dire predictions of a long and difficult labor, Paul Calvin Patterson arrived without a hitch at two minutes to ten that evening. Cal was with Jane and Leah, and Annie had dozed off against Lucas's shoulder when she awoke to the sound of an infant's wail and a jubilant shout of "Hot damn!"

Soon afterward, Cal burst through the bedroom door and let out a cry of sheer undiluted joy. "I got me a son!"

A round of hugs and tears followed, and soon the living room started to empty. Before she left, Annie went in to see her friend and hold the baby. Gazing down at the newborn, Annie experienced an ache of longing that reached deep inside her. Tears welled in her eyes.

"He looks just like Cal," she whispered, and brushed a finger over the fine soft hair.

"It's the big head," Lucas whispered from behind her, causing Annie to smile.

Annie rested on Lucas's shoulder again during the ride home. Rather than wake the girls, who were spending the night with Lucas's parents, they went back to the house alone.

Lucas sorted through the mail while Annie kicked off her shoes and poured them each a glass of wine. This was the first night they'd been without the girls since their honeymoon. After the long exciting day, they were both exhausted.

"I'm thrilled for Cal and Jane," Lucas said as they prepared for bed.

"This is the first time I've been at a birth," Annie

told him. "I've never experienced anything even close to this kind of feeling before." Annie had fallen asleep early in the evening and missed the actual birth—but she didn't need to be there every minute to experience the wonder and exhilaration.

She finished brushing her teeth, but remained standing in front of the bathroom sink, savoring the good feelings that had come with the birth of Jane and Cal's son.

"Annie, are you ready for bed?" Lucas joined her in the bathroom and stood behind her.

She turned to face him. Up to this point they'd exchanged chaste careful kisses. Now Annie's eyes locked with his as she slipped her arms up his chest and linked them around his neck.

Lucas inhaled sharply. "Annie—"

"Yes...I'm ready for bed," she murmured, and brought her mouth to his.

The raw hunger that exploded between them took her breath away.

They stood in the tiny bathroom with their arms wrapped around each other, sharing deep, uncontrolled kisses.

"Annie...Annie...Annie." Between each kiss Lucas whispered her name. "Oh, Annie." One hand bunched her cotton nightgown, while the other tenderly cradled the back of her head. One hand rough and urgent, the other gentle and loving.

They were on the bed before Annie even realized they'd left the bathroom, the light spilling like distant sunshine into the dark room. Lucas moved away from her and she watched as he tore off his shirt. Then he was kissing her again with an abandon that told her he'd been wanting her far longer than she'd known. Kissing her and impatiently unbuttoning her night-gown.

"Annie, I—"

"Yes, make love to me," she whispered.

After long minutes of kissing and caressing, of loving with hands and mouths, her excitement grew more and more intense. "Now, Lucas," she urged. He was about to enter her when he stopped cold, his face in torment.

"What is it?" she asked frantically.

"Your accident. Will I hurt you?"

Annie didn't know. "I suspect the pain will be worse if you stop now."

A smile relaxed his features, and he leaned forward and slowly, lovingly, joined their bodies. Annie did whimper, but the sound coming from deep in her throat had nothing to do with pain and everything to do with pleasure. It'd been so long for her. Years. That long for Lucas, too.

"Lucas, oh Lucas." All at once she understood how worthwhile the wait had been.

Annie slept in Lucas's arms all night, as content as she could ever remember being. The alarm rang at the usual time, but Lucas stretched out his hand and blindly turned it off. Grateful, Annie kissed the underside of his jaw, more than happy to return to the blissful oblivion of sleep.

Her reprieve was short-lived, however. Lucas kissed her eyes, then her nose, her cheek and finally her lips. Once, and then a second time. Their kisses lengthened and became more passionate.

"I've got three surgeries scheduled this morning," Lucas murmured between kisses.

Annie rubbed her hands down his bare back. "There's a shipment of books arriving before ten."

More kisses, more whispers.

"I'm going to be late."

"Me, too."

All the while they listed their protests, they were straining for one another. Soon their voices dipped to sighs and soft pants, followed by eager cries and more kisses, then softer less urgent ones.

Eighteen

The first thing Val did once she'd unpacked her suit-case was reach for a pad of paper and write a long newsy letter to Richard Weston. He wouldn't receive it until next week, since mail going into the prison was inspected first.

Val was more than a little attracted to him. They'd met when she'd been assigned as his defense attorney, a task she'd dreaded until she'd actually gotten to know Richard. He'd been charged with a number of crimes—smuggling illegal aliens, fraud and extortion among them. Richard was no innocent, but in Val's opinion he wasn't as bad as those charges suggested. The worst of his crimes—again, in her opinion—was that he'd been gullible. He claimed that he'd believed the men he'd worked with. They'd purported to help-ing the illegal aliens find jobs and decent housing. Richard said he'd been unaware of what was really going on. Val wasn't naive; she didn't buy his whole story. Nevertheless, she liked him. Liked him far more than she should—but then, she'd always en-joyed a man with a dangerous edge. Bad boys like Richard Weston had always tempted her. Interesting that the men she'd married weren't that type at all.

Richard had written her after he was sentenced. In

the beginning she'd ignored his letters, but his persistence had captured her attention. Almost against her will, and after maybe the fifth letter, she'd started answering him. It had begun as a game, a flirtation of sorts—and then she'd taken the next step. She'd set up a visit on the pretense of legal business. For all his faults, one quality Richard certainly didn't lack was charm. The things he said and wrote to her were enough to make her knees grow weak. She knew better, yet she still couldn't help herself.

Her marriage, which had been on the rocks for some time, was ending, and it felt good to be flattered, desired. He had a manner she found compelling, almost irresistible. Val didn't believe all of Richard's compliments, but she didn't care if he was sincere or not; she needed to hear them.

Naturally his undying devotion came with a price tag. Richard needed something from her, too. Her legal expertise.

The simple truth was that she'd fallen for Richard. During the months she'd been working on his appeal, she'd come to look forward to their brief visits.

In fact, her motives for traveling to Promise were all linked to helping Richard. He needed his family, and Val was here to make sure that his brother and sister would stand by him. She wanted to get a read on his family, figure out how much they'd be willing to help—with financial, as well as moral, support— when he came before the parole board. Richard was afraid the citizens of Promise might be tempted to take revenge on him. He seemed obsessed with Bitter End, too, although she couldn't quite understand why. He said he couldn't tolerate the idea of the ghost town being turned into a tourist trap, its historic value ruined. From his frequent descriptions of the place, Val had formed a mental picture of it.

Richard had spent a lot of time in Bitter End when he'd hidden out there, and he yearned to protect its integrity. It was this side of him, the one that others rarely saw, that Val had learned to treasure.

A knock on the door caught her unawares. She shoved the writing tablet beneath her pillow. "Come in," she called.

Travis opened the door and stuck his head inside. "Dinner will be on the table in fifteen minutes."

"Already?" Val glanced at her watch.

"I told you earlier that we eat at six."

Unable to resist, she thrust out her tongue in a childish display of temper. Travis had certainly proved to be a disappointment. He'd barely been cordial. From the moment she'd told him she'd be visiting Promise, he'd made it clear he'd rather she stayed in New York. His aversion to her company only confirmed what she'd always believed. He'd never gotten over their divorce, and although remarried, Val suspected he'd never stopped loving her. She was sorry he'd been hurt, but better opportunities had awaited her. Now those opportunities had faded and she was on her own again. Through it all, Val had been confident that Travis would always love her. She still thought so, even though he obviously didn't plan to act on his feelings. Maybe that was to punish her or—giving him some credit—to avoid hurting the second Mrs. Grant.

"I'll be right in," she said, refusing to let his lack of welcome dissuade her.

"Fine." He turned to leave.

"Travis." She leaped up and hurried after him. "I have some questions I was hoping you could answer."

"About what?"

He didn't slow his pace, and Val was forced to trot to keep up. This wouldn't be a problem for his new wife, she told herself. The little woman wasn't so little. Val had nearly laughed out loud at her first glimpse of his precious Nell. Six feet if she was an inch, with braids only Annie Oakley would envy.

"You don't want me here, do you?" she said, pouting ever so slightly.

"No." His answer was direct and brutal.

"Why not?"

He stopped walking and grabbed her by the arm. "You're after something."

"Don't be ridiculous." Val jerked her arm out of his grasp. She'd always resented the way he could see through her. "I haven't talked to you in ages—except when I phoned you about this trip."

His lips curled as if her words repulsed him. "We have nothing to talk about. And I still don't know why you came here."

"I'm curious about Promise."

"Why?"

She frowned. She didn't like having her motives questioned.

"What's come over you?" Val asked. "You never used to be like this."

"I don't want you here."

"So you've said." She crossed her arms and inhaled deeply, refusing to show him how much his words had wounded her. "Are you afraid, Travis?"

"Afraid of what?"

"Seeing me again, being near me. You used to love me, remember?"

"You've got that part right," he said without emotion. "I *used* to love you. Past tense. I don't any longer. I have a wife who knows the meaning of the word love. A wife who puts her family first, not her own self-centered desires."

"Are you telling me I don't know what love is?" Despite the years they'd been married, the man didn't have a clue about her. This entire trip was on behalf of someone else, but she couldn't very well tell Travis that. Despite the years they'd been married, he didn't know her, didn't appreciate her, not like Richard did.

"The only person you think about is yourself."

She lifted her chin at his insults, her pride rescuing her. "You've changed. I barely know you anymore."

"I *have* changed, thank God," he agreed. "Thanks to Nell and the people in Promise."

"I'd like to meet some of those people."

"Such as?"

She shrugged, unwilling to show her hand. "The people you mentioned when you first came out here."

"Such as?" he asked again.

"The Westons," she said casually. "Dolly, too."

"Dovie," he corrected, studying her, his eyes hard.

"Dovie," she repeated. "That's such an old-fashioned name." From what she'd seen of the hill country, the entire area could define the word "quaint." Sheets drying on a clothesline, homemade bread, flowers in a jar. And eating dinner at six! They probably went to sleep at eight—and got up at five. Boring, boring, boring. Val suspected there wasn't a single pizza franchise that would deliver to this dude ranch. If Nell was typical of Texas women, the entire state was populated with Amazons. Too bad they weren't around when poor old Davy Crockett was defending the Alamo.

"Does your sudden interest in Promise have anything to do with Richard Weston?" Travis demanded. "Tell me you aren't crazy enough to get mixed up with the likes of him."

"What do you mean?" she asked, playing dumb.

"You know darn good and well what I mean. Be warned—Richard is a user, and if he's had anything to do with your visit, you'd be wise to leave now."

"Don't be ridiculous!"

"As I recall, you were pretty intrigued with him three years ago."

"He's an interesting person."

Travis's frown darkened. "This *is* about Richard, isn't it?"

"Indirectly," she admitted, knowing he wouldn't believe her otherwise. Val couldn't afford to have Travis guess the truth—not yet, anyway. He'd become such great pals with all the people in Promise, people who hated Richard. So he wouldn't be pleased to hear that she was preparing an appeal. "He was full of talk about Bitter End. He went on and on about that ghost town. Remember how fascinating he made it all sound? You were intrigued enough to come here yourself." The ghost town was a good distraction. Val knew Travis couldn't argue, seeing that Richard's stories had prompted his own first visit to the Texas hill country.

"So?"

"So, as you know, my marriage fell apart and, well, I don't know.... I guess in my own way, I'm looking for the kind of happiness you found. This seemed like a place to start."

She could tell he thought she was lying. But the back door opened then, and Nell stepped outside. She paused when she saw Val and Travis.

"Hello, Nell." Val waved, making sure her smile was wide and generous. "I understand dinner's about ready."

"It's on the table now."

"Is there something I can do to help?" she asked, hurrying toward the other woman. She was willing to do anything that would take her away from this uncomfortable conversation with Travis.

As Jeannie went to the grocery to do her weekly shopping the following Saturday, everyone in town was talking about Cal and Dr. Jane's baby boy. She'd already heard the news from three different people, and while she'd enjoyed her conversations with the school secretary, Martie Caldwell, as well as Dovie and Caroline, there was one person she was waiting to hear from. But Adam hadn't called.

The sheriff certainly kept her on her toes wondering and worrying. She hesitated to call him herself, a rather old-fashioned idea in this day and age, but after the way he'd spurned her, then kissed her and now ignored her, she needed reassurance. With school out, she was doing volunteer work at the county nursing home, helping the residents record their family histories. She was especially struck by their stories of courting and marriage—and heartened by the fact that some of these women *had* taken romantic matters into their own hands.

The message light on her answering machine was flashing when she returned. She set her grocery bags and mail on the kitchen counter and pushed the button. At the sound of Adam's voice, she experienced a rush of excitement and relief.

"Hello, Jeannie, it's Adam Jordan," he said rather formally. "I'm calling about Sunday afternoon—tomorrow—and was wondering if you'd be interested in having dinner with me—say six-thirty. I'm on duty until six. If you'd give me a call here at the office, I'd appreciate it."

For about two seconds, she considered making him wait for an answer—but she found herself incapable of suppressing her own eagerness to talk to him. Adam picked up his phone on the first ring.

"Sheriff's office." The dispatcher must have been on a break.

"It's Jeannie. I got your message."

"Does dinner work for you?" he asked in the same businesslike voice he'd used on the answering machine.

"Dinner would be wonderful."

"The Chili Pepper?"

"That'd be great."

The best restaurant in town, no less. She was suddenly feeling much better about everything. "Um, why'd you wait so long to call?" She probably shouldn't ask. Her mother had always warned her not to ask a question if she wasn't going to like the answer.

Adam hesitated. "Did it bother you that I didn't phone?" he asked.

"Answer my question and I'll answer yours." She felt the tension building. She liked Adam and needed to know if this relationship had a future.

"I didn't think it was a good idea to call you too soon," he said at last.

"Why not?"

Again he hesitated. "Because I like you too damn much," he snapped, as if he resented being forced to admit it.

"But, Adam, I like you, too. I thought you knew how I felt. After we kissed and all..."

Once Annie and Lucas had made love, Annie wondered why they'd waited so long. She soon discovered that Lucas had a vigorous appetite for lovemaking. He seemed almost apologetic for wanting her as often as he did, although she had no objection.

"I never thought it'd be this good," Lucas told her late one night. Content, Annie lay in his arms. The room's only light came from the moon, a cool and silvery glow that crept between a small crack in the curtains.

"I don't know if that's a compliment or an insult," Annie said, smiling softly.

"I meant it as a compliment."

"I know." She lifted her head enough to kiss his throat.

He paused, then added in a low voice, "Julia was

sick for months before she died and we couldn't..."
He let the rest fade.

Lucas so rarely mentioned his first wife that Annie
wondered if his doing so now was significant. Since
their marriage, she'd mentioned Billy only once. They
were coming to trust each other, slowly exposing the
most painful parts of their pasts, yet yearning to move
forward.

"Until you and I got married, I'd assumed all of
that was over for me," he continued. "Making love,
being with a woman like this..."

Annie pressed the side of her face against his shoulder and wrapped her arm around his middle. "I, for
one, am most appreciative that it isn't." She felt his
smile and knew her words had pleased him. He
rubbed her back in long gentle strokes.

"I wasn't sure what to expect, you know."

"Me, neither."

"It'd been years."

"For me too," she reminded him. The car accident
and subsequent surgeries had made lovemaking impossible for her. By the time she was physically capable, her husband had found someone else and
wanted to end the marriage. It used to be that Annie
couldn't think of Billy without feeling pain. Recently
all she'd experienced was sadness. Not for her, amazingly, but for him. He was looking for the perfect
wife, the perfect job, the perfect *everything*—an attitude that meant he was destined to be disappointed.

For herself, Annie felt blessed beyond measure.
This marriage had been a precious and unexpected
gift, for which she would always be grateful. The
pregnancy she so desperately wanted would happen

in time, but she didn't think it would be soon. Not with all the medical problems she'd had, all the different medications she'd taken. She drew comfort from knowing that one day she would bear Lucas's child. Then something occurred to her, something she hadn't considered.

"Lucas…after I'm pregnant, will you…will we continue to make love?"

His hand stilled as if this thought was new to him, too. "Would you mind if we did?"

"No, of course not. I'd like to."

The tension left him, and Annie felt it ease from her own limbs. Their lovemaking was wonderful and she would have missed it dreadfully had he decided otherwise, but their time in bed was only a small part of their marriage. The physical intimacy paled next to the emotional intimacy she shared with him. This was all part of the gift she'd been given, part of life's compensation for all she'd endured. Sometimes it almost felt as if this joy, this contentment, was more than one person could possibly deserve.

The room darkened, and with her head on her husband's shoulder, Annie closed her eyes and let herself drift off to sleep. Sometime later, a loud crash of thunder startled her into wakefulness, and she heard rain pounding against the window.

"Daddy!" Hollie's cry echoed down the hallway.

Lucas moved his arm and was about to toss aside the blankets when Annie sat up. Storms had frightened her as a child, too. She'd always felt certain that other little girls didn't need to be afraid because they had mothers. Her father had told her she was being childish—but she *was* a child. He'd forbidden her to disturb his sleep, so many a night she'd hugged her arms about her and let her pillow absorb her cries.

"Daddy? Annie?" Heather and Hollie stood framed in the doorway.

"Come here, both of you," Annie said, throwing back the covers, inviting them to join her and Lucas.

Not waiting for their father to second the invitation, the two little girls raced across the carpet and bounced onto the bed, looking for the same comfort Annie had sought all those years ago.

"I was so scared," Hollie whispered, rubbing her cold feet against Annie's legs as she slid in beside her.

"I wasn't," Heather said, crawling from the bottom of the bed to the middle.

"You were, too," Hollie countered.

Lucas yawned loudly. "If you're sleeping in here, you'd better both be quiet."

One warning was all they needed. The storm continued to rage.

"Daddy, tell the storm to be quiet," Hollie said.

"Quiet out there."

Both girls giggled as if he'd said something outrageously funny. Annie laughed, too.

"Hey, quit with the noise," Lucas told them. "Annie and I have to go to work in the morning, and you girls have day camp."

"Yes, Daddy," Hollie said and it wasn't long before both sisters had fallen asleep. Her heart full, Annie stretched her arm protectively over their small bodies. Soon Lucas's fingers connected with hers.

"You awake?" he asked in a hushed whisper that was more breath than sound.

"Barely."

His hand covered hers completely now. "Thank you," he said in the same low tone.

"For what?"

"For this," he answered. "For making my girls feel safe and happy." He paused. "For everything."

Annie didn't bother to tell him that she was the one who should be giving thanks.

Nineteen

This time with Gordon had been heaven, Nessa mused as they sat in the taxi taking them to the Kansas City airport. They'd spent three days together. And for those three days she'd lived a life of enchantment and perfect happiness. Perfect romance. She and Gordon had been nearly inseparable. Every night he'd escorted her to her hotel room, kissed her good-night, then proceeded to his room, directly down the hall. It came to be a matter of much amusement that once he got to his room, he'd phone her. Habit, they decided, was hard to break.

In their time together, they'd laughed and talked and joked and kissed. If Nessa hadn't already been in love with Gordon, these few days would have had her falling head over heels.

Unfortunately the days had flown past far too quickly, and now they had to return to their separate lives. Reluctantly, delaying as long as possible, they'd departed for the airport with only an hour to spare.

"You're being unusually quiet," Gordon said, her hand in his.

"You should treasure the silence," Nessa joked. "It's rare for me."

"I treasure everything about you."

Nessa forced a smile and swallowed around the lump in her throat. Glancing down, she said, "I never knew a man who said such beautiful things."

Now it was his turn to look away. "Not since my wife died have I known anyone I wanted to say them to."

They'd decided that first day not to make up their minds about what they felt for each other until they were both home again. If they were indeed in love, they needed clear heads to sort through their feelings. Any decision about their future had to take the realities of the present into account. Because they were older and had children and complete lives in different places, there was more to consider. A lot of people could be affected by their decision.

The entire time, Gordon hadn't mentioned his son. Taking her cue from him, Nessa hadn't talked about her children, either. More than once she wondered if they should have discussed their families; she knew very well that her children wouldn't easily accept the idea of her marrying Gordon Pawling.

Sight unseen, and without even knowing his name, Sylvia had taken a dislike to Gordon. Nessa could only pray that Miles didn't have any preconceived prejudices against *her*. Gordon had told her his son wanted him to remarry, and it was the same with her own children. But Nessa was beginning to suspect her children weren't being entirely honest. They might have convinced themselves that remarriage was the best thing for their mother, but she doubted they'd thought it through. Bringing a man who wasn't their father into the family was more upsetting than they'd expected, as their reactions to this situation seemed to prove.

The taxi pulled up to the departure area, and while Gordon paid the driver and dealt with the luggage, Nessa took care of the tickets. Since they were traveling on two different airlines and her flight left first, Gordon walked her to her gate.

They waited in the departure lounge, holding hands, neither of them inclined to speak.

"I'll call you tonight," he promised as the time neared for her flight.

"You can wait if you like," Nessa said, knowing he'd be tired after the long trip. "Call me tomorrow, instead."

"It wouldn't feel right if I didn't call you this evening."

It wouldn't for Nessa, either....

"Leave a message on my answering machine as soon as you're home to let me know you arrived safely," he said. "I'll check it as soon as I get in."

"Okay." The lump in her throat seemed to grow thicker as boarding for her flight was announced.

Gordon stiffened, and Nessa knew this because she stiffened, too, not wanting to leave him and knowing she must. More difficult would be doing it with a smile.

"I won't board the plane until the very last minute," she whispered.

His hand tightened around hers almost painfully. Then, as if he seemed to realize what he was doing, he relaxed his grip.

The passengers for the San Antonio flight formed

a long straggling line. Not until the line had completely vanished did Nessa finally say, "I should go."

Gordon nodded.

She picked up her carry-on and Gordon accompanied her to the attendant at the gate. Smiling was as impossible as she'd known it would be; she dared not look at him for fear he'd see the tears in her eyes.

"Thank you," she whispered. "I had such a wonderful time. I'll always remember these days with you."

They hugged, and Gordon kissed her. Knowing how he felt about public displays of affection, she was surprised.

"I realize we agreed to wait before we made a decision," he said, easing her out of his arms, "but it isn't necessary. Not on my end. I love you."

"Oh, Gordon, I love you, too."

"I didn't plan to do it now, but I can't let you go, not like this. Marry me, Nessa."

She pressed her fingers to her lips in an effort to forestall the rush of tears. "Oh, Gordon."

"Excuse me," the airline clerk said, glancing toward the empty jetway, "are you on this flight?"

Nessa nodded, barely breaking eye contact with Gordon to answer the young man.

"You should board right away, ma'am," he said politely.

"I will." She reached for Gordon's hand and clasped it tightly. The thought of leaving him now was unbearable.

"Marry me, Nessa," Gordon pleaded a second time.

"Hurry up and say yes," the young man urged.

"Yes," Nessa said.

Gordon and Nessa clung to each other. "I love you," he whispered again.

"I love you, too."

"Is everyone on board?" A second clerk came out of the jetway.

"Not yet," the other man answered.

"They're ready to close the door," the second man warned.

"Tell them to hold on. We're in the middle of a marriage proposal here." Not waiting for the other man to do it, he spoke into the intercom. "Hold the plane," he said urgently. "We've got an engagement about to happen."

"I'll tell Miles tonight."

"Wait," Nessa advised. "Sleep on it."

"I know what I want, and that's to be with you for the rest of my life."

And that was exactly what she wanted, too.

Gordon kissed her one last time, and the young man who'd become her guardian angel gripped Nessa's elbow and hurried her into the jetway. "Are you going to marry him?" he asked just as she boarded the plane.

"Yes." Nessa had no hesitation in her voice.

"Great. Now make sure I get an invitation to the wedding."

"I will," she promised. But when she located her seat, she realized she hadn't gotten his name.

The happiness that filled her lasted the entire flight. She didn't know exactly when the lump in her throat had disappeared, but she guessed it was shortly after

Gordon's proposal. She felt giddy with love and so damn happy it was all she could do to sit still.

The flight landed in San Antonio, and Nessa was scheduled to take the shuttle bus to Promise, a ride that took nearly ninety minutes. It was dark by the time the Boeing 737 touched down. Nessa didn't relish the long trip home, but nothing could destroy this wonderful feeling inside her.

Almost nothing, she revised as she reached the baggage-claim area in the San Antonio terminal—and saw her daughter, glaring at her.

"Welcome home, Mother," Sylvia said in a cold uninflected voice. As if Nessa were some disobedient schoolgirl who'd been caught skipping classes.

"Sylvia! What are you doing here?"

Her daughter didn't answer. "Just where were you?" she demanded, instead.

"Kansas City." The flight information should have told her that. Or was she testing her mother, hoping to catch her in a lie?

"With who?"

"With *whom*," Nessa corrected.

"And don't try to tell me you were at a bridge tournament."

Nessa giggled. She didn't play bridge, and Sylvia knew it.

"This is no laughing matter," Sylvia said once they'd retrieved Nessa's bag and were on their way to the parking lot. "You were with a man, weren't you?"

"Yes," Nessa admitted.

That seemed to be more than Sylvia could bear.

She stopped in midstep and cast Nessa a horrified look.

"You needn't worry," Nessa assured her daughter. "We had separate rooms."

"Excuse me, are you Jeannie French?"

Jeannie, who was volunteering at the library, was through for the day. She glanced up from the picnic table in the park to find an attractive woman dressed in a green silk pantsuit and high heels. "I'm Val Langley, and Travis Grant suggested I talk to you."

Jeannie closed the book she'd been reading and set her half-eaten apple aside. The day was warm but not humid, a pleasant late-July afternoon, and she'd wanted to spend her free time sitting in the sun, enjoying her novel. Later she'd be meeting Adam at the theater—and the anticipation added a touch of excitement to her day. Adam had phoned earlier in the week and asked her to the movies. After their dinner date, they'd been out twice—bowling and on a picnic—but they were still uneasy with each other. Adam often waited several days between dates to call her again, as if he feared she'd change her mind about him. They were taking this slow, and in truth, Jeannie didn't mind. As long as he didn't wait *too* long between calls.

"How can I help you, Ms. Langley?" she asked.

"Please, call me Val. Apparently you're familiar with the history of the area?" Val made the statement a question.

Jeannie was stunned that Travis would send someone to her, seeing that he knew more about local history than anyone around here. "I know a little bit," she said warily.

"Would you mind if I asked you a few questions?"

"Not at all." As the woman sat carefully on the bench, first brushing it off, Jeannie couldn't help wondering about her. She remembered hearing that Nell and Travis had a female houseguest and vaguely recalled that she was related to Travis somehow. His sister, possibly. Jeannie was flattered that Travis had thought she could answer Val's questions.

"You've been to Bitter End?" Val asked.

"Once," Jeannie told her. "I've only lived in Promise a year." She explained she was a first-grade teacher and that she had a long-standing passion for Texan history.

"I was out at Bitter End myself this morning," Val said.

Jeannie suspected she hadn't been wearing her high heels then, and when the woman didn't elaborate, she wondered what Val had thought of the ghost town. "What brings you to Promise?" she asked.

"This is a vacation of sorts. I'm an attorney and I'm trying to help a friend. I don't suppose you've heard of Richard Weston, have you?"

"Is he related to Grady and Caroline?"

"Grady's brother. He has a sister, too."

"That would be Savannah Smith."

"Yes," Val said. "But I haven't managed to speak to either one." She shook her head. "I'm glad you're willing to talk to me, especially as no one else seems to be."

Jeannie couldn't understand why and said so.

"It's all rather complicated," Val said, folding her

hands on her crossed knees. "You see, Richard's in a New York prison. He'd been charged with...various crimes and made the mistake of running from the law. He came back here, and for a while he hid out at Bitter End."

"Really?" Jeannie's interest rose. She'd heard the occasional vague remark about Richard Weston, but little else. It was as if the entire town had decided to pretend he'd never existed. "For how long?"

"A few weeks. It's apparently because of Richard that the old hotel is boarded up. The staircase collapsed on him, and he was badly injured. From what I was told, it's a miracle he survived."

"I don't mean to pry," Jeannie said, "but what does any of that have to do with you?"

"I'm a friend, as I said. I'm also the attorney appealing Richard's conviction. I hope to file soon after I get back to New York."

"Oh."

"The prosecution made at least one legal error that I've been able to use in forming a case for an appeal. This often happens when a number of defendants are charged with the same crime. My belief is that Richard Weston played a relatively minor role in what happened, but received most of the blame."

"Well, then, I hope you can help him."

"I do, too," Val said, "since I'm investing my own time and money in this. I want to see Richard released as soon as possible."

"That's very generous of you."

"I want justice to be served. But even if the appeal is denied, Richard could appear before the parole board in as little as two years," Val continued. "He could get out early for good behavior. Another factor is overcrowding in the prisons. In any event, when he does go before the board, he'll need the support of his family.''

''Savannah and Grady are wonderful people,'' Jeannie offered without reservation. She'd met both of them quite a few times and couldn't imagine that they wouldn't be willing to help their brother in any way possible.

Val brightened considerably. ''The situation with Richard Weston is unfortunate, but I'm doing everything I can to see that he's vindicated.''

''It must give you a wonderful sense of pride and accomplishment to work on a case like this and see real justice done.'' Jeannie frowned. ''I mean, if he's been treated unfairly...''

''It's very rewarding,'' Val was quick to tell her. ''Anyway, part of the reason I'm here is that Richard asked me to personally check on the ghost town. He's afraid the historic value of the place might have been destroyed since his incarceration. He'll be pleased to hear that the town's basically been left intact.''

''I'm sure he will be.''

They chatted for nearly an hour. Val gave her a little more background on Richard, and Jeannie told her everything she'd learned about Bitter End, as well as a few other stories, including the ones she'd shared with Nell and Travis.

By then, it was time to prepare for her date with Adam. Jeannie and Val parted company, with Jeannie warmly wishing the attorney good luck in her efforts.

''You'll never guess who I talked to this afternoon,'' she told Adam as they walked into the theater fifteen minutes before showtime.

He grinned. "You're right, I'll never guess." They sat in a middle row, and he tipped the popcorn in her direction.

Jeannie helped herself to a handful. "Val Langley."

"What did she want?" Adam asked flatly.

"She's the attorney—"

"I know who she is."

Jeannie was surprised by the coolness of his tone. She liked Val and admired her dedication to her client. Val's big-city sophistication impressed her, too.

"She's working on an appeal for Richard Weston and had some questions."

"An appeal? That's the first I've heard of it."

"What's wrong?"

"I don't think it's a good idea to talk with her again."

"Why not?"

"Richard Weston hurt this community."

"I know. But Val told me he regrets what happened and wants to make it up to everyone. Actually, I think she might be a little sweet on him."

Adam frowned darkly. "Richard Weston's bad news."

"Val doesn't think so." She didn't mean to be argumentative, but his attitude irritated her.

"You *like* Val?" The way he said it insinuated she shouldn't.

"As a matter of fact, I do."

"A word of friendly advice, Jeannie. It'd be better if you didn't give her any more information about this town or the Westons.''

"I can't believe you're talking to me like this."
She crossed her arms stubbornly. "Val is an intelli-
gent woman and a successful attorney, and she's
taken on Richard's cause."

"You weren't here. You don't know what he did."

"You weren't here, either," she said.

"I'm not going to argue with you about Richard
Weston," Adam replied, and it was as though he'd
closed a door in her face. He turned his eyes to the
screen, which was still dark, and refused to look at
her.

"It's too late," Jeannie said with a hint of sarcasm.
"We're already arguing."

"I think you should stay away from Val."

"She's my friend."

"A piss-poor choice, if you ask me."

"I didn't." Arms still crossed, Jeannie glared at the
screen. Perhaps Adam wasn't the man she'd believed
him to be. Val was trying to help Richard Weston.
Jeannie thought Adam would be interested in seeing
justice done. Obviously he wasn't.

"I still don't understand how you knew I was with
Gordon," Nessa said as she poured Sylvia and herself
a cup of tea. The drive from the airport to Promise
had been an uncomfortable one. She'd said little to
Sylvia, beyond telling her who Gordon was—a widower and retired judge from Toronto. Her daughter's
attitude practically implied that Nessa deserved to
wear a scarlet letter. Maybe "F" for fool, since "A"
for adulteress hardly applied.

Her love life was her own business, and she had
no intention of discussing it with her daughter. Nor
did she feel she owed Sylvia any explanations. As far
as she could figure, when Sylvia hadn't been able to
reach her, she'd called Dovie who'd divulged her
whereabouts—although not, apparently, Gordon's
name. Nessa hadn't asked Dovie to keep her trip a
secret, but she certainly hadn't expected this kind of
reaction to a three-day absence.

"How well do you know this man, Mother?" Sylvia asked, picking up the delicate china cup. "This
Gordon Pawling from Canada?"

The distaste in her voice angered Nessa. "Well
enough to marry him," she snapped. She realized she
hadn't called yet to leave him a message; she'd do
that as soon as Sylvia left.

"Marry him!" Sylvia's cup hit the saucer with a
clang, spilling tea; Nessa was amazed it hadn't shattered. "You're..." Speechless, Sylvia stared at her.

"Engaged," Nessa supplied.

"To a Canadian?"

Nessa nearly laughed out loud. Sylvia made it
sound as if she'd agreed to marry a man from another
planet. "Yes, a Canadian," she returned evenly.
Nothing could destroy this joy that had been with her
since Gordon's proposal.

"Did you have him checked out?"

"Gordon?" Nessa asked. "Checked out? Whatever
for?"

"He could be after your money, Mother." Sylvia
seemed to think that should be obvious. Nessa was
reasonably well off, with enough retirement money to
live comfortably but by no means extravagantly.

"He's not after my money," Nessa said.

"You don't know that."

Sylvia could call her a fool if she wanted, but Nessa knew Gordon wasn't interested in her small stock portfolio. "I understand your concern, sweetie, but—"

"Where will you live?"

"Ah..." Nessa didn't know what to say. There hadn't been time to discuss any of those details. All they'd decided was that they loved each other and wanted to be together.

"Have you ever spent a winter in Toronto?" Sylvia asked aggressively.

"No, but it can't be any colder than the winter I spent with your father in Prudhoe Bay."

One look told Nessa her daughter didn't appreciate the comment.

"You're so in love with this man..."

"...you aren't thinking straight." Miles continued his tirade until it was all Gordon could do to restrain his temper.

"If you'd listen—"

"To what?" Miles challenged. "You know next to nothing about her."

"I know everything that's necessary."

Miles began pacing the library. "I expected much better from you."

"Better? You've never met Nessa. When you do, you'll see what a wonderful woman she is."

"You might have let me know you were leaving for Kansas City!"

Gordon was guilty as charged, but he knew that if

he'd discussed the trip with Miles, his son would've tried to talk him out of going. And now that he'd had this time with Nessa, now that he knew his heart, Gordon was willing to do whatever it took to marry her. Even if it meant standing up to his own son.

"I don't need your permission, Miles."

His son glared at him. "Are you saying you'd marry this...this gold digger, no matter what I think?"

Just off the plane, Gordon was tired and emotionally drained. The last thing he wanted was an argument with his only child. "Miles, listen."

"I had her checked out."

"You *what?*"

Miles's shoulders went back. "I hired a private detective."

Gordon couldn't believe it. How dared Miles presume he had the right to interfere like this? What he'd done was insulting. Intolerable.

"Don't you want to know what he found out?" Miles asked as though he'd uncovered enough dirt to take the case to the Grand Jury.

"Absolutely not." Gordon was outraged and prayed Nessa would never learn what Miles had done. He pounded his fist on the top of his desk. "I think it'd be best if you left *now*."

Miles's jaw sagged open. "You're kicking me out of the home where I was born and raised?"

Gordon didn't reply.

Miles grabbed his umbrella and headed out of the library. When he reached the door, he turned back. "Well, I guess it's true what they say—there's no fool like an old fool."

"Thank you for those words of infinite wisdom," Gordon muttered.

Miles shook his head, then rushed out, making sure the front door slammed in his wake.

Sitting down, Gordon drew in a deep breath to slow his racing heart. Not since Miles was a teenager had they argued like this. On most issues they were in full agreement. Gordon hoped Nessa hadn't been subjected to the same kind of inquisition from *her* children. Only a few hours earlier they'd been in each other's arms. He could still see the tears of happiness shining in her eyes when she'd whispered her love. The memory was enough to calm him.

Upon his return from the airport there'd been no message from Nessa, which concerned him. He punched in her phone number.

"Hello?" a woman answered. One who sounded almost like Nessa. "Who is this?"

"Gordon Pawling," Gordon said, certain he must be speaking to Sylvia. "Is Nessa available?"

"No," came the curt reply. "And she won't be for a long time." Sylvia lowered her voice. "I want you to know I found out about the inquiries you made into my mother's financial affairs."

Gordon groaned inwardly. He was about to explain that the private detective had been his son's doing and not his, but he wasn't allowed to finish.

"You can forget about marrying my mother, Mr. Pawling. Neither my brothers nor I will allow it."

With that, she slammed down the phone and Gordon heard nothing more—except the irritating buzz of a disconnected line.

* * *

Grady Weston walked from the barn toward the main house. He'd put in a long day repairing a wind-mill that supplied a watering hole for his cattle. Knowing he'd be able to spend the night relaxing with his wife and family made up for all the hard work and the worries that accompanied a rancher's life. For years he'd worked with no end in sight, no purpose, beyond simply surviving and holding on to the Yellow Rose Ranch. Caroline had added a miss-ing dimension to his life, and his marriage was— His thoughts came to an abrupt halt when he noticed a sheriff's department car parked in the yard. Frank Hennessey had been a family friend for many years, and Grady was sorry not to see him as often since he'd retired. He liked Adam Jordan, but because Adam had been away from Promise for more than a decade, he wasn't well acquainted with him yet.

Grady continued toward the house and Caroline met him at the back porch. "Sheriff Jordan's here."

"I saw the car. Is there trouble?"

Caroline's gaze held his. "I don't know. He wants to talk to you."

"About what?" Grady was a man who didn't take kindly to surprises.

"I'm not sure, but I have a feeling this has to do with Richard."

Grady closed his eyes. Would he never escape his brother's reach?

"I'll bring you a glass of iced tea," Caroline told him, and then before he could turn away, she stopped him. "I love you, Grady," she whispered, easing her arms around his neck and bringing her mouth to his. He didn't know what had prompted the kiss, not that he objected. The eagerness of her embrace was an unexpected pleasure.

Wrapping his arms about his wife's waist, he lifted her from the ground and swung her up. It felt damn good to hold Caroline. Every day he thanked God he had her in his life—her and Maggie and Roy. And now this baby to come...

"Howdy, Sheriff," he said, joining Adam Jordan a few minutes later. Adam waited for him on the front porch, which overlooked the rolling green pasture. A row of pecan trees, a recent addition, edged this side of the property.

"Grady." Adam stood and the two men shook hands.

"Anything I can do for you?" Grady asked as they lowered themselves into the white wicker chairs. The very ones his parents used to sit in almost every night.

"Has Travis mentioned that Val Langley's in town?"

The name was oddly familiar, but Grady couldn't remember where he'd heard it. "He might have, but if so, I don't recall." Val Langley. Val Langley. He just couldn't place it.

"She's his ex-wife."

Grady nodded. But he knew there was some other reason for this sense of familiarity.

"She also defended Richard against charges in New York three years ago," Adam said.

So that was why the name rang a bell. Because of her connection with Richard. Without so much as meeting the woman, Grady instantly distrusted her. He didn't allow himself to like or trust anyone connected with his brother. "What's she doing in Promise?" he demanded.

"I don't know. Do you?"

Grady frowned. "I wouldn't have asked you if I did."

"I don't mean to be blunt, but I read your brother's file and—"

"You don't need to worry about sparing my feelings. There's no love lost between Richard and me."

"I just found out that Ms. Langley's filing an appeal on his behalf."

Grady shrugged. He was no legal expert, but he'd talked to the prosecuting attorney by phone several times during the trial. The evidence against Richard and his accomplices had been overwhelming. "More power to her, but I doubt it'll do much good."

Adam nodded. "I hope you're right." He stared out over the pasture. "I don't mean to pry, but have you heard from your brother recently?"

Grady nodded. "For the first time in three years. He claims he's a changed man and wants our forgiveness."

"Do you believe him?"

Grady snorted. "About as much as I believe pigs fly."

A brief smile touched Adam's mouth. "Were you aware that your brother might be eligible for parole in less than two years?"

"You're kidding, right?" His brother had been sentenced to twenty-five years, and he deserved every second of that time, in Grady's opinion. Aside from everything he'd done to his family and the people of Promise, he'd committed unforgivable crimes against poor people—illegal immigrants he and his accomplices had lured into the U.S. and then exploited. The men had been forced into criminal activities and the women into prostitution. Several had died under suspicious circumstances. Murder was never proved, but Grady could no longer be sure that his brother was incapable of such a crime. And now he was being told that despite all the pain he'd inflicted, Richard might end up serving only five years? It wasn't right.

"Apparently, because of overcrowding and other factors, it's quite likely that he could come before the parole board within the next couple of years."

Grady shook his head in disgust.

"He also appears to be concerned about what's happened to Bitter End. Ms. Langley said he was afraid Promise would use it to attract tourists."

"I hate to play dumb here, Sheriff," Grady said, "but the only person my brother's ever cared about is himself. If he's interested in the ghost town, then it's for his own selfish reasons."

"Do you know what those reasons might be?"

Grady shook his head again. "I don't have a clue."

The sheriff left shortly afterward. Caroline stepped onto the porch beside her husband as the patrol car headed out of the driveway.

"You were right," Grady said, slipping his arm around her waist.

"Richard?"

Grady nodded grimly. "He could be up for parole in as little as two years."

"Two years?" Caroline sounded as incredulous as he'd been.

"Not only that, he has an attorney working on an appeal."

"Val Langley? Nell mentioned she was visiting, but I didn't realize that had anything to do with Richard.

Grady had forgotten that the women of Promise had a news network more effective than any spy ring.

"She's been going around town asking a lot of questions," Caroline informed him.

"I hope she got an earful—especially if she asked about Richard."

"Don't worry." Caroline laughed. "I doubt she learned a thing. People prefer not to discuss him."

"Did you hear about his supposedly deep concern for Bitter End?" The sarcasm in his voice was unavoidable.

Caroline stared at him. "Richard's concerned about Bitter End?"

"That's the word."

"But why?"

"I wouldn't know."

"Could he have left something behind?"

"Like what? We found where he'd been sleeping and the things he'd stolen. He didn't have anything all that valuable."

"Mommy, Daddy." Maggie raced onto the porch with three-year-old Roy tagging behind. "When's dinner?" Maggie asked.

"Just as soon as you wash your hands."

"You, too," Grady told his son, and then with his arm about his wife, walked back into the house that was his home.

Twenty

Nessa hadn't spoken to Gordon in two days. Two very difficult days. Sylvia had hounded her constantly, until she felt she had no choice but to delay the wedding. She decided to explain this to Gordon by writing a letter. She wanted no room for misunderstanding between them. She fully intended to marry him and only wanted to postpone setting the day—just until her children had the opportunity to meet him. That wasn't an unreasonable request. It would help if she met Miles, too.

What she didn't tell Gordon was that he had a lot to make up for in the eyes of her daughter. Sylvia had taken such delight in telling her that Gordon had hired a private detective, who'd investigated her background, her life and her finances. Nessa could say nothing in Gordon's defense and decided it would be best if Gordon did the explaining himself. She decided she wouldn't mention the detective directly; she'd hint at it by discussing Sylvia's concerns.

The letter required a great deal of thought and several handwritten drafts.

My dearest Gordon,

It pains me to write this letter, but I want everything to be as clear as I can make it. Most important of all, please know that I'll always treasure our time together in Kansas City.

We'd talked earlier about giving ourselves time to analyze our feelings before making any decisions regarding the future of our relationship. Neither one of us is young and neither one of us expected to fall in love.

So often in life what seems right one moment can seem wrong the next. We're both mature enough to recognize the consequences of our decision to marry. In the airport, marriage seemed such a logical and wonderful next step. I knew then and I know now how much I love you, but there are other considerations, other factors neither of us can ignore.

My children, mainly my daughter, have raised a number of valid points, and I'm sure Miles has his own concerns. It's because of our children that I feel we should postpone the wedding. This is an important decision and one that shouldn't be rushed. I know what you're thinking but, my darling. Believe me when I tell you how much I love you. I don't want to wait, either, but I think we have to—at least until everyone in my family has the opportunity to get to know everyone in yours, and vice versa.

Please don't be upset with me. I sincerely feel this is for the best. I love you and I want to marry you, but right now, I'm not sure when.

Please call me so we can discuss all of this. I've missed hearing from you.

Love,
Nessa

She reread the letter three times and then before she could change her mind, she walked over to the post office to mail it. Nessa was worried about Gordon's silence and depressed about putting off the wedding, but she didn't know what else to do.

Much as she hated to admit it, Sylvia's concerns were valid. Nessa had accepted Gordon's proposal impulsively. It was too soon; they hadn't taken their families into proper consideration. And there was another major question Sylvia had raised: Where would they live?

When she returned from the post office, the phone was ringing. Rushing to reach it before the answering machine came on, she was out of breath when she answered.

"Nessa?" the male voice asked hesitantly.

"Gordon, oh, Gordon, it's so good to hear from you! Why haven't you phoned?"

"Why haven't *you* phoned *me?*" he challenged.

His defiant tone took her by surprise. "That was because—"

"For the record, I did phone," Gordon said, breaking off her explanation, "and talked to your daughter. I take it she didn't relay the message."

"No. I'm very sorry. Had I known, I would have called you back immediately."

Her apology was followed by a short strained silence. "I'm sorry, too," he murmured. Then, "How are you?"

She almost gave in to the impulse to lie and tell him everything was fine, but she didn't. Because it wasn't. "Not so good. How about you?"

"I'm holding up. What's happening on your end?"

Nessa sank into a chair, more miserable and lonely

than ever. "My daughter met my plane. She was furious with me."

"My son wasn't pleased, either."

"Sylvia and her brothers insist we delay the wedding."

"In other words, she doesn't want you to marry me."

She understood his anger and disappointment; she was experiencing the same emotions herself.

"What did you tell her?"

Nessa bit her lower lip, calling herself a coward for letting him down, for not standing up to her family.

"Nessa?"

"I...I agreed to a delay. What could I say when you had a private detective asking questions about me?" she said in an anguished voice. "Don't you realize things like that get back to people? Why did you do such a thing, Gordon? Why?"

His lack of response told her everything. Sylvia had enjoyed filling in the ugly details, and it had been both painful and humiliating to listen.

Finally he said, "You told Sylvia you'd put off the wedding?"

"Yes."

"What you really agreed to do was to break off the relationship with me entirely," Gordon said in a calm cold voice.

"That's not true! I told you in Kansas City that I love you and I meant it."

"But apparently not enough to refuse to listen to your daughter."

"That's unfair! All I'm asking is that we hold off until we can answer a few important questions."

"Such as?"

"Well, where we'll live…"

Gordon sighed. "The answer seems perfectly obvious to me. We can spend winters in Texas and summers in Toronto. These are excuses, Nessa, not reasons. What I said earlier is true, isn't it? You agreed to abide by your daughter's wishes and in the same breath turned your back on me."

"I didn't!"

"Please don't tell me you love me again. You'll do us both a disservice. As for that private detective, you don't have a lot of room to talk."

"What's that supposed to mean?"

He ignored her question. "I suspect the next thing that'll happen is a polite note in the mail, explaining your decision."

Nessa's heart sank, since that was exactly what would take place.

"You'll tell me as diplomatically as possible that we both need time, and frankly, I agree with you. We do need time. Perhaps it'd be best if we didn't talk for a while. I'll tell you what, Nessa, next time around you can phone me."

"Gordon, please listen—"

"Goodbye."

She wanted to shout at him to come back, to let her explain, but the line had gone dead. Slowly she replaced the receiver, so much in pain she actually felt numb.

A day was all she could stand. Twenty-four miserable hours was all it took before she realized they had to settle this, or they were both destined for heartache. She thought it best that Gordon meet her children and they could judge him for themselves.

It hurt that not one of her three children trusted her

ability to recognize a man of character. She was sure that once Sylvia and the boys met Gordon, they'd have all the answers they needed. If they didn't... well, she mused with a deep sigh, they'd cross that bridge when they came to it.

With her pulse raging, Nessa waited until evening and then punched out Gordon's phone number. Three rings later, a man answered. It wasn't Gordon.

"May I take a message?" he asked with stiff politeness.

"Please," Nessa said. "My name's Vanessa Boyd."

"Oh." His voice, already cool, dropped to subfreezing temperatures. "This is Miles Pawling. Gordon's son."

"Hello, Miles," she said, refusing to allow his unfriendliness to deter her. "Your father's mentioned you often."

"I'll bet he has. Has he also mentioned that I'm opposed to this wedding you've supposedly planned?"

So Gordon had faced family disapproval, as well. That explained a great deal. "No, he hasn't, but I'm hoping you'll give me a chance, Miles. I happen to love your father very much."

"You love his bank balance more, though, right?"

"I beg your pardon?" Nessa struggled with her composure. What a cruel and ugly thing to say.

"My father's a wealthy man, but then you already know that, don't you, Mrs. Boyd?"

"Yes," she agreed softly. "Your father is rich— in strength of character, intelligence and grace. The truth is, I wasn't aware of his financial standing, but now that I am, this all makes a lot more sense. You're worried that I'm only interested in him because of his money.''

''Isn't that so?''

''You vastly underrate your father, Miles.'' And her too, but she didn't say that. Nessa heard a voice in the background and knew it was Gordon. ''You don't need to tell him I phoned,'' she said quietly. ''Goodbye, Miles, and don't worry, I won't trouble either of you again.''

She didn't wait for a response, and with tears stinging her eyes, she broke the connection.

Glen Patterson saw the For Sale sign posted in the front yard of his parents' bed-and-breakfast when he parked his truck. His father had talked over the decision with both sons, but seeing the realty sign was almost more than Glen could bear.

Phil opened the door for him, and Glen had to admit he looked better than he had in months. They'd hired a caregiver to come six days a week, which provided him with some help and much-needed relief. Caring for his wife had been demanding enough, but hiding her illness and keeping up appearances in the community had taken a terrible toll on his own health.

''How's Mom?'' Glen asked, following him into the kitchen.

''She's not doing too badly today.'' Phil shrugged. ''Tomorrow might be worse. It changes.... But right now she's a little more aware, remembering a few things. I value days like this when they happen.''

Glen loved and admired his father, and never more than in the past few weeks. His optimistic outlook in the face of ongoing tragedy were far and above anything Glen had thought possible.

"I see the house is listed," he said casually.

Phil nodded. "The agent thinks it'll sell quickly."

"Good. Have you decided where you want to move?"

Pulling out a chair at the kitchen table, Phil shook his head. "As little as two weeks ago I assumed a smaller house and a caregiver would be the best solution, but now I don't think..." He paused and pinched the bridge of his nose, then looked away, tears glistening in his eyes. "Pretty soon your mother's going to need more care than I and a single caregiver can provide." He paused. "We were at the doctor's this afternoon."

"Dr. Curtis?" The geriatric specialist in San Antonio. "What did he say?"

"Unfortunately your mother's not responding as well as he'd hoped to the medication."

"What does all this mean?" Glen asked, fighting back his own emotions.

"I won't be able to care for her at home much longer," his father said quietly.

"What if we hired a second caregiver?"

"Glen, I can't afford it." Glancing down at his hands, he muttered, "The cost of even one is crippling me financially. The insurance doesn't cover this."

"But family and friends could pitch in," Glen knew that now that Dovie and Frank were aware of Mary's condition, they dropped in nearly every day. Reverend Wade McMillen had become a regular visitor and spent part of the time with his mother, but much of his visit was with Phil.

"You and your brother have your own lives. The

same with Dovie and Frank. I won't ask that of any of you."

"But this is Mom," Glen argued.

"Sometimes she barely recognizes you."

"It doesn't matter. I recognize her," Glen returned. "We can't put her in a home. That's not what you're thinking, is it?" Glen wouldn't stand for it. He loved his father and acknowledged that this was a difficult time, but he wouldn't abandon his mother.

His father wouldn't meet his eyes.

"Dad, please. I'll help more. Just tell me what you need me to do."

"You have a family of your own, and then there's the ranch. Cal's a new father and Jane needs him."

"This is our *mother*. Your wife."

"You think I don't know that?" Phil's voice cracked. "You think this is an easy decision? I pray to God it's not a decision you'll ever have to make. It'd be easier to rip out my own heart than see your mother in a home." He looked directly at Glen. "Do you know what happened yesterday? She went in to take a bath and forgot how to turn off the water. The entire bathroom was flooded by the time I realized something was wrong. Glen, we can't go on this way!"

The air throbbed with anguish as both men struggled to hold back their tears.

"I was at a retirement complex in San Antonio this afternoon," his father said, his voice raw. "The place has a number of small apartments, so we could move in there and keep some of the things your mother's treasured over the years. It would feel like home to her, and frankly, I don't think it'll be long before she can't tell the difference."

"What about...later?" It went without saying what "later" meant.

"There are medical facilities and staff available for when that time comes. She won't be able to stay in the apartment with me, but...but I'll just be a few floors away. Whenever possible, I'll be with her."

With her, but without the grueling responsibility constant care demanded. It seemed a good solution. The only solution. Better than anything Glen could come up with.

"Dr. Curtis recommended I check out the facility, although he had nothing but good things to say."

"The cost?" Glen knew he'd be willing to do whatever he could to help financially. So would Cal.

"It's not as bad as I thought. The apartments, all utilities, meals and some of the medical expenses are included in a flat rate." He named a figure that seemed exorbitant to Glen, until he took into account everything it covered. "I'll have the money from the house, don't forget."

Glen nodded, looking regretfully around the charming kitchen his mother had decorated.

"I'm doing the best I can," his father whispered.

"I know, Dad. I know."

A few minutes later Glen went in to see his mother, who smiled up at him expectantly, as if waiting for him to identify himself. Her earlier awareness was evidently gone. They sat and watched television together, and then Glen rose to leave.

His father walked him to the door. Glen hugged his father for a long moment. "The retirement place is a good idea, Dad."

Phil nodded and they broke apart.

* * *

Amy McMillen, the pastor's wife, came into Tumbleweed Books and gleefully told Annie, "Wade has the children for the day, and I've got instructions to indulge myself with a good book."

"That sounds heavenly," Annie said as she stepped toward the cash register. Now that she, too, was both a wife and mother, her own reading time was severely curtailed—but she had no regrets. "Any special reason he's giving you a free day?"

"It's my birthday, and when he asked me what I wanted, I told him twenty-four hours to myself."

"It'll be good for him, too," Annie told her. "He'll have a greater understanding of all the work you do—and appreciate you even more."

"Yes, I'm sure he will," Amy said, smiling softly. She wandered about the store and after twenty minutes or so, set the book she wanted on the counter. "How's married life treating you?"

"Wonderful," Annie said and felt her cheeks heat. "Really wonderful."

Amy glanced up from the check she was writing. "Wade said this would happen."

"What do you mean?"

"Early on he told me that he felt your marriage to Lucas would be a strong one."

During their counseling session before the wedding, Wade had told them that as long as they were open and honest with each other and willingly agreed to the terms they'd set forth, their marriage would remain healthy.

"Well, I'm incredibly happy," Annie said, almost afraid to say the words out loud.

"Everything about you tells me that." Amy reached across the counter to squeeze Annie's hand.

"It's the way I felt when I realized how much I loved Wade...and yet at the same time I was terrified." She finished writing the check and handed it to Annie. "I'm so glad you came to Promise."

"Me, too. Jane was right—the town needed a bookstore."

"That's true, but I was thinking that you needed Promise and we needed you."

"Thank you, Amy," Annie said, remembering that Jane had said something like this the very first day she'd arrived in Promise.

The conversation was on Annie's mind all day. Amy's description of happiness tinged by fear fit her own emotional state. She supposed the fear was of loss, of losing what she'd gained but had never expected to have.

She did a brisk business that afternoon and was ready to close for the night when Jane entered the store, carrying Paul in his infant seat. He was sound asleep, and his innocence, his vulnerability, clutched at Annie's heart. She breathed in his baby scent, smiling as Jane put the seat on the counter between them.

"No one told me it'd take half an hour to get a baby ready for a trip into town," Jane said, slipping the diaper bag off her shoulder and putting it on the floor.

"Don't tell me you're complaining already?" Annie teased.

"I'm not complaining," Jane said. "It's just that I started to rely on having a couple of pairs of extra hands while Mom and Dad were here. I really miss them."

Annie missed them, too. Because she and Jane had been close friends for so many years, Annie had come to think of Stephanie Dickinson as a substitute mother. She hadn't seen nearly as much of the Dickinsons after Jane left for medical school, but they'd kept in touch. Their recent visit had been good all around, and Annie experienced a renewed sense of closeness with her friend's parents.

Jane picked up the infant seat and carried it to one of the big overstuffed chairs. "I'm worn out already," she said as she sank into the cushions with a sigh. But her energy was rejuvenated when Paul awoke, looked around him and, not seeing familiar surroundings, let out a lusty wail.

"Feeding time?" Annie asked.

"He's probably got a messy diaper." Jane scooped up her son, and after a brief inspection, expertly changed his diaper. When she'd finished, she placed him over her shoulder and gently rubbed his back. Not more than five minutes passed before he'd returned to sleep.

Annie wondered if she'd be as natural a mother as Jane. Then without warning, the room suddenly felt too hot. Perspiration moistened her brow and she fell into the chair across from Jane.

"Annie?"

"Jane... Oh, my goodness."

"What is it?"

"I'm feeling light-headed."

"Have you been unusually tired, as well?"

Now that she considered it, Annie realized she had. "Yes."

Jane asked her several other questions, and Annie wondered if her friend recognized these symptoms. She'd been needing to use the bathroom more frequently and recalled that was a symptom of diabetes.

She didn't remember there being any diabetics in her family, but—

"Annie," Jane said, interrupting her thoughts, "my guess is you're pregnant."

"Don't be ridiculous!" Annie said. "It's much too soon." But was it? Could she possibly be pregnant? They hadn't practiced birth control, but Annie had assumed that because of her medical history, getting pregnant would take a while.

"How can it be too soon?" Jane asked, sounding perfectly reasonable.

"It's just that..." Words deserted her, and Annie had no idea how to describe what she felt. She'd read all the books, knew all the symptoms, but no one had mentioned what should have been the most obvious. Joy.

A baby. That explained the boundless happiness she'd experienced of late. This protective barrier that kept problems at bay. The irrepressible feeling that everything was right with the world. Perhaps it also explained the fears that nibbled away at her, telling her that something this wonderful couldn't last.

"Does Lucas know?" Jane asked.

Annie shook her head. "How could he when I didn't know myself? Yet in a way, I suppose I did...."

"You can get a pregnancy kit and find out today," Jane said.

"No," was Annie's immediate response. If she was pregnant, then she was barely so and her body would soon catch up with the knowledge in her heart. By the end of the month, she'd have missed her first period; she would make an appointment at the health clinic then. If she wasn't pregnant, she didn't want to destroy the illusion this quickly.

"You've got a funny look," Jane said, breaking into Annie's thoughts. "You used to get the same look when we were kids."

Annie decided Jane was being fanciful. "Don't be ridiculous."

"We spent as much time together as sisters," Jane said, "and I know you. You never could keep a secret from me. I could always tell. It shows in your eyes."

Annie realized it would do no good to argue. "All right, I'll get the test. If you insist."

"I do," Jane returned with all the fervor of a woman who knows when she's right and isn't afraid to say so.

That night, Annie was tempted to mention the possibility that she was pregnant to Lucas, but it would be premature to say anything just yet. Besides, he'd want to tell the girls right away, and Annie was afraid of disappointing them. So she said nothing.

After preparing dinner, cleaning the kitchen and reading to Heather and Hollie, there hardly seemed time for a private conversation.

When she finally climbed into bed beside her husband later that evening, Lucas put down his book and looked at her.

She picked up her own novel, then realized her husband was still watching her. Slowly she lowered her book and met his eyes. "Did you want to say something?" she asked.

"Yes," he said, and continued to stare.

"Lucas—" she was blushing "—you're embarrassing me."

"You're so beautiful," he said softly and fervently.

"Lucas, stop. You don't need to say these things."

"Annie, I'm serious."

"If I'm beautiful," she said, closing her book and turning off the bedside lamp, "it's because I'm happy."

Lucas turned off his light, too, and they reached for one another, not in a frenzy of passion, but in love and gratitude for the miracle of second chances.

Summer was always busy for a veterinarian in a ranching community. It wasn't unusual for Lucas to work fifteen-hour days. When he did arrive home, he always found Annie waiting for him and his dinner warming in the oven. He didn't know how he'd managed all those months without her. Late hours meant he saw less of Heather and Hollie, but that didn't appear to trouble his daughters nearly as much as it did him.

Knowing that Annie was waiting at home made the long days tolerable. In the six weeks since their wedding, he'd come to rely on seeing her, spending time with her, no matter how brief, and sleeping with her in his arms every night. This marriage provided benefits he hadn't fully considered when he'd proposed.

Sometimes he worried that he might be too demanding physically, not that Annie complained. Often, in fact, she was the one who came to him and lovingly whispered her desire in his ear. She was his wife, she said, and being married meant they could make love whenever they wanted....

The next morning Cal Patterson put in a call to Lucas, but it took Lucas until late in the afternoon to get back to him. Fortunately it wasn't an emergency. One of his horses suffered from an eye ailment known as ophthalmia or moon blindness. Unusual though the ailment was, Lucas had seen it before. When the moon was full, the horse's eyes clouded and filmed over. This problem lasted the length of the full moon and then mysteriously disappeared.

"How about a cup of coffee?" Cal suggested after Lucas had finished with the mare.

"Sounds damn good about now," Lucas agreed, and headed toward the house with Cal.

"I guess you're pleased about Annie," Cal said casually.

Lucas found the statement odd.

"I'll say one thing—it sure didn't take you two long," Cal joked, elbowing Lucas in the ribs.

"What the hell are you talking about?" As far as Lucas was concerned, Cal must've gone too long without sleep.

"Annie's pregnant—isn't she?" Cal asked. "I overheard Jane talking to her on the phone. When I said something about it, she said I should talk to you."

Annie's pregnant? Lucas stopped in his tracks.

"You didn't mean to keep it a secret, did you?"

Lucas felt as though he'd been sucker-punched. It was all he could do not to reveal his shock. His friend shouldn't be the one giving him this news; his wife should. He was about to become a father, and he couldn't imagine why Annie hadn't told him herself. She must know he'd be pleased. Surely she knew that.

"I hope I wasn't speaking out of turn," Cal said, cutting into his frenzied thoughts.

Lucas shook his head, but it wasn't until he was driving home from the Lonesome Coyote Ranch that the full reality of what Cal had said hit him. Annie was pregnant. For the third time in his life he was going to be a father.

Actually, it shouldn't come as such a shock, considering how often they made love. In retrospect, Lucas realized this explained a lot, like the fact that Annie had been so pale lately. And some nights, she'd fallen asleep before he got home. Perhaps she was waiting for him to say something. The truth was, he enjoyed gently waking her, having her open her arms to him, warm and sleepy. Warm and loving.

With that realization came another. Lucas's hands gripped the steering wheel with such intensity his fingers grew white. He'd really done it now. What he thought was impossible had happened.

He'd gone and fallen in love with Annie.

Twenty-One

Sunday morning, Nessa sat through the entire church service in a daze. On past occasions she'd found the music stirring and the minister's message inspiring. She'd always come away feeling renewed and refreshed.

Not this morning. It was all she could do to smile and exchange pleasantries with friends. All she could do to pretend her heart wasn't breaking. Her life, which had been perfectly satisfactory until the day she met Gordon, now felt empty. Flat. Lonely. And more empty lonely years stretched ahead.

At the end of the service Wade stood in the vestibule and shook her hand as she left the church. As if he'd been able to read her thoughts, his gaze held hers a moment longer than necessary. "It's good to see you, Nessa," he said.

"It's good to be here." She did her best to offer him a dazzling smile. And failed. Her lips quivered and she quickly looked away. If not for the crowd, Nessa was certain Wade would have plied her with questions. She wasn't sure what she would have told him.

As she walked toward the parking lot, she thought she heard someone call her name, but she didn't stop.

She didn't want to encourage friendly conversation. Not today. All that mattered was returning to the safe cocoon of her home.

"Nessa!" Dovie's call was louder and more insistent this time.

Given no option, Nessa turned and waved.

"Wait up!" Dovie pressed her hand over her heart when she reached Nessa. "My goodness," she said breathlessly, "I don't know when I've seen anyone leave a church faster."

"Where's Frank?" Nessa asked, wanting to distract her sister-in-law. She dearly loved Dovie, but the woman did tend to meddle.

"Talking to Grady and the Patterson brothers," Dovie answered, studying Nessa until she grew uncomfortable with the scrutiny. "Okay, what's wrong?"

Nessa pretended surprise. "Wrong? Why, nothing."

"Okay," Dovie said again, frowning. "When was the last time you spoke to Gordon?"

The question hurt. Nessa didn't want to think about Gordon, and yet she was constantly besieged by thoughts of him. He'd been upset with her for giving in to Sylvia's demands. At the same time, he'd chosen not to tell her about his own son's opposition to their marriage. In thinking it over, she was convinced Gordon's investigation of her finances had been instigated by his son. He'd also made some vague remark about her not being one to talk, which she hadn't understood at the time.

"Gordon?" She repeated his name as if he was of little importance in her life. "Oh, we spoke last week sometime."

Dovie's expression told Nessa her sister-in-law wasn't so easily fooled. "How did he take the news about delaying the wedding?"

Nessa sometimes forgot what a big mouth her daughter had. Apparently Dovie knew everything.

"He...he said..." She paused for a moment to regain her composure. "He thinks what I really want is to call the whole thing off."

"Do you?"

"I... His son doesn't approve of me, either."

"You didn't answer my question," Dovie said.

"Call it off? Of course not, but...but there are complications if I marry Gordon. We have different backgrounds and live in different places, and we each have opinionated children who seem to think we don't—"

"Your children are more than opinionated," Dovie cut in. "They want to control your lives. Are you going to allow your family to stand between you and Gordon? To interfere with your happiness?"

Nessa knew her daughter meant well, and she was certain Miles's concern was also for his father's well-being. Nessa had eventually come to the conclusion that her children were afraid of the changes that would occur in their own lives if she married Gordon. Afraid she'd be taken from them to live in another country. Afraid she'd love them less. Because they hadn't met Gordon yet, they were suspicious. Sylvia and Miles had grown up in a world less trusting than the one Nessa knew.

"Are you going to stand for it?" Dovie asked.

Nessa looked away. She didn't want to discuss any of this right now—not with anyone. She felt trapped between her children and the man she loved. "If Gordon and I are meant to be together, it'll happen," she said, trying for a nonchalant shrug.

"Is this the same woman who defied her family and moved to Promise without so much as a word until the deed was done?"

Nessa found the conversation increasingly difficult. It hadn't been hard to buy a home in Promise because she'd known she was making the right decision. Marrying Gordon, though—that raised questions she couldn't answer.

"Maybe you don't love Gordon as much as you thought," Dovie suggested in a sly voice. "Maybe you aren't that interested in marrying him."

But Nessa did love him, did want to marry him. Her heart pounded with the truth of it until she could no longer remain silent. "I do love him, Dovie. I want to be his wife."

"Then tell him."

Dovie made everything sound easy. It wasn't as though Nessa hadn't stood up to her children before, but they'd been so adamant this time, so sure they knew what was best for her. So confident that they were protecting her from herself.

"Gordon is a good man. Are you willing to lose him?"

Nessa had lost so much already. How could she allow the possibility of happiness with Gordon to slip away like this? "You're right!" she cried. "This is *my* life. Sylvia didn't seek my approval when she got married. My boys didn't, either."

"I don't know why Sylvia feels the way she does, but it's her problem," Dovie insisted, "not yours."

Nessa felt as if a weight had been lifted from her heart. Dovie was a voice of reason in circumstances that had seemed hopelessly confusing only minutes earlier.

"Dovie, thank you, thank you so much," Nessa whispered, so grateful she felt close to tears.

Her resolve didn't desert her as she drove home. She walked into her house, set her Bible on the kitchen counter and, without stopping, headed directly for the telephone. If Miles answered, Nessa would demand to talk to Gordon. She wasn't a woman who made demands easily, but she refused to be manipulated anymore.

She was so determined and so prepared to do battle with his son that when Gordon answered on the third ring she was caught unawares. "Gordon?" she said.

"Nessa?"

Taking a deep breath, she spilled out the secrets of her heart. "I love you. I'm sorry Miles doesn't approve of me. I profoundly regret the way my own children have treated you. But I refuse to allow anyone else to make my decisions for me."

Her statement was met with silence, then, "Are you saying you're willing to marry me?"

"Yes." She couldn't be any more direct than that.

"When?" He didn't sound as if he entirely believed her.

"Today. Tomorrow. Next week. Whenever you want."

"I want you with me right now."

Nessa closed her eyes at the burst of joy that flowed through her.

"I've been miserable without you," he confessed.

"Me, too," she told him, and then some of her defiance revived itself. "I love my children, but this is *my* life."

"I told Miles the same thing, but I didn't hear from you and I was sure you'd changed your mind."

They talked for nearly an hour, and when they hung up, Nessa felt wonderful. Her heart was full, too full to keep such joy inside. Too full to stay home on a bright and beautiful August afternoon.

When she arrived at Dovie's house, Nessa was amused by her sister-in-law's startled look.

"Come in," Dovie said, opening the screen door.

Nessa shook her head. "I only came by for a minute," she told her, and Dovie stepped onto the porch. "Just wanted to see if you'd like to go shopping with me," Nessa explained.

"Shopping?"

Nessa's grin stretched wide. "It seems I'm in need of a wedding dress."

Dovie gave a holler and threw her arms around Nessa, hugging her fiercely. "Tell me what happened."

"I phoned Gordon. Wonder of wonders, he loves me and still wants us to get married. He's making his flight arrangements this very minute and he's doing everything he can to get here this week."

"This week!"

"He isn't giving me a chance to change my mind." As if she would. Nessa was a woman on a mission. She was determined to marry Gordon Pawling and spend the rest of her life loving him. Despite what her children thought. Despite Miles. Despite private investigators. Despite everything.

"When's the wedding?"

"Soon," Nessa replied. "Just as soon as we can

find a preacher to marry us. Of course, I'm hoping Wade will agree..."

"I don't think I've ever heard anything so romantic. It's like you're eloping."

"That is kind of what we're doing," Nessa said, and laughed with the sheer amazement of all that had happened in the past couple of hours. "Only we aren't running away from our parents. We're escaping the wrath and disapproval of our children."

"What's all the noise out here?" Frank asked, walking out to the porch.

"Nessa's getting married," Dovie explained, dabbing at her eyes.

"And you're crying?" her husband muttered. "I don't know what it is about you women." He shook his head as though this was beyond his comprehension. "How's a man supposed to know what to do? You cry when you're happy. You cry when you're sad. Haven't I told you before now that tears don't solve a thing?"

Laughing and weeping at the same time, Nessa and Dovie hugged each other again.

"What'd I say to get this kind of reaction?" Frank asked of no one in particular. Then he turned and headed back into the house.

Lucas had never intended to love Annie. He'd been careful to ensure that it wouldn't happen. He'd done everything he could to make their marriage as advantageous to her as possible. That only seemed fair. All the while, he'd carefully guarded his heart, because this relationship hadn't been about love. It was supposed to be about meeting certain needs, providing certain kinds of satisfaction. Love had nothing to do with it.

Refusing to love her had been a calculated decision. In fairness to Annie, he'd been honest with her, making sure she understood how he felt.

It wasn't that he *couldn't* love her, but that he'd purposely chosen not to. He was afraid of what might happen if he did. Julia's cancer had left him damaged. Emotionally damaged. In some ways, he knew he'd never get over her death. He couldn't forget his own helplessness and anger in the face of her suffering. In the lonely years that had followed, while he'd struggled as a single father and a widower, he'd vowed he'd never allow himself to be that vulnerable again.

So much for vows. He'd kept all the ones he'd ever made, except those he'd made to himself.

With love came the incredible risk of loss. He'd buried one wife and, God help him, he didn't have the strength to bury another. If anything happened to Annie, he'd be destroyed.

Several days had passed since Lucas had learned that Annie was carrying his child. Still Annie said nothing. Everyone in town seemed to know. Glen Patterson and Frank Hennessey had both congratulated him. Still Annie kept this secret to herself while Lucas struggled to deal with emotions that confused and frustrated him.

Lucas found himself watching Annie, waiting for her to enlighten him with the news. He didn't know what prompted her silence, couldn't begin to guess at her reasons. The longer she delayed, the more confused he became, and with his confusion came a slow-burning resentment.

At night, when Annie turned off the light, he

waited, wondered, only to be disappointed again, only to face the frustration of her silence. Perhaps she didn't trust him, and with that lack of trust, his desire for her decreased. But if Annie noticed, she said nothing, which annoyed him even more.

Monday night, following a meeting with the Cattlemen's Association, Lucas got home late. He expected Annie to be asleep, wanted her to be. When he drove toward the house and saw light shining from the kitchen, he was grateful she'd left it on for him. Then Annie's face appeared in the window; she must have heard the sound of his truck and come to check.

Despite all his resolutions, he felt a surge of gladness that she'd waited up for him. He tried not to show any of his contradictory feelings when he walked into the house.

"How'd the meeting go?" she asked, tilting her head back to smile at him. She touched her palm to his cheek so lovingly he was forced to look away.

"Fine."

"Did you eat?"

"No." There hadn't been time, so he'd grabbed a doughnut and a cup of coffee when he'd stopped for gas. Now the sugar-coated doughnut sat like a lump of lard in the pit of his stomach.

"I was afraid of that," Annie said. "There's a plate for you in the oven."

A chill went through Lucas as the war continued to rage inside him. He couldn't allow her thoughtfulness to influence him, couldn't let her know his feelings, couldn't let her know he'd been told about the baby.

Humming softly to herself, Annie brought his dinner to the table, then fussed about the kitchen while he ate. Lucas watched her, wondering, as always, if she'd tell him.

"How were the girls tonight?" he asked casually. School had started that week.

"Wonderful." She glanced up and smiled. "But they missed seeing you."

"They didn't give you any trouble about going to bed, did they?"

"None whatsoever. Heather wrote you a note and Hollie drew you a picture." She retrieved both treasures and handed them to Lucas.

He read the short note and studied Hollie's picture of a horse, and despite his mood, couldn't help grinning. He loved his daughters with everything in him, and he would love this new child growing inside Annie, too.

"Heather's note says she got an A on her spelling test." He was proud of his oldest daughter, who'd had some trouble with reading and the rules of written English.

"I went through the spelling list with her last night," Annie said as she cut him a slice of Dovie's apple pie. "She was really proud of that A."

Then it occurred to him—a reason for Annie's secrecy. Perhaps she wanted out of the relationship. He shook his head, chasing the thought away. It made no sense; she loved Heather and Hollie, and she wasn't the type of woman who'd abandon him and the girls. Especially after what her first husband had done to her.

When he'd finished his dinner, Lucas carried his plates to the sink.

"I'm tired," she murmured. "Will you be up much longer?"

"Go on to bed," he said. "I'll join you shortly."

She hesitated, as if she preferred they retire at the same time.

"I'll be there in half an hour or so."

Annie nodded.

That didn't sound like a woman planning to walk out of his life, Lucas reasoned, and the tightness in his chest began to ease.

When Annie had disappeared into the bedroom, Lucas sorted through the mail and tried to read the evening paper.

Dammit, what was he going to do? He was in love with her, and his confused emotions were tearing him apart. He was so frightened—he *couldn't* lose Annie, couldn't let her go.

Annie, who took his emotionally hungry daughters and loved them unconditionally. Loved them in a way that allowed them to remember their mother without trying to replace her. Annie, who'd walked straight into his stubborn heart, who'd effortlessly given him back his life.

He should have been more careful. Should have realized what was happening and put an end to it while he still could. Should never have allowed himself to slip this far.

Now that he was in love with her, he didn't know what he was going to do.

Lucas assumed Annie would be asleep by the time he slipped beneath the covers. As soon as he was in bed, she rolled over and tucked her head against his shoulder.

"There's something I've been meaning to tell you," she said. "It seems... I know it's unexpected and all, but it...it looks like I'm pregnant."

Now that she'd actually told him, he no longer knew how to react.

He opened his mouth to tell her how glad he was, but nothing came out. Nothing. Instead, he experienced a sense of panic, of dread and then of bitter resignation, as if he were going down for the third time and had no choice but to accept the inevitable.

"I had an appointment at the health clinic this afternoon," she was saying, "and it's official. I suspected earlier, but wasn't sure enough to say anything."

Lucas felt as though his jaw had locked, leaving him unable to respond.

"Lucas, did you hear what I said?"

His fears were multiple, and intensifying every minute. "I heard."

"Isn't there anything you want to say?"

He couldn't think, couldn't reason. "Jane knew. Cal, Glen and Frank, too. You might have told me sooner."

"But...I wasn't sure."

"Sure enough to tell Jane, though—and not me." Lucas drew apart from Annie and onto his side.

He hadn't intended to push her away, but that was what happened.

Grady Weston had learned early in life that if he had a question, the best way to get an answer was to go right to the source. His wife and his sister could speculate all they wanted about Val Langley's presence in Promise, but not Grady. He intended to ask Ms. Big City Attorney herself.

He waited until after dinner, then headed for Nell and Travis's ranch, ten miles east of his own spread.

For some reason, this New Yorker was acting on Richard's behalf. Of that Grady was convinced. His crafty manipulative brother was trying to sneak back into their lives.

He'd suspected something was up when Richard wrote him a letter, after three years of silence. Richard wanting his forgiveness—now that was a laugh. Grady was aware that Savannah had routinely sent Richard news of her family, and money for his birthday and Christmas. But as far as Grady was concerned, Richard could rot in that prison cell. It was what he deserved.

Grady had phoned ahead of time, so Travis was waiting for him. The two men exchanged hearty handshakes. "Nell's giving the twins a bath and getting them down for the night."

"Is Val around?" Grady asked as they walked across the yard toward the house.

"Inside. I told her you were coming."

"Thanks."

Travis stopped just before entering the house. "Would you prefer to talk to Val alone?"

Grady shook his head. "Not particularly."

Travis grinned. "Be careful, she's a lawyer."

"What's that supposed to mean?"

Travis looked as if he was about to explain, then changed his mind. "You'll find out soon enough."

Val sat on the living-room sofa with her long shapely legs crossed, drinking coffee out of a mug. She glanced up when Travis and Grady came into the room. "You must be Grady Weston. I understand you had a few questions you wanted to ask me," she said.

"I do." Grady removed his hat and sat on the edge of a chair, leaning forward. "I'll get straight to the point. I understand you're working on an appeal for my brother.''

''That's correct.''

''On what grounds?''

''There are a number of factors I've considered but—''

''I'd appreciate it if you didn't use a lot of legal jargon.''

Val took five minutes to explain that Richard had failed to receive the proper legal representation at the time of his arrest. According to police documents, Richard had been grouped with the other men involved, and she felt he'd been denied his rights.

Grady listened politely and nodded a couple of times. ''In other words, you're going after technicalities because you have a weak case.''

''There are valid grounds for an appeal, Mr. Weston.''

But her body language told Grady he was right. She didn't hold out much hope.

''Why are you doing this?'' Grady asked.

Her spine stiffened. ''I believe in justice.''

Grady caught Travis's look of amusement, but pretended not to notice. ''Is my brother paying you?''

''No,'' Val admitted with some reluctance.

''Richard couldn't afford your fees,'' Travis inserted.

Val shifted her weight and uncrossed her legs. ''Actually, I've been working on his case without compensation.''

''Why?'' Grady suspected the reason. Somehow Richard had been able to charm and cajole this sophisticated attorney into accepting his innocence.

He'd seen it happen before—had, in fact, fallen for Richard's clever lies himself.

"I believe in Richard," she answered just as bluntly.

"I wouldn't if I were you," Grady advised. "My brother isn't a man to be trusted."

"I'm fairly confident I can handle your brother, Mr. Weston." Val's smug expression told him she wasn't going to consider a word he said.

Well, if that was the case, so be it. Travis's ex-wife would learn the same way everyone else did exactly what kind of man his brother was.

"Richard Weston's the sole reason you decided to visit Promise, isn't he?" Travis asked.

"Did you think I came to Promise because of *you?*" Val widened her eyes, gazing at Travis with a look of pity.

"No." Travis's tone was emotionless. "I knew better."

"Richard did ask me to do this," she said, surprising Grady. "He loves his family and wanted me to do what I could to build a bridge between him and his brother and sister."

Unable to hold back his amusement, Grady snickered loudly. The only time Richard ever loved his family was when he needed something.

"What does he want now?" he asked.

"What I already told you." Val sighed as if she regretted the path their conversation had taken. "And you must know, he asked me to find out how the community feels about him."

"Why should he care?" Grady shook his head. None of this made sense to him, but he knew Richard had a reason, a reason he wasn't going to like.

"I think I can answer that," Travis said. "This has to do with the parole hearing, doesn't it?" Travis's question was directed at Val. "Because the crimes Richard committed were against illegal aliens who are no longer in this country and therefore can't testify, you're hoping to inundate the judge with testimonies of what a fine upstanding citizen Richard Weston is."

One glance at the attorney told Grady that was indeed the case. "You're joking, right?"

"It would be of considerable value if you were to write a letter on your brother's behalf," Val said, batting her baby blues in his direction.

Grady was immune. He found it hard to believe Richard would dare to even ask. "You can forget that, and my guess is there isn't a man or woman in this town who'd be willing to help him."

"Because of your own insecurities, Mr. Weston." She heaved a deep sigh. "Richard told me how jealous you were of him while you were all growing up, how you resented his popularity and good looks. You stole his inheritance, didn't you, for your own selfish reasons? Yet Richard's willing to overlook that, and in exchange all he wants is a helping hand."

"I'll help him, all right," Grady said from between clenched teeth. Richard could lie as much as he wanted; Grady knew the truth. And so did everyone else in Promise.

"Richard wanted you to check out Bitter End, too," Travis said, cutting in.

"Yes…" Again Val revealed her reluctance to discuss the purpose of her visit. "He's worried about what's happened to the ghost town."

"I'll just bet he is." Grady made no effort to conceal his sarcasm.

"You underestimate your brother, Mr. Weston," Val said. "Richard wants to protect the town."

"Does he now." It was difficult to keep a straight face, but Grady managed. This poor woman had lost all sense of the truth. Richard had completely taken her in. The word "bamboozled" came to mind.

"I don't think this conversation is going anywhere," Val murmured, setting down her coffee cup. Without another word, she strode from the house.

After she'd left, Travis walked Grady back outside. "What do you think?" he asked.

"He's using her."

Travis nodded. "That much is obvious."

"Do you understand this business about Bitter End?"

"No," Travis admitted. "Nell and I paid a visit there recently. We both feel there's something we're missing."

"I can tell you right now, if Richard's interested in the ghost town, there's a reason."

"But what could it be?"

"I wonder if we'll ever know," Grady said with a shrug. "Do you think he might've left behind something of value?" That was all Grady could think of. "I know he didn't have any money."

"Then what?"

"Hell if I know." Grady studied Travis. "You're the one who unraveled the mystery. This should be child's play for you."

Travis chuckled. "I'll give it some thought."

"Do that."

"You know," Travis said, shaking his head, "I find it hard to believe I was ever married to Val. I almost feel sorry for her now."

Grady did, too, knowing that Val Langley was in line for a rude awakening. Anyone who'd ever befriended Richard ended up regretting it sooner or later. Usually sooner...

Twenty-Two

Jeannie hadn't seen Adam since their disagreement at the movies. In retrospect she recognized that the argument had been about much more than her conversation with Val Langley.

What she'd been telling Adam was that she admired the woman for her suave sophistication, her intellect and cosmopolitan attitude. Val Langley was everything *she* wasn't. Frustrated, Jeannie thought of herself as simple and homespun—while Val was anything but. Like fried chicken versus coq au vin. Bowling versus nightclubbing.

When Jeannie walked down the street, she longed to have men look at her the way they did Val, who wore double-breasted business suits with tight short skirts. Or sleek silk pantsuits. As a first-grade teacher, Jeannie often chose long loose dresses for work, which made getting down on the floor with the children a lot easier.

The thing was, Jeannie got the feeling that Adam wasn't impressed by Val, which seemed to suggest, somehow, that he doubted Jeannie's judgment and disapproved of her aspirations.

As for Richard Weston—okay, she had to admit Adam had a point there. Jeannie had since learned more about Weston and the crimes that had landed him in prison. She hadn't meant to defend him, and wouldn't have if Adam's attitude hadn't irritated her so much.

The rest of the afternoon had been even worse. She decided her initial instincts were right; there was no future in this relationship.

Adam had apparently reached the same conclusion. He'd taken her home as soon as the movie ended. Then, standing back, his fingertips tucked into his belt, he'd told her goodbye. He hadn't said another word, simply turned and walked away.

Her initial reaction was a mixture of fury and self-righteousness. Adam was high-handed, arrogant, just plain wrong.

But in the week since their movie date, she'd had plenty of time for serious thinking, and she'd begun to revise her opinions. She'd come to see that her reactions resulted from hurt pride that he'd questioned her judgment, from resentment at his giving her orders and from a misplaced dissatisfaction with her life.

Her resentment had quickly dissolved and she'd learned the truth about Richard, the truth about Val and, most importantly, the truth about herself. Her life, homespun though it might be, *was* right for her.

To fill in the gap Adam had left, Jeannie was doing more reading than ever. Exploring Bitter End had piqued her interest in the period after the Civil War. Late Thursday afternoon, she stopped by Tumbleweed Books to pick up a new volume on Western history that Annie had ordered for her.

She stepped out of the bookstore and nearly collided with Adam as he was leaving his father's western-wear shop. Her breath caught in her throat at the unexpectedness of their meeting. She thought at first that he meant to ignore her, then realized he was as flustered as she was.

She, for one, could be civil about this. "Hello, Adam."

"Jeannie." He touched the brim of his hat.

"How are you?" they asked simultaneously.

Jeannie didn't know how to answer him. She felt torn—wanting to resume their relationship but uncertain about the wisdom of doing so. After the things he'd said, the things he'd suggested, their continual misunderstandings, she should just walk on.

Instead, she stayed.

He stayed, too.

Before either of them had the opportunity to say anything more, Adam's father came out of the store and confronted them both.

"You two going to stare at each other like a pair of lost puppies or you going to settle this squabble?"

"Dad..." Adam warned, glaring at his father.

Max ignored his son and turned to Jeannie. "You know what Adam's problem is, don't you? That boy's been besotted from the minute he first laid eyes on you. I swear, I've never seen anything like it. His mother and I've been after him to find a good woman, but up until now he's—"

"Dad, stay out of this!" Adam sounded angry now.

"I'd be happy to," Max said in exasperation, "if I felt you were going to clear up whatever's wrong between you and Jeannie." Then, turning to Jeannie again, he added, "You *do* want to set things straight, don't you?"

Adam seemed to be interested in her response, too.

"I..." She'd almost managed to convince herself she didn't want Adam back in her life. It seemed the most sensible course, a way of avoiding heartache. And yet...

"That answers that," Adam muttered, and started to move away.

"I want to resolve this!" Jeannie cried urgently. "I really do."

Adam hesitated.

Max evidently considered himself vindicated and cast his son a glance that seemed to suggest Adam listen to his advice more often. "Perhaps you two should go have a cup of coffee," he suggested. "Talk everything out. Share an order of nachos at the Mexican Lindo."

"Jeannie?" Adam looked to her.

"With jalapeños on the side, okay?"

He agreed with a quick grin and a sexy lift of his eyebrows.

Max Jordan was obviously pleased with himself. He ushered them toward the Mexican Lindo, one hand on Adam's back, the other on hers. "Take your time," he urged. "No need to rush. Talk everything out. You two belong together. Margaret thinks so, and she's always right about these things."

As soon as they were out of earshot, Adam grimaced and said, "You'll have to forgive my father."

"Actually, I was planning to thank him."

Adam's eyes narrowed slightly, but he didn't speak again until they entered the restaurant. The owner and his wife sat at a table going over some paperwork.

Adam raised his hand in greeting. "Carlos, Aracelli."

"What can I get for you, amigo?"

"Nachos, with jalapeños on the side, and iced tea."

Carlos slipped out of the booth and headed for the kitchen.

Jeannie was grateful they were the only customers, but at the same time she felt oddly self-conscious. She and Adam being alone established an immediate mood of intimacy.

"Where would you like to start?" Adam asked after their drinks had been served.

Jeannie knew how she *thought* the conversation should go. "I'd say an apology is in order."

"All right," Adam said, his face tightening. "I apologize. I was overbearing and opinionated and should never have said the things I did."

Jeannie's mouth fell open. "You're apologizing to me?"

"Isn't that what you wanted?"

"Yes...no. I was about to tell you how sorry *I* was."

"You?"

She nodded. "Oh, Adam, I was so foolish. I was defending someone I didn't even know be-cause...because..."

"Because I was so high-handed," he supplied on a rueful note. "I put you in a position where you were forced to defend Richard Weston."

"I wasn't defending Richard as much as Val Lang-ley," Jeannie admitted, remembering their conversation. "And I was wrong, so wrong. I knew it last week, but I assumed you'd washed your hands of me."

"I figured you were just as glad to be rid of me."

That was exactly what she'd tried to tell herself, exactly what she'd wanted to believe. But it wasn't true. She'd missed him, missed his friend-ship...missed his kisses.

Their order arrived and Jeannie reached for a na-cho, dripping with melted cheese. The chip was half-way between the plate and her mouth when Adam said, "What my dad said is true."

"You're besotted with me?" Jeannie said with a delighted smile. She loved the old-fashioned words, loved the way they sounded and the way they made her feel. Most of all, she was thrilled and reassured because of what this told her—that Adam cared as much as she did.

"I'm crazy about you, Jeannie. It's no good to pre-tend otherwise. You don't have to say anything, but I wanted you to know I love you."

"But, Adam, don't you see?" she whispered. "I love you, too, but I've been so afraid I'd ruined ev-erything. I was afraid you wouldn't want anything more to do with me. Um, I should tell you I...have a bit of a stubborn steak."

Adam hooted with laughter. "I hadn't noticed."

"Hey, you have your share of faults, too, Mister Sheriff."

He raised both hands. "Guilty."

"We're going to have to put a lot of time and effort into this relationship if it's going to work," she said seriously. The practical side of her was showing, but she didn't think Adam minded.

"I'm willing," he told her with a slow lazy grin that stirred feeling deep inside her.

"I am, too." He wasn't perfect, but then neither was she. And he loved her just the way she was.

The door to the restaurant opened and Travis Grant entered. "They're in here." He tossed the words over his shoulder. Grady Weston and Val Langley followed close behind him.

"You looking for me?" Adam asked in crisp businesslike tones. He grabbed his hat. "Trouble?"

"Actually, we need to talk to both of you," Grady said, sliding into the booth next to Adam.

Val claimed the seat beside Jeannie, and Travis pulled up a chair. Adam indicated that they should all help themselves to nachos. Grady and Travis had no qualms, but Val regarded the pile of cheese-coated chips with distaste.

"You had a question?" Adam asked.

"More a difference of opinion," Val said, folding her arms as though to put distance between herself and the others.

"Tell me the story of One-Eyed Jack again, would you?" Travis asked Jeannie.

"I've already told you everything I know," Jeannie said. "He lost his eye in the Civil War and later became the leader of a band of renegade soldiers who rode across Texas, wreaking havoc wherever they went."

"But you said he robbed a Union paymaster, right?"

"As I recall. Left the poor guy for dead."

"Whatever happened to the gold coins?"

"You're asking me?"

"So you don't know if that gold was ever recovered or not?"

Jeannie shrugged. "No, I don't have any idea."

"I do," Travis said. "I have a very good idea what happened to it."

It was useless to try to work, and Lucas knew it. Saturday afternoon, he returned to his office, pulled down the shades and closed the door. He sat in the semidark room trying to sort through his thoughts.

When Annie told him about the baby, Lucas had reacted with anger. He'd hurt her, but she'd hurt him, too. He'd felt confused and betrayed. And he'd felt like a fool, a laughingstock. It seemed everyone in town knew his wife was pregnant before he did. Well, maybe that was an exaggeration, but he felt he should have been the first to know.

That morning, he'd awakened to the sound of Annie vomiting. He'd wiped her face with a warm washcloth, then brought her a glass of water and two soda crackers, saying Julia had found those helpful. She'd nodded and thanked him.

Heather and Hollie had guessed something was wrong, but didn't ask questions. Annie had already left for the bookstore accompanied by the girls, who were helping her with Story Time. Lucas headed for his office. But he hadn't been worth a damn all day, and he knew he wouldn't be until he'd settled this with Annie. Abruptly he got up and started out.

Lucas arrived at the store, sincerely hoping Gina was there that afternoon; he wanted to talk to Annie without the interruption of customers.

The bell above the door jangled when he entered Tumbleweed Books. His wife glanced up—and froze when she saw him. She recovered quickly, turning her gaze away.

"Is Gina here?" he asked, knowing it was a stupid question. Clearly she wasn't, much to his disappointment. "Where are the kids?"

"Gina isn't working today," Annie explained. "She's helping her mom with a big flower order. And the girls went out for ice cream with Caroline and her two.''

He took a couple of steps farther into the store. "Can we talk?''

She nodded, but still refused to look at him.

"I'm sorry, Annie.''

"For what?'' she asked with a thin smile.

"For everything. Mainly for the way I acted when you told me about the baby.''

"I was the one who wanted a child,'' she reminded him. "It was my stipulation for the marriage, not yours. There's no reason for you to be happy that I'm pregnant.''

"But I am! I'm thrilled.''

The bell went as a customer entered the store. Lucas turned around and groaned at the sight of Louise Powell. The town's biggest gossip—just his luck. The older woman glared at him, defying him to challenge her right to be in the store.

"Hello, Annie,'' Louise said. "Lucas,'' she added with less enthusiasm.

"Louise.'' Lucas nodded in her direction.

"The book you ordered should be in on Monday afternoon,'' Annie told her.

"But Louise doesn't have time to linger, do you, Louise?'' Lucas muttered.

"As a matter of fact—''

"As a matter of fact,'' Lucas interjected, "Annie's about to close the store.''

"I am?''

"You are,'' Lucas returned sweetly.

"She is?'' Louise asked.

Lucas nodded. "I apologize for the inconvenience. I really am sorry, but I need to talk to my wife.''

Louise's eyes lit up. "Oh, you should, you should, and don't either of you mind me while I browse around the store." Her spectacles slid down her nose as she smiled benevolently at Lucas and Annie.

"Unfortunately this is a private conversation." Lucas walked over to the door and held it open for her.

Louise glanced from Annie to Lucas apparently trying to gauge how much of a fuss she should make about being kicked out of the bookstore, not once but twice.

"I'm sorry, Louise," Annie told her customer, "but my husband's right. We do need to talk."

The woman seemed to gather her composure. "Well, I've never been treated so rudely in all my life." Her nose was aimed at the ceiling and she sailed through the door.

"Louise," Annie called out to her in a stage whisper.

Louise paused, her back to Annie.

"I'm pregnant."

"You are?" Louise whirled around. "Does anyone else know?"

"Jane Patterson," Annie told her.

"Cal and Glen," Lucas added. "Frank and Dovie Hennessey."

"No one else?"

Annie grinned conspiratorially. "Not yet."

"Congratulations," Louise said, and was gone so fast she was practically a blur. As soon as she'd left, Lucas turned the sign in the window to Closed and latched the door.

Now that they weren't likely to be interrupted, he found himself at a loss as to where he should start.

"I didn't think I'd get pregnant this soon," Annie said, easing the way for him.

"I didn't, either, but that doesn't matter. I'm happy about it."

Her gentle smile touched him. "It wasn't part of our agreement that I love you," he said, "but I—"

"I know." She cut him off. "It doesn't matter, really it doesn't. I've accepted that, but I didn't stop to think—didn't stop to consider the baby. I do hope you'll love our child."

It never occurred to Lucas that he wouldn't. "I already do, the same way I love his or her mother."

Annie went still, as if she wasn't sure she'd heard him correctly. "Are you saying you love *me?*"

"That's exactly what I'm saying. That's what I came here to tell you." The distance between them dissolved as she raced toward him. Lucas met her more than halfway, hauling her into his embrace, finding her mouth with his own and kissing her with an intensity that left her in no doubt of his feelings.

"We need to call Pastor McMillen," he whispered, holding Annie against him.

"Wade? But why?"

"I want us to get married."

"We are married."

Lucas heard the smile in her voice and felt like laughing himself. "I want us to repeat our vows. Only this time I'm not going to delete any words. I love you, Annie, heart and soul."

"Oh, Lucas, I love you, too."

He continued to hold her, his arms wrapped about her waist. "For the life of me, I can't imagine why you should, but I'm grateful, so very grateful that you do."

"I can give you a hundred reasons why I love you," she insisted, "but, most important, you're the father of my children."

Children. Annie included Heather and Hollie as her own. The motherless little girl had grown up to become the mother of two lonely children. Had brought light and life back to a hurt, struggling family. He knew that Heather and Hollie were the children of Annie's heart, and she'd love them and guide them as she would the child who grew within her body.

A knock at the glass door interrupted them, and Lucas turned to find both his daughters with their faces pressed against the window. Caroline stood behind them, pointing, then waved when she caught his eye. She headed off, across the street.

"Hi, Dad," Heather said when he unlatched the door. "What are you doing here?"

"Visiting Annie."

"You and Annie were kissing again," Hollie said.

"Yup." Lucas brought his daughters into his embrace. "Annie and I have some news for you."

"I bet you're gonna have a baby," Heather said.

"When did you get so smart?" Lucas asked her.

"Are you really?" Hollie's eyes lit with excitement. "This time I want a brother, okay?"

The bell jangled again and Louise Powell stuck her head inside. "Are you open for business or not?" she demanded.

"Open," Lucas answered for Annie.

"You're leaving?" Annie asked him.

He loved the disappointment he heard in his wife's voice. "Sorry, but I've got to see a man about a wedding." Feeling almost light-headed with relief, Lucas hurried out the door with Heather and Hollie in tow.

He whistled "The Wedding March" all the way to the parsonage.

Gordon Pawling had never packed his suitcase faster. He was going to marry Nessa Boyd, and he wasn't about to let his son or her daughter stand in the way.

Unfortunately he'd had to delay his flight until Saturday morning. His instinct had been to grab the first available plane out of Toronto, but he'd had several obligations to meet first. He was not a man who shirked his commitments, ever. Besides, he reminded himself, he had the rest of his life to spend with Nessa.

After booking his ticket for Texas, he phoned Miles. "Are you sitting down?" he asked his son.

"Why?" That reserved tone was back, as if Miles had already guessed he wasn't going to like what he heard.

"I'm getting married."

Gordon had fully expected Miles to rant and rage. Instead, his announcement was greeted with silence and then a calm "I see."

"I'm leaving on Saturday morning for Texas."

"When's the wedding?" How civil he sounded, how cordial.

"As soon as I can arrange it," Gordon answered.

"I'd like to fly down with you."

Gordon debated the merits of that idea. His son's intentions were questionable at best, but refusing could complicate an already rocky relationship. "All right," Gordon agreed. "I'll arrange for a second ticket."

The flight proved to be rather pleasant. Gordon had

half expected Miles to spend the time haranguing him with questions and accusations. But it would have done nothing to dissuade him, and apparently his son had accepted the inevitable.

Nessa was at the gate waiting for him when he stepped out of the jetway in San Antonio. The instant he caught sight of her, he experienced a surge of rightness, of certainty, that left him almost weak with relief. They hurried into each other's arms.

"You must be Miles," Nessa said to his son when they'd finished hugging.

Judging by the look on his face, Miles hadn't expected a woman as lovely and charming as Nessa. Heaven only knew what type of woman his son *had* expected.

"I have a bit of news myself," Nessa told him as they walked through the crowded airport toward the baggage claim area. "Sylvia's arrived."

"Sylvia is Nessa's daughter," Gordon explained to his son.

"She isn't any more thrilled about this marriage than you are," Nessa said, teasing Miles.

"There goes the elopement," Gordon joked. He wrapped his arm around Nessa's waist. It felt so damn good to be with her. He tightened his hold, signaling to Miles that he wouldn't allow him or anyone else to interfere with their plans.

As predicted, Nessa's daughter was waiting at her mother's house in Promise. She whirled around when the door opened, as if she'd been pacing the living room.

"We're back," Nessa said cheerfully. Taking Gordon's hand and clasping it firmly in her own, she looked directly at Sylvia. "This is Gordon Pawling. Gordon, this is my daughter, Sylvia Munson."

"And who are you?" Sylvia asked, pointing at Miles.

"Sylvia, I won't tolerate rudeness," Nessa warned.

"Miles," his son answered. "Miles Pawling."

"My son," Gordon added.

Sylvia ignored Gordon and crossed her arms defiantly. "I won't stand for it."

Unfortunately, Gordon thought, the poor girl had no choice in the matter, since he and Nessa weren't changing their minds.

"I'm no keener on this marriage than you are," Miles said.

"All your father's interested in is my mother's money."

"Sylvia!" Nessa cried, embarrassed and outraged. "How dare you say such a thing. Either you apologize or I'm afraid I'm going to have to ask you to leave my home."

Sylvia seemed ready to burst into tears.

"I'll have you know my father is considerably wealthier than your mother. If anyone's interested in marrying for money, it's your mother."

"That's insulting!" Sylvia cried, her hands on her hips. "Give me one good reason why there was a private detective prying into my mother's financial records."

"You made inquiries of your own, didn't you?" Miles accused Nessa's daughter. "But it didn't do you any good, did it?"

"Oh, dear," Nessa murmured, embarrassed beyond belief. She could only imagine what Sylvia had done. And, she thought with a flash of insight, that explained Gordon's remark during that terrible phone call—about her having no room to talk.

"Would you two kindly stop sniping at each other?" Gordon had to yell to be heard above their arguing. Nessa was evidently upset and he'd had enough of this nonsense from Sylvia and Miles.

The doorbell rang, diverting everyone's attention. The air was thick with hostility as Dovie walked in, with a man who was obviously her husband. Frank Hennessey, the former sheriff. Dovie glanced from Nessa to Gordon to Sylvia.

"Thank heavens you're here." Sylvia threw up her hands. "Please talk some sense into my mother, would you?"

Gordon caught Dovie and Nessa exchanging a look. "I already did," Dovie said.

Sylvia wore a puzzled frown.

"I advised her to marry Gordon," Dovie went on.

"Aunt Dovie!" Sylvia wept, "how *could* you?"

"How could I?" Dovie repeated. "They're in love."

"I don't like this, either," Miles interjected.

"You'll get used to it," Dovie told him. "Just the way Sylvia and her brothers will."

"You mean to say there are two more like her?" Miles muttered with ill-concealed distaste.

"You're all about to become one big happy family." This came from Frank Hennessey.

"You always claimed you didn't want to be an only child," Gordon reminded his son, with a light shrug.

"It's a little late, don't you think?" Miles shot back.

"It's not too late," Gordon said, smiling in Nessa's direction. "Not too late at all."

It seemed everyone in the room had an opinion— and they all chose to express them at once. Gordon found it impossible to listen anymore. He took Nessa by the hand and the two of them escaped into the kitchen and closed the door. Apparently no one noticed them leaving.

"It's a miracle you're willing to marry me," he whispered, urging her into his arms.

She hugged him close, and Gordon experienced the full wonder of her love.

The doorbell rang a second time. "Let someone else answer that," he said as his lips met hers.

They were deeply involved in the kiss when the kitchen door creaked open and Frank Hennessey entered the room. The arguing continued, voices growing increasingly louder.

"It's Pastor McMillen," Frank said. He extended his hand to Gordon. "I'm Frank Hennessey."

"Gordon Pawling. Good to meet you."

"Yeah, you too. Want me to ask Wade to come back at a more convenient time?" Frank asked.

"Send him in," Nessa said, glancing at Gordon for approval.

"By all means, send him in."

The door opened again and Miles stuck his head into the kitchen. He began to say something, but Gordon cut him off. "Just remember that woman you're arguing with is about to become your stepsister."

Miles swallowed and closed his eyes. "God help us all."

"He does young man, that He does," Wade said, stepping around Miles.

Nessa introduced Gordon.

"I understand you two are interested in having me perform a wedding ceremony. Is that right?"

"Yes," Nessa answered.

"Most definitely," Gordon concurred. "And right now would be just fine."

Twenty-Three

Travis grinned at the people assembled before him, nachos and drinks forgotten. Ever since Val had sent word of her impending visit, something had been niggling at the back of his mind. Especially when he discovered that Richard was responsible for Val's sudden interest in Promise and the ghost town.

Nell shared his suspicions, but it wasn't until after they'd run into Jeannie and Adam at Bitter End that everything had started to come together. Travis wasn't sure even now if his conclusions were correct, but he certainly had everyone's attention. Either he was about to be labeled a hero a second time—or a world-class fool.

"You know something about that gold?" the sheriff asked, studying him from the other end of the booth.

"As soon as I heard about Richard's interest in the town, I suspected it had to be for one of two reasons. He left something of value in Promise or he found something he doesn't want anyone else to know about. Otherwise he wouldn't give a tinker's damn about Bitter End."

Everyone nodded in agreement, except Val, who gave an unladylike snicker. "I sincerely doubt that."

"So you think Richard found the gold?" Jeannie asked. "What gave you that idea?"

"When you told us the story of One-Eyed Jack, I decided to do a bit of research."

"Hold on," Val, said, raising both hands. "As far as I'm concerned, this is utterly ridiculous."

"If you'd hear me out—"

"You people are so quick to blame Richard Weston for every crime that's ever been committed around here, you're willing to charge him with a robbery that happened 130 years ago?" She rolled her eyes.

"No," Travis said patiently. "I'm just saying I believe Richard found the stash when he was rooting around the town—and that's what he wants now. It's why he sent you to snoop around, Val."

"Oh, for..." she sputtered. "This is *so* ridiculous."

"You don't know Richard," Grady insisted, his voice dark.

"If this wasn't so crazy, it'd be sad," Val said under her breath.

"Is anyone interested in hearing what I found out?"

"I am," Jeannie told him.

"Me, too," Adam said.

"Okay," Travis began. "Do you know if anyone ever learned the name of the man who hanged the preacher's son?"

"The preacher's what?" Val demanded.

"That's what the mystery was all about," Jeannie explained. "At one time Bitter End had a thriving population, and then a group of rowdy drunken men hanged the preacher's son because he defended a saloon girl. When his father returned and found his son murdered, he stood at the end of the street by the church, opened his Bible and swore that God would bring vengeance upon the town.''

''After that,'' Travis said, ''Bitter End was cursed with a variety of plagues.''

Val was laughing at them. ''In Biblical proportions, no doubt. Cecil B. DeMille all over again, right?''

''Whatever happened—and why—we can't say for sure,'' Grady told her, undaunted by Val's sarcasm. ''We do know that shortly afterward, grasshoppers came through the area and destroyed the crops.''

''Something happened to the water supply, as well,'' Travis said. ''We know all of this from pieces of a story quilt that several of Promise's founding families passed down from one generation to the next.''

''It was Travis and Nell who managed to figure out what those quilt squares meant.''

Val turned to him. ''You're basing all this on a *quilt?*'' She sounded incredulous. ''Travis, your imagination is more creative than I'd realized.''

He ignored her insulting words. ''It was what Nell and I discovered in the graveyard that made everything clear,'' he said.

''And what, pray tell, was that?'' Val asked in a long-suffering tone.

''The grave markers revealed that a number of children had all died within a short time span. Whether or not the curse was real, we're not here to say, but the citizens of Bitter End began to believe they *were* cursed. They'd remained in the town, withstood one hardship after another. Hung on no matter what until…''

"Until *what?*" Val asked.

"Until the children started to die," Jeannie said quietly.

"This is all extremely interesting, but I still don't know how it's supposed to tie in with Richard." Val folded her arms defensively. "I realize he hid from the law up in Bitter End, but this seems a stretch even for you, Travis. You haven't established a link between the town and that stolen gold shipment, let alone between Richard and the gold."

"Tell us what you found out," Jeannie said.

"I will in a moment," Travis replied without emotion, "but I'll repeat my earlier question first. What was the name of the man responsible for the hanging?"

"I don't follow you," Grady said.

"All this time we've assumed a few men in town had too much to drink and got carried away." Travis looked around the table and saw Adam, Grady and Jeannie nod their heads in agreement.

"Are you suggesting it *wasn't* the locals?" Jeannie asked.

Travis shrugged. "Oh, I think a few men from Promise were involved. When I researched Jeannie's story about One-Eyed Jack and that Union payroll, I discovered that the date of the robbery was only a week or so before the hanging." He paused, glancing around. "The men and women who settled the town were hardworking decent folks, not unlike the people here today. From what I could learn, there hadn't been a lot of trouble in Bitter End. My guess is that One-Eyed Jack and his band of renegades were on the run and stopped in the town."

"You can't prove that!" Val cried.

"True, but it all adds up." He grinned. "Perhaps it's my creative imagination, Val. I'm a writer, so I tend to look for endings. I want to see how the story comes out."

"I think you're right about something else, too," Adam added as though thinking out loud. "The people in Bitter End weren't murderers. Someone must have driven them into a frenzy to hang that innocent young man."

"If it was One-Eyed Jack's men, you think they had the gold with them?" Grady asked.

"I'm guessing they did."

Val shook her head. "And now you're suggesting Richard Weston found the gold and hid it somewhere in the town?"

"Well, it makes sense, doesn't it?" Travis said.

Grady nodded. "And I know for a fact that Richard came to Promise with nothing."

Travis remembered that when he'd first met Richard, the man had fed him a crazy story about the town and its background to pique his interest. He'd relayed only a few details—all of which proved to be untrue—in an effort to get Travis to pay him for more information. Travis had refused, and the two men hadn't been in touch since. In an effort to discover whether there was any truth to Richard's outrageous claims, Travis had flown to Texas...and met Nell.

"This is beyond belief!" Val shouted.

"But where could he have hidden it?" Travis continued as if she hadn't spoken.

"There are no gold coins in Bitter End," Val said, "and if there were, don't you think Richard would have mentioned them to me?"

"Why should he?" Travis asked.

"Well...because. I've befriended him. For the last couple of years I've put countless hours into his defense without a penny's compensation. Trust me, if he had access to that kind of money, he would have told me about it."

Grady's eyes went cold. "It's time you woke up and realized the truth about Richard. You don't know what he's like."

"You're the one who doesn't know Richard," Val hissed at Grady.

He shook his head sadly. "I'm afraid you're about to learn a painful lesson."

"Fine," Val said defiantly. "If you actually believe such a preposterous idea, then I suggest we all go out to Bitter End and look for this gold ourselves."

Travis watched as everyone around the table nodded in turn. While Adam paid the bill, Grady, Travis and Val headed outside and got into Grady's truck. Adam and Jeannie followed them in the patrol car.

Travis admitted that the idea of Richard's having found something in Bitter End was mere speculation, but the more he thought about it, the more he believed he was right. And even if it wasn't One-Eyed Jack's stolen gold, Travis was absolutely certain that Weston's interest in the ghost town wasn't altruistic.

Once they'd parked on the hill above Bitter End, they all made the arduous trek down the steep grade that led into the old town. They stopped at the outskirts, unsure where to start the search.

"Well," Val challenged, hands on her hips, "show me the gold." She rolled her eyes as though she found this entire episode ludicrous.

"You're in love with Richard, aren't you?" Jeannie asked suddenly.

Val ignored the question for a moment, meeting the other woman's look defiantly. "Let's put it like this," she finally said. "I believe that if Richard had found a strongbox of gold, he would have said something. He wouldn't keep it from me. You see, Richard and I trust each other. We've come through a lot together. There are no secrets between us."

"Not unless he plans to dump you the minute he's free," Grady suggested without malice.

"I've heard enough of this craziness." Val started to walk away. "Tell me when you're finished with this wild-goose chase." Having said that, she stalked over to the rocking chair outside the boarded-up hotel.

"The hotel," Grady said triumphantly, pointing at it. "That's where Jane and Cal found Richard. The stairway collapsed on him and he'd been trapped for nearly three days."

"You've got the story all wrong, but I'm not going to argue with you," Val told them.

"But he wasn't sleeping there," Grady said, paying no attention to Val.

"That's true." Travis remembered that Richard had set up house in one of the other buildings, a stone structure that wasn't likely to topple in a strong wind.

"Yet he risked his life to climb those rickety old stairs," Grady said thoughtfully. "At the time I wondered what could have possessed him to take such a foolish chance. He had to know just by looking at them how dangerous they were."

The small party gathered in front of the hotel and stared at the dilapidated half-fallen building. "Even if the gold's hidden somewhere on the second floor, that place isn't safe," Jeannie remarked. "Besides, there's no way of reaching it now."

"Sure there is." Adam glanced about. "Get me a rope and I'll give you a short demonstration of my Airborne training."

"Adam!" Jeannie cried, putting her hand on his forearm. "It's too dangerous!"

"You love him, don't you?" Val taunted her.

Jeannie didn't hesitate. "As a matter of fact, I do."

It did Travis's heart good to see her set Val back a step with her honesty. Jeannie, at least, had nothing to be ashamed of in the man she'd chosen to love.

"I've got a rope in my truck," Grady volunteered, and took off at a trot up the path to the limestone bluff where the vehicles were parked.

Grady returned twenty minutes later, sweating from the exertion of his climb, the rope draped over one shoulder. He handed it to Adam and they all stepped back and watched as the sheriff expertly swung the rope to the hotel's second-story balcony and anchored it on the railing. He tested it carefully, then decided it would support his weight.

Adam hadn't exaggerated his climbing skills, and Travis watched in amazement as the younger man hauled himself up onto the balcony.

Jeannie stood there, hands covering her mouth. It was obvious she didn't want to watch Adam in danger, but at the same time couldn't stop herself. "Be careful," she called, once Adam had made it safely.

"Don't take any unnecessary chances," Travis shouted.

"Just find something," Grady added.

Val glared at them all and shook her head. "You're out of your minds, every last one of you."

Adam disappeared into the hotel and a few minutes later, they heard the sound of wood splintering. Travis felt a jolt of alarm. If anything happened to the sheriff, he'd feel personally responsible.

"Adam," Jeannie screamed, moving forward.

"It's okay." The sheriff's voice was steady.

"This is crazy," Val said, directing the comment at Travis.

Much as he hated to admit it, Val was right. Proving his theory wasn't worth injury to Sheriff Jordan or anyone else. It occurred to him now that if word of a hidden treasure got out, it'd spread through the community like wildfire. Before long, strangers would swarm the countryside in search of lost gold coins. Their community, indeed the entire hill country, would never be the same—and it would be his doing. His fault.

"What's happening?" Jeannie asked anxiously.

"Adam's fine," Grady said confidently.

"How can you say for sure?"

"We'd know." Travis stood next to Jeannie, who gazed intently at the hotel.

It couldn't have been any longer than fifteen minutes, but it felt like hours before a triumphant Adam appeared, holding up a leather pouch. "I found it!" he shouted. "He'd hidden it just the way Travis suspected. It was tucked in a cupboard. I might never have stumbled on it if the weight of it hadn't broken through the rotting wood."

"What is it?" Grady called up to him.

Adam laughed. "Gold! Pure gold!"

Grady stared back in astonishment, slowly shaking his head.

Travis's hunch had been correct. The date of the robbery and the date of the hanging in Bitter End—that was the link. How and when the renegades had hidden the gold in Bitter End, and why they never retrieved it, would probably always be a mystery. Travis figured he might never know exactly how Richard had gotten his hands on it, either.

Travis suspected that Grady's brother must have discovered it while exploring the town during those weeks he spent there. Perhaps One-Eyed Jack had placed it at the bottom of a well or under the boardwalk. The possibilities were endless. Once Richard had located it, he must have secured it in the hotel, knowing few would risk investigating the second floor. But his plan had backfired when the staircase collapsed on him.

Trapped as he was now in a prison cell, Weston must have been frantic that someone would uncover his find. All his supposed concern about people's safety and not "commercializing" the ghost town had been a futile effort to keep anyone else from finding the gold.

"I don't believe it," Val murmured repeatedly. "I just don't believe it."

"Believe it, Ms. Langley," Grady advised. "Now you know the truth about Richard. He planned on dumping you as soon as you got him out of prison. Join the club. We've all been used by Richard. You weren't the first and you surely won't be the last."

Val couldn't wait to leave Texas. The very minute Travis dropped her off at the ranch, she began packing her bags, stuffing her clothes roughly into the suitcase. Dammit, she'd actually believed Richard Weston. Believed in him. The bastard!

The worst of it was she'd fallen for Richard, opened her heart to him. She wouldn't have traveled to this back-of-beyond town if she hadn't trusted him. She'd even told that bumpkin of a schoolteacher that she and Richard had no secrets from each other. He'd made a fool of her. An utter fool.

As far as Val could figure, everything Richard had told her was a lie. Everything. Including the way he felt about her, and dammit, that hurt. More than she wanted to admit.

A polite knock sounded on the bunkhouse door.

"Who is it?" Val snapped.

"Nell."

Oh, great, Ms. Jolly Green Giant. "What do you want?"

"I just need to know if you're planning on staying much longer."

Val walked across the room and threw open the door. "Frankly, I can't get out of this state fast enough."

"I'm sorry to hear that."

The last thing Val wanted to deal with was a Merry Sunshine attitude. "Spare me the bull. You're just as glad to be rid of me."

Nell shook her head. "That's not true."

"Whatever." Val searched for her purse, buried beneath the clothes flung across the bed. "How much do I owe you?" she asked once she'd found her wallet. She begrudged every cent she'd wasted on this trip. Richard had been after her for weeks, urging her to meet his family, to see Bitter End for herself. His biggest concern had been the ghost town—and now she understood why.

"Listen, Val, your stay is on the house."

Val stiffened. "I don't need your charity."

"It isn't charity," Nell said. "I was grateful for the

opportunity to get to know you. You might not think so, but we actually have something in common. We both love or have loved the same man.''

"I'll pay you what I agreed.''

"If you insist,'' Nell said with a certain sadness. "But I do want you to know I'm sorry Richard hurt you.''

It would have been easier for Val to deal with ridicule from Travis's wife than her kindness. The tears that sprang to her eyes felt like acid. It'd been years, literally years, since she'd broken down and cried. Sinking onto the edge of the bed, she covered her face with both hands.

"Oh, Val.''

"Just leave me alone,'' she said angrily, and not having a tissue handy, she reached for her purse and scrambled through it.

"Here,'' Nell said, handing her a tissue from her apron pocket.

Val blew her nose and still the tears came. "I was such a fool,'' she sobbed, "such an idiot.''

"It's all right,'' Nell said in a soft comforting tone. "We're all fools at one time or another.''

The compassion, the understanding, was more than Val could take and she shocked herself by turning toward Nell.

The woman she'd considered the Jolly Green Giant, Miss Merry Sunshine, an unsophisticated hick, gently placed her arms around Val and patted her back.

"Richard's going to pay for this.'' Val was sobbing openly.

"Life has a way of setting things straight,'' Nell said.

Val pulled herself together a little. "I'm going to make sure it does." She didn't intend to waste a minute, either. She was going to set the wheels of vengeance turning as fast as she could. She'd begin working on it during the flight home. Before she was through, Val would ensure that Richard Weston spent a very long time in prison. No one was more familiar with his case than she was. In all the months she'd spent studying the legal aspects, she'd seen a number of points of law she could get him on. He'd been fortunate to have several charges slip through the cracks. It would be easy to shine a light on those areas.

That wasn't all. She was well aware of the activities Richard participated in behind bars. Little things most prisoners did to make life easier. Smuggling and trading contraband, turning snitch, stealing. Nothing really serious. But perhaps it was time someone let the parole review board know about Richard's prison involvements. He was going to pay, by heaven. Richard Weston would rue the day he'd used and abused Valerie Langley.

"How about a nice hot cup of tea?" Nell asked.

Val sniffled and nodded. "That sounds great."

Together the two women headed toward the main house, talking as they went. With tea and womanly conversation, it wasn't long before Val's spirits lifted. This had all been a valuable lesson and one she wouldn't soon forget. Neither would Richard by the time she was finished with him. The bastard.

With her bags packed and her airline ticket in hand, Val bade farewell to Travis and Nell the next morning.

"Thanks for putting up with me," she said, and

meant it. If the situation had been reversed, she wasn't sure she would have been nearly this gracious.

"It was a pleasure to meet you," Nell said.

Travis had his arm around Nell's shoulders. They were a handsome couple, Val admitted. Nell was a much better match for Travis than she'd ever been.

"Goodbye, Val," Travis said.

But it was Nell who hugged her, and Val returned the hug. The unspoken communication between them was clear.

Who'd ever think her ex-husband's wife would turn out to be the most understanding woman Val had ever met?

Epilogue

Annie gently rocked her sleepy child, cradling him in her arms and humming softly. She'd lived in Promise nearly two years now, and the town was everything Jane had said. Everything and more. She'd left California looking for a new life and she'd found it— new work, a new home and, most important, a husband and family.

The bookstore was doing well financially, although Annie was working only part-time these days. Louise Powell had always been one of her most regular customers, and soon after Annie discovered she was pregnant, she'd approached the older woman about accepting a part-time position. Louise had been thrilled and said yes almost immediately. As the pregnancy progressed, they'd reversed roles, with Louise working full-time and acting as the store's manager. Annie took on even fewer hours to stay with her newborn son. The arrangement suited them both. Annie loved her time at home. And, busy at the store, Louise had less time to spread gossip; as a result, she'd formed several close friendships with women her age.

"Is he asleep?" Lucas asked, tiptoeing into the baby's room.

Annie smiled lovingly at her husband and nodded.

Gently she brushed the dark curls from little Luke's brow, then stood and placed him in his crib. Lucas joined her and tucked the blanket about his sleeping son's shoulders.

As noiselessly as possible, they moved out of the room and closed the door.

"I just got an emergency call," Lucas told her, regretfully.

"Go," she told him, wondering at his hesitation.

"But I was looking forward to spending a Saturday afternoon with my wife."

Annie never tired of hearing him refer to her as his wife. It was a word she loved, and a role she loved. Just as wonderful as the other role she'd accepted when she agreed to marry Lucas: mother.

"I'm not going anywhere," Annie told him, walking him to the front door.

He kissed her. "I'll call you as soon as I can."

"I'll be waiting."

"Don't forget to pick up Heather and Hollie at two from the movie theater."

As if she would. "I won't forget." She giggled. "Now go. Scoot. Be gone with you."

"I really do love you, Annie."

"I know."

And she did.

Nessa Pawling sat in her kitchen with brochures from a number of different cruise lines spread across the table. She just couldn't decide.

The back door opened and Gordon walked into the room, setting his golf clubs aside. "The Panama Canal," Gordon whispered enticingly from behind her. Leaning forward, he kissed her cheek. "Frank and I talked it over, and since you women can't seem to make up your minds, we're doing it for you."

"But there's no shopping in Panama," Nessa argued.

"You and Dovie have a dozen or more Caribbean islands where you can spend your money, and every store on every one of them takes Visa and American Express." Gordon opened the refrigerator and brought out a pitcher of iced tea.

"I married you for your money, you know," she teased.

Gordon laughed. "That's all right, because I married you for yours."

"Sylvia believes it to this day." Actually, Gordon and Sylvia had called a truce soon after the wedding, just as Nessa had with Miles. Gordon's son had given their marriage three months. Nessa wanted to laugh every time she thought about it. They'd been married for a year and a half now, and the honeymoon didn't show any signs of ending.

"The kids are just worried we're going to squander their inheritance," Gordon said, pulling out a chair and sitting down next to her.

"We are, aren't we? Every last penny of it."

"It might take some real effort, but I'm willing to try if you are."

It went without saying that she was.

"The Panama Canal, then?" Gordon asked, flipping through the colorful pages of the brochure.

"Looks like that's the general consensus." Nessa knew she'd enjoy the cruise, especially since Dovie and Frank would be joining them. In truth, it wouldn't have mattered if Gordon had decided to circumnavigate the globe; Nessa would have gone along for nothing more than the pleasure of his company.

Gordon kissed the back of her hand. "Thank you, sweetheart."

"I'd better give Dovie a call," Nessa said, standing up. "We'll have to plan our wardrobes. Oh, Gordon, this is going to be such fun."

Her husband reached for a second brochure. "What would you think of a trip down the Amazon?"

"Next year, darling, next year." She wondered if anyone in Brazil took American Express.

Cal Patterson drove the pickup through the stone gate and down the one-lane road that wound its way through Promise Cemetery. The older grave sites with their ornate markers dominated the front half, those of more recent years were situated in the back.

It'd been a month since he'd been to see his mother's grave. Mary's dying had been a long good-bye. But although they'd all expected it, known it was coming, Cal hadn't been ready. Glen, neither, and certainly not their father.

Once his parents had sold the bed-and-breakfast and moved into the retirement center in San Antonio, his mother's health had quickly deteriorated. Within a year she was gone.

Cal parked the truck and walked across the freshly cut lawn to his mother's grave.

"Hello, Mom," he whispered as he laid a bouquet of bluebonnets next to her headstone. "It's been a while since I last stopped by." He could see that his father had paid a recent visit. Whenever he came, he brought a rose.

"I have some news," he continued in a whisper.

"Jane's pregnant again. We're really happy. Ellie's pregnant, too, but I imagine Glen's already told you that." He swallowed tightly and looked toward the sky. For years his mother had wanted him to give her grandchildren. Now she'd never know them, but Cal chose to think of her watching and loving them all from heaven.

"If we have a girl this time, Jane said she wanted to name her after you." They'd call her Mary Ann, after his mother and Jane's closest friend, Annie Porter.

"Dad's adjusting. It isn't easy, but he's managing." Phil had returned to Promise and was living in a brand-new retirement complex. The seniors' center in Promise had helped. Frank Hennessey had taken him under his wing and gotten Phil involved in various activities. He was trying to talk him into learning golf. Gordon Pawling was keen on it and had organized a group of retired businessmen to investigate the possibility of building a golf course right outside town. Cal had to smile every time he thought about a golf course in Promise. Those men were serious about it, though, and it wasn't uncommon to find one or more of them practicing putting techniques in the town park.

"It's Dad's birthday next week, and I wanted you to know I'm getting him a set of clubs." If Gordon, Frank and the others got their way, Phil would soon be joining them on a golf course, and Cal wanted to encourage that.

He stood with his hat in his hand for several minutes, communicating silently with his mother, struggling with the fact that their long goodbye hadn't been long enough.

* * *

The diamond on Jeannie French's left hand sparkled in the light of her first-grade classroom.

Adam stood in front of the children as he did every year, discussing safety and talking about a sheriff's work, ending his talk with a demonstration involving his handcuffs. It was this part her six-year-olds always enjoyed the most.

After class, Adam lingered and helped her clean up for the day.

"I'd like a pair of those handcuffs myself," Jeannie told him once the classroom had emptied.

"Any particular reason?" he asked with more than a hint of suggestion.

"I have a few ideas, Sheriff Jordan," she said, doing her best to make her voice deep and sexy.

"Ms. French, you shock me."

"Do I now?"

"What exactly would you do if I was foolish enough to give you my handcuffs?" He dangled them in front of her.

Jeannie stood next to her desk, head tilted, and planted her hands on her waist. "You mean you don't know?"

He waggled his eyebrows. "I can guess."

"Guess again, Adam Jordan." This was the moment she'd been waiting for. "I want us to set a date for our wedding. We can work on our relationship until kingdom come. If you aren't ready to marry me now, you never will be."

Adam looked stunned. "If it was up to me, we would've been married a year ago."

"Then why aren't we?"

"Well...because, you never said..."

"You never asked! Am I *always* going to have to

be the one to do the asking?'' Jeannie demanded, pouting just a little. "I love you, and I want us to be married.''

"I want us to be married, too.''

"Well...you should've said something sooner.''

"Are you willing to set the date or not?''

"Yes,'' Jeannie said without hesitation.

"Good.''

They glared at each other, then Jeannie asked, "Why are you standing over there when I'm standing over here?''

Adam shook his head. "Hell if I know. Did we or did we not just agree to set our wedding date?''

"We agreed.''

Adam pulled her into his arms, joining his hands at the small of her back. "That's what I thought. What are you doing next weekend?''

Jeannie stared at him. "You want to set the wedding for next weekend?''

"No, I just wanted to know if you had any plans.''

She was about to let out a cry of protest, but he cut her off with a deep heartfelt kiss that robbed her of both breath and reason. When he'd finished, he looked down at her and his eyes grew serious. "Next weekend, we'll choose a date. Okay?''

Jeannie laughed and nodded, crazy in love with the best-looking sheriff she'd ever known.

Grady had been expecting his sister to show up all afternoon and he wasn't disappointed. Savannah sought him out in his office.

"You heard?'' he asked.

She nodded. "There was a letter from Richard in

today's mail. The parole board's denied his request, and he blames Val."

"Interesting, seeing that the only person he has to blame is himself." But this was a familiar scenario with Richard.

Savannah agreed with a nod, then took the chair across from Grady. "I wish I knew why Richard went so wrong. I've asked myself that a thousand times over the years, and I've never found an answer that made sense."

Grady had wondered, too.

"His letter was so full of anger," Savannah said, and Grady heard the hurt in her voice.

"I didn't know you still wrote to him."

She avoided eye contact. "I do every now and then."

"And he writes back?" Grady knew the answer, but wanted his sister to admit the truth. Richard would write his family only when he needed something.

"He does keep in touch," Savannah replied, "but mostly to request money or ask me to do him some favor."

"And do you?"

"Laredo prefers that I only send Richard money on his birthday and Christmas, and frankly I agree. For the rest, I tend to ignore his requests. Did you hear from him, too?"

Grady nodded. "It isn't only Val he blames."

"Why you?"

"I refused to write a letter to the parole board on his behalf."

"Neither would I," Savannah admitted.

"Yes, but he isn't about to bite the hand that feeds him." Oh, no, Richard was much too smart for that.

"How's Val?" Savannah asked. "Have you heard from her recently?"

"Travis and Nell do frequently." Once she'd learned the truth about Richard, Val was hell on wheels, doing everything possible to make sure he served his full sentence. She'd been helpful to the people of Promise, too. Working with another attorney, she'd helped with the return of the gold coins to the federal government. But her assistance hadn't stopped there. Because of her efforts, money had recently been raised to build a small hospital in Promise.

A golf course, a hospital. Grady wondered if he'd recognize the town in a few more years. Then again, he knew he would. Changes would come; the town was destined to grow. His own family certainly had since the birth of his second daughter. But the heart of Promise—the strength and faith that had led the original settlers to leave Bitter End and start over in a new place—that heart would never change.

A story of home, happiness and hardheaded men.

SHERRYL WOODS

When he was alive, Tex O'Rourke was a sneaky old coot. Now that he's dead, he's even worse.

Jake Landers came home to Whispering Wind, Wyoming, to put down some roots. But seeing Megan O'Rourke, the woman who shared his troubled past, is a shock: Megan's become a driven, stressed-out powerhouse who's forgotten what's really important.

Megan has to make some big decisions, and Jake is only too happy to help. Because he's beginning to recall some old dreams—and the best one begins with Megan.

AFTER TEX

On sale mid-September 1999 wherever paperbacks are sold!

MIRA®

Look us up on-line at: http://www.mirabooks.com   MSHW5

New York Times Bestselling Author

ELIZABETH LOWELL

CHAIN LIGHTNING

They were strangers, stranded in a breathtaking land where nature wields a power of her own.

For Damon Sutter, the trip to Australia's Great Barrier Reef is a chance to escape civilization… alone. And Mandy Blythe, a beautiful woman haunted by her past, is the last person he wants to share the beautiful island retreat with. Though Mandy's been tricked into the trip, she's not fooled by Sutter. The arrogant womanizer is the last man she'd ever fall in love with. But the tropics are a different world, where emotions run as deep as the ocean and paradise is only a heartbeat away.

"For smoldering sensuality and exceptional storytelling, Elizabeth Lowell is incomparable."
—*Romantic Times*

On sale mid-September 1999 wherever paperbacks are sold!

MIRA

Look us up on-line at: http://www.mirabooks.com   MEL538

From *New York Times* bestselling phenomenon

BARBARA DELINSKY

DREAMS

For five generations Crosslyn Rise has been the very heart of one of Massachusetts's finest families. But time and neglect have diminished the glory of the once-majestic estate. Now three couples share a dream…a dream of restoring this home.

For Jessica Crosslyn and Carter Mallory, Gideon Lowe and Christine Gillette, and Nina Stone and John Sawyer, Crosslyn Rise has become their mutual passion. And as they work to restore the house, that passion turns personal, making their own dreams come true.…

Join these three couples as they build their dreams for the future in Barbara Delinsky's unforgettable Crosslyn trilogy.

On sale mid-September 1999 wherever paperbacks are sold!

MIRA®

Look us up on-line at: http://www.mirabooks.com   MBD627

If you enjoyed what you just read,
then we've got an offer you can't resist!

Take 2 bestselling love stories FREE!

Plus get a FREE surprise gift!

Clip this page and mail it to The Best of the Best™

IN U.S.A.	IN CANADA
3010 Walden Ave.	P.O. Box 609
P.O. Box 1867	Fort Erie, Ontario
Buffalo, N.Y. 14240-1867	L2A 5X3

YES! Please send me 2 free Best of the Best™ novels and my free surprise gift. Then send me 3 brand-new novels every month, which I will receive months before they're available in stores. In the U.S.A., bill me at the bargain price of $4.24 plus 25¢ delivery per book and applicable sales tax, if any*. In Canada, bill me at the bargain price of $4.74 plus 25¢ delivery per book and applicable taxes**. That's the complete price and a savings of over 10% off the cover prices—what a great deal! I understand that accepting the 2 free books and gift places me under no obligation ever to buy any books. I can always return a shipment and cancel at any time. Even if I never buy another book from The Best of the Best™, the 2 free books and gift are mine to keep forever. So why not take us up on our invitation. You'll be glad you did!

183 MEN CNFK

383 MEN CNFL

Name	(PLEASE PRINT)
Address	Apt.#
City	State/Prov. Zip/Postal Code

* Terms and prices subject to change without notice. Sales tax applicable in N.Y.
** Canadian residents will be charged applicable provincial taxes and GST.
   All orders subject to approval. Offer limited to one per household.
   ® are registered trademarks of Harlequin Enterprises Limited.

BOB99

©1998 Harlequin Enterprises Limited

Debbie Macomber always enjoyed
telling stories—first to her baby-sitting
clients and then to her own four children.
As a full-time wife and mother and an avid
romance reader, she dreamed of one day
sharing her stories with a wider audience.
In the autumn of 1982 she sold her first
book, and that was only the beginning.
Debbie has been making regular
appearances on the *USA Today* bestseller
list—not surprising, considering that there
are over forty million copies of her books
in print worldwide!

MDMBIO99